DISCIPLINE? OR BRUTALITY

"You're naive, Sanders. You act as though Bennett and I are the only two DIs on this island who raise our hands against recruits. And you know why we're 'brutal'? Because we have only ten weeks to prepare these clowns for combat, and the quickest way—"

"Is not by brutalizing them," Sanders interrupted.

"Sanders, your trouble is you keep mistaking discipline for brutality. The Corps is a fraternity of professional killers, and boot camp is merely the initiation, the rites of passage. . . ."

TO KEEP OUR HONOR CLEAN

"A critical but loving look at the corps."
—*The New York Times*

"Somewhere between *Dress Gray* and *From Here to Eternity* . . . a true-to-life portrait of the Corps."
—*Publishers Weekly*

TO KEEP
OUR
HONOR CLEAN

Edwin McDowell

BANTAM BOOKS
TORONTO · NEW YORK · LONDON · SYDNEY

ꚛ

TO KEEP OUR HONOR CLEAN

*A Bantam Book / published by arrangement with
Vanguard Press*

PRINTING HISTORY
*Vanguard edition published May 1980
Bantam edition / January 1982*

PRINTED IN THE UNITED STATES OF AMERICA

0 9 8 7 6 5 4 3 2 1

For
Sathie Akimoto
from Lavinia, Brazil,
my wife, companion,
and best friend,
with deepest love and appreciation

First to fight for right and freedom,
 And to keep our honor clean,
We are proud to claim the title
 Of United States Marine.

> —The Marines' Hymn

. . . but man, proud man,
Drest in a little brief authority,
Most ignorant of what he's most assured . . .
Plays such fantastic tricks before high heaven
As make the angels weep. . . .

> —SHAKESPEARE,
> Measure for Measure, II, 2

Chapter
1

The moment the Marine sentry waved the bus past the checkpoint with a smart, fluttery motion, the expressions of most of the youthful passengers became even more grim and attentive.

During the thirty-mile ride from Yemassee, where the staff sergeant in charge of the receiving barracks put the forty-three recruits aboard the bus with a warning not to utter a sound, most of the youngsters had just stared idly out the window at the passing scenery.

Now, as they cleared the gate guarding the sole land entrance to their destination and had time to consider the significance of the bright gold-and-red sign proclaiming: "U.S. Marine Corps Recruit Depot, Parris Island, South Carolina," a sudden tension gripped them. It was as though they realized for the first time the finality of their decision to join the Marines.

A few of the newcomers managed nervous grins. But most just watched apprehensively as the blue, bobtailed bus of the Palmetto Bus Line wound its way along the mile-long road through the marshes, past rows of close-cropped palm trees and green, well-kept shrubbery.

Soon the road widened and buildings came into view: The civilian motor pool, the office of the provost marshal, the photo lab. As if on cue, all eyes swung left as the bus approached the main parade ground, which echoed with the rhythmic sound of marching feet. A half-dozen recruit platoons were drilling at various sections of the large, paved parade field, exhibiting varying degrees of precision.

Recruit Thomas Dutton studied the marchers intently. Even

1

at that distance he marveled at their angular grace, their split-second obedience to commands. He was especially impressed with the one or two leaders of each platoon, whom he did not yet identify as drill instructors, who manipulated the marchers much as a skillful choreographer manipulates a chorus line, with precise, confident commands.

The parade ground faded from view as the bus continued down Blvd. de France, past the veiled Iwo Jima Monument that would be dedicated in two more months, past the red brick Marine Corps Exchange, past the impressive statue of a World War I Marine with a raised pistol in his left hand and a machine gun slung across his right shoulder.

This was "Iron Mike," a landmark at the Recruit Depot, Dutton managed to read the inscription on it as the bus rolled along slowly:

IN—MEMORY—OF
THE—MEN—OF—PARRIS—ISLAND
WHO—GAVE—THEIR—LIVES
IN—THE—WORLD—WAR
ERECTED
BY—THEIR—COMRADES

Shortly thereafter the bus swung left down a narrow side street and came to a halt at the Recruit Receiving Center. The instant the bus door hissed open, a large khaki-clad figure swung abroad, his massive shoulders completely filling the doorway. He hovered forebodingly on the top step, his eyes shadowed by the bill of his frame cap as he surveyed the newcomers. Tucked up under his left armpit was a dark club, about two and a half feet long and three-quarters of an inch in diameter. His five stripes, three over and two under, identified him as a technical sergeant and therefore someone of authority. But his confident, almost imperious bearing identified him further as someone who exuded authority irrespective of rank.

"Listen up, you Privates," he commanded. The harshness of his loud, low-pitched voice jolted the attentive newcomers. "When I give you the word you will get out of this bus on the double, you will run inside this barracks, and you will line up quickly at attention in front of the nearest empty rack. And when I say move, I mean just that. Now *move!*"

The recruits immediately sprang from their seats, surged

into the aisle, and began pushing toward the front of the bus. Outside the vehicle two other voices began shouting, "Move, move," even though it was obvious the confused youngsters were making every effort to do exactly that.

The tech sergeant, who meanwhile had positioned himself at the foot of the bus, began pulling some of the slower or hesitant youngsters out of the doorway, jerking them forward, then shoving them toward the building. "You had better move, boy, when I tell you to move," he said evenly, his voice just below the level of a roar.

Near the steps leading to the building another figure in khaki—a buck sergeant, a three striper, with grim expression—was cursing and shouting, indiscriminately knocking recruits off balance. When one bewildered youngster went sprawling, the buck sergeant moved toward him menacingly. "You better get on your feet, lard ass, or you're gonna wish you had. Get in that door," he scrowled, leveling a poorly aimed kick in the direction of the recruit, who by then was up and scurrying toward the steps.

Thomas Dutton leaped up from his window seat the instant the tech sergeant ordered them to move, but his path was blocked by the sudden surge toward the door. Even at that he made his way to the front quickly by finding himself directly behind a brawny recruit who, in his race for the door, toppled several other recruits back into their seats.

Dutton waited impatiently as his unwitting benefactor leaped from the top step, preparing to take off toward the security of the building amid the increasing shouts and threats. But just as the brawny recruit hit the ground the tech sergeant moved toward him. Without altering the position of the club, which was still sheltered in his armpit, he drove his right fist deep into the recruit's stomach, sending him crashing to the ground.

"You better get up, Private," the tech sergeant said, standing over the stunned and angry recruit. His tone was calm and measured, in striking contrast to that of only a minute before.

Enraged, the recruit began scrambling to his feet, looking as though he would confront his attacker, who, although he was about the same height and weight, somehow appeared bigger. As the tech sergeant inched closer, letting his right arm sink to his side, he said through clenched teeth, "Get in that barracks, Private, I don't intend to repeat myself."

Halfway to his feet the recruit hesitated. When he saw the

drill instructor's cold, unflinching eyes squinting at him, magnified behind thick eyeglasses, his anger began draining away. Instead of springing right up, now he hung back cautiously, finally rising and dusting the knees of his modified pegged pants with several swipes of his hand. Then he took off on the double for the building, working his lips in a silent oath.

The entire incident lasted only seconds. Yet so completely did it surprise Dutton that he was still standing in the doorway of the bus, trying to make sense of what he had just witnessed, when he saw a blur and then felt himself being hurtled forward.

"Goddamn you, Private," shouted the buck sergeant, who had lunged at him, grabbing Dutton by the necktie and pulling him out of the bus, "you want a taste of the same treatment?" Without waiting for an answer, he half-pushed, half-dragged the recruit toward the building, then flung him toward the stairs.

Inside the building Dutton, more humiliated than hurt, saw the other recruits lined up in front of the double-decker racks at what they hoped was attention. Stunned by the violent reception, he hesitated, unsure of where to go.

"Down here, Private, on the double," commanded another figure in khaki, a corporal, standing with hands on hips in the middle of the two wings of the squad bay. Dutton ran to the nearest empty bed and tried to emulate the other recruits, who were staring straight ahead, hands at their side, most of them likewise wondering what they had done to cause such a flare-up.

Outside the door the shouting continued. After a distinctive dull thud, another recruit was propelled unceremoniously through the open door as the volatile buck sergeant shouted, "Jesus H. Christ, if you aren't a clumsy son-of-a-bitch. Get in there before I *really* help you in."

In another few seconds all the recruits were inside, including a number who had not arrived on the bus from Yemassee with Dutton. The threats and oaths subsided as quickly as they had begun. The only sounds were those of a door banging closed and the driver revving up. As the bus began pulling away, apprehension among some recruits gave way to alarm.

The corporal paced back and forth between both columns of youngsters. Like his colleagues outside, he walked fully erect with his shoulders pinched back, a posture that stopped just short of being a strut. Also like them, his form-fitting uniform was newly starched and pressed. But instead of the frame hat, he wore the brimless garrison cap that revealed his entire face. His stern visage made him look older than he was, but Dutton guessed him to be no more than twenty-four or twenty-five.

The momentary silence was instantly shattered as the two DIs bounded up the steps, the tech sergeant bellowing even before he reached the doorway. "So this is the sorry bunch they sent me to try to make Marines of," he yelled, striding toward the middle of the squad bay. As if by a prearranged signal, all three drill instructors began denouncing the recruits, cursing the fates that conspired to deliver this motley crew to their care, promising to make them regret the day they ever set foot on Parris Island.

For several minutes—minutes that seemed endless to the frightened recruits—the frenzied trio dashed back and forth threatening, haranguing, and, in the case of the buck sergeant, cursing profusely. The noise from the metal cleats on their double-soled shoes, resounding against the bare wooden barracks floors, added to the confusion and disorder.

Twice the tech sergeant smashed his club down just inches away from recruits, banging the iron rung across the foot of the upper rack and vowing to smash it on their skulls if they didn't shape up quickly. "You better lock those thumbs along the seams of your trousers while you're at attention," he roared to no one in particular.

Only the corporal, berating the newcomers for "acting like civilians," didn't threaten outright violence.

"You think you'll ever be a Marine, boy?" the tech sergeant asked scornfully, thrusting his face into that of a lanky recruit who was doing his best to continue looking straight ahead. "Do you?"

The youngster fumbled for an appropriate answer, "I th—"

"Yes or no, Private? I asked you a question and you had better answer up."

"No," he muttered.

"No? NO? No *what*, boy?" he demanded, grabbing him by the neck with one massive hand and pressing his thumb into the private's throat.

"No, sir," the fearful boy replied as his face began to discolor.

"You had *better* say 'sir,' you understand, lad?"

"Yes, sir," the recruit wheezed, gasping for air.

With that the tech sergeant relaxed his grip, turned, and announced, "From now on you will address everyone who is not a lowly recruit as 'sir.' Do you understand?"

Several recruits overcame their dismay sufficiently to respond, "Yes, sir."

"Sergeant Krupe asked you if you understand," screamed the buck sergeant as he stepped toward an overweight recruit and caught him in the ribs with the open edge of his hand, making him double over. "What's the matter, you lard-assed son-of-a-bitch, didn't you hear? Now answer up, all of you."

"Yes, sir!" came the collective reply, much louder this time.

"I can't hear you, Privates," the buck sergeant said.

"YES, SIR," they hollered, the noise reverberating throughout the barracks.

"That's better," he said sarcastically. "Now you better goddamned well listen up, ever' last one of you. I'm Sergeant Bennett, but God help you if any of you call me that—or if you ever call me anything but Sir. Is that understood?"

"YES, SIR."

"This," he said, pointing to the bespectacled drill instructor who stood with his hands on hips, his left hand gripping the handle of the club whose business end was tucked under his left armpit, "is Technical Sergeant Krupe. And that," he continued, pointing to the far end of the squad room, "is Corporal Sanders."

As Bennett spoke, a dark-skinned youth next to Dutton turned to watch. Suddenly he felt a sharp pain in the pit of his stomach; then he slumped to the foor.

"Who told you to turn your eyes, Private?" Krupe demanded angrily, brandishing the club that he had rammed into the boy's solar plexus. Without waiting for an answer, he said: "No one turns his eyes until one of us gives you the word. No one does anything but breathe until we tell you to, and maybe we'll even tell you to do that. Is that understood?"

"YES, SIR." The shaken youth, who meanwhile had risen from the floor and partially recovered his breath, joined weakly in the reply. He was bronzed rather than dark, and had the high cheekbones of an Indian.

"Continue, Sergeant Bennett."

"Thank you, Sergeant Krupe. As I was telling you half-assed clowns, we are your three Drill Instructors. For the next ten weeks one or all of us will be with you night and day. We'll tell you what to do, when to do it, how to do it, and where to do it. And you will obey—immediately, automatically. Is that understood?''

"YES, SIR."

"Sergeant Krupe is your—" Bennett stopped. For several seconds he stared at a red-haired, freckle-faced youth slightly off to his left. Then he sauntered toward him, as though he had nothing better to do. "What's your name, boy?" he asked nonchalantly.

Surprised, the youth hesitated, "My name, sir?"

"Didn't you hear me, lad? Or maybe you don't have a name. Which is it?"

"Sir, my name is James Gillian."

"*Sir, my name is James Gillian,*" mimicked Bennett, his voice deliberately pitched an octave higher than usual. "Your rank, Mr. Gillian, if you please—what is your rank? Are you a Sergeant? A Major, maybe? Or maybe you're a *real* big wheel— the kind that dogs piss on."

"I'm *Private* James Gillian, sir," the youth replied.

"That's better, Private Gillian," Bennett said, squinting and inching closer until he was almost pressed against the youngster. Thrusting his face into the recruit's face, he said, "You were staring at me, Private. Why were you staring at me? Do you love me, Gillian?"

The recruit hesitated, unable to think of a suitable answer.

"I asked you a question, goddamn it, Private, and you had best give me an answer. Do-you-love-me?"

"Sir, I don't I—" Gillian began, but Bennett interrupted.

"You mean you *don't* love me, Private?" he asked ominously, moving forward slightly and backing the youth against the bed.

"Yes, sir, I do," the befuddled Gillian replied.

"I *thought* you were a queer," Bennett spat. "A goddamned redheaded queer in the United States Marine Corps. A freckle-faced fairy, and we have to get him. Now, isn't that just too goddamn sweet for words."

Gillian, although humiliated, held his tongue—to the apparent chagrin of the drill instructor.

"Don't worry, Private Gillian, the Marine Corps knows how to handle queers—gently, and with tender loving care. You," Bennett said, turning to the recruit who was at rigid attention alongside Gillian. It was the brawny youngster who had run interference on the bus for Dutton and who had been sent sprawling by Krupe. "Come closer to Private James—I mean Jane—Gillian." Both recruits were visibly embarrassed. "From now on you two are going steady, is that understood?"

"Yes, sir," stammered Gillian, hoping Bennett would soon leave so he could lapse into obscurity.

"What about you, Private? I gave an order and I want to know if you're going to carry it out."

"Sir, I—"

"God*damn* it," Bennett shouted with an air of sudden exasperation. "Just answer yes or no. When I want any shit out of you I'll squeeze your head. Is that understood?"

"Yes, sir."

"What's your name, boy?"

"Private Stanley Tew, sir."

"Now isn't that nice? Well, thank you, Private Tew." He bowed slightly, then turned and strutted toward the center of the squad bay. He seemed to be enjoying himself immensely, although Krupe appeared impatient of all the theatricals.

"When Jane interrupted me," Bennett resumed, looking with undisguised amusement at the two mortified recruits, "I was about to tell you boots that Sergeant Krupe is Senior Drill Instructor of this sorry excuse for a platoon. Corporal Sanders and I are Assistant DIs. All three of us are mean, all three of us agree we've never seen a more raggedy-assed bunch of civilians, and all three of us are determined we'll make Marines out of you or die trying. Correction—*you'll* die from us trying. Sergeant Krupe, wanna say a few words?"

For almost an entire minute Krupe looked from one side of the aisle to the other, scrutinizing all seventy-one recruits. Each continued staring straight ahead, fearful even of breathing loudly lest he be heard and singled out for punishment or ridicule. As he stood at rigid attention, careful not to let his thoughts wander, Dutton mused that the cardinal law of boot camp—the recruits' Iron Law of Survival—must be to remain forever anonymous. He resolved to act upon that assumption as best he could.

At infrequent intervals Krupe transferred his club from one hand to the other. Acquired some years earlier from a veteran of one of the Marine Corps's Caribbean campaigns, the mahogany *cocomacaque* was a fitting complement to its present owner: Both of them inspired immediate respect.

"Until you hit this godforsaken island," he intoned, "you

were civilians, regardless of what your orders say. As of—'' he paused to check his watch—''as of twenty minutes ago you ceased being civilians, which means you ceased having minds of your own. At that minute you became the property of the United States Marine Corps.''

He began pacing, making no effort to soften the sound of his cleats on the shiny wooden floor. ''But you Privates are not Marines, in any sense of that much-abused word. Some of you will never become Marines, that I can promise you here and now. *None* of you will make it until I've taught you the fundamentals of being Marines—how to obey orders instantly . . . how to march and drill . . . how to use a bayonet and a rifle . . . how to stay alive under combat conditions. Above all, you will learn how to act and fight and die like Marines, whether you are stateside or in Korea.''

As Krupe spoke, Bennett and Sanders also began pacing, although not so loudly, occasionally stopping in front of particular recruits as though to see if they could spot some transgression. Dutton prayed silently for them to bypass him.

''A lot of good men have fought and died for this uniform,'' Krupe continued, ''and I intend to see that you don't disgrace them. Let this be a warning: I will personally squash the first one of you who gets out of line.'' He stared at Tew, but the recruit never diverted his gaze fixed straight ahead. ''That,'' he said ominously, ''is a promise I will sign in blood—*your* blood. Now, Sergeant Bennett . . .''

''All right, goddamn it,'' Bennett shouted, ''empty all your pockets, take everything out of your bags and wallet, remove your shoes, put them in front of your rack, hold your money in your left hand, and when you're finished stand at attention in front of the rack. When we come by, turn around, place both hands along the top rack, and lean forward while we frisk you. *Move!*''

''Get moving,'' the DIs shouted as they charged back and forth among the recruits. ''Goddamn it, lad, I said move,'' commanded Bennett furiously, pushing a confused, bespectacled recruit.

''Get a move on, you Privates,'' hollered Sanders as he dashed from one end of the line of recruits to the other. ''You're taking too much time.''

Krupe moved swiftly toward Tew and Gillian. ''Didn't you hear Sergeant Bennett, you sweethearts?'' he demanded.

"Sir—" Tew began apologetically.

Krupe cut him off. "Let go," he demanded, grabbing Gillian's wrist and pushing him away. "You have exactly twenty seconds to do as you're told or God help you," he threatened.

"Move, move," Bennett screamed, punctuating his orders with punches and occasional kicks.

One recruit, who had the misfortune to be wearing hightop shoes that laced midway to his knees, was sent sprawling by Krupe. "Get those clodhoppers off and be quick about it. Get 'em off."

Another recruit had trouble opening the zipper on his gym bag; Bennett pulled the leather handles in opposite directions until he tore a gaping hole in it. "It's easy to open, isn't it, Private?" he demanded.

"Yes, sir," replied the crestfallen youth.

"Fifteen more seconds, Privates, and you had better all be standing at attention in front of your racks," Krupe warned, his deep voice rising above the muffled sound of the recruits racing against the clock.

James Gillian was frantically trying to beat the deadline. He had emptied his wallet, his pockets, and his gym bag, and was now untying his shoes when Bennett approached.

"Hurry it up, Private Jane," he commanded. Then he glanced at Gillian's feet. "Well, I'll-be-go-to-hell," he exclaimed as he spotted the recruit's soiled white shoes. "What in Christ's name do you call those, honey?"

"Bucks, sir," Gillian replied as he yanked off the second shoe and immediately lined up at attention.

"Bucks? Don't you mean does? They're fruit boots, that's what they are—fruit boots. Oh, you're one goddamned peach, you are, Gillian," he said. Casting a lingering glance, he turned and joined the other drill instructors in the middle of the squad bay.

"You Privates are too slow, entirely too slow," announced Krupe, glancing at his watch. "You better never be this slow again, is that understood?"

"Yes, sir."

"I said, is that understood?"

"YES, SIR!"

"Now, when we come around, turn and face your racks, bend forward, and spread your legs."

At that, the drill instructors began frisking the recruits, then examining the items spread across the beds. "Get rid of this," Kurpe ordered whenever he came across toilet articles, personal effects, or extra items of clothing. "Send it home, you understand?"

Sanders, too, ordered the recruits to send home everything except their wallets, telling them they wouldn't be needing anything for the next ten weeks. Only Bennett operated differently. He ordered a recruit to follow him with a drawstring laundry bag to collect other recruits' electric razors, radios, cameras, and valuables other than money.

"Ho—what's this?" exclaimed Krupe as he discovered a bright red and white package inside an otherwise empty wallet. "Just what is this, Private?" he demanded of its owner, a freckled youngster.

"It's . . . it's a rubber, sir."

"A rubber, is it? And what did you plan to do with it, Private?"

"Nothing, sir. I mean—"

"Nothing? You don't know what rubbers are for, Private?"

The youth, braced rigidly at attention, replied: "No, sir. I mean, yes, sir. I do know, but it wasn't for here. I thought while I was in Washington on the way down here—"

"Oh, Washington. I see. You thought maybe you'd see what kind of man you are, is that it?"

"No, sir. I mean, I don't know, sir. I—"

"How old are you, Private?"

"Seventeen, sir. I'll be eighteen in October."

"Wonderful, Private, that's wonderful," said Krupe caustically. "You're a real man, aren't you? Well, we'll see how much of a man you are during the next ten weeks. You know what you can do with this? There's a head just around the bulkhead there." He pointed toward the passageway. "Move out on the double and flush this down the can, you understand?"

"Yes, sir."

"Well, then, move out—go, get."

The youngster did as directed, running as fast as he safely could on the newly waxed and buffed floor, and was back in a moment. By then Krupe had moved on; each drill instructor was methodical and fast, wasting scarcely a movement.

When Bennett got to Gillian, he grinned. "Turn around, sweetheart," he said. As he frisked the recruit, checking his legs, he taunted, "I'll bet you like this, don't you, Dolly?"

Gillian, on the verge of tears, said in a low voice, "I don't mind it too much, sir."

"I'll *bet* you don't mind it, Dolly. And you better hadn't. Because by the time I get through with you you'll be praying that's the worst thing's ever happened to you. Now, let's see your wallet."

The wallet was empty, its contents atop the bed as ordered. Bennett thumbed through the cards, which included the youngster's driver's license, his high-school graduation picture, and a photograph of a young, pretty Oriental girl on which was inscribed: "Jim, to you my darling. I'll love you always, Nancy."

"Who's this?" Bennett demanded. "Your sister?"

"No, sir, it's my girl friend," Gillian replied.

"Girl friend's ass," ridiculed Bennett. "The only kind of girl friends queers have are boy girl friends. Is it your sister?"

"No, sir," Gillian insisted, "it's my girl."

"Balls!" Bennett spat out. "If she's your girl friend then she's one of those transvestites. You know what a transvestite is?"

Tears welled in Gillian's eyes. He feared that if he answered he might break down, yet he was scared to remain silent. "Yes, sir," he replied, his voice almost inaudible.

Bennett was amused at the sight of the boy's tear-rimmed eyes. "You're not getting ready to cry, are you, Janie?" he taunted. "Are you?"

Gillian had been, but he'd be damned if he'd give his tormentor the satisfaction of knowing it. He swallowed hard and replied, "No, sir, I'm not."

"That's a good girl. Because the Marine Corps doesn't like sob sisters, Janie. In fact, we hate sob sisters almost as much as we hate queers."

"Sir," Gillian replied, "I'm *not* queer. I'm—"

"Are you trying to tell me I'm a liar when I say you're a pansy?" Bennett was trying his best to provoke a showdown, but Sanders, who had been working his way down the line of recruits, nudged the sergeant as he passed by.

"Hurry it up, you boots, we don't have all day," the corporal yelled, ostensibly at the recruits. The sergeant hesitated. He looked at Gillian, then at Sanders, who by now was busy frisking Tew. He decided maybe he was wasting too much time.

"We'll see about you later," he scowled at the recruit. Then he turned quickly away.

After the boots had been frisked, Krupe ordered them outside on the double. On the way, driven by threats and Bennett's curses, several recruits were bounced against the wall by Krupe just as they approached the doorway. Among them was the seventeen-year-old who had just been dressed down by Krupe.

Once again Krupe ordered the platoon to form two ranks of equal length. "Eyes right, looking at the lead Private, your left arm extended straight, the fingertips of your left hand touching the shoulder of the man to your left," ordered Krupe. "Hurry it up, you Privates."

Without warning, Bennett broke through the front rank, scattering two recruits as he did so. He grabbed Gillian by the collar and shook him vigorously.

"Straighten up, you little pussy," he hissed through clenched teeth. "You're supposed to be a Marine, not a goddamn girl scout."

Krupe also shook several boots for not straightening up properly, not lining up with the man directly to their right, or not fully extending their left arm. Then, satisfied for the time being, he walked to the front of the column, midway between the ranks, and commanded: "Turn right."

When they did so he commanded again: "Turn right." Then once more he ordered: "Turn right."

"Now you idiots are headed in the proper direction," he said. Bennett smirked when he realized Krupe had deliberately ordered three right turns rather than one left turn. He made a mental note to add that to his own repertoire.

At the command, "For-ward . . . harch," some recruits stepped off on the proper foot, others stepped off on their right foot, and still others had to scramble to keep from being walked on from behind as they tried to interpret the barely intelligible command.

Krupe didn't bother to count cadence, nor did the drill instructors try to enforce even a semblance of military precision; instead, the platoon straggled along in dual ranks. As Bennett passed within earshot of Sanders as the two of them brought up the rear of the platoon, he spat, "How we gonna make Marines of this crummy bunch in ten weeks?"

Sanders shook his head. "It looks like Coxey's Army," he

replied. Sighing loudly, as though asking how he ever got stuck with such an assignment, Bennett continued ahead and took up a position midway along the ranks.

Krupe ordered a halt outside the entrance to a large tin warehouse with sliding double doors. "Form one line," he commanded, "and stand up close, with your toes touching the heel of the person in front of you, thumbs at your side, looking straight ahead."

They did as ordered, hastily lining up in one serpentine rank that the drill instructors undertook to straighten out with appropriate force. When Bennett reached Gillian he deliberately shoved him into the recruit in front of him.

"You like this, Private Jane?" he mocked.

"Yes, sir," the boot replied, trying not to betray any emotion.

"I'll bet you do. Sex you up, does it, Private?"

There was an awkward silence. Gillian set his jaw, as though he did not intend to answer. Just as he did so, Bennett laid into him, pulling the recruit from the ranks and crashing a knee into his groin. Gillian fell as though he had been poleaxed. Stretched out on the floor, he began gasping for air in quick sharp wheezes.

A staff sergeant, wearing a T-shirt but his rank stenciled on his dungaree cap, emerged from the warehouse and strolled over toward the prostrate youth. "What have we here, Sergeant?" the amused supply sergeant asked Bennett. "A salty boot on his first day at our vacation resort?"

"Not salty, Sergeant," Bennett explained. "Queer. A fairy nice boy." He paused. Gillian's gasps were louder now, but the wheezes had diminished.

"Sounds like he has asthma," volunteered the staff sergeant.

"Wouldn't it be just my luck to get an asthmatic fairy—a wheezing queer," Bennett said contemptuously. "A panting, puffing pussy."

"Sergeant, do you mind if we get started?" Krupe broke in impatiently, addressing the supply sergeant. "I've got to get these idiots to chow by seventeen forty-five and it's sixteen ten already."

The smile faded and the supply sergeant looked as though he were about to respond with a wisecrack. But if so, the sight of Krupe—unsmiling, forcefully gripping his *cocomacaque* at the

ends with each hand—caused him to change his mind. Instead he
blared, "When I give you the word you will run inside on the
double, line up in front of a stall, and look straight ahead. Take
off!"

When the recruits were inside and standing as directed, the
supply sergeant walked forward and climbed atop a raised
platform.

"In front of each one of you you will find two laundry bags
like so," he began, holding up a white drawstring bag. "When I
give you the word you will take one in your right hand, one in
your left hand. When I give you the word again you will hold
them up in the air. Now, take one in each hand."

"God*damn* it, Private," Bennett hollered, slapping a recruit
across the face for raising the bags, "you weren't told to hold
'em in the air."

"Okay," said the supply sergeant, "get 'em in the air."

The recruits did as directed.

"Now lower the laundry bags and put the one in your left
hand inside the one in your right hand, and be quick about it."

Sanders, walking back and forth as though on a scouting
mission, upbraided one recruit: "Private, don't you know your
right hand from your left hand? You've put the bag in your right
hand inside the bag in your left hand. Let's see you do it right."

The recruit obeyed, although there was no discernible difference between the two bags. Several other recruits hastily withdrew the bags they had also tucked away incorrectly, and
repeated the procedure as ordered.

"Privates, you will find one bar of soap and one scrub
brush. Take one in each hand. Now get 'em up, way up high.
Come on, damn it, Privates, you're too slow. If you don't know
what you're looking for, look at the man next to you. All right,
drop your hands and put the items in your laundry bag. Let's go,
let's go.

"You will also find one tube of shaving cream and one
double-edged razor. Take one in each hand, any hand. Get 'em
up in the air. Come on, way up, way up. Okay, put 'em away."

This procedure was repeated until the recruits had tucked
away a can of Kiwi shoe polish, a combination lock, a sewing
kit, a brush for cleaning rifles, a shoe brush and laces, three
wooden pencils, a ballpoint pen, and a toothbrush. When these
items were safely enclosed in the laundry bags the supply
sergeant said, "Now all that remains in front of you is your

Guidebook for Marines. Hold it up, quick. Take it and put it in your rear pocket. You jitterbugs who don't have rear pockets, you can carry it wherever it's convenient for the time being, but Christ help you if you lose it. Those of you who smoke hold up your hands.''

The response, from perhaps half the platoon, was guarded, nervous. ''You smokers hustle up here and form one line.'' When they did so, they were issued two cartons of cigarettes and several packs of matches. ''Get back to your bins and put those cigarettes in your laundry bags.''

Then the supply sergeant said, ''Now all of you, shake your bags . . . come on, be quick about it, shake your bags. Tie the ends like so,'' he said, demonstrating a simple wrap-around knot.

When the bags were tied the drill instructors hustled the recruits outside, cajoling and threatening them as they ran to form into two lines. Again they lined up in no particular order, striving merely to stand at some semblance of attention in alignment with the person to their right. After Krupe and Bennett jostled several unaligned recruits, warning them to straighten up, the platoon moved out in route-step, the recruits carrying laundry bags slung over their right shoulder.

They walked for about ten minutes in silence unbroken except for the sound of their feet on the warm asphalt as they moved along the company streets. It was now midafternoon and the hot Carolina sun was causing perspiration to form on brows, necks, and wrists. At each intersection Krupe ordered the two recruits in the front of the lines to jump out of ranks and post themselves as lookouts, somewhat like school-crossing guards, until the platoon was safely past. Occasionally an interested bystander stopped to watch the newcomers straggle by, conspicuous in civilian clothes. But for the most part few passers-by paid them other than cursory attention.

They continued down a road and past a tent area, its several recruit platoons nowhere in sight. Finally on Krupe's command they stopped alongside four Quonset huts. In front of the huts were several cement washracks, and just beyond them was a series of rectangular-shaped pipes between which ran strands of wire clothesline. Perhaps fifty yards farther, beyond clumps of bushes and trees that partially obscured the view, was the company drill field. And far in the distance, way across Blvd. de France, was the main parade field, or ''grinder.''

"This is the Sixth Battalion," Krupe announced. "This is where you'll live until we move to the rifle range . . . or until they cart you off in a basket because you weren't Marine material. When I tell you, you will get inside your Quonset hut on the double, you will tie your laundry bag around the first empty rack you come to, then you will double-time back outside and line up again. Is that clear?"

"Yes, sir," they responded.

"All right. Now I want you to begin counting." He pointed to the first recruit in the front rank. "Begin."

"One," the youth replied.

"What's the matter, lad, can't you count?" Krupe asked the next recruit.

"Two," the second recruit hastened to respond.

"Three," said the third.

"Four."

When they reached twenty-four, Krupe said, "You first twenty-four will get in that hut. But don't move until I tell you to. Start counting again to twenty-four."

The second group, which included Dutton, Tew, Gillian, and the Indian youth, was assigned to the next Quonset hut. The remaining twenty-three recruits were assigned to the third hut, alongside the drill instructors' Quonset that doubled as platoon office.

On Krupe's orders the seventy-one recruits scurried toward their assigned huts. There was momentary confusion as each recruit raced to get inside, tie his laundry bag to an empty rack, and return. Dutton found an empty top rack, looped his laundry bag around the end of it and secured it with an improvised knot, then sped outside. None of the drill instructors was in sight, so he and the dozen or so recruits who returned at approximately the same time lined up as before.

Less than a minute later all the recruits were standing silently at attention. The sun was even warmer now, almost uncomfortable. Suddenly Krupe stormed from the DI hut, followed closely by Bennett and Sanders. "Just what do you call this?" Krupe demanded. "You are supposed to be studying your Guide-books, not standing here meditating."

He approached Stanley Tew and thrust his face right on up into that of the recruit. "Private, repeat your fourth General Order."

"Sir?"

"I said, Private, repeat your fourth General Order—or your sixth . . . or your second . . . or your fifth."

"I don't know them, sir," Tew said contritely.

"You don't know? Then why are you just standing here not studying?"

"Sir, I thought—"

"You thought! I don't care what you thought, Private. I already told you that you're not to think—we will do your thinking for you. I seem to have forgotten your name, Private. Perhaps you can enlighten me."

"Private Stanley Tew, sir."

"That's right, Private Tew?" He repeated it as though making a mental note. "I'll remember from now on. You're pretty tough, aren't you, Private Tew?"

"No, sir. I mean, I don't know what you mean, sir."

"Tough, Private Tew, t-o-u-g-h. Is the word so hard to understand? You're a tough guy, aren't you?"

Careful to subordinate self-confidence to caution, the recruit replied: "I could usually take care of myself, sir."

The drill instructor scrutinized him, trying to decide whether any disrespect was implied, even unintentionally. But the recruit continued standing perfectly erect, betraying no hint of impudence. Momentarily at a loss whether to smash Tew or ignore him, Krupe decided on the latter—for now. "Good for you, Tew," he said. "That's a Marine Corps specialty, taking care of tough guys. We'll see how tough you are over the next ten weeks."

He looked at the diminutive recruit next to Tew. "What's your name, Private?"

"Private Gabriel, sir," came the timid reply. "Private Jonathan Gabriel, sir."

"Well, Private Gabriel, since Private Tew here most likely can't read, suppose you read for all of us the fourth General Order. It's in Chapter Six of your *Guidebook*."

Fumbling nervously, Gabriel had difficulty finding the page. Sanders, standing nearby, walked over, took the *Guidebook* from him, and returned it open to the page marked "Orders for Sentries."

"Thank you, sir," Gabriel muttered. Relieved that he wasn't about to be pummeled, he scanned the page until he found what he was looking for. "Sir," he began, "the fourth

Gen—'' He was interrupted almost immediately by Krupe, which caused Gabriel to flinch and almost drop the book.

"I can't hear you, Private Gabriel, and neither can anybody else. Sing out."

"Sir, the fourth General Order is—"

"Louder," Krupe said.

"Sir, the fourth General Order is, 'To repeat all calls from posts more distant from the guardhouse than my own.'"

"That's right: 'To repeat all calls from posts more distant from the guardhouse than my own.' What does that mean, Private Gabriel?"

"I—I don't exactly know, sir," he replied.

"Do you *un*exactly know, or approximately know?"

"I don't think so, sir."

"How old are you, Private Gabriel?"

"Seventeen, sir."

"Why did you join the Marines?"

"Sir, I've always wanted to be a Marine," Gabriel replied trembling, the sweat streaming down his cheeks. "I want to fight in Korea."

"Oh Jesus," groaned Bennett. "Another candy-ass who watched too many John Wayne movies. If I had a dollar for every . . ." His voice trailed off and he shook his head disgustedly.

Krupe had neither raised his voice to Gabriel nor softened his inquisitorial tone; he merely stared at the diffident bespectacled recruit. He seemed about to say something, apparently thought better of it, then announced:

"We're on our way to the mess hall. You will not say a word the entire time unless one of us talks to you. Move through the line quickly, eat quickly, then get out the back door and line up where you see one of us. Take whatever you want. But there will be no seconds on anything as long as you are a member of my platoon, and you will eat everything on your plate. Be sure to be out of the mess hall by the time the last Drill Instructor leaves."

When Krupe's platoon arrived, several other platoons were lined up in front of the mess hall, so he marched his to the tail end of the line. All the other platoons consisted of two sections of three squads each; only Krupe's platoon was in civvies and in two ranks.

"Well, well, if it isn't Sergeant Bad-ass Krupe himself,"

boomed a voice in front of them. Dutton watched from the corner of his eye as a huge buck sergeant stroke into view. Like every drill instructor Dutton had seen thus far, the newcomer was crew-cut, his hair shaved off almost completely except for a thin layer covering his scalp.

"Hello, Pepper," the tech sergeant replied coldly. "Is one of these platoons yours?"

"That little ol' platoon over there," Pepper said with feigned enthusiasm, pointing to the recruits lined up ahead of Krupe's. "Platoon Four eighty-four, Sixth Battalion. The meanest, toughest platoon on this island. That is, they gonna be at the end of ten weeks. In fact, they don't know it yet, but they gonna be at the end of the month before we leave for the rifle range, or you can bet your sweet katookus I'll know why."

At that Pepper began scanning Krupe's platoon. "Where did you get these yardbirds?" he laughed loudly.

"They just arrived today."

"What platoon?"

"Four eight-six." He paused. "Sixth Battalion."

Pepper's forced smile disappeared immediately. "Well, then," he said finally, lowering his voice, "that means we'll be rivals for the Post Honor Platoon, won't we?"

"I guess so," answered Krupe.

"This time, buddy-roll, it'll be a different story—unless, of course, my platoon has to qualify in the fog again while your platoon shoots in the sunlight."

"You still using that excuse? It already sounds old."

"Too bad. You're gonna hear it until I'm tired of telling it," Pepper said belligerently.

Dutton guessed Pepper was about 230 pounds, 6'4, or about 15 pounds and three inches taller than Krupe. But Krupe just stared at him impassively. Finally he said, "Don't pin your hopes on winning Post Honor Platoon, Pepper. You haven't seen the day you can surpass me on the rifle range or on the grinder, in the fog or on a sunny day."

Corporal Sanders had never seen Pepper before, and he was astonished that the DIs would express their mutual contempt so openly in front of each other's recruits. He wondered what had happened to provoke such smoldering hostility.

Just then another platoon cleared the mess hall doors and the mess sergeant, standing outside the double-door entrance, yelled to Pepper, "Sergeant, let's get your platoon moving, they're holding up the works."

Pepper shot a malevolent look at the mess sergeant, then turned back to Krupe. "I expect we'll be seeing a lot of each other, Sergeant Bad-Ass," he said.

"I hope so, Pepper, preferably at arm's length. I was afraid you'd request transfer to a different training battalion before I could make you eat your words."

Pepper spun away angrily. "Move, goddamn it," he hollered at his recruits, shoving one and sending him sprawling. "Get in there and eat and get outside on the double."

Sanders sidled up to Krupe. "What was that all about?" Without taking his eyes off Pepper, Krupe replied: "That is Sergeant LeRoy Pepper. We're old, old friends." And he walked toward the front of the platoon.

The recruits moved quickly into the west wing of the mess hall while another platoon filed into the east wing. After passing through the screen door they extracted metal trays from a nearby large rack, selected silverware from metal containers, then filed past messmen—recruits who had completed at least two-thirds of boot training—who placed the food onto any of the tray's six sections.

As James Gillian reached the end of the chow line, Bennett who had quietly positioned himself there moments earlier, grabbed him by the shoulder and turned him toward a large stainless-steel vat. "See this, Private Gillian?" he said, pushing the recruit's face down and almost into the red-colored liquid.

"Yes sir," the youth gasped.

"I want you to drink at least four cups of this a meal, do you hear? The cook here"—he grinned and nodded toward a perplexed corporal—"he calls this 'fruit drink,' but everyone else calls it Panther Piss." The cook smiled, but without conviction.

"The reason I want you to drink so much with every meal is because it contains saltpeter"—at that he winked at the amused corporal, who nodded in solemn agreement—"and I want to be sure you don't put it to one of your buddies during the night. Is that clear?"

"Yes, sir," Gillian replied, willing to agree to anything if he could slink away.

Dutton made it a point to sit at the table with him. He

caught the recruit's eye and smiled ever so slightly, hoping to boost his spirits. The Indian youngster also tried to catch Gillian's eye, but he didn't look up from the tray throughout the meal except to refill his cup as ordered.

The recruits ate quickly, yet none had finished by the time Bennett rose from his table in the section reserved for drill instructors and NCOs. He ordered a messman to remove his tray, then strode toward the exit. His departure alarmed the recruits, who began swallowing and gulping their food.

As soon as Bennett left through the back screen door, the bronzed recruit gathered up his cup and silverware and headed for the scullery near the rear exit. He had taken no more than three or four steps when a voice boomed throughout the mess hall: *"Where do you think you're going, lad?"*

Krupe slowly pushed back his chair, then rose ominously. The recruit, shaken by the realization that he had done something wrong but unaware of what, thought his best defense lay in silence. The mess hall was deathly quiet as Krupe, retrieving his *cocomacaque* from beneath the chair, strolled toward him.

"What did I tell you about eating everything on your plate?"

Silence was now out of the question. "Sir, you said to eat everything."

"And did you eat everything on your plate?"

The boy gulped. He dropped his eyes toward the tray, which he held in both hands fully extended downward. "No, sir."

"Bring the tray up close to your chest and then put your face all the way down in those mashed potatoes."

One look at the drill instructor's eyes convinced the boy it was no joke. Gingerly he did as ordered, pressing his face slowly into the potatoes.

"Get that face down in there," Krupe ordered, swiftly rapping the bottom of the tray with his *cocomacaque*. The recruit stumbled backward, fought to regain his balance, then collapsed on the floor. The tray landed on his chest; an unsightly mixture of potatoes and gravy clung to his face and shirt.

"Get outside on the double," Krupe ordered. After he picked himself up the youth began scrambling after his utensils, but at Krupe's order he stopped his search and started running toward the scullery door. "Come back here," Krupe hollered after him.

"Sir," the youth protested, "I thought you ordered me—"

"Don't think, Private. Pick up your mess gear before you move out. There are no waiters here."

Most of the drill instructors watched the performance with amusement and respect approaching awe, befitting Krupe's reputation as one of the toughest and best DIs in the Marine Corps. Even Pepper grudgingly admitted to himself that the mashed potatoes routine was a good gimmick.

The messmen and other recruits watched with varying degrees of fright as the confused boy scurried to collect his silverware. After what seemed an eternity, he dashed toward the scullery, emptying his tray in the prescribed manner before racing out.

The line started moving again. Dutton, Gillian, and the six others at the table wolfed down the rest of their meal, filed into the scullery, cleared the few scraps of food from their trays by whacking them over a sturdy GI can, then deposited silverware and trays in the appropriate slots before leaving through the screen door.

Outside, the Indian and several other recruits were lined up at attention reading their *Guidebooks*. Dutton fell in alongside the Indian, withdrew his *Guidebook*, opened it to Chapter Six, and began memorizing the General Orders. Bennett and Sanders posted themselves near the scullery door, talking nonchalantly, seemingly indifferent to the mad scramble around them.

Soon after all Platoon 486's recruits were lined up at attention studying, Krupe emerged. "Where's your *Guidebook*, Private?" he demanded of a recruit far down the line in the back row.

"He's speaking to you, pinhead," Bennett said, directing his remark to a recruit who had tried to escape detection by looking straight ahead. The recruit, who did have an elongated head, set off by predominant, hooded eyes, turned toward Krupe. "It's on my bed, sir," he confessed. "I left it there with my laundry bag."

"Oh, you left it on your *bed*, did you, Private? That's interesting," Krupe said as he walked casually toward the offender, "because we don't have beds in the Marine Corps. We have racks or bunks, and you had best get that through that thick pin . . . through that thick skull of yours, is that clear?"

"Yes, sir."

"Good. Now, Private," he said, pushing aside a recruit in

the front rank in order to have an unobstructed view of the miscreant, "we don't tolerate forgetfulness in the Marine Corps. A man who forgets his *Guidebook* in boot camp is the kind of malingerer who forgets his helmet or bayonet in combat, or falls asleep on guard duty. He's the kind of numskull whose thoughtlessness gets other Marines killed in battle. You wouldn't want to be responsible for killing another Marine, would you, Private?"

"No, sir," the recruit replied.

"I believe you, Private . . . What's your name, lad?"

"Private Loyal Reese, sir."

"I believe you, Private Reese. But I have to be sure. I can't risk others' lives by sending you into combat without being sure. Don't you agree?"

Reese was only too happy to agree.

"Very well. In that case you will walk fire watch from midnight to two every night this week, just to remind you never to forget again. Is that clear?"

"Yes, sir."

"Good. Sergeant Bennett, Corporal Sanders," he said, turning toward his assistants, "you'll help Private Reese remember, won't you?"

"You bet your sweet ass," Bennett said, his face twisted in a malevolent half-grin. Sanders merely nodded.

"All right, Privates," Krupe said. "Right face. For-ward . . . harch."

*   *   *

As soon as they arrived back at the barracks the recruits were ordered inside, warned to stand at attention in front of their racks, and told to memorize all eleven General Orders. Sanders selected three recruits from each hut to line up in front of the drill instructors' quarters to draw linen and blankets for their Quonsets. Dutton was one of the nine picked for this detail. As they stood silently outside, Bennett, who had been inside the hut talking and laughing with the other two DIs, walked over to the door and said irritably, "Well, what the hell you waiting for?"

One of the recruits mistook the question as an order to step inside—at which point Bennett rushed at him and bowled him over, tumbling him outside the door. "Don't you know better than to set foot inside my home without knocking?" Bennett demanded, squinting and blinking rapidly. "What in Christ's name is this civilian crap, walking into someone's home unannounced?"

"I'm sorry, sir," replied the startled boot as he rose from the asphalt, his trousers torn and his knee bloodied.

"Sorry's ass," Bennett spat. "From now on when any goddamn recruit wants to enter our home you will knock loudly three times, wait for an answer, then say, 'Sir, Private John Smith requests permission to speak to the Drill Instructor.' You think you can remember that?"

"Yes, sir," the recruit said.

"Well then, do it."

The recruit approached the doorway, reached inside to knock against the open door, and rapped loudly three times.

"Speak!" Bennett demanded.

"Sir, Private Paul Thorn requests permission to speak with the Drill Instructor."

"About what?"

"Sir, we were ordered here to collect the linen and blankets, sir."

"Get in here," Bennett replied, directing Thorn to two piles of linen. "Where are the other two idiots from your hut?"

"Here, sir," answered a voice from outside.

"Here, sir," echoed another voice.

"Get in here."

After the recruits announced themselves in the prescribed manner they were admitted and each was told to count out forty-eight sheets, twenty-four pillow cases, and twenty-four blankets. Then they were directed to carry them back and distribute a set to each recruit.

"Whose hut has only twenty-three men in it?" Bennett demanded. No one answered. "Goddamn it, Privates, which of you bastards are in the hut closest to this one?"

"Here, sir," came the simultaneous replies from three recruits outside the Quonset.

"Get in here, Privates, let's go."

The lead recruit started to enter unannounced but caught himself at the last minute, knocked three times, and was admitted. The other two followed his lead. After they counted out their allotment of linens and blankets, Dutton and the two recruits from his hut repeated the procedure. The nine recruits were each required to make two trips, then they also fell in at attention in front of their racks, their *Guidebooks* opened to the General Orders.

After about ten minutes, Corporal Sanders opened the door of the middle Quonset hut. There was total silence for a moment, then Sanders said angrily, "From now on the first boot to see a Drill Instructor in the doorway will yell 'Attention.' Is that understood?"

"Yes, sir."

"Now I'll go out and we'll try it again."

He returned several minutes later. This time three or four recruits spotted him and hollered. "That's better," Sanders said as he strode toward the middle of the hut. "Private," he said to Jonathan Gabriel, "attention means that both arms are at your side, including the arm holding the *Guidebook*." Gabriel, eager to obey, stood stiffly and awkwardly in a rigid semblance of attention.

"All right," the corporal announced, "at ease." The recruits relaxed only slightly. "We're going to learn to make our racks the Marine Corps way. So gather around up here," he said, walking toward the bed at the front of the hut. "Hurry it up."

"You," he said, beckoning to Gillian, "come up here and give me a hand." Afraid of what was in store, the boot made his way to the front.

"This is your mattress cover," Sanders explained, pointing to the contoured sheet already covering the mattress. "The first thing we do is take a sheet this way and open it full length over the mattress. Then we make hospital corners, like this," he explained. When he finished he ordered Gillian, observing from the other side of the bed, to repeat the procedure.

"That's right, Private," he said encouragingly. Then he demonstrated how to pull the sheets tight, how to fold hospital corners at the bottom of the blanket, how to roll down the sheet from the top and stretch it taut until every trace of a wrinkle disappeared. "This," he said, slapping the completed rack, "is the way you will make your rack the first thing each morning, before you go to the head to wash, shave, and clean your teeth."

He ordered the recruits to do so now, saying he would return in a few minutes to inspect. If they had spare time, he said, they should break out their *Guidebooks* again and resume studying.

As soon as he left, the frantic recruits hurried to make up

their racks according to Sanders' directions. As he raced against
an unseen clock, Dutton suddenly realized Private Gabriel was in
the rack below him. "I'm Tom Dutton," he said, thrusting out
his hand for a hurried introduction. Gabriel accepted it with a
limp handshake and a mumbled expression of his name. "I took
the top bunk because I'm tall and can climb into it easily,"
Dutton said. "But you can have it if you want."

"No thanks," replied Gabriel, "I better keep this one. And
I've got to make it up before he comes back," he said, looking
around warily. "He'll kill us if it isn't made up."

"It's not that bad," Dutton said reassuringly, although he
was beginning to wonder exactly how bad it would be. Certainly
he had not been prepared for the violent reception he had
experienced so far. "But you're right, we better get them made
up."

The recruits worked rapidly, comparing the results with
their neighbors. When Dutton smoothed away the last trace of a
wrinkle with a satisfied swipe, he looked down to check Gabriel's
progress. He almost wished he hadn't, for his bunkmate's efforts
were clearly unsatisfactory.

"Can I give you a hand?"

Gabriel looked at him pleadingly but replied, "Maybe you
better not."

"Just this once, until you get the hang of it," Dutton said
offhandedly, hurriedly pitching in. When the rack finally looked
presentable they joined the others at attention, studying their
Guidebooks.

Fifteen minutes later they heard a commotion in a nearby
Quonset hut, followed by occasional loud metallic noises and
muffled shouts. After a few minutes everything was silent again.
All at once someone yelled, "Ten-shun," and the drill instructors charged into the hut.

"What do you call this, lad?" demanded Krupe as he
approached the first rack, grabbing the turned-down blanket and
sheet and in one motion dumping the entire mattress on the floor.
"Make it the way you were shown."

Bennett, meanwhile, raced to the rear of the hut and began
tearing apart each rack at that end, while Sanders worked the
middle sector. Not a single rack escaped their wrath, not a single
recruit was spared threats, criticism, or loud denunciation.

"Make them up again," Krupe warned. "We'll be back

shortly and you better have them right this time." The trio departed as suddenly as it appeared, en route to the remaining Quonset hut.

"Yours looked perfect," Gabriel whispered to Dutton as they began all over again.

"I thought they were both okay," Dutton said, darting around the end of the bed to smooth the wrinkles in the sheet. "But I guess we did something wrong. Or maybe they just wanted us to practice."

"Nobody could be that mad who just wanted us to practice," Gabriel said as he struggled with his bottom sheet. "We must have really done something earlier today to make them mad. I wish I knew what it was."

"I do too, Jonathan. Is that what you want to be called?"

"I prefer Jack," Gabriel whispered, as if to say this wasn't any time to be socializing. Sensing he was on edge, Dutton didn't continue the conversation. But after he finished making his own bed he again gave Gabriel a hand, this time without any pretense of helping out just this once.

Once again the puzzled boots were trying to concentrate on their *Guidebooks* when the DIs returned.

Once again the drill instructors berated the results of their labors as pitiful and inadequate.

Once again they methodically tore up each rack, tossing the linen on the floor.

And once again the puzzled recruits remade their racks and stood at attention, studying.

"Ten-shun," someone hollered as Krupe bounded through the doorway. He moved quickly but no wrinkle passed unnoticed as he scanned racks top and bottom. He tore up four bunks before retracing his steps and stopping in front of James Gillian.

"What is your second General Order, Private?"

Without hesitating, Gillian replied: "Sir, my second General Order is 'To walk my post in a military manner, keeping always on the alert, and observing everything that takes place within sight or hearing.' "

"Your seventh General Order."

"Sir, my seventh General Order is . . . is, 'To talk—to talk to no one except in the line of duty.' "

"Your twelfth General Order."

Gillian hesitated. "Sir," he replied cautiously, "I believe there are only eleven General Orders."

"You *believe* there are only eleven or there *are* only eleven? Which is it?"

The recruit was undecided how best to reply. Finally he said warily, "Sir, there are only eleven."

Krupe stared at him without expression. To Gillian's immense relief he turned and walked away, coming to a halt in front of Dutton.

"What is your third General Order, Private?"

"Sir, my third General Order is, 'To report all violations of orders I am instructed to enforce.'"

Krupe moved on to the next rack, where one of the recruits was straightening the blanket Krupe had stripped from his bed only minutes before. "What is your sixth General Order?"

The Indian lad, whose memories of the mess-hall incident were still vivid, tried hard to remember. "Hurry up, Private," Krupe ordered. "Your sixth General Order?"

"My sixth General Ord—" the recruit began. But Krupe reached out, seized him by his gravy-stained lapel, and spun him into the nearby rack.

"What did you forget, Private?" Krupe demanded, hovering over him. "What have I told you time and again not to forget?"

At last it dawned on the boy. "Sir, I forgot to say 'sir.'"

As Krupe grabbed him again and pulled him upright, he said, "You won't forget again, will you, Private?"

"No, sir."

"You bet you won't, Private—not if you know what's good for you. What's your sixth General Order?"

"Sir, I . . . I haven't memorized them that far yet."

"Why not? You've had almost enough time to memorize the entire *Guidebook*. How far have you memorized them?"

"To number—I mean, sir, I've memorized them to number four."

"Let's hear them, Private."

"Sir, my first General Order is to—"

"Wait a minute, wait a minute," Krupe interrupted. "This isn't a monastery. Open your mouth when you talk and share your brilliance with your fraternity brothers."

"Sir," the recruit began, exaggeratedly loud, "my first General Order is, 'To take charge of this post and all government property in view.'

"Sir, my second General Order is, 'To walk my post in a

military manner, keeping always on the alert, and observing everything that takes place within sight or hearing.'

"Sir, my third General Order is, 'To report all violations of orders I am instructed to enforce.'

"Sir, my fourth General Order is 'To repeat . . . to repeat from posts—I mean, to repeat . . . all calls from posts' ''—he hesitated, then finished with a flourish—'' 'more distant from the guardhouse than my own.' ''

Krupe was unimpressed. "Tomorrow I expect you to know all eleven General Orders, is that understood?"

"Yes, sir."

"And your rack will not be messed up ever again, is that also understood?"

"Yes, sir."

"Very well, Private, we'll see," his voice both threatening and skeptical. Then he turned to Jonathan Gabriel, who had spent the entire time trembling inwardly while the drill instructor was in the vicinity. "What's your name, Private?"

"Private Jonathan Gabriel, sir."

"That's right, Private Gabriel," Krupe repeated coldly. "Private, who is the President of the United States?"

Taken aback by the question, the recruit couldn't think clearly for several seconds. All he was aware of was a massive, hostile figure hovering over him, wielding a formidable club and demanding an answer. Then Gabriel heard himself replying, "Sir, the President of the United States is Harry S Truman."

"Who is the Vice President?"

"Sir, the Vice President is Alben Barkley."

"Who is the Secretary of State?"

"Sir, the Secretary of State is Dean Acheson."

"Who is the Secretary of the Navy?"

"Sir, the Secretary of the Navy is . . . I believe . . . Dan A. Kimball."

"Who is Secretary of the Marine Corps?"

Gabriel, still inwardly frightened but somewhat emboldened by the ease with which he was answering, replied, ''Sir, if I'm not mistaken, there is no Secretary of the Marine Corps. The Marine Corps falls under the jurisdiction of the Secretary of the Navy."

"What party do the President, Vice President, Secretary of State, and Secretary of the Navy belong to?"

"Sir, they belong to the Democratic Party."

"What is your opinion of the Democratic Party?"

Gabriel was confused and fearful that he was about to be set upon once more. "Sir," he replied cautiously, "I'm not sure I can answer that question—"

"You better be sure you *don't* answer, Private. As long as you're in my platoon—and for some of you that isn't going to be much longer," he added parenthetically, scrutinizing some of the faces before him—"I don't ever want to hear a political opinion of any kind. Is that understood?"

"Yes, sir."

Krupe turned toward the door as though preparing to leave. He stopped in front of the bunk across the aisle from Dutton. "Private Reese, who is the Commandant of the Marine Corps?"

The youth furrowed his brow, accentuating his elongated head as he tried hard to remember. Finally, sensing the drill instructor's growing impatience, he replied, "I don't know, sir."

"Why don't you know?" Krupe demanded. He shifted his *cocomacaque* from hand to hand several times. Then, before the recruit could reply, the tech sergeant aimed the end of the club at the boy's solar plexus.

The startled recruit involuntarily raised his knee across his groin, simultaneously drawing up his body into an awkward protective shell. When the edge of the club came to rest less than an inch from his body, he was caught completely off balance. Krupe tapped him and he toppled backward, falling to the floor, one arm sprawling across the lower rack as he fell.

Krupe moved toward him, smashing his club against the bunk and missing the recruit's outstretched hand by inches. "Get your hand off that rack, Private," the drill instructor ordered. As he did so, Krupe announced: "None of you will put so much as a finger on a rack before lights out. Is that clear?"

"Yes, sir," came the reply, from no one louder than Loyal Reese, who at that very moment was scrambling to his feet.

"When I give you the word you will fall in outside," he said, turning his back on them and walking away.

Less than a minute later Bennett shouted, "Platoon Four eighty-six, fall in."

Dutton didn't remember having been told his platoon number, but he raced for the door determined that if he was in error it was better to err on the side of overreaction. The other recruits apparently felt the same way, for they scurried into the platoon street from the three Quonset huts and lined up in two columns, as before. The drill instructors surveyed them for a few moments in silence, then Krupe announced:

"From now on you people will line up like Marines. When you fall in, you fall in in two sections of three squads each, the tallest recruits up front, the feather merchants in the rear. You will line up this way every time. Sergeant Bennett and Corporal Sanders," he said, "let's see if we can bring some order from this chaos."

The three of them undertook to align the platoon properly. Krupe designated Stanley Tew as platoon leader, Bennett appointed Dutton and two other recruits as squad leaders and ordered them to the front of the platoon. The appointments were based on the recruits' height, so that the platoon sloped gently downward from front to back, and was divided in the middle. The Indian recruit was appointed leader of the second section, which was separated from the front section by about two yards.

The platoon was rearranged to the accompaniment of jostling by Krupe and continuous swearing by Bennett. "Study the man to your right and to your left, because this is where you'll be every time you fall in," Krupe said. "You people were too slow getting into formation. You need more practice. When I say so you will get back inside on the double and line up in front of your racks. Then when I tell you, run outside fast and line up properly. Is that clear?"

"Yes, sir."

"All right. Now get in those huts."

There was a frantic dash for the doorways. Because the platoon had been rearranged according to height, rather than proximity to assigned huts, confused recruits scrambled from the huts at one end of the platoon to huts at the other end. As they did so the drill instructors spurred them on, tongue-lashing them and occasionally adding a shove.

No sooner did most of the recruits reach their racks when they were ordered outside, and took off running again. Dutton slipped into the front of the line quickly amid the general confusion of trying to decide where to go.

"Where do you belong?" Krupe demanded of Jonathan Gabriel, who was wandering around aimlessly.

"I'm not sure, sir," Gabriel replied, fearful that his earlier success in answering Krupe's questions was in imminent jeopardy.

"You're down the end, Private," Krupe said, pointing

toward the second section, where everyone else was standing at attention.

As Gabriel started to run around the platoon in order to slip into line from the rear, Bennett grabbed him and shook him violently. "Goddamn it, what are you milling around for?" he screamed. "Get in ranks before I stomp your ass." Gabriel spotted an opening in the middle squad and ducked in.

"This platoon is still too slow," Krupe announced. "I want to see some speed. Get in those huts."

As Gillian raced toward his Quonset, Bennett stuck out a foot and tripped him. When Gillian realized what had happened, he wanted to get up and try to rearrange Bennett's idiotic grin. But he knew any such move would be suicidal, so after regaining his feet he headed for the hut, pursued by Bennett's derisive laughter.

Even before all the recruits made it to their racks, Krupe ordered them to fall in. Once again they turned and ran back outside.

"Get in the huts," Krupe demanded the instant they formed into their assigned ranks. Then, again before most of them reached their racks, in fact while many were still struggling to get throught the doorways, they were ordered outside once more.

At least a half-dozen more times Krupe ordered the recruits in and out of the huts at intervals ranging from seconds to ten minutes. Once he batted a laggard recruit across the mouth with the back of his hand, splitting the recruit's lower lip. Another time he approached a recruit who hadn't come fully to attention, grabbed the supraclavicular nerve between the youth's neck and shoulder, and squeezed with his thumb and forefinger until the youngster sank to the ground on one knee in pain.

But most of the time he merely stood there magisterially, clutching his *cocomacaque*, scowling from behind his thick lenses, his very presence awesome and intimidating.

Bennett, on the other hand, kept up a running stream of oaths—here thumping a confused recruit, there pushing or slapping another, all the while grinning fiendishly. Corporal Sanders merely hollered at the recruits, demanding they speed up.

Content that for the time being the platoon had had enough practice getting in and out of the huts, Krupe summoned Jonathan Gabriel front and center and ordered him to repeat the chain of command, starting with the President, through each Cabinet member, through the Commandant of the Marine Corps, the

Commanding Officer of Parris Island, and the Commanding
Officer of Recruit Training. As early twilight grudgingly gave
way to dusk and then settled into darkness, the platoon remained
at attention, responding in unison to such questions as, "Who is
the Secretary of Labor?" or "Who is the Secretary of the
Treasury?"

At 9:00 P.M. Krupe ordered them inside to get their toilet
articles, then hasten down to the wooden building beyond the
end Quonset hut to shower and clean their teeth. "There will be
no cruds in this platoon," he warned. "You will shower each
night, you will clean your teeth morning and night, and you will
shave each morning whether you think you need it or not. Is that
clear?"

"Yes, sir."

After warning they had ten minutes to be back from the
head and standing in front of their racks studying their General
Orders until lights out, he dismissed them with a curt, "Get out
of my sight. Get."

The recruits hurriedly soaped themselves, then rinsed off
beneath rows of open showers that operated by pulling an
overhead handle. Dutton cleaned his teeth and moved silently
into line to await his turn at the shower. There was little talking;
most recruits were busy soaping, soaking, or drying, rushing to
get back in the allotted time. But just before he stepped into the
shower, the recruit ahead of Dutton complained about going all
day without a cigarette. No sooner were the words out of his
mouth when a massive arm reached into the shower, enveloped
the recruit's bicep, and slammed him against the wall.

"Who told you to talk?" Sergeant Krupe demanded. Too
frightened to reply coherently, the youth stammered meaningless
word fragments. Krupe grabbed his right wrist and jerked him
forward, then smashed him with a forearm that knocked him flat
on the wet floor.

"Get off that deck," Krupe commanded. The recruit merely
gasped heavily. "Get up," Krupe insisted.

When he still did not obey, the DI grabbed the dazed
youngster by the arm and dragged him across the cement floor on
his back and slid him under the shower, face up.

"You'll either get up or you'll drown," Krupe said for the
benefit of the other recruits. Then, turning toward them, he
threatened: "Don't ever let me hear any of you talking in this

head again. This is a place to clean up, not a place for socializing." With that he stomped out, banging the front screen door as he departed.

Dutton helped the semi-conscious youth to his feet, guiding him toward the wooden benches heaped with shoes, socks, underwear, and towels. Still shaken, the recruit tried to gasp his thanks but could not squeeze out the words. So he leaned forward and hung his head limply between his knees.

After Dutton showered he helped the unsteady recruit to his hut, the closest one to the head. The youngster thanked his benefactor; still bent over slightly, he wove his way through the door.

Inside all three Quonset huts the recruits, clad only in skivvies, stood at attention in front of their racks, studying their General Orders. From time to time Sanders or Bennett wandered through, pacing up and down as though in search of the slightest infraction.

At 9:40 P.M. Bennett ordered Loyal Reese, Gillian, and another recruit to dress and report to the DI hut. There he explained their fire watch assignments: The first recruit would continuously walk the prescribed boundaries around the area of Platoon 486 from 10:00 P.M. ("twenty-two hundred" is the way he said it) until midnight ("twenty-four hundred"), Reese would walk from midnight until 2:00 A.M. ("oh, two-hundred hours"), and Gillian from 2:00 until reveille at 4:00 A.M. ("zero four-hundred").

Sanders gave each recruit a duty belt—a cartridge belt with ten pockets plus a canteen hanging from the right hip and a first-aid kit from the left. Then he showed them the area to be walked, described how to alert the drill instructors in case of emergency, and explained how to rouse everyone in the event of fire, how to challenge intruders, and how to remain alert. He warned that it was an automatic court-martial offense to sleep or otherwise goof off on duty.

After showing them the location of each fire extinguisher, he told the first two fire watches to learn the bunk location of their relief men on fire-watch detail. Then he ordered the first recruit to begin his patrol.

Shortly before 10:00 P.M. the recruits, still at attention studying, heard the DIs talking and laughing outside the huts. Precisely on the hour, someone in Dutton's hut yelled for attention as Bennett entered. "All right,, you sorry sons-of-bitches," he hollered, "get those *Guidebooks* away and get in those racks. Now."

He flipped the light switch several times while recruits stuffed the books in their laundry bags, stashed them under mattresses, or placed them on the wooden locker boxes beneath the racks. Before most of them had time to hop in the rack he flicked the lights off for good.

Seconds later the lights flicked off in the nearby Quonsets. It was completely silent. Then Bennett bellowed, "I don't want to hear one word out of you girls."

Dutton was exhausted, but because he was keyed up he had difficulty falling asleep. He tried to reconstruct all that had occurred from the moment the bus door swung open at Recruit Receiving, but everything seemed to be a jumble. He thought perhaps it was just as well, for he had little wish to relive those moments of confusion, fear, and terror.

Remembering that he hadn't had a cigarette all day—in almost twenty-four hours, to be exact, since just before the train had pulled into Yemassee—he was overwhelmed by the desire to smoke, even a drag or two.

Suddenly the squad bay was ablaze with lights so bright he had to shield his eyes. Standing by the light switch with that half-grin, half-sneer on his face, Bennett snarled, "Get out of those goddamn racks before I get you out. Get out!"

There was a frantic scramble to obey. Dutton jumped to the floor and came immediately to attention. Even those who had fallen asleep in the ten-minute interval since the lights clicked off managed somehow to stagger to their feet.

"Private Gillian, front and center," Bennett hollered. The sleepy recruit hesitated. "Did you hear me, Gillian?" Bennett screamed.

"Yes, sir."

"Then you better haul your tender ass up here, lad. I mean lass."

Gillian took off running, pulling to attention in front of the drill instructor.

"How do you report, Private?"

"Sir?"

"Sir, balls!" Bennett squinted his eyes as though measuring the recruit for size. "I said how do you report?"

"I don't know, sir."

"You don't know. Isn't that nice? You say, 'Sir, Private Janie Gillian reporting as ordered.' Is that clear?"

"Yes, sir."

"Then say it."

"Sir, Private Janie Gillian reporting as ordered."

"Janie, let me look you over." He scrutinized the recruit, who was clad only in his shorts. Finally he asked, "Do you have an erection, Private Gillian?"

"Sir?"

"Goddamn it, Gillian," he said menacingly, the semi-smile disappearing altogether, "I asked whether you have an erection. You know what an erection is, don't you, Private?"

"Yes, sir. I mean, I know what it is, sir, but I don't have one."

"Why don't you have one, Gillian? Here you are, sleeping with twenty-three tender young men. The odds are twenty-three to one in your favor and you mean to say you haven't got a hard-on?"

The recruit realized he was expected to answer every question, no matter how degrading. "No, sir."

"What happened, Private? Did you beat it down? Did you do the wash by hand? Or did you already put the boots to somebody?"

"No, sir," Gillian insisted. "Nothing happened. I just finished my prayers and was beginning—"

"Your what?" Bennett interrupted. "You just finished your what?"

"My prayers, sir."

"Well Je-sus H. Kee-rist on a cross! Your prayers. What did you pray for, Private Gillian? A nice warm male ass beside you each night?"

"No, sir."

"Then what *did* you pray for?"

Was there no respect even for one's religion? Dutton wondered as he kept his eyes straight ahead. But he knew Bennett's bullying would end only when it ran its course. "I . . . I prayed for my family and friends, for world peace—"

"Piece! I knew it, Gillian. You prayed for a piece, just like I thought." Turning to address the entire hut, Bennett said, "Gillian is one girl I know who really means it when he—she—

says she wants a piece of ass." He began laughing raucously, but his laughter soon trailed off. It seemed not to have occurred to him that his performance was not humorous.

"Private Gillian," he said, his tone hostile once again, "what lullabies do you know?"

"I'm . . . not sure I know any lullabies, sir."

"You better goddamn soon think of one. How about 'Lulla-by and Good Night'? You know that?" He was squinting and blinking rapidly, almost like a semaphore.

"No, sir. I . . . I think I probably know 'Away in a Man-ger.' "

"That's wonderful, Private Gillian. 'Away in a Manger' is one of my very favorite songs. I'll tell you what let's do, Private Gillian. You get back in that rack, understand? And when I turn out the lights you begin singing 'Away in a Manger' loud enough to be heard all through the barracks. Sing it six times, you understand?"

"Yes, sir."

"Good. Now move. The rest of you get in those racks."

Before Gillian reached his rack Bennett flipped off the lights. He waited at the door until the recruit began singing in a halting, uncertain voice. Before he had finished the song Bennett interrupted. "Private Gillian?"

"Yes, sir?"

"Good night, Private Gillian."

"Good night, sir."

"Private Gillian?"

"Yes, sir?"

"Don't play with it any more tonight, Private Gillian."

There was a breathless silence that Dutton feared would invite another lights-on session and public humiliation of the recruit. Finally Gillian muttered, "No, sir."

Bennett left, the screen door banging behind him. The recruit picked up where he had left off, intoning "Away in a Manger" as he struggled to hold back tears.

Dutton was asleep before Gillian finished singing. The last thing he remembered was saying a brief prayer that tomorrow be different, that the insults, the torment, the humiliation, the cuffings, the shouts, the vulgarity, and the threats be a thing of the past. He was anxious to begin the sort of training Marines were famed for, the kind he expected when he had affixed his signature to the enlistment paper only a few days before.

Chapter 2

"All right," said the captain after the six youngsters finished signing their names, "raise your right hand and repeat after me the oath up there on the wall." Dutton, like the others, swore to bear true faith and allegiance to the United Satates.

"That's it," said the captain with a satisfied smile. "That doesn't mean you're Marines yet. It only means you've enlisted in the Marine Corps. There's a world of difference, as you'll find out when you get to Parris Island."

Their official enlistment date was July 7, 1952, although they wouldn't board the train for South Carolina until the next morning and probably wouldn't arrive at Parris Island until Wednesday.

Dutton was pleased to learn he would have two days seniority (two days toward retirement, he noted wryly) by the time he reached boot camp. Yet he was impatient. Despite what the captain said, he already considered himself a Marine. Nevertheless he didn't feel any different, and he was still in civilian clothes.

The captain said they must be back by midnight or they would be counted AWOL. Even the Philadelphians among them had to spend the night in Marine barracks rather than at home, since all had to be at 30th Street Station in time to catch the 7:11 A.M. train.

It was just after 3:00 P.M. when Dutton walked out of the recruiting office. There was more than enough time to go down and back to the Jersey shore, but he had already said his good-bys last night and early this morning. He decided instead to explore some bookstores and see a couple of movies downtown.

The hours went swiftly, even though his thoughts lay elsewhere, and during the motion pictures a familiar face kept reappearing in front of him, as though on the screen. The youthful apparition was not a ghost, however, but a memory—the memory of Tim Conway, "Tim the Terror," as Dutton had affectionately dubbed his best friend, who had been killed in combat a little more than a year before. The months since were the longest, saddest, and most confusing year of Dutton's life, and it was because of what had happened to Tim that he was now a Marine himself—at least nominally a Marine.

It was a wonder that he and Tim ever learned to tolerate each other, much less become best friends. For their initial meetings, soon after Tim arrived that summer from Philadelphia to spend a vacation with his grandparents, had resulted in mutual animosity. And the animosity remained even after Tim tried out for the local baseball team and so impressed the manager with his fancy fielding that he broke into the starting line-up in the very next game.

What Tim lacked in size he made up for in determination and brass. He wasn't a troublemaker exactly, but neither was he the sort to shy away from trouble. As he later explained, if you backed away from a showdown in "Fishtown," the Kensington neighborhood from which he hailed, you'd better keep on running.

His immediate estrangement from Tom Dutton was precipitated by two incidents: While Dutton was coaching first base in a game against Port Republic, awaiting his own turn at bat farther down in the line-up, Tim smacked a line drive over the shortstop. Since they were trailing by two runs, Dutton signaled for him to stay at first. But on the very first pitch Tim lit out for second base and was thrown out easily.

The manager showed his displeasure by promptly relegating Tim to right field, the position often reserved for goof-offs or misfits. He would have removed the brash newcomer from the line-up altogether except that only nine players showed up that night.

But if Tim was concerned, he didn't show it. On the contrary, during the very next inning he stood in the outfield casually downing a soft drink between pitches. At age thirteen, Tim Conway was serving notice that he was not one to be pushed around.

After the game Dutton advised Tim that his particular brand of independence was unwelcome on the team. One word led to another. And although Dutton was almost a year older, several inches taller, and perhaps fifteen pounds heavier, Conway took a final drag on a cigarette and said wearily, "Listen, Ace, either get off my back or take a poke at me, 'cause I'm not in any mood to be lectured."

Dutton was so taken aback that he merely stared at the pipsqueak newcomer who, cradling his glove in his left armpit, casually began lighting another cigarette. He was obviously unworried. Finally Dutton said, "You wouldn't be worth the effort," picking up his glove and walking away, convinced that only his maturity and restraint prevented a disaster.

During the next few games neither acknowledged the other's presence, although whenever Dutton got a hit or made a play the least bit out of the ordinary Tim would yell, "Way to go, Ace," or "Good shot, Ace." It was pure Fishtown patois, disconcerting to Ocean Point natives but intended as a compliment all the same. Soon Dutton returned the compliments. Then they began walking home from games together—in semi-silence at first, but as they forgot what they were sore about, eventually by replaying much of the game.

Then, after spending the morning caddying at the local golf course, Tim began visiting the public beach where Dutton was a lifeguard and they resumed where they had left off the day before. Dutton soon helped get Tim a job in the snack bar at the beach, and the two usually swam together after work. By the end of the summer no one would have guessed they had once been antagonists.

Tim returned to Philadelphia at summer's end. But each June he reappeared in Ocean Point and their friendship resumed as though it had never been interrupted.

It wasn't until Dutton visited Tim that he understood why the façade of toughness was necessary: "Fishtown" was as different from Ocean Point as anything he had ever seen. It wasn't a slum and maybe not even dangerous, but its lower-class Irish-Slav residents were visibly marked by their daily struggle against economic and social forces they understood only dimly, if at all. The Conways lived in one of the small, faceless brick row homes that stretched endlessly in every direction. Like most of these homes, its exterior was clean but in need of a face lifting. Inside, like the great majority, the home was dingy but immaculate—as spotless as Tim's mother could keep it, despite her long struggle with poverty, privation, and recurrent illness.

Tim's dad was a truck driver for a rendering company, collecting grease, bones, fat, and suet from restaurants and packing houses. It wasn't ennobling work, perhaps, but it was a steady job, and few residents of Fishtown could boast anymore.

For years it had been Hilda Conway's dream that one day they would move away, perhaps to Mayfair up Frankford Avenue, or maybe out to Upper Darby. Not so much for her sake as for Tim's. More than anything in the world she wanted him to acquire the education and opportunities circumstance had denied her and Al.

Then she fell ill, and with mounting medical bills it was all Al could do to keep Tim in high school. Tim knew all along that college was out of the question, except maybe for night school.

Soon after the war erupted in Korea, Tim decided to join the Marine Corps. He arranged to have a monthly allotment check sent home, and since he had heard talk that the GI Bill would be reintroduced to cover Korean veterans, he hoped to attend college after his discharge while working part time. Meanwhile, he could earn college credits through the Marine Corps Institute extension program.

In early August, at almost the very moment the first contingent of Marines sailed for Korea from California, Tim Conway left Fishtown for Parris Island. During the next few months he periodically requested a transfer to the infantry, but each request was denied without explanation and he was assigned as an instructor at the Parris Island rifle range.

Then in February 1951 he was ordered to report for duty with the First Division in Korea.

Less than a month later he was dead, blown apart by a grenade thrown from the darkness while he was on night patrol.

A piece of Dutton died with Tim on that frozen wasteland. For days he walked around in a stupor, stopped attending classes, ignored his studies, and took to passing long hours with his girl Julie in virtual silence. At times he imagined Tim was still alive, other times he was sure of it: It wasn't conceivable that his friend had died thousands of miles away, in a country Dutton knew nothing about. By the time he finally accepted the fact of Tim's death, thereby acknowledging his own mortality, his mind was made up: He was going to enlist in the Marine Corps.

It wasn't a judiciously weighed decision, but neither was it purely impulsive. It involved considerable soul-searching; yet overriding every other consideration was the wish to follow Tim's trail in the hope of discovering whatever purpose there might have been in his friend's decision to join the Marines.

Tom's parents were incredulous. And until the day he drove to Philadelphia to take his physical, they were hopeful that the arrival of summer and the lure of the seashore would change his mind. Julie was stunned. But she understood his feelings for Tim, and she knew that once he made up his mind, nothing could change it. So she did not try very hard to talk him out of it.

But others tried: His teammates, who pointed out that he had an excellent chance to be drafted by the Warriors . . . family friends, who couldn't understand why such a promising student and athlete would throw it all away to enlist in the Marine Corps, of all places, when he could probably avoid military duty altogether . . . and his friends on the Ocean Point Beach Patrol, where he had put in six carefree summers as a lifeguard. With few exceptions, they couldn't imagine anyone joining *anything*— the military, the monastery, the Foreign Legion—before draining every drop of pleasure from summer's bountiful cup.

For Julie, the few weeks before his departure were already lonely. The two seldom discussed their impending separation, yet it was tacitly expressed in almost every caress, every conversation, every kiss.

Their last night together Julie broke down, her reserve finally crumbling before the awful realization that tonight was the end of their relationship as they had known it. Ten weeks of boot camp, probably a month or more of advanced training at Pendleton or Camp Lejeune, then . . .

Tom comforted her as best he could, but his attempts at reassurance were unconvincing. During the several hours they were parked near the sea wall along the ocean there were two or three prolonged lapses during which they hardly talked. He cuddled her in his arms protectively, trying to kiss away her fears. Then it was time to take her home. On the drive to her house the car radio was playing and Julie sang along with it softly, afraid to sing louder lest she go to pieces:

> "Ev'ry time we say goodby,
> I die a little.
> Ev'ry time we say goodby.

> *I wonder why a little.*
> *Why the gods above me,*
> *Who must be in the know,*
> *Think so little of me*
> *They'd allow you to go. . . ."*

He looked at her, realizing how much he loved and would miss her, and he was suddenly overwhelmed by sadness. Afterward, as he drove across the causeway leading over the bay, he thought of all the things he should have said. But this night— when he should have been able to tell her so much more easily, when he owed it to her to tell her again—he could only hope she would understand.

After the movies he walked one last time through the near-deserted streets of downtown Philadelphia, then hailed a taxicab to drive him to the barracks. On the way, he thought about Julie, about how she would be worrying tonight the way Mrs. Conway had worried the night Tim left for Parris Island. Dear, sweet, kind, unspoiled Julie, a girl at once so worldly and wise, so ingenuous and naive.

And he thought about Parris Island—what it looked like . . . whether boot camp was really as tough as he had been told . . . whether he could endure those ten weeks . . . whether he would be sent to Korea as he hoped to be.

*   *   *

The next morning he boarded the Atlantic Coast Line's Everglades bound for Washington. A recruiting sergeant escorted the seven Philadelphia-area inductees to the 30th Street Station, handed Dutton a sealed brown envelope containing their service records, and warned him not to let it out of his sight until he surrendered it to the recruit receiving sergeant at Yemassee. He wished them all good luck as they boarded the train.

They crowded into adjoining seats and immediately began to speculate about what sort of reception awaited them at "P.I.," the training center famed since before the First World War for turning soft civilians into tough Marines. No sooner had they begun swapping rumors when a loud voice interrupted. "You guys on your way to Parris Island?"

"Yea, man, how'd you know?" one of the Philadelphians asked.

"I seen you talking with the six-striper before you got on

the train," he replied. "My name's Tew, Stanley Tew. From Buffalo. We got four more of us back in this next car from around Buffalo, Tonawanda, that area. And another five or six gyrenes from Boston are in the car behind us, but they seem to want to stick to themselves. Afraid maybe us bad New Yorkers will corrupt them." He laughed loudly, then began puffing on a large cigar.

"Kee-rist, are all the guys from Buffalo as big as you?" another of the Philadelphians asked, awed by Tew's size and apparent strength.

"Yea, we're all as big as Buffalos," he laughed, nudging one of the group. "Hey, how about you guys joining us, maybe play some cards or just shoot the shit? That is, if you ain't stuck-up like them Boston blue bloods."

"Hell, I'm game," one of the Philadelphians replied. "Let's go."

All except Dutton rose to follow Tew. "I'll join you later," he said. "I want to finish a letter."

"A letter?" Tew asked in a voice that could be heard throughout the entire coach. "He ain't been gone ten minutes and already he's writing home. You'll never make a good Marine that way, buddy-roll."

Dutton smiled, although he was mildly annoyed by the intrusion. "Guess you're right," he said agreeably, hoping it would send Tew on his way. "But it won't take long. Then I'll be back to win everybody's money at poker."

"You're on, man," Tew replied. "But hurry, because I intend to finish off these fish pretty fast." Then he turned to the others. "What are we waiting for? Come on, time's money."

Dutton knew he wouldn't get very far with his letter, with its belated endearments. Somehow he seemed incapable of sentiment at this moment, and since he was in no mood for cards or a bull session he merely stared out the window as the train made its way past Main Line Philadelphia, then headed southwestwardly.

Eventually he opened the newspaper to the sports section and studied the baseball standings. Here it was only midseason and his Phillies were already 17½ games out, while his A's were eleven games out. Wait until next year, he thought with a frown. Then he remembered how Tim suffered whenever the Phillies lost—which, except for winning the pennant two years ago—was most of the time.

Tim, he thought as he stared absently beyond his drooping

newspaper. Tim dead. *Dead.* He tried to concentrate on the word but he had trouble grasping its significance. It hurt to remember that he had never once told Tim how much he cherished their friendship. What was it about him, he wondered, that he found it so difficult to express affection?

"Hey," one of the Philadelphians hollered above the noise of the train as he burst through the coach door, "Tew wants you to come back and join the game. Man, he's some card player. He just about cleaned me."

"I think I'll wait," Dutton replied. "We'll be in Washington in about forty-five minutes. I'll contribute my share to the Tew Welfare Fund after we change trains. Tell him not to worry, I won't spend it in D.C."

Dutton's visitor laughed. "Hey," he said. "you know what somebody said back in that train? They said some of the Drill Instructors at Parris Island beat on you."

"Tew tell you that?"

"Hah, not Tew. He says anybody beat on him is gonna get his ass stomped. This was one of our guys from Philly. Said he had a buddy who's just finishing up boot camp and he wrote and told this guy not to join because some of these DIs were meaner'n hell and liked nothing better than to beat on guys from New York or Philly. You believe that?"

"To tell you the truth, I think thy guy's buddy is probably exaggerating to show how tough he is. But even if he's right, there isn't much we can do about it now. By the way," he said, extending his hand, "I'm Tom Dutton."

"Herb Beeks. A and Allegheny."

"A and Allegheny?"

"You're not from Philadelphia, I see."

"Ocean Point—sixty miles away."

"Yea, man, I know where it is. Myself, I go to Wildwood a couple times a year. I mean I did go. I guess none of us will be seeing much of the seashore this summer."

"You know it. Now, what's that about A and Allegheny?"

"That's my neighborhood."

"I had a friend not too far from there. Front and Berks, you know where that is?"

"Sure, Fishtown, ain't it? Near Frankford Avenue. Is he a Polak?"

"No, he's . . . he was Irish. He's dead now."

In Washington they were met at the train by a master sergeant. Tew began calling him "Top" until the sergeant sharply reprimanded him. Since they had only an hour-and-a half wait before changing to the Atlantic Coast Line's Washington-Jacksonville through train, no one was to leave the terminal. They could visit the newsstand, the coffee shop, or make telephone calls. But they were to be at the designated track no later than ten-thirty.

Everyone dispersed as if on command. Dutton visited the barbershop and had his shoes wax-shined to a high gloss. Afterward he strolled across the terminal to the newsstand where he bought the local papers and a paperback book. Then he plunked down on a bench to await the boarding announcement.

As the train sped southward through Virginia and North Carolina, he put his book down often and studied the unfamiliar surroundings, the mile after mile of rich farmland. Occasionally he'd wave to barefoot youngsters with poles slung over their shoulders, modern-day Huck Finns probably on their way to some nearby fishing hole.

Tew had discovered three or four other recruits bound for Parris Island, so he forgot about Dutton. But Dutton wasn't allowed to forget Tew's presence. Although they were at opposite ends of the coach, every few minutes he heard the card players erupt in shouts and laughter. Periodically, usually at Tew's instigation, they broke into an off-key version of the Marines' Hymn.

Shortly before 11:00 P.M., minutes after their scheduled arrival time, the train hissed to a stop outside a small, unlighted station.

"Yemassee, Yemassee," the porter announced, moving through the cars. "All off for those going to Parris Island. Last stop before Savannah."

Dutton slipped his book into his hip pocket and removed his utility bag from the overhead rack. It was dark when he alighted. The train was perhaps thirty yards from the depot's umbrella shed, a rickety structure unsteadily supported by a series of old posts. Eventually Dutton could make out the silhouettes of several buildings up the hill to the right, but it was too dark to tell what they were. It was a sultry evening, and an agreeable fragrance—magnolias, he wondered?—permeated the air.

"All recruits, line up in two rows, on the double." A staff

sergeant, standing in front of them alongside the train, watched
with growing impatience. "On the double, " he repeated, as the
recruits hastened into some semblance of formation.

"I want those of you who are carrying orders to hold them
in the air in your right hand." Dutton and three other recruits
obeyed. The staff sergeant snatched them away. "All right, now
no talking. Follow me."

He led them alongside the tracks to an intersection, then up
a street toward a dimly lighted building. He ordered them inside
the white wooden fence and through the two front doors. As
Dutton passed inside he could just make out the sign over the
outer door:

U.S. Marine Corps
Receiving Barracks

The front portion of the barracks was partitioned off into a
duty room containing a desk and a cot for the duty NCO. Behind
the partition was a blue-green squad bay supported by four
wooden beams running from the floor to the ceiling in the center
of the building. Fifteen double bunks and lockers completed the
meager furnishings.

Recruits were issued linen and ordered to make their bunks.
They were given fifteen minutes to shower and use the head to
the right of the quad bay entrance. After roll call the staff
sergeant picked three recruits at random to walk fire watch
during the night. Then he flipped off the lights with a warning
not to talk.

They were awakened by the third fire watch at 5:00
A.M., ordered to shave and wash, turned in their bed linen, then
were divided into work teams to wash windows, clean the lawn
and walkway, wash Venetian blinds, and scrub the floor. At
eight-thirty they were ordered to wash up and were led in double
file down past the depot, across the tracks, and toward a row of
buildings containing five drab stores. "You will eat in the
Yemassee Cafe," the staff sergeant announced, as if reciting.
"You will eat what you are served and there will be no
complaints. You can talk, but keep it down. Now, fill up those
booths before you sit at the counter."

As they filed in, the staff sergeant intercepted a bronzed
recruit, said something to him, and led him three buildings

away—past the drugstore and the Bank of Yemassee to the St. Clair Cafe. Sixteen recruits quickly filled the four small booths in the Yemassee Cafe while the remainder sat at the counter or waited for a seat. The owner, a Greek, helped the two waitresses serve scrambled eggs, two strips of bacon, hominy grits, toast, butter, and individual packets of jelly.

After eating, Dutton wandered outside, hoping to buy a paper in the adjoining drugstore. He saw the bronzed recruit standing off by himself.

"Did you eat yet?" he asked.

The youth nodded. "Where?" Dutton asked, less out of any real interest than in an effort to be pleasant.

"There." He nodded toward the St. Clair.

"How come?"

The youth shifted uncomfortably, then replied, " 'Cause I'm an Indian."

Dutton regretted the question because the youth was visibly discomfited by it, but he decided he couldn't just drop it at that. "I knew there was segregation down here against Negroes, but I didn't know Indians were discriminated against too."

"Sergeant said he wasn't sure, but it was best not to take a chance."

"Well, how come the St. Clair serves you if the Yemassee won't?"

"It's owned by a Negro. It's a Negro cafe."

"And the Negro served you?" It was Dutton's first exposure to *de jure* segregation and he was confused by its nuances, but the Indian recruit appeared resigned to it, although he seemed to be growing restless with the questions.

"He said he didn't know whether he could, but he talked to the Sergeant and finally said okay."

"I'll be go to hell," said Dutton. "You're good enough to go to Korea and have the Commies blow your head off, but you're not good enough to eat in the Yemassee Cafe. What kind of sense does that make?" When the Indian didn't reply, he said, "I'm Tom Dutton."

"Robert Begay," the Indian replied, returning the handshake.

"Look, I was just going in here to buy a paper to see who won the All-Star game yesterday," Dutton said. "If they don't have a law against it, want to come with me?"

"Thanks, but I'll wait out here. No sense getting anybody upset."

Dutton returned shortly, folding the paper back at the sports section as he did so. When the Indian boy didn't speak he said, "National League, won three to two. Called after five because of rain. But look at this," Dutton said. "Curt Simmons gave only one hit in three innings and Bobby Shantz struck out Lockman, Robinson, and Musial in the only inning he pitched."

As the Indian made a move to look at the box score, the sergeant emerged from the depot and strode across the street. "Fall in," he hollered. "Get those people out of that restaurant. You," he said, turning to Dutton, "throw that newspaper away. You won't need to know what's going on where you're headed. And you," he said to another recruit, "who said you could smoke? Get that cigarette out and don't light up again until you're told you can. As of this minute, the smoking lamp is out."

He led them back to the receiving barracks and again assigned them to work details. Then he walked down to the depot as another train pulled in and soon returned with four more recruits in tow. They were also assigned to work parties.

At about eleven o'clock, when the barracks and surrounding area were sparkling, they were given study folders containing General Orders and Marine Corps terminology and told to memorize them: Henceforth a wall was to be called a bulkhead, stairs were to be called a ladder, the floor was a deck, the toilet a head, a bed a rack or a bunk, a gun a rifle or weapon or piece.

About an hour later a northbound train stopped long enough to unload a dozen more passengers. After they were processed, all forty-three recruits were taken to the Yemassee Cafe. Once again Robert Begay was directed to the St. Clair. After lunch they were hustled aboard the blue, bobtailed bus of the Palmetto Bus Line for the journey to Parris Island.

As the bus rolled along the narrow back roads, the Spanish moss hanging from the overhead trees gave the illusion that they were traveling through a dim tunnel. Dutton studied the ramshackle roadside stands, their crude hand-lettered signs advertising fruit and vegetables for sale. He watched ancient blacks picking corn in nearby fields. He wondered who lived in the broken houses surrounded by weed-covered yards, yards decorated by wrecked pickup trucks, old tires, and rusted farm implements.

As they neared Beaufort, just outside the depot gate, the thick, green foliage gave way to swamps and occasional palm trees. The road leading to the gate was a sprawl of trailer parks and subdivisions. A jumble of billboards advertised the wares of auto dealers, finance companies, and insurance agents. Soon Dutton noticed a checkpoint up ahead and saw that it was manned by a Marine sentry. As the bus drew nearer he made out the gold-and-red sign proclaiming that this was Parris Island. As the sentry waved the bus through, an involuntary shudder passed over Tom Dutton.

Chapter
3

Somewhere in the distance he heard shouting, accompanied by an almost unbearable whirring sound. The shouts grew louder, yet they remained indistinguishable. Dutton blinked. Out of the corner of his eye he saw something hazy off to his left.

He jumped up, even before he remembered where he was. Then, as a whirlwind stormed through the barracks tearing off sheets and blankets, tipping over racks and knocking recruits onto the floor, he recognized Tech Sergeant Krupe.

"Get up, get up!" Krupe shouted. As the drill instructor dashed back and forth, stalking up and down the Quonset hut, the fire watch obeyed his command to whirl an empty pop bottle vigorously inside one of the large metal trash cans. The noise was excruciating.

"What are you standing there for?" Krupe demanded of the recruits who automatically fell in at attention. "Get those racks made up, then get down to the head, shave, and clean up. Hurry it up before I make you wish you had."

Dutton didn't have to be told a second time. Still half-asleep, he quickly made up the rack. Then, after fumbling inside his locker box for the toilet articles, he slipped on his boondockers, slung a towel around his neck, and took off running. It was dark outside. Dutton was wearing his watch, but he did not pause to check the time until he was cleaning his teeth and was reasonably sure none of the drill instructors was around.

Five after four! A.M. Good God, Dutton thought, are they kidding? Five after *four?* He hoped the watch had stopped, but the sweep hand was moving steadily. What an hour to awaken anyone! He heard several muttered curses and whispered complaints, but he washed and shaved in silence, then double-timed back to the Quonset hut.

It was still dark out, and as Dutton dressed he thought of Julie back in Ocean Point. She would be sleeping for several more hours. He tried to visualize her as she slept, probably wearing some sort of little-girl-type pajamas bedecked with ribbons or bows. A wave of nostalgia swept over him, and for the first time since he left, although it had been only two days, he felt desperately lonely.

After dressing, Dutton straightened out Gabriel's poorly made-up rack, stretching the blanket to rid it of wrinkles. Then he broke out his *Guidebook* and, standing stiffly in front of the rack, began reviewing his General Orders.

" 'Ten-shun," someone hollered as a sullen Bennett strode in the door, looking as though he had just awakened.

"You first five men," he said in a fractious tone, pointing across the aisle from Dutton, "get down to the head for cleanup detail. You'll be told what to do when you get there. You three," he pointed to Dutton, Gabriel, and a nearby recruit, "report to the Drill Instructors' hut, on the double. The rest of you, break out the brooms and mops and clean this place down fore and aft. And it better sparkle when I come around to inspect. Now, snap shit."

Corporal Sanders admitted the trio after each recruit executed the prescribed ritual of knocking three times. "The brooms and mops are in that closet," Sanders said, pointing. "Clean it up on the double, then get back to your huts."

They worked silently. Sanders, seated at a desk, studied what looked like their orders. Occasionally he jotted down something on a white tablet. As Dutton worked, he sized up the room furtively. On the wall near the front door was a large topographical map of Korea. Superimposed on it were colored discs apparently indicating the movements of enemy troops, and Marine and other UN forces.

There were two racks, one on each side of the room; three overstuffed chairs and a makeshift coffee brewer; and two long benches supporting dozens of books on military strategy, military history, and histories of Korea, Japan, and China. A large Hallicrafters radio, capable of picking up short-wave broadcasts, occupied a table alongside the desk in the corner of the hut. Also in that corner was a typewriter, a bulletin board containing orders and directives, and a smattering of recent copies of the *Leatherneck*, the *Marine Corps Gazette*, *Time*, *Newsweek*, *U.S. News & World Report*, and several newspapers.

Sanders ignored the recruits. Whenever Dutton glanced at him out of the corner of his eye, or looked toward him when turning to mop in a corner, the drill instructor was absorbed in his work. As the recruits neared completion, Krupe and Bennett returned. The tech sergeant glanced at them, turned toward Sanders, and asked, "Corporal, are you about finished with that roster?"

"Almost, Sergeant. Be right with you." Dutton sensed that the formality of addressing each other by rank was for the benefit of the recruits.

"How about you, Sergeant Bennett? Does your tally jibe with the roster?"

"Christ knows how, but it does."

"Good. What time are we expected at the mess hall?"

"Zero six thirty," Bennett replied.

"Okay. Give them another ten minutes, then break them outside in formation."

"What's up?" asked Sanders.

"A little jog, something to stimulate the appetite."

"Sounds like a good idea, Sergeant," Sanders replied, "but remember, none of these jokers has even been issued sneakers yet. They're still wearing street shoes."

"Yea, I know. Just our lousy luck that some goof-off in the motor pool screwed up the transportation to Yemassee so our civilians didn't arrive until afternoon. Now we'll waste most of the day doing what should have been done yesterday. But don't worry, we won't run far—today. Remind me after chow to put on report whoever fouled up the pickup."

Sanders wondered if Krupe was kidding, but one glance assured him he was not. Absorbed by the conversation, Dutton also looked toward the senior DI. At that instant Bennett sprang at the recruit, knocking him into the locker.

"What in Christ's name do you think you're doing, boot?" Bennett demanded. "Who do you think you are that you eavesdrop on our conversation in our home?"

The locker arrested Dutton's fall, but he was still off balance as Bennett moved toward him, his eyes flashing angrily. He struck Dutton across the face with the back of his hand. Instinctively, the recruit ran his hand across his mouth.

"Is it bleeding, boy?" Bennett demanded.

"No, sir," Dutton replied.

"That's too bad, Private. Really too bad. Because the next time I catch you goofing off, you better believe you'll bleed, real bad-like. You know what I mean?"

"Yes, sir." Dutton stared directly ahead, but he felt Krupe and Sanders watching. For a brief instant he thought about smashing Bennett in the mouth, but he realized it would be suicidal, so he just stood at attention.

"What's your name, boot?"

"Private Dutton, sir."

"You have a first name, Dutton?"

"Sir, my name is Thomas. Private Thomas Dutton."

"Where you from, Private Dutton?"

"New Jersey, sir. South Jersey . . . Ocean Point."

"New Jersey." Bennett spat out the words distastefully. "That's near New York, isn't it? Where all the hoodlums and switchbladers come from?"

Dutton knew Bennett was baiting him. His lips were beginning to smart. He decided he better get away before Bennett alone or with his partners, began to work him over. "I suppose so, sir," he said.

"You suppose so. One thing you'll learn before you leave here, Dutton—that is, if you ever leave here—is that you will give direct answers to questions. You will snap out of your old civilian crap immediately or we will snap you out of it. Is that understood?"

"Yes, sir."

"Okay, put away that goddamn cleaning gear and get out. Move."

*   *   *

Krupe led the run, jogging effortlessly at the front of the formation as the platoon wound through unfamiliar streets and out onto an open field. Sanders positioned himself between the two sections, while Bennett, breathing heavily after they had run only a block, brought up the rear.

As they came near Platoon 484's area, a familiar voice rang out: "Hey, Jack Armstrong, where you going?" Krupe recognized Pepper's voice so he didn't slow his pace or bother to look around. "Haha," the voice mocked as 486 jogged out of sight, "Jack Armstrong and his candy-assed civilians."

Altogether the run covered less than a mile. Because it was still early—it had been light only a few minutes when they had begun the run—the broiling midsummer Carolina sun had not yet added to their discomfort. Nevertheless, the recruits' civilian clothes were soaked with sweat.

Dutton managed the pace and distance handily. But several recruits staggered into the platoon area panting and gasping for breath. Jonathan Gabriel and an obese recruit, Orme Beacotte, staggered in fifteen or twenty seconds behind everyone else, prodded by threats from Bennett, who was himself panting heavily.

"Front and center, you two Privates," Krupe demanded when they finally joined the formation. Although exhausted almost to the point of collapse, both stumbled to the front of the platoon. "What's the matter with you, Private?" he demanded of Gabriel, who was trying not to gasp. "Was the run too much for you."

"I . . . I don't know, sir."

"You don't know? Can you run a mile, Private?"

Struggling to regain his breath, the recruit couldn't answer for several seconds. Then he replied, "I'm not sure, sir, I never tried."

"How about you, fat boy?" Krupe demanded of Beacotte. "Can you run a mile?"

"I think so, sir," the recruit replied.

"I didn't ask you what you think or don't think. I asked you a simple question. Can you run a mile? *Have* you ever run a mile?"

"No, sir, I never have," Beacotte admitted.

"That's wonderful, just great. What right have either of you misfits to join the Marine Corps in such rotten shape? What did you think you were going to be called on to do down here, pussy-foot around all day? Did you think this was the Navy? Or worse yet, the Army?"

Hoping the questions were rhetorical, the recruits remained silent. Then Krupe turned his attention to the entire platoon. "Now listen up, all of you. You Privates are here to become United States Marines, and I'm here to see you become just that . . . if it is humanly possible to make Marines out of such poor raw meterial. You can't become Marines unless you are physically fit. So each morning we are going to fall out before chow for a morning run. You will be issued sneakers today, and you will fall out in them each morning. Is that understood?''

"Yes, sir."

"We will begin with a mile *run* tomorrow, not a jog, and we will stay at a mile for the rest of the week. Each week from now on we will increase it by a quarter mile. By the time you leave this island you will be running three miles a day. Those who can't," he said, looking toward Gabriel and Beacotte, "will remain here until they can."

He stopped for a moment, then continued. "You people probably think being a Marine means dressing up in your blues and charming some impressionable girl—playing the role. But I have news for you. A Marine is someone who is always mentally and physically fit for combat—*combat*, do you understand? Killing the enemy before he kills you.

"Or don't you glory hounds think Marines get killed? Let me tell you something. Yesterday the Defense Department reported that five hundred and twenty-two Americans were killed and wounded in Korea *just last week*, and we're not even fighting any major battles there now. It's only probing action—patrols trying to take prisoners, gather intelligence, feel each other out. Five hundred and twenty-two—that's this platoon multiplied more than seven times. And a lot of those casualties were Marines—Marines who paid attention in boot camp and Marines who didn't, Marines who worked themselves into condition and Marines who just coasted through boot camp."

He began pacing, warming to his subject, ramrod erect as though his shoulders and chest were welded into position.

"Well, none of you will coast through boot camp, I promise that. All of you will be in condition when you leave here; whether you remain that way is somebody else's responsibility. Most of our casualties in Korea, the ones who don't make the Defense Department statistics, are guys who suffer heat exhaustion or other non-battle ailments.

"You may think it's hot down here in the middle of the summer, but you don't know what heat is until you're crawling around the Korean hills in August, when the sun burns a hole right through you and the heat and stink are rising from the rice paddies. Then you'll think Parris Island was a picnic—only then it'll be too late. So listen carefully: During the summer at Parris Island and in Korea, your body needs more water than you probably want. So you have to force yourself to drink even when you don't want to. Each morning and noon, before you leave the mess hall, be sure your canteens are full. Is that understood?''

"Yes, sir."

"You will swallow at least two salt pills with each meal. Is that clear?''

"Yes, sir.''

"And anybody who disobeys can expect to hear from me. Is *that* understood?''

"Yes, sir.''

"It better be. Now," he said, turning to Gabriel and Beacotte, "I'm going to give you both the opportunity to work yourselves into shape, to become Marines. Would you like that?''

"Yes, sir," they answered in unison.

"All right, let me see you run in place," he said, demonstrating by alternately pumping his knees in a high, exaggerated motion. The recruits obeyed awkwardly. Krupe studied them disapprovingly. "Higher," he demanded, "and faster. It won't do any good the way you're doing it.''

After a minute or two Krupe ordered the winded recruits to halt. "From now on, when I give the platoon parade rest, the two of you will practice running in place—in front of the barracks, outside the mess hall, on the drill field, or whenever standing in line. Is that clear?''

"Yes, sir.''

"Get back in line," he ordered, glowering after them for having wasted precious time.

After chow the recruits were marched back to the platoon area and ordered to stand at attention while Gabriel and Beacotte ran in place. Then the drill instructors departed. Twenty minutes later they reappeared, in time to prevent the imminent collapse of Gabriel, who was gasping loudly as he strove to keep pumping his knees.

*   *   *

The forming period, those several days known as Hygienic, began with the recruits being marched to a drab wooden building, directed to line up in front of stalls, and ordered to strip. They were told to wrap up their civilian clothes and were given the choice of mailing them home or signing a waiver authorizing their donation to charity. After putting their money and wrist watches in canvas bags, they marched single-file into a room with three barber chairs, each presided over by an unsmiling civilian barber who methodically shaved them completely bald with electric clippers. The shearing operation required less than thirty seconds for burr-heads and less than a minute for Herb Beeks and others with longer hair.

Ordered out of the straight-backed chairs, the naked recruits were directed toward several open showers by another recruit who first brushed the loose hairs off them with a foxtail brush. They were told to soap their entire bodies, then they were given towels and told to queue up in another line. Here they were issued a durable olive-drab seabag, white underwear, brown socks and the green dungaree jackets, trousers and caps that would be their uniform throughout most of boot camp. They also were measured for shoes—dress shoes and two pairs of boon-dockers to march in—by a PFC who viewed their bone structure through an x-ray machine.

During this entire process they were hectored by Krupe and Bennett, by the supply NCOs', and by the privates and PFCs—themselves only recent graduates from boot camp—who were assisting with the supplies.

During the forming period each recruit was issued a laundry bucket, packs and equipment, and a rifle, the serial number of which he was required to memorize at once.

Recruits were instructed never to discard cigarettes without first "field stripping" them by unraveling the paper, rolling it into a tiny ball, and discarding the tobacco.

Bennett taught them how to mark their clothing, and showed how to wear the cartridge belt with the canteen on the right hip, bayonet along the left side, and first-aid pack in the rear.

Navy corpsmen simultaneously jabbed needles in both arms.

Sanders showed how to spit-shine shoes, and how to make belt buckles sparkle after an application of steel wool, Blitz metal-polishing cloth, and elbow grease. He cautioned them never, *never* to call their M-1 a gun, or anything other than "rifle," "piece," or "weapon." And he told them to memorize the Marine creed: "This is my rifle. There are many like it, but this one is mine. My rifle is my best friend. It is my life. I must master it as I must master my own life. . . ."

Throughout all this, an impatient Krupe managed to squeeze in time each day to drill them in the platoon street. He taught them the various formations and commands, demonstrated the differences between quick time (120 steps a minute), double time (180 steps), and slow time (60). He taught them how to line up at normal interval (30 inches between each recruit) and close interval (4 inches). He taught them the difference between the half step and back step (both 15 inches), and between steps taken in quick time (30 inches) and in double time (36 inches).

Each morning they ran a mile, steadily increasing their speed. Each evening before chow they did push-ups, chins, and sit-ups. At every opportunity each day, Gabriel and Beacotte ran in place, so that by the end of the fifth day they no longer felt as though they were about to faint.

Each day, too, Krupe and Bennett discovered violations that brought them charging into the middle of the platoon to deal summarily with offenders. Bennett continued picking on Gillian, although the recruit carefully obeyed the letter of every law and tried to make himself as inconspicuous as possible. And Krupe, all the while gripping his ominous club, continued to berate and threaten, chafing while waiting for Hygienic to end.

After evening chow the recruits were marched to a nearby hut and shown again and again how to dismantle and assemble the M-1. Krupe drilled them endlessly on its components, its weight . . . length . . . firepower . . . clip capacity . . . and range. Sanders taught them how to clean it, explained how it functioned, and drilled them on what to do should the rifle fail to fire or feed. Then they were given just enough time to shower, briefly review their notebooks, and prepare for lights out at 10:00 P.M.

Much of the instruction of those first few days was wasted. The constant threats, intimidation, and bullying had created a state of confusion for a number of recruits, rendering them incapable of grasping much of what was said. Gabriel and one or two others appeared almost shell-shocked: Their ability to reason, or to obey other than mechanically, was literally suspended. Their eyes were glazed. Reticent from the beginning, they now withdrew even further into themselves.

Several days after their arrival on the island, it dawned on Dutton that though they were together eighteen waking hours a day, the recruits had not had an opportunity to talk with one another. In fact, there had been no time for anything except listening to an endless procession of orders. From the second the lights flipped on at precisely 4:00 A.M. until they turned off at 10:00 P.M., the recruits were not given a free minute. Twice during the first three days they were allowed to smoke part of a cigarette after a meal. Otherwise they were kept scurrying from one formation to another, from one lecture to another. For diversion they ran in the morning, drilled for brief periods in the morning and afternoon, and exercised in the evening. And always under a stifling summer sun that bathed the recruit depot in never-ending, oppressive heat. Tender civilian feet developed blisters on the hot parade ground that became calloused after a few painful days.

Dutton drew fire watch the third night, the 2:00 A.M. until 4:00 A.M. shift, and had to fight the entire time to keep awake. A half-dozen times his eyes flickered closed as he patroled, but somehow he managed to overcome an almost irresistible urge to sit down briefly and rest.

He had been kept so busy he forgot he hadn't heard from Julie. He hadn't had time to write, and the form letter sent home by the Recruit Training Regiment Headquarters—saying that Marine So and So had arrived safely, and giving the number of the platoon, company, and battalion to which he had been assigned—probably had not yet arrived in Ocean Point. He knew his mother would notify Julie as soon as it did, and that Julie would write to him that very same day. He hoped there would be a letter from her at the first mail call, but at the moment he didn't know when he would ever get a chance to read it.

*   *   *

Boot training did not begin seriously until that weekend, which most recruits had hoped would be devoted to letting them rest, write home, or review part of what they had been told. But Saturday morning they were up as usual at 4:00 A.M. Once again they cleaned themselves and the barracks, studied their *Guidebooks*, ran a mile, marched to chow, then began a full day of serious drill.

During the next week Krupe constantly warned them not to anticipate commands—to move only when actually ordered to do so. And time and again he charged into the midst of the platoon to manhandle recruits who, having heard him say, "Right . . . ," executed a right-facing movement—only to have him withhold the second half of the command. He often resorted to ruses: Hollering "For-ward . . . ," then hesitating, waiting to catch someone stepping off on the left foot. Or ordering "Parade . . ." without adding "rest," hoping to see a recruit relax. His patience was usually well-rewarded.

When there were too many offenders to punch or jostle, often by cracking them across the shins or buttocks with his *cocomacaque*, Krupe ordered them to exercise in front of the rest of the platoon, until one or more collapsed. This punishment took several forms. One of Krupe's favorites was up-and-on shoulders: The recruit gripped his M-1 with both hands, palms pointing upward and facing outward at chin level, elbows at the side. On the count of one he raised the rifle as high above his head as he could... on two he brought it down behind his neck... on three back up high again... and on four back to the original starting position.

Recruits soon discovered that it didn't require many repetitions before the rifle's nine-and-a half pounds felt like ninety-five pounds, especially when the weapon was not allowed to touch the neck in the number two position. Sooner or later at least one recruit would collapse on the deck—or worse yet, from Krupe's viewpoint, drop his rifle in agony. Those who fainted were assigned to walk fire watch from midnight until 2:00 A.M. But anyone who dropped or otherwise abused rifles was made to atone for this cardinal sin by sleeping that night atop four rifles laid sideways across the rack, bolt tangs facing upward. Or by trying to sleep, since no one punished in this manner ever managed more than a few minutes of unbroken sleep at a time.

Krupe and Bennett, different in many ways, complemented each other as drill instructors. If one somehow overlooked a violation, the other usually spotted it. And neither wasted any time before exacting swift, oftentimes vicious, retribution. Nevertheless, Dutton observed important differences between them.

Krupe, for example, played no favorites, nor did he single out particular recruits for punishment. He lashed out swiftly but impartially. He appeared to be interested in punishing the violation, not the violator.

Bennett, on the other hand, although prepared to punish any recruit, clearly enjoyed punishing some more than others. His treatment of Gillian was the most glaring example, but it was not the only one. Bennett hectored several other recruits almost as mercilessly, taunting them, threatening, kicking, and punching them even when they did as instructed. He rushed to their racks the moment the lights flipped on in the morning and tossed the groggy occupants onto the deck. He sneaked up behind them while they were in the head and punched them if he caught them talking. He hovered over them during chow, a minatory, distracting presence.

Dutton couldn't understand why Bennett had singled out for punishment those particular recruits, since there didn't seem to be any singular geographic or religious overtones to his hostility. He enjoyed baiting Robert Begay, yet he didn't pick on any of the three black recruits. Nor did he pick on only the better-educated recruits, as Dutton had been told career servicemen sometimes did. If there was a pattern to Bennett's volatile behavior, Dutton was unable to fathom it.

Then there was Corporal Sanders, in some ways the most enigmatic of the three. What was different about him, Dutton finally realized, was that in spite of the maltreatment dished out at every turn at Parris Island, *Sanders had not hit or physically abused a single recruit.*

Dutton didn't know whether anyone else was aware of his discovery, which came to him like a revelation. Probably nobody bothered to differentiate among the three drill instructors; they just lumped them into the same category, as symbols of unbridled authority and ferocious tempers. He himself hadn't thought about it until the night he took a shortcut back to his hut from the head, just before lights out, and came upon Sanders standing between two of the Quonsets smoking a cigarette.

At first Dutton thought it was a recruit sneaking a smoke, but as he came toward him he noticed the crisp khaki uniform. He slowed down as he advanced, then said, "By your leave, sir."

The corporal had been deep in thought, and he was momentarily taken aback. Finally he said: "Private, don't you know you say 'By your leave' only when you pass a Drill Instructor or an officer from the rear?"

"Sorry, sir, I forgot."

Sanders' face relaxed. "That's okay." He stared at the recruit, whose face was partly illuminated by the lights from the Quonset windows. "What's your name, Private?"

It was the first time since his arrival that Dutton heard a question that wasn't framed as a threat. "Private Dutton, sir."

"Dutton . . . Dutton." Sanders was turning the name over in his mind. "Oh, yea, Penn, right?"

The recruit smiled. Penn. Suddenly the sound of the word, the sound of the sentence in which it was uttered, seemed almost musical. They were the first civil words he had heard from anyone in authority since he had left the outside world several days before. "Yes, sir, Penn. Did you go there, sir?"

"Nope. Columbia, Class of nineteen-fifty. But I'm from Wynnewood."

"I know where it is, sir. On the Main Line—near Merion and Bala Cynwyd. But I don't know much about it."

"I'm not sure I do either," Sanders replied vaguely as he crushed his cigarette butt and field-stripped it. Then he looked at his watch. "Three minutes, Dutton. You better get moving."

"Yes, sir," the recruit replied, and took off running. Later, while mulling the conversation over in the rack after lights out, he thought how strange it was that he had been so elated by a brief encounter that in civilian life would have had little meaning. But in the southeastern corner of South Carolina on this summer night in 1952, it was charged with . . . What? Not meaning, perhaps, but with emotion.

That's when he became aware that Sanders had not laid a hand on anyone; that all along it had been Bennett and Krupe who had manhandled recruits. The worst Sanders had done was yell and threaten, but he had not lifted a hand in anger. Dutton wondered why.

*　　*　　*

Platoon 486 received an unexpected gift on Sundays: Recruits were permitted to sleep until 5:00 A.M.

After chow on that first Sunday, Sanders demonstrated several of the simpler movements of the manual of arms: left shoulder, arms; port arms; and present arms. Then Bennett emerged from the DI hut and announced, "All right, you Privates, listen up. You have five minutes to wash and square away. You bastards who are going to church fall in two ranks when you get back here, one rank for Catholics, the other for Protestants. You atheists will be put to work, so you better goddamn well decide right now whether you're Catholic or Protestant. Begay," he said, his face wreathed in his familiar sardonic smile, "we don't have any medicine men on this base, so you damn well better fall in one or the other. Maybe you better pretend you're a Catholic, and you can tell me if that communion they eat tastes like pauite, or payute, or whatever in hell it is you Indians eat or smoke or snuff."

"Sir," the youth replied softly, "I want to go to Protestant services." When Bennett cocked an eyebrow as if to ask why, he added: "Sir, I'm a Mormon."

The drill instructor walked toward him slowly, quizzically, as though he were hearing things. "Come again?"

"I'm a Mormon, sir."

"A Mormon? What . . . in . . . the . . . fuck . . . is . . . that?" he demanded, slowly accentuating each word. "What kind of exotic things do *they* drink and smoke?"

"Sir, Mormons don't drink or smoke anything."

"Bullshit. Who are you trying to kid? An Indian who don't drink?" When the youth didn't reply, he said, "You trying to tell me you don't drink firewater, Injun?"

"No, sir I don't."

Bennett wondered if he were being strung along. Warily he said, "And you're really an Indian, boy?"

"Yes, sir."

"From where? Brooklyn?" He said it disdainfully.

"Sir, I'm originally from Arizona."

"Then how come you didn't go to boot camp in San Diego?"

"Sir, I had just finished my second year at Dartmouth College, in New Hampshire, when I joined the Marines."

"College?" For a moment Bennett stared, trying to put everything in proper focus. It looked as if he were preparing to say something more but was unable to do so. Finally he bellowed, "All right, goddamn it, you Catholics move out to church."

Dutton fell in with the Catholics, who were marched to the interdenominational chapel by Sanders. Afterward, while returning to the platoon area, they ran into Bennett, who was leading recruits to Protestant services. As the two groups passed, the sergeant hollered, "Corporal Sanders, I hope them Pape bastards of yours asked Big Daddy in Rome to pray for them, 'cause they're gonna need it." He roared with laughter, but Sanders pretended not to hear.

Back in the platoon area, while awaiting return of the remainder of the recruits, Sanders drilled his group steadily. When everyone was present, Krupe took over.

Throughout the morning-long session the drill instructors alternated counting cadence, demonstrating flanking movements, about-faces, and other maneuvers. The purpose was to familiarize the recruits with each DI's technique while instilling in them instant, unquestioning obedience to commands.

The DIs were alike in calling cadence and in their rigid military posture, yet there were marked differences in style and technique. Krupe's voice was much the most authoritative, the loudest, the lowest pitched, and the most rhythmic. Bennett's was shrill but his diction was clearer—perhaps because he called cadence according to the familiar singsong "Awn, hup, a-reep, reep, fah ya lep," whereas Krupe didn't follow any familiar pronunciation pattern. His commands, "Platoon...halt," "Forward...harch," "to the right flank...harch," were distinguishable only occasionally, and sometimes they ranged in pitch as much as an octave. But always he was perfectly erect, his shoulders pinched back as he fairly strutted along, always looking cool and his uniform immaculately pressed despite sweltering heat and humidity.

Sanders, assigned to his first recruit platoon, was understandably less sure of himself than either of his senior colleagues. His cadence was authoritative and rhythmical enough, having been honed during the five weeks he had spent in DI school, but he was less certain of himself than Krupe or Bennett. Yet even he was beginning to develop confidence.

One morning during the first week of serious drill, after Krupe stopped to answer another senior DI's questions about administrative procedure, Sanders took charge of the platoon as it drilled on the large practice field in the company area. The recruits were still ragged, still had a tendency to anticipate commands, and their responses were still studied and deliberate rather than automatic. Aware that Krupe was observing every movement, Sanders was absorbed in doing a good job so he paid scant attention to another platoon that suddenly appeared on the drill field. But Krupe could see that, although still unpolished, its movements were more precise than those of 486 and that its senior DI radiated an aura of total control.

As the platoon came closer, Sanders recognized Sergeant Pepper, but it took him a while to realize Pepper was leading his platoon on a converging course with 486. Just before the two would have crashed head-on, and when it finally became apparent that Pepper had no intention of altering his platoon's direction, Sanders ordered 486 to execute a left flanking movement that narrowly averted a collision. As he did so, Pepper taunted loudly, "That's the idea, Corporal. You better move when

Platoon 484 comes marching by, 'cause we're just mean enough to walk all over you.''

Before Sanders had a chance to reply or deliver another command, Krupe appeared at the front of the formation. His face was contorted with rage yet he managed somehow to keep his voice under control. "I'll take over now, Corporal," he said firmly.

He promptly ordered the platoon to the rear, then ordered a right oblique movement that headed 486 in the direction of Pepper's platoon. When 484 flanked left, Krupe ordered his platoon to execute a left oblique; although 486 was thirty yards or more behind, it was staying right on 484's tail.

When Pepper saw what Krupe was up to, he kept his platoon pointed straight ahead. Perhaps Krupe's grim visage dampened Pepper's eagerness to create an incident. Because 484 had a sizable head start, and because of the vastness of the drill field, Pepper could have dodged 486 all day—and apparently intended to do so. He ordered his platoon around the outer edges of the drill field, and for the remainder of the drill period he discreetly kept as far away from Krupe as possible.

Only when Krupe was satisfied that he had made his point did the anger drain from his face.

* * *

During a break later that morning, Bennett noticed Gillian sharing his canteen with Paul Thorn. "What's the meaning of this?" he demanded. "Is this some sort of sex symbol between fairies, drinking out of the same canteen?"

"No, sir," Gillian replied as Bennett moved menacingly toward them.

"Then what's it all about?"

Unwilling to reveal that Thorn had forgotten to fill his canteen, the recruit stammered, "Sir, he . . . he ran out of water."

"Who you trying to shit, boy?" Bennett threatened, stomping hard on Gillian's instep. "This is our first water break today, our very first. So if he ran out of water he ran out because he didn't remember to fill his canteen, right?"

Standing at rigid attention despite the pain, Gillian frantically searched for an answer that wouldn't incriminate either of them. Finally he replied, "I don't know, sir."

"What do you mean, you don't know?" Bennett demanded,

pulling Gillian out of line and knocking him to the ground with a short right jab in the midsection. Then he began kicking the recruit—in the ribs and back, along the buttocks, and finally hard in the right heel. Only this time his outburst seemed somewhat controlled, less given over to random wildness.

"Maybe if I mark you up a little bit your ass won't seem quite as appealing to those queer playmates of yours," he sputtered as Gillian lay curled up on his side, alternately gasping and coughing. "Now you, you son-of-a-bitch," he said, turning to a frightened Thorn. "Now it's your turn."

But Krupe interrupted. "I have a better idea, Sergeant," he said. "We'll let Private Thorn run around the drill field the rest of the morning. That should remind him a Marine has a full canteen every morning and night."

"Good idea, Sergeant Krupe," agreed Bennett, with only partial conviction. "But let's send his girl friend Gillian with him."

"Very good. And let's see, what are the names of our two jumping jacks?"

"You mean Gabriel and Beacotte?"

"That's it. Privates Gabriel and Beacotte, get up here, on the double."

"Begay, you get up here too," ordered Bennett, although it was not clear why he singled out the Navajo recruit.

Gillian struggled to his feet, slowly and painfully. Then Krupe ordered the five of them to run until he sent word to quit or until someone fainted. But he warned them not to try to sandbag him about fainting.

Afterward, Krupe resumed the drill, putting the platoon through an increasingly dizzying series of flanking and turning movements. Whenever anyone missed a count or stepped off on the wrong foot he exploded in anger. He bellowed constant reminders for them to dig in their heels. He warned them never to anticipate commands.

All the while Gillian, Thorn, Beacotte, Begay, and Gabriel circled the hot, steaming field. They began at approximately the same pace, but Gillian soon dropped behind because of an injured Achilles tendon, where Bennett had kicked him. Then Gabriel began to falter on the third lap, soaked through with perspiration and gasping for breath, and by the sixth lap he was weaving as though punch-drunk.

Whenever the runners came near the platoon, Bennett in

tercepted them long enough to threaten them not to dare fall. Once he ran alongside Gillian, threatening the limping recruit until he thought better of running any farther around the steaming drill field. Besides, he rationalized, Gillian would be around again; it wasn't like he was going anywhere.

At eleven-thirty Krupe told Sanders to march the platoon back to the hut area, have the recruits wash up, then fall in for chow. He ordered Dutton and Dave Hall to remain behind to carry to the DI hut the first runner who fainted. Dutton had hoped Krupe would eventually decide the quintet had had enough and would send word for them to quit after several laps. But when he was ordered to act as a stretcher bearer, he knew he and Hall had to produce at least one body before the marathon could be called off.

Dutton began pulling silently for Gillian, Gabriel, and Begay, his hutmates and friends. Then he remembered that Beacotte hadn't done anything; if anyone was to blame it was Thorn, for forgetting to fill his canteen. So even though standing at attention, he began whispering encouragement to the other four as they trudged past.

"You got a bet or something?" Hall asked, his voice sullen and annoyed.

"I don't bet on other people's misfortune. Why?"

"You seem to be rooting for everybody but Thorn."

"Somebody's going to have to pass out, and I figure he's the person it should be."

"How do you figure that?"

"If he had filled his canteen, these guys wouldn't be running now."

"What about that queer Gillian and that screw-up Gabriel? They've been nothing but trouble since we got here. Don't defend them just because you're all in the same hut."

Even though they were supposed to be at attention, Dutton turned and looked at Hall. "What's that got to do with it?" he demanded. "I don't give a damn whose hut they're in. They've been picked on enough since they've been here."

"They deserve it. The best thing could happen would be if those two get left behind. At least that's the opinion of Quonset Hut Number One."

"Yea? Well you tell Quonset Hut Number One to mind its own business. This has nothing to do with what hut somebody's in, it's a case of simple justice."

Hall snorted. "Justice? Is that supposed to mean something here? It's a question of whose ass gets in a sling, and so far your two buddies have been screwing up the works and making us all suffer."

"Look, fella, you haven't suffered one single bit compared to what those two guys have gone through. If—"

As Gabriel approached, he suddenly gasped, then pitched headfirst onto the ground. Dutton was at his side in a second but the recruit was out cold, glasses sprawled in front of him, mouth agape, and his breathing labored.

When Hall reached the prostrate recruit he merely stood open-mouthed. Dutton, who was bent over checking Gabriel's pulse, turned and glared at him. Then, clinching his fists, he rose and said, "Does this make you happy, you son-of-a-bitch?"

*   *   *

After Sanders marched the platoon back to the Quonsets he returned to the DI hut. Bennett was stretched across his bunk reading a comic book, Krupe appeared to be busy writing a report. The corporal dropped heavily into a chair, hot and exhausted. When he looked up, Krupe was glaring at him. "Sanders," the tech sergeant said through clenched teeth, "don't you ever again back away from a challenge by Pepper or anybody else—not while you're my assistant."

Sanders was speechless. Back away from a challenge? The thought hadn't occurred to him. The order he gave to avoid a collision with 484 had nothing to do with bravery but with concern over the safety of his recruits. "What would you suggest I do next time? Keep the platoon on a collision course?" he asked angrily.

"Exactly—only it isn't a suggestion, it's an order!"

"Very well . . . *Sergeant*," he said, emphasizing Krupe's rank. As an afterthought he asked, "Does that order hold in every case, or only when it involves Pepper?"

As he sat back in his chair, Krupe studied his assistant. "What is that supposed to mean?" A curious Bennett interrupted his reading in order to listen.

"Exactly what I said. Remember, I was there when you and Pepper had that set-to outside the mess hall."

"So?"

"So it's obvious you don't have any love for each other. It's also obvious you think I allowed him to show you up."

Krupe frowned at the suggestion. "He didn't show *me* up, Corporal, he showed *you* up. You and Platoon 486."

"Your platoon."

"My platoon, Corporal, but your honor. Or what's left of it. You dishonored mostly yourself by turning away from Pepper's challenge. You dishonored the platoon only incidentally."

Sanders looked at him in open-eyed amazement. "You can't be serious, Sergeant. You can't really be serious making such a production out of something as insignificant as exercising judgment on the drill field. Honor, you say. Is it honor to march a platoon of kids into another platoon of kids merely to prove a point—a point that eludes everybody but you? What would it have proved—except that some recruits would have gotten hurt and bled?"

"What you don't seem to realize, Corporal, is that honor isn't measured by outward appearances. It's something within you that reacts instinctively to compromising situations."

"How did I 'dishonor' myself by protecting your platoon against Pepper's tactics? And how did you intend to redeem that honor if you caught up with him?" When Krupe didn't reply immediately, Sanders continued, "For your information, Sergeant, I don't feel as though I let down either myself or the Marine Corps. I may be bound by your orders, but I'm sure as hell not bound by your peculiar honor code."

"You were—"

At that moment there were three loud raps at the door. "Speak," hollered Bennett, who had been carefully following the dialogue.

"Sir, Private Dutton requests permission to speak to the Drill Instructor." Behind him, sprawled on the ground, was Gabriel. Surrounding Gabriel were Hall, Beacotte, Begay, Gillian, and Thorn.

"Then speak, goddamn it, spit it out."

"Sir, we are returning Private Gabriel, who is still unconscious."

"Bastard must not be taking his salt tablets," Bennett said with a broad grin.

Krupe arose slowly from behind the desk and started toward the door. "Do *you* have a full canteen, Private Dutton?" he asked.

"Yes, sir."

"Good. Now, Private Dutton, you unscrew the cap from

your canteen and empty its contents on Private Gabriel's face.''

Dutton glanced at the scowling Bennett, then turned toward Sanders as though seeking support, but the corporal was impassive. "What are you waiting for?'' Krupe demanded. "Pour.'' He stood in front of Dutton menacingly, hands on hips, his *cocomacaque* tucked under his armpit.

Dutton did as ordered. The water gurgled out, the irregular spurts splashing onto Gabriel's face and glasses, bounding off onto the dry ground where they formed large, dusty beads of moisture.

The recruit made sounds as though he were struggling for breath. His eyes opened and he blinked several times, but he made no move to prevent the stream of water from drenching and choking him.

Krupe ordered Dutton and Hall to carry Gabriel to the head, clean him off, make him drink from his canteen, then stretch him out on the deck beside his rack. He ordered the others to do push-ups. When Beacotte could no longer push himself off the floor, despite several sharp prods in the ribs from Bennett's shoe, Krupe ordered the three remaining recruits to help him to the head and give him the same treatment decreed for Gabriel. He also ordered Thorn, Begay, and Gillian to walk fire watch the next two nights.

Sanders and Bennett accompanied the platoon to noon chow. Outside the mess hall exit a youngster from a nearby town was selling Sunday papers. After making sure the two drill instructors were still inside, Otis McGraw stopped to look at the front page. He bent over, facing the scullery door so he could see whoever approached. Suddenly he was propelled headlong into the door, striking his head against one of the four wooden horizontal slats covering the screen. He dropped to one knee, then tried to right himself, but a powerful forearm smash in the chest sent him reeling.

McGraw landed on his back. Instinctively he raised both legs, as though to ward off his attacker. At that instant the *cocomacaque* caught him behind the left knee. He yelled in pain, drew both knees up to his stomach and grabbed his injured part with both hands. Krupe hovered over him, watching, expressionless.

By then Platoon 486's recruits were all out of the mess hall and lined up at attention. Sanders and Bennett sauntered out the door in time to see McGraw moaning and thrashing about, clutching the back of his knee as though the pain were excruciating.

"Apparently some of you people thought you joined the Army," Krupe scowled, after ordering McGraw to be quiet. "You thought you came here to keep up on current events and the latest sports news. Well, as far as you're concerned, the outside world no longer exists. It ended the minute you drove through that gate. All that exists is Platoon Four eighty-six of the Sixth Battalion at the Marine Corps Recruit Training Battalion at Parris Island, South Carolina."

He glanced down at McGraw but quickly resumed addressing the platoon. "The Korean War exists too," he said, "but it's not something you read about or listen to on the radio. It's something you learn about by following orders, by obeying commands. And the first order you learn here is that you don't do a thing until you're told. Is that understood?"

"Yes, sir."

Turning to McGraw, Krupe ordered, "Fall in, Private."

The recruit hobbled to his feet, his face wreathed in pain. Krupe ordered him to the rear of the platoon and watched impassively as the recruit dragged himself back in line. Then he marched the group back to the platoon area. McGraw managed to keep up only by half-running, half-scrambling, dragging his damaged leg with considerable effort.

Back at the huts the recruits were ordered to break out buckets, scrub brushes, and bring their laundry bags outside. Then they were told to line up in front of the washracks and scrub until their clothes were spotless.

The two washracks—large, flat table-like platforms made of a sandstone substance—each contained two rows of spigots, twelve on each side. Some recruits shared a spigot, others washed underwear, socks, cartridge belts, dungaree jackets, trousers, and caps in their buckets.

At frequent intervals the drill instructors wandered in and out of the wash area, instructing recruits in the proper method of tying clothes on the wire lines. Bennett warned that they would be punished if they stole anyone else's clothes, or if their own clothes were stolen.

About the time the last recruit finished hanging his clothes, Krupe began his inspection. "This is filthy," he said, pulling an undershirt from the line and grinding it beneath his heel. "Wash it." He ordered most recruits to wash out their socks again. He trampled towels and dungaree jackets into the ground. Few articles were still hanging by the time Krupe completed his rampage.

An hour later the platoon was back on the drill field, once again practicing endless repetitions beneath the blazing noon sun and high humidity. But fear helped the recruits keep their minds off the heat—fear and warnings not to run their sleeves over their sweaty faces, or slap at the eternal sand fleas, or scratch random itches.

Krupe used the afternoon drill to re-evaluate individual recruits. He kept Stanley Tew as platoon leader but replaced two other squad leaders. Dutton remained a squad leader in the first section and Begay was assigned to march in front of the entire platoon, carrying a tall, slender pole bearing a crimson and gold banner with the familiar globe-and-anchor insignia.

Despite the presumptive advantage of being made platoon or squad leader, the titles did not stave off punishment whenever Krupe or Bennett chose to inflict it. That very afternoon Krupe grabbed Dutton and shook him repeatedly for missing a count when he ordered the platoon to halt after marking time. Tew was upbraided for executing a sloppy right flanking movement.

Tew relished his position, which afforded him a limited opportunity to exercise the authority he coveted. But Dutton disliked being singled out for the dubious honor, since his ambition had been to draw as little attention to himself as possible. He had abandoned his self-imposed cautionary rule when he had talked with Sanders several nights previously, but he hoped that momentary lapse wouldn't upset his overall strategy. Still, he took some comfort in the fact that Krupe had designated him by pointing, rather than calling him by name.

When the platoon returned from the drill field, Gabriel and McGraw were hanging their clothes. Neither looked to be in especially bad shape, but McGraw limped noticeably and Gabriel appeared more frightened and withdrawn than ever. For a moment Dutton wondered whether perhaps Hall had been right—whether the platoon *would* be better off without Gabriel. But he dismissed the thought, remembering the resolution he had made that very morning, as he watched Gabriel suffer during his ordeal at the drill field, to do everything possible to see that Gabriel *did* make it. This would be his special project—to save Gabriel from certain failure in the face of enmity from Hall and his hutmates and cruelty from Krupe and Bennett.

During the few minutes they were allotted to sort their laundry before falling in for chow, Dutton talked with Gabriel long enough to realize that he had recovered physically but that his sense of failure had heightened. He tried to cheer Gabriel by saying that by the time he left P.I. he'd be eligible for Boston's annual marathon race, but his bunkmate remained disconsolate. He knew he was being put to the test of becoming a Marine and that already, in only about a week, he was failing that test.

On the march back from chow McGraw's limp became more pronounced. Without the slightest hint of contrition, Krupe warned that if the leg didn't improve overnight the recruit would be sent to the infirmary, then withheld from training until he was physically able to join another platoon at the beginning of its ten-week cycle. Ordinarily a recruit might be expected to welcome the opportunity to escape from Krupe and Bennett. But Dutton knew McGraw was asking himself whether it was worse to remain where he was or spend as much as one extra day on Parris Island. Especially since he couldn't be sure any new DIs would be any improvement over Krupe and Bennett.

Chapter
4

Early one evening in the second week of training Platoon 486 held its first field day.

After changing into bathing suits, the recruits were directed to lift locker boxes onto their racks and move everything, racks and all, into one half of the hut. After they fell in outside with their buckets they were marched to a sandy area adjoining Platoon 484, and half the recruits were ordered to fill their buckets with sand. Afterward they were all marched back to the huts, where the others were ordered to fill their buckets with water from the washracks. Then everyone was ordered back inside.

Each drill instructor took one Quonset hut. Standing in the center of the middle recruit hut, Krupe ordered sand scattered across half the deck. Next he ordered buckets of water dumped on the sand. Then each recruit was made to get down on hands and knees and begin scrubbing.

When one end of the hut was spotless, after the mud and sand were completely washed away, the other part of the hut was given the same treatment.

It was an agonizing job. Before it turned to mud, the sand cut into bare knees. When it finally did coagulate, it splattered and began to cake on the recruits' bodies. Furthermore, Krupe kept a close vigil, reappearing regularly to be sure no one was goofing off. He emptied a bucket of water over the head of a recruit he accused of malingering. He grabbed another by the shoulder and the waistband of his bathing suit and sent him slithering across the slippery deck through the mud and water.

As the night dragged on, Krupe began staying away as much as twenty minutes at a time. During those interims, Stanley Tew gradually arrogated to himself Krupe's supervisory function. Walking among the wet, perspiring recruits, he began demanding they scrub harder, "Quit playing grab-ass," or "Get with it." When he told a perspiring Herb Beeks to scrub harder, Beeks sprang up in front of him and demanded, "Who the hell are you to tell me what to do? You're no better than the rest of us, so where do you get off ordering me around?"

"Listen, punk," Tew said to the 5'9" Beeks at the top of his voice, wanting everyone to hear, "I'm leader of this platoon and that means I'm responsible to the DIs, on the drill field or in the barracks. Now, you better turn to, or you've had it."

Beeks wasn't fazed in the slightest. "Power really *has* gone to your head, Tew," he said. "You're even beginning to *sound* like a Drill Instructor. But you're still nothing but a boot and I'm not about to take orders from you after taking crap from the rest of this goddamned island all day."

Tew flushed, then doubled up his fists. "I shit you not, you're asking for trouble."

"Are you going to give it to me?" Beeks asked defiantly.

With that Tew fired a hasty right-hand punch, hitting the Philadelphian a glancing blow high on the side of the head. Beeks was stunned but still managed instinctively to flick out a polished left jab as the much larger recruit charged. It landed flush against Tew's nose, snapping his head backward and momentarily halting his advance. But after partially blocking another left jab, Tew bulled his way inside Beeks's defense and overpowered him, driving him against the wall. He pounded him repeatedly in the ribs with powerful short rights while trying with his left hand to push Beeks far enough away from him so he could go to work on his face.

The smaller recruit clung close to Tew as long as he could, despite the force of the blows landing on his ribs. But Tew finally managed to get a hand beneath Beeks's chin and pushed violently, sending him reeling backward with Tew stumbling after. Both of them tumbled to the deck, Tew landing on top. He pinned Beeks's right arm beneath his left knee, then aimed a vicious right at his face.

Luckily, Beeks turned away at the last second, because even though Tew still was unable to exert maximum leverage, his fist crashed into the side of Beeks's head with a hollow thud that

echoed throughout the barracks. "You son-of-a-bitching-bastard,"
Tew repeated as the clubbed Beeks twice more. As he measured
him for a third shot, Dutton stepped in, grabbed Tew's arm just
as it started forward, and yanked it back so far that Tew yielded
his grip on the dazed Beeks.

"What, do you want some too?" Tew bellowed, his voice a
mixture of surprise and resentment.

"Don't threaten me, Tew," Dutton replied, surprisingly
calm for someone who appeared to be next in line for the huge
platoon leader's ire. "You proved your point. What more do you
want?"

"I want to teach this bastard a lesson he'll never forget,"
Tew raged, scrambling to his feet in anticipation of another
go-around.

At that instant a shout rang out. " 'Ten-shun!'"

"What's going on here?" Krupe demanded, charging into
the room and bounding over to where the bleeding Beeks lay
sprawled on the muddy floor.

"Nothing, sir," Tew replied. "Beeks here, he just got
dizzy and collapsed."

"Tripped over a locker box, is that it?" Krupe demanded,
carefully eyeing the combatants. "Is that it, Tew? Did he trip
over a locker box? Or was it the heat that got to him?"

Tew finally replied, "Sir, I think it was the locker box,
sir."

The drill instructor studied the bloodied Beeks, who began
rising slowly, holding the swelling left side of his head. "What
happened, Beeks?"

"Sir," he replied through swollen lips, "I did trip over a
locker box." Then, realizing the locker boxes were all atop
bunks, he added, "Or maybe it was the edge of a rack. I'm not
sure."

"You were fighting, weren't you, Beeks?" The drill instructor looked toward Tew, who was likewise wet and muddy
and whose right cheekbone was swollen and bruised.

"No, sir."

"If you had been fighting you'd admit it, wouldn't you,
Beeks?"

"Yes, sir," he replied.

"And you'd tell me too, wouldn't you?" the tech sergeant
challenged Tew. "As platoon leader, you'd feel duty bound to

report any fighting among members of this platoon, wouldn't you, Tew?''

When Tew agreed he would, Krupe replied: "Good. Because I won't tolerate fighting among yourselves. It's bad for morale. It disrupts concentration. It may become habit-forming.'' He stared again at Tew, who remained at rigid attention. "Now, get back to your field day.''

Tew resumed his self-appointed supervisory pose for the remainder of the evening, fastidiously inspecting every square inch of the deck. But he was virtually silent. He ignored Beeks completely, only flashing a malevolent look at Dutton as the latter returned from fetching a bucket of water. Dutton returned the look until Tew angrily looked away. Soon afterward, after twice scrubbing down each Quonset hut with sand and water, the recruits were ordered to secure the field day. They were given fifteen minutes to shower and hit the sack.

* * *

During the next two weeks Krupe and Bennett berated and belabored the recruits with renewed determination. Bennett's profane vocabulary, adequate for every normal circumstance, seemed to increase in content and frequency, prompting Dutton to dub him "Golden Throat." And Krupe devised some ingenious methods of punishment. When he caught two recruits sneaking a smoke inside the head while they were supposed to be washing up for noon chow, he made them stand in front of the platoon, inhale, drink from their canteens, and exhale. They repeated the procedure until both of them threw up a half-dozen times. Then, while the platoon remained at attention in the hot sun, they were ordered to scrub down the area they had despoiled with their vomit. At chow they were told to take a regular portion of every item, including fried liver and bacon, and Bennett hovered over them to make sure they ate every scrap. When one of them threw up again after the platoon returned to the Quonset area, the entire clean-up process was repeated.

Another time, when Paul Thorn fell in one morning without having shaved, Krupe sent him for his razor and ordered him to dry-shave in front of the platoon without benefit of a mirror and while double-timing in place. By the time the whiskers were removed, blood streamed down the recruit's face and neck from a dozen nicks and superficial cuts.

Because Recruit Jackson T. Hosse from Winston-Salem, North Carolina—he automatically affixed his home town whenever he was asked his name—spat while standing at parade rest outside the mess hall, Krupe made him get down on all fours at mail call and push a letter along the asphalt with his nose. By the time he returned to his original place in ranks, his nose was raw and bleeding, his trousers torn, and one knee lacerated.

Bennett enjoyed these punishments almost as much as if he had devised them; he could be depended on to laugh at and mock the pained recruits as they went through their paces. His was a malevolent laugh that rose as the victim's discomfort or agony increased.

Occasionally Bennett devised original punishments of his own. Once when he overheard three recruits whispering in ranks, he made them place buckets over their heads and ordered recruits on each side of them to pound the buckets with their sheathed bayonets. However, his usual punishment was the surprise punch or swift knee into the stomach or groin. Otherwise he was content to emulate the punishments devised by Krupe or to require the objects of his wrath to do push-ups until they passed out.

Once he ordered Gillian to do twenty-five push-ups from atop four locker boxes spaced at proper intervals for each hand and foot. Directly below, its handle embedded in a bucket of sand, a bayonet thrust upward from the deck at about chest level. When Bennett later boasted about the incident to Krupe, the senior DI exploded in anger. For the better part of fifteen minutes he chewed Bennett up one side and down the other, warning that he'd have him transferred off the island if he ever again did anything so risky and imbecilic.

One of Bennett's favorite pastimes was to call the platoon to attention and, while waiting for Krupe or Sanders, light up a cigarette without lighting the smoking lamp for the recruits. Or he tried to make them laugh in hopes they would abandon their military bearing. Sometimes he strolled back and forth in front of the platoon singing:

> *Six pounds of titty in a pink brassiere*
> *A twat that twitches like a moose's ear*
> *A condom and a beer . . .*
> *These foolish things remind me of you.*

or

I remember old Alice Blue Gown
And especially when Alice lay down
She was bashful and shy
'Till I unzipped my fly,
When she saw by budini
I thought she would die.

                              or

Have a baby by me
Have a baby by me
I'm big and strong
And it won't take long,
So have a baby by me.

The recruits learned soon enough not to laugh, even when Bennett grinned from ear to ear at his imagined cleverness. In fact, when a buddy of Tew's let a slight smile cross his face in an attempt to ingratiate himself, Bennett pounced on him and knocked him down, saying no one gave him permission to smile in ranks.

Although it seemed their ears were constantly being assailed with profanity from every direction, Dutton noticed Bennett was the source of almost all of it. To the best of his recollection, Krupe, although he was forever shouting and threatening, rarely cursed. And Sanders almost never punctuated his orders with more than an occasional "hell" or "damn."

But "Golden Throat" Bennett rarely uttered a complete sentence without obscenities. Moreover, he constantly waited until he had a captive audience to regale Sanders or Krupe with his latest conquest: Recalling "that little ol' piece in Myrtle Beach who has the kind of legs I love, the kind that go all the way up to her ass." Or telling about "the pig I got stuck with one night while pulling liberty in Oceanside. Man, if anybody told that bitch to haul ass, she'd have to make two trips."

Krupe and Sanders tried to ignore Bennett, but their unresponsiveness didn't inhibit or deter him. He never missed an opportunity to refer to the Women Marines—known throughout the Corps as BAMs, an unflattering acronym for Broad-Assed Marines—as "crack troops." He usually referred to sailors as "ball-bearing WAVES." After each attempted witticism he scrutinized the ranks in hope of catching someone stifling a smile.

But smiles were few and far between throughout the platoon, or throughout other platoons with which 486 came in contact. The typical recruits Dutton saw in the mess hall looked similarly confused and scared. Those he saw on the drill field also appeared cowed and submissive, and their drill instructors equally harsh and volatile.

About the only ones who acted at all assertive were the recruits on mess duty. These recruits were, in the vernacular of the Marine Corps, "salty"—omniscient old hands. Although they too were mere privates, they were often insolent and sometimes abusive toward other recruits who passed through the chow lines, recruits who were less experienced but usually no more than six weeks behind them in the training cycle. Encouraged by the cooks, messmen routinely slopped food on the trays of passing recruits, demanded they hurry it up, and occasionally—if a recruit's drill instructors were not around and if the mess sergeant was out of range—berated them in language befitting Sergeant Bennett.

But only the messmen assigned to the recruits' serving line acted that way. Those assigned to wait on the drill instructors, officers, and other permanent personnel were every bit as meek and docile as the newest recruits. Nevertheless, some drill instructors and other NCOs still ordered them around as though they were newly arrived, abusing them verbally and sometimes even physically.

Drawn to cataloguing the differences among Krupe, Bennett, and Sanders, and attuned to the differences in nuance as well as style, Dutton studied their behavior in the mess hall.

Krupe, imperious as ever, read the mimeographed menu thoroughly but quickly. He spoke to the messman only long enough to order. When he wanted anything more, he told the recruit precisely what. After eating, he never lingered or engaged in small talk; instead, he pushed away his chair, excused himself, picked up his *cocomacaque* and cap, and departed.

Sanders emulated Krupe's impersonal style in the mess hall, neither fraternizing with nor berating recruits. Bennett, by way of contrast, belonged to the minority of DIs that seemed to be as interested in using the time to badger and humiliate the messmen as in eating.

He tormented the waiters, baiting them with barbed questions and insults. No matter how fast they brought his order, he accused them of being slow. He constantly found fault with the food, although he knew they had nothing to do with its preparation. If a messman was slow in clearing away his tray at the end of a meal, he cursed and threatened. If the messman cleared it away too quickly, he would shove him away or ask what in the hell he thought he was doing.

Whenever the humiliated recruits slinked away, Bennett grinned at his dining partners. But Krupe, while never interfering, never returned Bennett's smile. Sanders sometimes half-smiled, and then only because Bennett's expectant grin made him uncomfortable and he found that the sooner he responded, the sooner he could return to his meal.

*   *   *

Bennett monopolized every dinner conversation with much the same crude braggadocio he paraded before the recruits. Sanders' usual response was that embarrassed half-smile he reserved for Bennett's treatment of messman, and Krupe continued to ignore him. Sanders wasn't sure whether Krupe simply didn't care what Bennett had to say or was so preoccupied with other matters that he didn't hear. He suspected his indifference stemmed from a little bit of both.

The one thing Krupe was not indifferent about was Bennett's and Sanders' handling of the platoon. Early every morning and sometimes late at night he held strategy sessions to discuss the day's routine down to the smallest detail. He designated who was to handle what aspect of training, reminded them of the day's appointments, insisted that each DI change into freshly starched and pressed uniforms at least twice a day, and analyzed what he considered to be any recruit or drill instructor weaknesses.

In this latter category he included Bennett's inability to keep up with the platoon during the morning run, a shortcoming that greatly disturbed him and one he attributed to Bennett's being ten or fifteen pounds overweight.

Most mornings Krupe led the run. Sometimes, when he had not yet arrived—he lived on the base in an area reserved for married staff NCOs—Sanders led it. At those times Bennett usually found some pretext for remaining behind. Otherwise he tried to find pretexts for resting en route, such as stopping to talk to other DIs they met along the way.

Finally, however, Krupe said there were to be no more flake-outs—that Bennett was to run the entire distance each day, completing it in the same time it took the main body of the platoon. Should any recruits lag behind, as often happened during the first week or two of training, Bennett was to continue running while Sanders dropped behind to see that nothing went awry.

Bennett was resentful but resigned, although he still intended to malinger whenever the tech sergeant was absent. He knew Krupe would brook no insubordination, much less in something he considered as important as physical conditioning.

Bennett had returned from Korea in the best shape of his life, but had soon gone to pot after settling into a routine desk job at Camp Lejeune. Later he worked himself into reasonable shape once more while attending DI school, but that didn't last long either—not after he was assigned as a junior DI to a recruit platoon whose senior DI was as averse to running as he was. Then his sole physical activity was confined to drill sessions with the platoon. But even that was offset by nights spent drinking beer at the NCO Club, or at any of several favorite watering holes outside the gate, in Beaufort or Port Royal.

Gradually, though, like Gabriel and Beacotte, Bennett found the morning run endurable—although not as quickly as he would have had he run every day. When Krupe added to the difficulty by requiring runners to wear Light Marching Packs and carry rifles, he included drill instructors in his orders. Not for several weeks did he discover that Bennett's haversack was filled not with the prescribed toilet articles, undershirt, drawers, socks, mess gear, and poncho, but with cardboard shaped to give it the appearance of a full pack.

Even Krupe had to grin at Bennett's ingenuity, which he discovered quite by accident in the DI hut when he lifted the pack to move it out of the way. Before the run that morning he ordered the recruits to empty the contents of their packs on the ground in front of them. An item-by-item inspection revealed that Bennett alone had faked the contents. But several recruits had omitted certain prescribed articles or had placed soiled clothing in the packs, so Krupe decided to teach them a lesson.

He began by ordering the platoon in and out of the huts, as before. Only now his commands came faster than ever, even though the drill was much more hazardous because they were carrying rifles and bulky packs as they scurried to and fro.

But Krupe and Bennett kept at them, badgering them to knock over anyone who slowed them down. Stanley Tew personally decked three recruits, a feat he bragged about for several days afterward, and a number of other recruits were also sent sprawling. Gabriel was knocked flat twice, as was the injured Otis McGraw, each of them once by Tew.

Tew himself doubled over as though he had been poleaxed when Herb Beeks caught him just above the solar plexus with a rifle butt. The platoon leader was first of all incredulous, then enraged. Once he regained his feet he vowed revenge, but before he could retaliate, the drill ended abruptly when the front sight of James Gillian's rifle accidentally caught a recruit under the left eye and laid it wide open, causing blood to spurt all over.

It was obviously an accident, Bennett saw it was an accident, yet he shoved his way through the scattered recruits until he reached the apologetic Gillian. Then he began swinging wildly, slamming him in the ribs and face. When Gillian instinctively raised his rifle to protect his face, Bennett—claiming later the recruit threatened him with the weapon—grabbed the barrel with his right hand and crashed the outer edge of his left hand into the side of Gillian's neck.

When Gillian fell, Bennett stepped on the back of his neck, pinning the side of his face against the asphalt. "You tried to hit me, you no good son-of-a-bitch," he hissed, his face contorted with rage. "You tried to hit me, didn't you, you bastard?"

There was a muffled response, which prompted Bennett to grind his shoe into Gillian's neck and mutter, "Don't you answer me back, you goddamn queer."

Afraid Bennett might break Gillian's neck, Dutton glanced furtively at Krupe. The tech sergeant was watching, but he made no move. Then he sneaked a look toward Sanders, who was examining the gash under the eye of the injured recruit, Carson Duvail. "Sergeant Bennett," Sanders said, as though oblivious to what was taking place with Gillian, "I need your assistance with this injured recruit."

Bennett was irate when he realized what Sanders was doing. His face grew scarlet, but the corporal merely looked at him and calmly repeated his request. When Bennett looked beseechingly toward Krupe, the tech sergeant said, "Get that injured idiot to the dispensary and have him sewn up. And see he's back here by the time we return from the mess hall."

Reluctantly, Bennett removed his foot from Gillian's neck—yet not before grinding it with the ball of the foot, as though to emphasize that if it had been up to him he *would* break it. Then, knocking aside two nearby recruits, he walked toward Duvail, muttering and cursing. Again he glared at Sanders, who remained expressionless. Finally he ordered Duvail, who was holding the clean T-shirt from his pack against the cut, to follow him.

Dutton completed the run without exertion, conscious only of a numbness occasioned by the violence he had witnessed—senseless, random violence. When they marched to chow, he was still trying to comprehend Bennett's frenzied outburst.

*   *   *

Krupe decided to remain at the barracks and catch up on some paperwork while awaiting Bennett's and Duvail's return, so Sanders marched the platoon to the mess hall. As usual, 486 lined up in the street behind the platoons that had arrived before them—four or five of them this particular morning, some of which passed the time in drill, parading back and forth in uneven displays of marching ability.

Engrossed in the impromptu parade, Sanders paid almost no attention to an approaching platoon until it came to a halt alongside 486 instead of lining up according to the usual procedure. When he looked up he recognized Sergeant Pepper, who nodded and broke into an artificially wide smile. "Good morning, Corporal," he said agreeably. "And where might I ask is the illustrious Sergeant Krupe this fine morning?"

Uncertain of how to take Pepper, but inclined to feel he didn't like him, Sanders replied, "He's back in the platoon area. He may be over later."

"Whew," Pepper said, wiping the back of his hand theatrically across his brow. "For a minute you had me worried—I thought maybe Sergeant Krupe overslept. But Sergeant Krupe would never commit an infraction, would he? Besides, there are some around here who doubt Krupe ever sleeps. They say he's the original twenty-four-hour-a-day Marine."

Pepper's sarcastic tone didn't bother Sanders as much as the fact that the sergeant was talking at the top of his voice. So he tried to change the subject. "How's your platoon coming along?" he asked.

"This bunch of candy-assed civilians?" Pepper said disdainfully. "If it wasn't that I've seen your platoon drill, I'd say we were the worst on the entire island." He was still talking at the top of his voice, only this time his words were aimed at his own recruits more than at Sanders.

"Well, it's a long time until graduation," the corporal said mollifyingly.

"It sure as hell is," Pepper agreed.

"But I wouldn't underestimate Platoon 486. If you'll excuse me . . ." Sanders turned and walked to the rear of the platoon, crossing to the far side in order to see that everyone was at proper attention. Pepper, meanwhile, ambled back toward the center of his platoon, stationing himself midway between the two sections, off to one side on the grass. A minute or so later a recruit came double-timing up toward the mess hall. Beneath his left eye was a large white patch. As he approached Pepper, the sergeant snarled, "What do you want, boot?"

"Sir," the recruit replied timorously, "Private Duvail is looking for Platoon Four eighty-six."

"Four eighty-six? You mean Krupe's platoon?"

"Yes, sir."

"Yes, sir? Don't you mean *Sergeant* Krupe?"

Uncertain whether it was permissible to repeat titles, which were forbidden as direct forms of address, Duvail nevertheless replied: "Yes, sir. Sergeant Krupe's platoon, sir."

"Over there," Pepper said, waving vaguely beyond his platoon.

Duvail recognized some of his platoon mates across the way. "Thank you, sir," he said, and started toward them. But he pulled up short when he realized his path would take him between the sections of Platoon 484. Turning to Pepper he asked, "Sir, may I cross here?"

"What did Sergeant Krupe tell you about that?"

"I don't know, sir. Nothing, I don't think, sir."

"In that case," Pepper said pleasantly, disarmingly, "do what you want."

Duvail hesitated a moment longer, then started through the ranks. As he did, Pepper bellowed, "Get him." Almost immediately recruits from both sections swarmed all over Duvail and began swinging. One punch caught him flush in the face, another brought blood gushing from his nose. He fell back, raising his left arm to protect his injured eye, but the punches kept falling on him. By the time he struggled free from the middle of the ranks, only to be grabbed by Pepper, who pulled him to attention, his face was badly puffed and his lip was also bleeding freely.

Sanders had heard Pepper berating someone, but he assumed it was one of 484's recruits. When he nevertheless decided to see what the commotion was, he recognized Duvail at the exact moment Pepper pulled the bleeding recruit to attention. Even then it took a few seconds to comprehend what was going on, to realize that Pepper had ordered his recruits to pummel an unsuspecting recruit from another platoon.

Once it dawned on him, he crashed into the midst of Platoon 484, pushing aside several recruits who were in his path and stopping just long enough to freeze with a glance three other recruits who seemed to be trying to decide whether to gang up on anyone other than recruits who invaded their ranks. Then he charged toward Pepper, who was berating the bleeding Duvail. Stepping between the sergeant and the injured recruit, he demanded, "What the hell do you think you're doing?"

Pepper knew Sanders was seething, and although he was personally unafraid, he did not want to provoke a scene in front of the mess hall, even though he apparently had earlier tried to provoke one there with Krupe. So instead of responding with equal anger he said, "Maybe you didn't see that your recruit here tried to break another platoon's ranks."

"So what?" Sanders' tone was outraged.

"So what? I never expected to hear that from a Drill Instructor. Tsk, tsk. No wonder your boy here got himself hurt. Didn't Sergeant Krupe ever tell you it's a cardinal sin for a boot to break another platoon's ranks?"

The question disarmed Sanders, dissipating much of his anger. As a matter of fact, Krupe hadn't mentioned it, nor could he remember having heard of it when he was in boot camp. Still, maybe Pepper was stringing him along. . . . "I'm not defending breaking your platoon's ranks," Sanders replied evasively, uncertain of the seriousness of the transgression. "But that doesn't excuse ganging up on him. This recruit just came from the infirmary." It was a weak defense and Sanders knew it. What's more, he knew Pepper knew it.

"I *am* sorry about that, Corporal," Pepper said solicitously. "But how were my boys to know? One of the first things I taught them was never to break another platoon's ranks—and to attack anybody from another platoon who broke theirs. They were j st following orders. Ask Sergeant Krupe how important it is that recruits follow orders." He saw a chance now to rub it in. "My, I'm really shocked Krupe never warned his platoon about breaking another platoon's ranks; I thought every Drill Instructor taught that first thing. I guess you could say Sergeant Krupe is really to blame for this boy's beat-up condition."

Although outraged at Pepper, Sanders was also angry at Krupe for not warning Duvail and the others. But he was angriest with himself for allowing Pepeer to confuse him. When the sergeant offered a handkerchief to the injured recruit, an offer that appeared to be made in good faith, Sanders snatched it from the drill instructor's hand, squeezed it into a ball, and threw it on the ground. "He doesn't want anything from you," he said truculently. He drew himself up full, as though, despite his considerable height and weight disadvantage, he was preparing to attack Pepper.

But the drill instructor remained calm. "Very well, Corporal," Pepper said. "But you better do something for that lad before he bleeds to death on you."

Duvail's wounds did not seem to be serious, but he was bleeding profusely from the mouth and nose. The bandage under his eye, which covered sixteen stitches, had lost its antiseptic white look and was rapidly discoloring—the stitches had split under the pressure of the blows and the wound would have to be sewn again.

Sanders ordered 486 to move toward the mess hall. He offered his own handkerchief to Duvail, who was bent over trying to stanch the flow of blood. The corporal skipped chow in order to escort Duvail to the infirmary and left him there with instructions to return to the platoon area after being treated. Then he hastened back to the mess hall to lead the platoon back to the Quonset area. All the while he was seething. He would have preferred to keep from Krupe the knowledge of what had happened, but he had to account for Duvail's battered condition. He feared Krupe would explode and immediately confront Pepper, and he wanted to avoid, or at least postpone, any such confrontation as long as possible.

Chapter
5

Corporal Christopher Sanders was as shocked as were most recruits by the violent reception that greeted boots upon their arrival at Parris Island. He simply had been unprepared for the rough stuff. Threats, okay—and grueling physical tests to challenge their physical and moral reserves. But he could not reconcile punches, kicks, and beatings with military training in a democratic society, not even in wartime. And it didn't take him long to realize that mistreatment was widespread.

The irony was that nothing Krupe or Bennett had said, by way of preliminary introduction when Sanders reported for duty, prepared him for what followed. Instructors in DI school warned that the Uniform Code of Military Justice (UCMJ) explicitly prohibited maltreatment. And Sanders' own ten weeks in boot camp after he was drafted in September 1950 and assigned to the Marines, had been rigorous but not brutal. During and after boot camp he had heard persistent tales about DI brutality, but while his own two drill instructors were constantly bellowing and threatening, they never raised a hand against any member of his platoon.

Those serene memories of boot camp were jolted at Recruit Receiving as the nucleus of Platoon 486 arrived. And for several days afterward, while the recruits underwent Hygienic, Sanders tried to remember what he had heard about Krupe that should have alerted him to the surprise he was in for. It wasn't until late one night, during an unsuccessful attempt to drop off to sleep, that it came to him.

It occurred the day he completed DI school on the island.

When the graduates were discussing their new assignments, an instructor whom Sanders had grown to like during the five-week session looked at him oddly when Sanders said his orders were to report to a Tech Sergeant Krupe to begin duty as a junior drill instructor.

"*Floyd* Krupe?" the instructor asked.

"Let's see," Sanders replied, looking at his orders again. "Yea, Floyd Krupe. Why? You know him?"

"Not really—only by reputation."

He was puzzled. "What reputation?"

The instructor's face had suddenly become clouded. "I don't think it's a good idea to prejudge people. Anyhow, you'll soon know more about him than I do, so why not wait and find out for yourself."

Sanders thought the instructor was being unnecessarily enigmatic, but shrugged and said, "Okay."

"Just one word of advice," the instructor had added. "Don't judge the entire Marine Corps by Krupe—or by any one man."

In the aftermath of the farewell "beer bust" and the move to other quarters, Sanders forgot about the conversation. Although he was looking forward to his new assignment, he didn't have to report back until Tuesday morning. Four full days off, the most he had had in months. At first he planned to drive home, even though the highways would be jammed over the Fourth of July weekend. But his girl friend Linda was on a student tour of Europe and wouldn't be back until late August. So, rather than fight the holiday mob on the highways, he decided to remain in the area and visit some nearby places of interest.

That afternoon he checked out some books from the base library describing South Carolina's historical heritage and later he drove to an Italian restaurant not far from the base. It was a large and usually bustling restaurant, except on holiday weekends, but somehow it gave the appearance of intimacy. The rooms were illuminated by melted candles in wicker wine baskets, scenes of Italy adorned the walls, and a record player piped Italian love ballads.

"Good evening, may I get you something to drink?" the waitress asked cheerfully soon after Sanders settled into a chair in the far corner. "A small bottle of Chianti, please," he replied, almost without looking up. He wondered if he would be able to read the books he had brought with him even if he squinted, but before long his eyes adjusted reasonably well to the flickering candlelight.

After he drained the bottle the waitress returned. "Are you ready to order yet, sir, or may I get you more wine?"

"Excuse me?" he said, momentarily confused about where he was or what she was saying.

"I said—" She stopped as he looked up in sudden surprise. She laughed good-naturedly when she realized he had been so engrossed in his reading he didn't know where he was. "I said, it's almost time to report back to base, Lieutenant, so would you like to order?"

"Thanks for the promotion," he laughed when he recovered his wits, "but I'm only a lowly corporal." Then, remembering he was in mufti, he asked, "Hey, how did you know I'm a serviceman?"

She smiled, a shy but pretty smile that drew attention to her white teeth and large blue eyes. "For one thing, the crew cut—it's longer than the skin-head look of most recruits and shorter than the close-cropped look of most civilians."

"And for another?"

"For another, civilian shoes don't shine the way yours do."

He looked down and saw that his shoes were highly polished. "You're *very* observant," he said. "Are you always that way?"

"But I was way off in the matter of rank."

"Not way off—just premature. I'm going to Officers Candidate School at Quantico after I leave here in September. First I have to serve as a junior DI to one recruit platoon."

"Oh, that explains it. Now, what can I get you?" she asked, her tone suddenly impersonal and no longer smiling.

After she departed with his order, Sanders wondered what he might have said to offend her, but he couldn't think of anything. Neither could he concentrate on his book. He looked in her direction several times but she always appeared busy. He tried to shrug off her changed tone as inconsequential, but he kept thinking about it. And thinking about her. She hadn't Linda's kind of delicate beauty; in fact, she wasn't really beautiful so much as attractive, the kind of wholesome good looks he associated with a college campus rather than a military town.

"What's your name?" he asked as she set down his salad and dinner of veal Parmesan and spaghetti.

"Susan. Susan Brewer. Will there be anything else?" she asked, pleasantly enough but somewhat impatiently, as though she were much too busy to talk.

"I'd like another bottle of Chianti, please."

When she returned a moment later he asked, "Do you go to college in the winter or do you do this . . . or is this your . . . I mean—"

He was trying to understand her, but by so doing was just making matters worse. "No, I don't go to college. This is my occupation. I'm a career waitress."

This time the sarcasm was unmistakable. He searched for an appropriate reply. "I'm sorry," he began. "I didn't mean to offend you."

She moved away without a word, although she seemed on the verge of a reply. The bus boy refilled his water glass twice but she stayed discreetly away, moving quickly and efficiently from one table to another as two other waitresses in similar red-and-white checked uniforms crisscrossed the half-filled room. Eventually he returned to his book, but his concentration was broken. He decided to head back to the base, read a while before turning in, then maybe head for Charleston about midday tomorrow.

He asked the bus boy to ask the waitress for his check. She asked if he'd like dessert, totaled his bill at once, and thanked him. Then she was gone. He left a tip, paid the fat, congenial cashier, and walked out into the sultry evening. He paused alongside his car door to light a cigarette and suddenly she was there beside him. "I'm sorry, Corporal," she said, her eyes downcast. "My behavior was awful. I'm the one who owes you an apology."

"If you were really sorry," he began sternly, before his eyes revealed the smallest hint of a smile, "you'd knock off that Corporal business and call me Chris."

"Chris. It's a nice name. I'm sorry, Chris."

"Forget it. We all get days like that." Then, without intending to, he added, "I don't suppose you'd care to tell me why?"

"I'm not sure I know why." She tried to smile, but her eyes were etched with worry.

"It wouldn't hurt to try," he said.

She sensed it was an invitation to share her burden, rather than the usual proposition. She lowered her eyes.

"What time do you get off work?"

"Ten o'clock."

"I'll be back at ten, then. Meet you here."

"Make it ten-thirty."

As she started back toward the restaurant, he said, "In case you forget what I look like, I'm the one with the polished shoes and short hair." He smiled; she smiled back and walked quickly toward the back door. Before she opened it she turned and waved, then disappeared inside.

*   *   *

Later, waiting for her in the nearly deserted restaurant parking lot, he felt vaguely guilty—as though he were somehow being unfaithful to Linda. Then he laughed at himself for transforming an accidental and harmless meeting into a grand betrayal.

"Hi," she said, suddenly appearing alongside his convertible.

"Well," he said approvingly, seeing her in a white summer skirt and royal blue blouse, "it wasn't necessary to change, but I must say it looks nice."

She was obviously pleased, and before he could get out of the car to help her in she walked around to the side and let herself in. He drove a few miles down the road until he found a lounge that looked respectable, pulled into the parking lot, and parked the car. Inside they sat in a small booth back from the dance floor. After ordering they talked for a while, mostly in generalities. Eventually he learned she had been born and raised outside Muncie, Indiana, that she had moved to South Carolina two years ago, and that she liked it well enough, although she missed the sharply defined change of seasons of the North. But whenever he tried to probe deeper into her background she steered the conversation into other channels.

As they danced, she was warm and relaxed in his arms yet still seemed to be keeping her distance—at least her psychic distance. It was a pleasure to hold a girl again, even—here Chris had to smile at himself—if she was only a waitress.

"What are you thinking?" she asked, backing away slightly from his embrace and looking into his eyes.

"Nothing, really. Why do you ask?"

"No reason." Then she added with a sly smile, "Actually, I

thought maybe you were wondering how you ever wound up dancing with a waitress.''

He blushed deeply. How ever could she have known . . . ? When he mustered the courage to look at her she was laughing mischievously.

As the evening wore on, their conversation became more personal. Chris sketched his own background first, skirting mention of Linda and his family's prominence. But eventually that too came out, including his expectation to marry soon after his discharge. She seemed interested as he recalled his plan to enroll for graduate study in the fall, after receiving his B.A. in June 1950. As it was, he had received his draft notice in August. When he reported for induction in September, he was assigned to the Marine Corps.

He skipped telling her his father could have used his influence to protect him from the draft, or at least postpone it, but that Chris had refused to allow him to intervene. He didn't look forward to serving in the military, but he considered it—what, unjust, perhaps?—to pull family strings in such a situation. So off he went to Parris Island, emerging from boot camp none the worse for wear shortly before Christmas. Most of his platoon had been ordered to advanced infantry training at Pendleton or Camp Lejeune pending reassignment to Korea with the First Marine Dvision. But for reasons known only to the Marine Corps he was assigned to airman's school at the Naval Air Technical Training Center in Jacksonville, Florida. Afterward he was sent to Control Tower Operators School at the Naval Air Station at Olathe, Kansas.

At first he welcomed the prospect of attending school while he waited out his two years in safety, he told Susan. But elation gradually gave way to doubt, then to guilt. He became nagged by a feeling that perhaps his family's or Linda's family connections made it possible for him to be kept thousands of miles from the front lines while there was a war on. He had no burning desire to experience combat, but he could not shake the feeling that he was receiving special treatment.

He departed Olathe in mid-1951 and was assigned to the Second Marine Air Wing at Cherry Point, North Carolina. Then, without telling Linda or anyone, he requested a transfer to the infantry. His request was denied, as were several subsequent requests. Finally, in desperation, he composed a lengthy letter to the commandant, explaining that he felt he could contribute much more to the Marine Corps if he were a foot soldier in Korea instead of a control-tower operator at Cherry Point.

Two weeks later his commanding officer received a letter saying, in part:

"Please be advised that the Commandant wishes no disciplinary action taken against PFC Sanders, but trusts he will be fully advised as to the proper chain of command. . . ."

But if the reprimand didn't chasten him, neither did his letter persuade the powers-that-be, since two more requests for transfer were denied. That's when he realized his lone remaining hope was to apply for Officers Candidate School, since there was a critical need for second lieutenants. Soviet UN delegate Jacob Malik had recently proposed truce talks between both sides in Korea, but meanwhile the Marines were still attacking the northern rim of the Punchbowl in Korea, still pursuing the retreating enemy toward the Thirty-Eighth Parallel, and still suffering heavy casualties among junior officers.

"And so you signed up for OCS?" Susan asked as he paused to light a cigarette. "You decided to become a Ninety-Day Wonder?"

He nodded. "I'll be off to Quantico before long. I report to my new unit on Tuesday," he said, meaning Parris Island, "and the platoon begins forming on Wednesday."

"What about your parents . . . and Linda? How did they take it when you told them?"

"About like you'd expect. Every emotion from disbelief to anger to hurt, and back again."

"And your wedding plans?"

"Vague. Or maybe I should say indefinite. My 'irrational behavior,' to use my mother's phrase, has confused everything."

"Will she wait—Linda, I mean?"

"I didn't think you were talking about my mother," he grinned. "Oh, sure, she'll wait."

"You sound very confident."

"I didn't mean it quite the way it must have sounded. What I meant was that she'll wait because it's . . . it's sort of expected of us. We've been going together almost since either of us began to date, and our parents are good friends."

"The same social circle?"

"Yea, just about." He signaled the waitress to bring them both another drink, but Susan begged off.

"And how about you? Will you wait?" The question was rhetorical rather than personal, and he understood it as such.

"Oh, sure. It's expected of me. But time and circumstances change things," he said pensively, "and war—"

"You sound sure you're going to war."

"I am if the war's still on by the time I get out of OCS. That's about automatic for Marine second lieutenants. Hey," he said cheerfully, "I'd better go. That's why I signed up for OCS."

Becoming suddenly serious she said, "Let's not talk about war, Chris."

"Fine, so let's hear about you."

"Some other time," she said, looking at her watch. "I've had a hard day and I should be turning in soon." She finished her drink and waited for him to drink up.

As they were driving from the parking lot he said, "Where to? Where do you live?"

"My car's at the restaurant. You can drop me off there."

"Will I see you tomorrow? What time do you work?"

"I don't work, not for three more days. Beaufort's like a ghost town this weekend, with all the Marines heading home for a long weekend, so I get the days off. But I have a lot of things to do."

As they pulled up to her car she said, "Don't bother getting out." She opened the door.

"Look, Susan," he began hesitantly, "those books I was reading in the restaurant—they're all about South Carolina and its sights. I thought if you weren't busy tomorrow we could maybe drive to Charleston or somewhere and take in some of its history. As I said, I have a couple of days to kill and I'd like spending them with you."

"Thanks, Chris, but I can't make it. I really can't."

"How about Sunday?"

"Not Sunday either. But I enjoyed tonight, I really did." He leaned over and kissed her. At first she resisted, then she began to respond. After a moment, however, she pulled away. "Good night, Chris," she said, squeezing his hand and getting out of the car.

*   *   *

He had a difficult time sleeping that night, tossing and turning in a losing bout with restlessness. He kept seeing a girl who at times was Linda but at other times was Susan. It disturbed him that he thought about Susan at all, for even though he had enjoyed the brief time they'd spent together, he knew he could never be serious about her. Yet her face kept fading in and out—the haunting distant look in her eyes at once teasing and pleading.

He arose at mid-morning, groggy and still tired. Almost without thinking he showered, dressed and drove out to the restaurant. It was not yet open but he noticed movement inside and banged on the door. At first whoever was there ignored him, but he persisted and finally the figure walked toward the door. "We don't open until five," he said. It was the rotund cashier from last night.

"I know you don't, but I need some help," Chris said. "I was here last night, remember?"

The man eyed him quizzically. He furrowed his brow for a moment, then said, "Oh, you're the bookworm, right?"

"Yea. At least I had a couple of books with me."

The cashier slid the bolt apprehensively, opening the door a crack. "What kind of help?"

"I need to know where Susan Brewer lives."

"Oh, that kind of help. Nothing doing," he said, making a move to shut the door.

"Look, I know what you're probably thinking, but I just want to talk with her. We were out together last night after work—"

"You and Susan were out together?" His tone of voice expressed serious doubt.

"Yes, we were. But I don't know where she lives and I want to invite her to go for a drive."

The fat man looked Sanders up and down. "Why didn't she tell you herself?"

"Because I was dumb enough to forget to ask. I left her off at her car in the parking lot and . . . I don't know, I guess I thought a gentleman doesn't ask a nice girl her address on a first date, not without frightening her."

"A gentleman," the cashier repeated with a snort. Yet he reopened the door a couple of inches. "At least you don't look dangerous."

"Thanks for the vote of confidence. I'm not dangerous, only a lowly Marine corporal."

"Now, why'd you have to ruin everything by telling me you're a Marine?" the cashier moaned. "I was just about to see what I could do—"

"Please."

The fat man hesitated, eyeing Sanders carefully and seemingly turning the problem over in his mind, weighing the pros and cons. Finally he shrugged his shoulders and said, "She lives in Iwo Jima Park, a trailer park two, three miles up the road. It's set back off the road but you'll see a sign pointing to it. Number Forty-eight."

"Thank you, sir. I mean it—thanks," Chris said as he began backing off the porch. "I really appreciate it, I really do."

The fat man didn't reply; he looked worried, as though he still wasn't convinced he had done the right thing.

Sanders turned at the sign and followed the road another half mile as it wound past a grove of tall willow trees, then turned into the trailer park. He finally found Number Forty-eight several rows back, then recognized her car parked outside. As he approached, she opened her trailer door. "Good morning. I see you didn't have any trouble finding it. I was afraid you'd get lost."

"Afraid I'd—"

"Sal telephoned and told me you were on the way. He said he gave you my address." She paused. "He also said he didn't know why." She grinned mischievously at him.

"Because he's a good judge of character, that's why," Chris quipped. She smiled but didn't say anything. He was pleased that she was as pretty as he remembered her, and that the alcohol hadn't played tricks on him. "Aren't you going to invite me in?" he said finally. "I assure you my intentions are quite honorable, at least this time of day."

"Chris," she said, laying a gentle restraining hand on his arm as he approached.

"What is it?"

"Maybe . . . maybe it would be better if we called it off now, forgot each other. You have Linda, I have complications of my own, neither of us can afford to get serious, and I don't have time for—how do you say it, a dalliance?"

He whistled and then said, "You make it all sound so businesslike. I didn't come here to talk about the future, I came to talk about today and tomorrow. It's my last free weekend in weeks and I want to spend it with you—this weekend and whatever other time we can spend together until I leave for Quantico.''

She remained in the doorway, making no move to invite him inside. "I like your honesty, Chris, especially since I haven't been completely honest with you."

"In what way?" Suddenly his face clouded. "Is there someone I don't know about?"

She paused. "Yes, there is." He looked downcast, and then she asked, "Want to meet that someone?"

"You mean he's in there? Now?" he asked, pointing at the door.

"Follow me," she said, turning back into the trailer. He was surprised by her invitation, and couldn't decide whether it was a sign of candor or cruelty. He knew only that he would have preferred to avoid the embarrassment that seemed to be unavoidable, yet he really had no choice other than to follow.

"Chris Sanders," she said as he ducked inside, "I'd like you to meet Amy Brewer."

The sun was streaming through the living room window and the reflection blinded him. He looked for her boy friend but he couldn't see anyone. Only when he maneuvered his back to the light did he see a figure—a child, a virtual infant. "Your daughter!" he exclaimed. "Then . . . you're married?"

"Daughter, yes. Married, no. Not anymore."

"Divorced?"

"A widow." Her eyes began filling with tears. "God, I hate that word," she said. "No matter how many times I say it, each time I hate it."

"My God, a widow at your age?" He judged her to be no more than twenty-two. "Was he . . . was he a Marine?"

"What else?" she said with a touch of bitterness, dabbing at her eyes.

"That explains a lot," he said. "And Amy—that explains why you couldn't go to Charleston with me. Or is there more?"

"Isn't that enough?"

She moved into the kitchen and put the coffee pot on the burner. He followed and placed a comforting hand on her shoulder. They barely spoke as they drank their coffee, while Amy stared at the visitor. Finally he said, "Susan, I still have the rest of the day off, you have it off, Amy has it off—so let's go to Hilton Head Island. We'll have a picnic."

"Don't you want to hear the rest of it?" She didn't sound eager to tell, but she thought he might be curious.

"If you want to tell me. But not here, not now. On our way to Hilton Head. What do you say? It so happened I brought my bathing suit along."

"I think I'd like that," she said, making an effort to smile. Then she exclaimed, "Oh gosh."

"What's the matter?"

"I have to phone Sal."

"Sal?"

"I...I told him I'd phone within half an hour..."

"I see. Afraid of me?"

"Sal's just being cautious. He's like that."

"Well, then," he said, rising from his chair, "while you phone Sal and assure him I'm not Jack the Ripper, I'll go get some food." When he returned about twenty minutes later Susan was dressed and putting the finishing touches on her daughter. "Did Sal approve?" he teased.

"Not entirely. But he was so relieved you didn't turn out to be a madman that he would have approved of almost anything, I think. He told me all he could think of was why he ever gave you my address."

"My ineffable charm, most likely."

She pretended to frown as he began unpacking the food and drinks he had purchased. "I thought this picnic was just for the three of us," she said as she watched him.

"It is. Why?"

"There's enough food here for a platoon."

"You can never be too sure. Besides, what if we get marooned?"

"I'm wise to those tricks, Corporal," she said easily. "Besides, I can swim and row."

He winced. "Easy with that Corporal business. I'm a civilian this weekend, remember? All weekend. By the way, I hope Amy drinks beer, otherwise she's going to get mighty thristy over at Hilton Head—I seem to have forgotten milk or soda."

"Why, Corporal...I mean Mister Sanders. I'm shocked—I didn't know Marines drank anything stronger than R.C. or Coke."

"That's the new Corps, ma'am. Us old corps gyrenes have been known to bend an elbow or two," he said, opening a can of beer for them both.

She finished packing and before long they drove to the dock, rented an outboard motorboat, then set out down the Beaufort River past Parris Island, heading across Port Royal Sound. It was a warm, clear day with low humidity, a deep blue sky, and a gentle breeze that caressed their faces. Colorful sailboats and pleasure craft dotted the blue-green water of the Sound, but few of them were headed toward Hilton Head, the large ocean-front island inaccessible except by boat. Amy, clinging to her mother, was fascinated by the water and the gulls that hovered just above them, noisily screeching at the occupants for scraps of food.

They moored the boat right on the beach, then spread a blanket midway between the water's edge and the dunes that formed a protective barrier. Susan made a tentlike shelter for Amy from a large beach towel. The island was deserted except for people way off in the distance, a mile or more up the unbroken stretch of spacious beach. They talked, walked along the water's edge collecting sand dollars and driftwood, and took turns watching Amy as the other went for a brief swim in the surf. They relaxed and enjoyed the solitude amid a lush setting of palm trees, magnolias, and virgin pines. With only a tiny effort of the imagination Chris could conceive that this looked not unlike Saipan, Tinian, Kwajalein, and those other Pacific islands whose names were a source of pride to every Marine.

After lunch, while Amy slept beneath her makeshift tent shaded from the sun and lulled by the warm breezes, Susan felt Chris staring at her. When he made no effort to stop she said, "Chris, what's the matter?"

"I'm waiting."

"For what?"

"For you to fill me in on your life."

"Tell me all about yourself, is that it?"

"Not all about yourself—just the last twenty or twenty-five years," he quipped.

"It's really a dull story—"

"Good, I'll use it to relax by," he replied, bundling his clothing and a towel into a pillow, turning on his back, and settling his head as though preparing to take an after-dinner nap.

She laughed at his histrionics, but soon became solemn as she began her story. She was glad he had draped his arm over his eyes to shield them from the sun; that way he couldn't see her as she kneeled beside him.

"Dan and I met in high school," she began. "That was his name—Dan. We had a couple of classes together." She paused for a second. "Everybody in school knew him and all the girls were crazy about him. He was a good athlete, handsome, and he came from a prominent family in town."

"What town was this?"

"A little town outside Muncie, no place you ever heard of. His family owned a big farm within the city limits, we lived in a nearby township and rode the bus to the high school. We weren't poor exactly, except compared to the Brewers. They had money and position and influence."

Still shielding his eyes with his arm, Chris raised up just enough to put his head in her lap. She began soothing his cheek with her hand. "But none of that really mattered to me because I knew Dan was out of reach. Guys like him always pick girl friends from either their own church or social circle, or one of the cheerleaders. I was just another girl, a little bit above average in looks and brains, maybe—"

"A *little* above?"

"But for some reason he asked me out," she said, ignoring the interruption. "I was so surprised that I told him I already had plans. He told me later he knew I was lying, but I didn't know that then. I went home and cried all night about being so stupid, certain he'd never ask me out again. But he asked me the very next week and I think I blurted 'Yes' even before he had the words out of his mouth."

"And from that day on there was never any doubt you'd be married?"

"From that day on the two of us were engaged in a running battle with his parents."

"Why?"

"Because they had greater ambitions for him than for him to get involved with a . . . a—"

"A mere commoner?"

"Exactly. I was a commoner and they had groomed him for royalty, at least Indiana royalty. Anyway, they had much bigger things in mind for him."

"What sorts of things?"

"That's what was maddening about all of it. Whenever Dan

asked what they objected to about me, they'd never say anything specific. They just always gave him the impression he could do better. We'd laugh about it, but after a while it really did begin to hurt.''

''I can't imagine why,'' Chris twitted.

''We imagined they were hoping he'd meet some well-connected girl at college, and he wasn't likely to do that if I tagged along with him, as I planned to do. So he told me of his plan. We discussed it for several weeks and I tried to talk him out of it but he wouldn't listen. And I was so much in love I would have walked off a cliff with him. So the day after graduation we took a bus to Indianapolis, flew to San Diego, and drove to Tijuana to get married. His parents were furious when he telephoned them from California. They said we could get it annulled, they threatened to have me arrested—''

''How noble.''

''—They said a Mexican marriage was illegal and sinful. When Dan told them we'd be back in a week or so, after we saw a little more of the West, they said he was welcome to come home any time, but only if he came alone.''

''My God, they sound wacky.''

''Actually, they're quite nice people.''

''If you don't happen to marry their son.''

''Right.''

''Then what happened?''

''Then we went back home. Since I couldn't set foot in his parents' house, Dan didn't either. Instead, we moved in with my parents. They weren't in favor of the marriage either, but only because they thought we were too young. My mother told me later that for months afterward she'd cry whenever she looked at our bedroom and remembered that just a few weeks before I had shared it with my stuffed animals. But they were good about it and they gave us moral support. Dan's parents pleaded with him to go to college at their expense, but he said he'd never accept help of any kind from anyone who treated me as less than his lawful wife. They resisted, until one day out of the blue they telephoned and asked if we'd both come to a small party they were having that Saturday. Dan's father said let bygones be bygones. And they tried—even during the party they did their best. But Dan's mother was a very proud woman, and she couldn't bring herself to introduce me as anything but Susan—no last name, no hint I was Dan Brewer's wife, even though everybody there knew we were married. And halfway through the party she excused herself and went upstairs to bed. Nervous exhaustion her husband told the guests but we knew what was making her nervous.''

By this time Chris was sitting up, watching her as she fought back tears. He reached over and dug two cans of beer from the ice chest and opened them, struck by the fact that while her story was sad, somehow it was devoid of self-pity. She took a few sips, then, after checking to be sure Amy was still in the shade, she said, ''There isn't much more to tell. After that Dan decided we had to get away, to prove we could do it on our own. I agreed, but I blamed myself for jeopardizing his future. He laughed and joked about it. That's when I knew he was as much in love with me as I was with him. A few days later he said he had decided to join the Marine Corps.''

''And you agreed?''

''As I said, I would have followed him off a cliff. He was young and bright and adventurous. And it was peacetime. We weren't at war, remember? I'd never even heard of Korea until the Marines sailed for there a year after we were married. By that time we had spent a glorious twelve months together. He had graduated from boot camp, then I joined him at Quantico during OCS . . .''

''He was an officer?''

''A Second Lieutenant. And proud! How he loved the Marines! He joined because it seemed a glamorous and exciting way to get away from our personal problems, and he wound up with a second wife.''

Chris cocked an eyebrow awaiting an explanation. ''The Corps,'' she said. ''He was married to the Marine Corps.''

''Was he . . . did he . . . I mean how did—''

''He was killed in Korea. I went with him when he was ordered to Pendleton, and whenever he had a day off we'd try to revisit some of the places we'd visited on our honeymoon. Even with the shadow of his departure hanging over us, it was fun. I expected to be lonely but not . . . not a widow.'' Chris put his arm around her shoulder, trying to comfort her. ''We had it all planned,'' she said. ''During his first leave I'd fly either to Japan or Hawaii to be with him. We still had stars in our eyes, still thought our fairy-tale marriage could never end.'' She began sobbing and finally was unable to continue.

After a while she quieted down and Chris asked, "How did you end up here in Beaufort? Why didn't you go home?"

"By then I was three months pregnant and—"

"Did Dan know it?"

She shook her head. "I never told him," she said. "I didn't want to worry him before he went overseas. Since I was pregnant and we didn't have any money except his salary, I decided to remain in the Pendleton area. My parents would have welcomed me home, but I knew Dan would be proud if his child was born on a Marine base. And when I learned that two of my girl friends from our OCS days were in Parris Island, waiting for their husbands to come back from overseas, I decided to move here—at least until Amy was born."

She grew silent again, then finally excused herself and took another quick dip in the surf. After she returned, Chris followed her example. When he emerged from the water she was feeding Amy, who had awakened and demanded food and attention. Neither of them talked as they began packing. The sun was still high in the cloudless sky, but they wanted to get to the mainland long before dark. Finally, on the way back across the Sound, he said, "Susan, why have you remained in South Carolina? Why didn't you go home?"

"A lot of reasons, I guess," she said, raising her voice to be heard above the outboard motor. "For one, I figured I might have some trouble with Dan's parents when they learned about Amy. I heard they blamed me for Dan's death—"

"Blamed you for his death?"

"If we hadn't been married, he would have been in school and not in the Marine Corps. In a way they're right, I suppose."

"Nonsense," he said. "Arguing about what might have happened is hopeless—and fundamentally dishonest."

"Anyway, I also didn't want to burden my parents, especially since my father had had a stroke. Then I guess I had to prove to both sets of parents and myself that I could make it on my own. So once I got here and Amy was born in the Base hospital, I stayed, even after both my girl friends eventually packed up and moved home."

"How long do you plan to stay?"

"Until I straighten out my problem with Uncle Sam," she said, brushing the windswept hair from her eyes.

"What problem?"

"Nothing important—just a question of convincing the

Government I'm really Daniel Brewer's widow. It seems our Mexican marriage is open to question."

"But weren't you recognized as man and wife when he joined the Marine Corps?"

She nodded. "That's the strange thing. Dan was paid the same as any married man. We received quarters' allowance and I had a dependent's card entitling me to shop at the PX and the rest. But for some reason I'm tangled up in red tape trying to convince the Government I'm the rightful beneficiary of Dan's government insurance policy. Ten thousand dollars is a lot of money, but I almost think I'd walk away from it if it weren't for Amy. Well, I expect one of these days things'll get straightened out."

"Meanwhile you'll keep on working?"

"Sure. There isn't anything elegant about my job, but it pays pretty well with tips. The best thing, though, is that I only work four or five hours a day, so I'm really away from Amy just part of the day. Besides, I have a wonderful woman, Kennie Bletz, right in the trailer park who watches Amy every day and loves her. And Sal is really good to me."

Chris cocked a quizzical eye. "He's not a dirty old man, is he?"

She laughed. "Not Sal. He and his wife, Mary Rose, took a liking to me and they've helped me over some rough spots. Sal divides his time between watching over me like a father and the other half planning to introduce me to men who pass his approval. It says a little about Sal's standards that no one yet has ever met his approval—until you, that is. And he still has doubts about you. That reminds me, I have to telephone him as soon as we get back and let him know I'm safe."

"My God, again?" Chris laughed, shutting down the motor as the boat glided into the dock. At that moment Amy gurgled.

"See," she laughed, "she's telling you she's happy."

"Maybe she's just saying that Sal will be happy to hear from you."

"Oh, you," Susan said, playfully hitting him with her elbow.

He asked her to see if the baby sitter was free that night, and when Mrs. Bletz learned there was a young man involved she said, "Why, I'd cancel any engagement for something this important."

"I don't think it's that important, Mrs. Bletz," Susan said, "but it'll probably be good for my morale."

"Nothing could be more important than that," Mrs. Bletz corrected. "I'll be there on time and the two of you stay out as long as you want."

They went to a movie, the first she had seen in more than a year. Later they dropped by to see Sal, who greeted both of them like long-lost kin. Then they drove out to a roadside restaurant for dinner. She was dressed in a plain white skirt and scoop-necked print blouse, her medium-length dark hair set off by bangs. He thought she looked truly lovely, a loveliness that seemed enhanced by her enigmatic, faraway look.

He had an inkling why she hadn't hired a lawyer to pursue her claim against the Government, and she confirmed the suspicion by merely shrugging when he asked about it. But he pursued the subject, asking the date of their marriage, Dan's service number and enlistment date, and the current status of her claim, all of which he jotted down in a notebook. "I know someone I think might be able to help," was all he said by way of explanation.

She cuddled up alongside him as they drove back to the trailer park, the warm, scented breeze blowing against their faces as the open convertible sped along. For a moment he thought of those summer nights with Linda driving along the Ocean Highway to his family's summer home in Cape May, and he had to remind himself that this was South Carolina and Susan, not New Jersey and Linda.

Mrs. Bletz greeted them cheerily, gave a detailed report of Amy's every movement, then bade them good night, saying, "I hope I'll be seeing you soon again, Mr. Sanders."

"She's really subtle, isn't she?" he laughed after she left. Susan also laughed at the somewhat obvious attempt to promote a lasting relationship. There were a few cans of beer left, so they shared them sitting side by side on the sofa. She put on some mood music and before long they began dancing, both in their stockinged feet. He switched off the light and they opened the blinds. It was a clear moonlit night and the heavens were filled with stars. Chris held her tight and she rested her head on his shoulder. He stopped dancing, and as she raised her head he kissed her, gently at first, then with increasing passion. He drew the blind and led her over to the couch, setting her down gently and positioning his body firmly against hers.

"Please don't hurt me, Chris," she whispered between kisses.

"Hurt you? How?"

"I'm vulnerable," she said, "terribly vulnerable." He pressed closer to her. "I know I shouldn't tell you, but I am. I guess I need something to believe in again."

"I don't want to hurt you, Susan, ever," he said, pausing again to kiss her sensuously. "But I don't know if I can give you something to believe in. I can't promise—"

"I don't want any promises, Chris," she interrupted, the tears coming into her eyes. "I don't ever want any promises."

"Then what?" He was genuinely puzzled.

She kissed him ardently, then paused. "I just always need to know the truth about our relationship—not that I'm liked, or adored, or loved, or admired. None of that. I just don't want to be misled." She was clinging to him, almost as though for protection.

"I'll never mislead you, honey, you have my promise." It was the first time he had called her by other than her Christian name. "I'm no gay deceiver in the first place, and especially not with someone who's been through everything you've been through." He maneuvered his body directly against her and soon she felt the intensity of his passion. She started crying again, soft gentle sobs that originated in distant sorrowful memories, but she made no effort to pull away. His tongue eagerly explored her warm mouth and eventually he slid his hand gently between her thighs, seeking her hidden warmth.

She shuddered apprehensively but offered only token resistance. He was excited yet strangely composed as he removed her clothing. But as he gazed at her firm body his last vestige of restraint dissolved. For a brief moment he thought about Linda and about the possibility of holding back, but by then he was no longer capable of makeing a choice. He hoped only that Susan would never look back on this night with regret.

Chapter 6

When Sanders related what Pepper's recruits had done to Duvail, he fully expected the tech sergeant to dash out the door over to Platoon 484's area in search of Pepper. Instead, Krupe was uncharacteristically calm, interested only in Duvail's condition. "Do you know whose fault it is, Sanders?" he asked, assuming a didactic air.

"I suppose you'll say it's mine for not attacking Pepper right then and there and salvaging my—our, your—honor."

"Wrong, Corporal. Pepper was right for a change. It was my fault for not telling you or the recruits. Those cuts on Duvail's face might as well have been put there by me."

Sanders was astonished by the tech sergeant's contrition, yet he couldn't resist the impulse to rub it in. "But what about your honor code? Doesn't it require you to retaliate? Or does this fall under the heading of military Darwinism, survival of the fittest Marine?"

The reference to Darwinism caused Krupe to draw back slightly. Yet when he replied he ignored it. "Oh, I'll retaliate all right, Corporal, don't worry about that. But not for my oversight. Pepper was right about breaking ranks, but overall he's a poor DI. He doesn't have what it takes to prepare recruits for combat."

"And what does it take?"

"Dedication. Knowledge. Leadership." Krupe said it without embarrassment, without the slightest indication he was in effect passing judgment on himself as well as speaking in general terms.

"What is it between you and Pepper?" Sanders asked. "Why do you hate each other so much?"

"Now, don't go playing psychologist, Corporal," Krupe said irritably, "because your diagnosis is wrong already. Despite what you may think, I don't hate Pepper. The rare occasions that I even think of him, I feel pity, for his recruits mostly, but not contempt."

"You look like you hate him when the two of you are glaring at each other. But I don't think Pepper's scared."

"I think Pepper's too dumb to be scared. I told you he doesn't have good judgment—or if I didn't tell you, I'm telling you now. But he's not as reckless as he looks to you. He's actually relying on my judgment not to provoke a showdown, so he acts as though he's calling my bluff. And it'll work—up to a point."

"Unless he tried to march his platoon into yours, is that it?"

"That's it—until the minute he interferes with my handling of my platoon."

"He's a big boy, Sergeant."

Krupe smiled, a smile of utmost confidence. "All right, Corporal," he said, as if he no longer cared to continue so frivolous a conversation, "fall the troops out for drill."

*　　*　　*

Carson Duvail was missing the next morning when the platoon lined up to march to the mess hall. After Sanders and Bennett had searched the entire platoon area without success, Bennett telephoned Krupe at his home. Although he lived at the far end of the base, near Page Field, the auxiliary landing strip, he arrived within minutes, impeccably attired as always in his starched uniform. He immediately ordered a wider and more intensive search, pressing a half-dozen recruits into service under the direction of Robert Begay. Although Bennett warned the Indian to find Duvail even if he had to send up smoke signals, there was no trace of the missing recruit and Bennett was too preoccupied to carry out his vague threat.

Several recruits recalled seeing Duvail studying his *Guidebook* before lights out the previous night, but no one remembered seeing him that morning.

Finally there was no alternative but to report Duvail's disappearance to the commanding officer, Major Adam Knisely.

When the C.O. asked Bennett if he knew any reason for Duvail to go AWOL, the sergeant said he probably feared he couldn't measure up as a Marine.

"That's what I thought," Knisely replied, his suspicions confirmed. "You're bound to get the ten percent that can't take it—the mamas's boys, the slackers, the goof-offs. We'll take care of him, all right."

Sanders wondered how Krupe would explain Duvail's disappearance to the full platoon, and after 486 returned from chow he addressed them forthwith. "Now that Private Duvail has tendered his resignation from our exclusive little club," he said, "maybe others of you plan to join him. I hope you do. That will save me from carrying you on the back of this platoon any longer than necessary, and it will mean we won't be slowed down by the misfits.

"But let me explain what it means for Duvail and for any others who plan to take the easy way out. First of all, he'll be found before the night is out—or, if he's unlucky, he may hide out another day or two. But no one has ever escaped from Parris Island, because there's only one exit—the main gate. There are the swamps, of course, but you'd have to be better Marines than any of you yo-yos to find your way through them. And even if you did, there's nothing but shark-infested waters between them and the mainland—Beaufort River on one side, Broad River on the other.

"So you hole up somewhere, without food, without water and with nowhere to go. Right now Duvail is somewhere on this island wishing he had had the guts to stick it out . . . cursing his cowardice and stupidity for ever running away . . . wishing he were back with his platoon . . . and wondering what's going to happen once he's caught.

"I'll tell you what's going to happen when he's caught. He's going to spend a couple of years in the brig at hard labor. And if you think boot camp is tough, spend a day or two in the brig. There isn't one of you who wouldn't be praying before nightfall to be back with your platoon. Then Private Duvail is going to be dishonorably discharged—sent home in disgrace, hounded for the rest of his life by the realization that he couldn't cut it and that everyone at home knows he couldn't cut it.

"So run away, if that's what you want. Get out of my platoon, get out of my sight, get out of my Marine Corps. Most of you aren't even fit for the Army, much less a *real* fighting outfit.''

Duvail was discovered the next day, hiding in the vicinity of the Elliot's Beach training area. When the two MPs found him, he seemed relieved. Panic at not being able to escape from the island, fear of the consequences, hunger, and fatigue brought on by the suffocating heat—all combined to make him surrender meekly to await the consequences.

*   *   *

After several weeks Platoon 486 began looking less like stragglers and more like a nascent drill team. Its rifle drills were still sloppy, and Krupe invariably tricked at least one recruit each time he unexpectedly ordered flanking or turning movements. Yet for the very first time the platoon was beginning to respond in unison rather than as seventy individuals. Moreover, most of the bald heads now sprouted a thin covering of peach fuzz, which a seemingly unbelieving Herb Beeks ran his hand through at every opportunity.

Bennett, meanwhile, continued to torment Gillian, so that at times it was all the recruit could do to hold his temper. The day after Duvail was reported missing, Bennett blamed his disappearance on a lovers' quarrel between them—claiming they had a falling out over whose turn it was to act the part of the girl friend that night. When Gillian grimaced at the accusation, the DI knocked him down and kicked him several times in the back for expressing "silent contempt." After Duvail was imprisoned, Bennett demanded to know whether Gillian wanted to join his lover in the brig. When something in the recruit's "No, sir" displeased him, he ordered him to stand outside the mess hall exit after evening chow and sing as much as he knew of "I'm In Love with a Wonderful Guy."

Bennett's badgering and frequent accusations and insinuations had some effect on other recruits, who eventually did begin wondering about Gillian's masculinity. Several ignored him, others were barely cordial, and a couple of Dave Hall's buddies pointedly turned away whenever Gillian came near.

This latent hostility flared to the surface one night when Bennett ordered a four-hour-long field day, claiming Gillian had marred the day's drill. Everyone understood that Gillian was simply a scapegoat, but as the hours passed and they were still on their knees scrubbing the mud-caked floors, sweating from exertion and the high humidity, some of them began grumbling, rationalizing that they might have been spared this drudgery if it hadn't been for Gillian.

Two recruits from a nearby hut entered Dutton's Quonset to borrow a squeegee. Seeing Gillian down on the floor scrubbing, one of them spat, "Thanks a helluva lot, you queer bastard." Afraid of getting in worse trouble than he was already in, Gillian pretended at first not to hear; he knew Bennett was somewhere in the area, unexpectedly popping in and out of huts, and he hoped to avoid giving the DI an excuse for smashing him.

Dutton appreciated Gillian's contretemps, so he rose from his mud-soaked knees and said, "That's enough out of you, fella. Get the hell out of here while you're still in one piece."

"Why?" snorted the intruder. "Afraid Janie might slap me on the wrist?"

Before his detractor could utter another word, Gillian lunged at him, smashing him above the eye with a wooden scrub brush. The wounded recruit gasped as blood spurted out of a deep, ugly cut and flowed down his face. When his companion started forward toward Gillian, Gillian discarded the brush, smacked him flush in the face with two sharp left jabs, then followed up with a right elbow smash to the chest that knocked him sprawling across the wet floor.

As Gillian turned back to confront his original antagonist, who was still standing dumfounded and helpless with the bottom of his blood-stained T-shirt pressed against his brow, Dutton moved in to restrain him. "Easy, Jim," he said, "he got the message. I don't think we'll hear anything more out of him. Will we?" he asked the bloodied visitor.

"Jesus Christ, you bastards," the kid said, almost in tears. "There was no goddamn need to cut me up. I didn't mean anything by it. Hell, it was only a joke."

"Then the joke was on you," Dutton said, as a crowd began to gather.

"Yea, some joke," the kid replied. "He hit me with a scrub brush."

Gillian pushed forward but Dutton restrained him. "Here, you son-of-a-bitch," Gillian challenged, "this time you take the scrub brush and I'll use my fists." He picked up the brush and offered it.

Dutton had no intention of letting the fight continue but,

eager to prevent any repetition of the provocation, he said to the intruder, "That's fair, isn't it?"

"How about it?" Gillian persisted. "You use the scrub brush or whatever else is handy, and I'll take you on with my fists—you and your buddy together," he said, looking toward the other recruit, who had picked himself up and was looking for a face-saving way of departing. The bleeding recruit didn't answer. Instead, he looked at Gillian, then at Dutton. Finally he lowered his eyes, signifying he had enough.

By this time several other recruits had pushed their way into the circle that had gathered to watch the fight. "What the hell do you call this noise?" It was Dave Hall, accompanied by three buddies who had previously treated Gillian as though he were a pariah. "Who the hell did this to a man from my hut?"

"Gillian done it," replied Stanley Tew, who had been outside when the trouble started and who had been as surprised as anyone by the redheaded recruit's angry reaction. "Now, get the hell out of here, all who don't belong in this hut, before I lose *my* temper."

"Gillian?" Hall was incredulous. "That'll be the god—"

He glanced toward the recruit, who looked as though he hoped Hall would finish his statement. But he didn't, so astounded was he by the startling transformation in Gillian. "Finish what you were going to say," Gillian demanded.

Still confused by the unexpected development, Hall didn't know what to say. Finally he said, "Did you do this?"

"Do you feel like mouthing off too?" Gillian asked, ignoring the question.

Hall raised his hands in a friendly "I surrender" motion, smiling as though to show he was a reasonable guy. "Man, don't go bad-mouthing me," he said in a spuriously friendly tone, "I'm just concerned with the guys in our Quonset hut. Hell, we need every able body to pitch in on the field day."

"Then get these two punks out of here and keep them out of my sight. If they even talk to me again, I'll beat hell out of them."

When Hall and his troupe departed, Dutton grasped Gillian's hand. "Nice going, Jim," he said. "They deserved it, and a lot more."

Also impressed by Gillian's performance, Tew said, "Damn, man—you're all right, you know that? I always thought you wasn't qu— I mean, I always thought you was a gung-ho jar head."

Gillian understood Tew was being complimentary, so he smiled civilly. "That's good, Tew. Now all I have to do is convince Bennett."

But Bennett continued as before. During formation for chow the next morning he announced, "It seems that our Platoon Pin-up likes to use scrub brushes in ways not authorized by the *Guidebook*." He walked menacingly up to Gillian. "Is that right, Janie?"

Resigned to the prospect of another thumping, Gillian replied, "Yes, sir."

"Well now, Miss Jane," Bennett said, pitching his voice artificially high, "that's a serious breach of etiquette—like not straightening the seams on your nylons, or flying the flag on your honeymoon. And so that we don't misuse government property again, I want you to sleep with your scrub brush every night from now on. Is that clear?"

"Yes, sir."

"Good. And Janie," Bennett said ominously, "I have big plans for you. Why, before you leave here, you'll be the most famous woman Marine in the entire Corps, a real big BAM."

*   *   *

When platoon 486 finally held mail call, Dutton received a letter from his mother and three from Julie.

Julie! His pulse quickened as he carefully, lovingly opened the letter with the earliest postmark. Julie—even her name was like a musical interlude that soothed the harsh reality of boot camp. They were typical Julie letters—an irrepressible mixture of chitchat and seriousness, of implicit sentiments and explicit expressions of love, written in a clear, flowing hand he would have recognized anywhere.

His anticipation awaiting mail call reminded him of the many times he had rushed to his college postal box between classes in hopes of finding a letter or note from her. Even when they had talked on the telephone that day, had spent the previous weekend together, and planned to meet the weekend after, more often than not there would still be a letter.

As he sat on his locker box slowly absorbing every word, trying to stretch out her letter, he pictured her alone at the seashore, as lonely as he was, as full of doubts about the future, as saddened by their separation. He saw her in a thousand different poses—romping with him on the beach like a frisky

cub; the cute way she shook her head to flip the hair out of her way before holding the receiver to her ear when talking on the telephone; her sun-browned, desirable body in a bathing suit.

In her third letter she said she was thinking about visiting him at Parris Island some Sunday, and wondered if it would be all right. When he read those words his heart almost stood still. More than anything in the world, he wanted to see her. But not at Parris Island, not at a place so totally removed from her own innocent world and comprehension. He resolved to write her that very night and dissuade her, telling her visitors were not permitted.

Bennett enjoyed mail call more than almost any part of the training day. Since newspapers were prohibited in boot camp, he delighted in summoning Private Sam Bayard front and center. Then, from a distance of no more than six feet, he threw at the recruit's face the home town newspaper to which Bayard's parents had entered a subscription. Luckily for the recruit, Bennett was uncoordinated and erratic, so he often missed Bayard altogether.

Whenever packages arrived containing candy, cakes, or other sweets, Bennett ordered the recipients to open them in his presence. After expropriating whatever he wanted, he ordered the remaining "pogey bait" eaten that night so not a crumb remained by morning.

When Gillian raced to the front of the platoon in prescribed fashion to claim his letters, Bennett put him through the usual humiliation. The first time he demanded, "Who's that from?" Gillian replied the letter was from his girl. Bennett snorted "What's his name?"

"It's a she, sir," Gillian insisted. "Her name is Nancy Akimoto."

"Don't lie to me, you homo bastard," Bennett said, blinking rapidly. "I'm going to keep this letter until you tell me the truth." This routine was repeated several times, until Sanders convinced Bennett it was a serious offense to withhold or otherwise tamper with someone else's mail. He finally returned the letters unopened, but not before scattering them on the ground and making the recruit drop to his knees, clasp his hands behind his back, and retrieve them in his mouth, using only his tongue and teeth.

Another time he made Gillian put two letters between his knees and walk with them back to his assigned place in ranks, warning that if they fell he would have two extra nights of fire watch. As Gillian maneuvered thus encumbered, Bennett ridiculed the exaggerated walk. "Thay, you're beautiful, you are," he lisped, convulsed by his own cleverness. And then Gillian dropped the letters—probably intentionally, Dutton thought, in order to escape further humiliation even at the price of having to walk fire watch. Oddly, though, Bennett didn't attack him. For whatever reason, that time he seemed content merely to gloat.

* * *

After about three weeks most of the recruits slowly emerged from the trauma that accompanied their terrifying reception at the recruit depot. There were several reasons why. For one thing, the physical assaults were less indiscriminate, and now the more vigorous workings-over were usually reserved for real rather than imaginary foul-ups. Equally important, however, by now most recruits did everything possible to avoid antagonizing Krupe or Bennett. Finally, although the drill instructors never hinted at it to the recruits, the platoon was progressing satisfactorily.

Not all the boots overcame the paroxysm of fear and confusion that had greeted their arrival. Some, like Jonathan Gabriel, remained bewildered and scared. His responses were too deliberate, too studied, and it still required too much time for him to grasp even such relatively uncomplicated tasks as disassembling and reassembling his M-1. Others, like Orme Beacotte, were not yet sufficiently physically fit to keep up without enormous physical exertion. Although Beacotte had lost fifteen pounds since his arrival, he was still at least twenty pounds overweight.

But it was Gabriel who worried Dutton the most, especially after he twice expressed fear that he'd end up in Simple City, the nickname given to the area where failures, psychotics, and misfits marked time awaiting medical or general discharges. Dutton did his best to bolster the timid recruit's confidence, but Gabriel was inconsolable. And fear of his failure was increasingly etched in his pallid face.

One Sunday afternoon, during a rare free hour for shining shoes, cleaning rifles, and polishing belt buckles, Gabriel uncharacteristically confided to Dutton that all his life he had been meek and withdrawn, that he instinctively shrank from any challenge that threatened to reveal his frailty, and this merely reinforced his sense of worthlessness. His father, who in his

dropped the letters—probably intentionally, Dutton thought, in order to escape further humiliation even at the price of having to walk fire watch. Oddly, though, Bennett didn't attack him. For whatever reason, that time he seemed content merely to gloat.

*   *   *

After about three weeks most of the recruits slowly emerged from the trauma that accompanied their terrifying reception at the recruit depot. There were several reasons why. For one thing, the physical assaults were less indiscriminate, and now the more vigorous workings-over were usually reserved for real rather than imaginary foul-ups. Equally important, however, by now most recruits did everything possible to avoid antagonizing Krupe or Bennett. Finally, although the drill instructors never hinted at it to the recruits, the platoon was progressing satisfactorily.

Not all the boots overcame the paroxysm of fear and confusion that had greeted their arrival. Some, like Jonathan Gabriel, remained bewildered and scared. His responses were too deliberate, too studied, and it still required too much time for him to grasp even such relatively uncomplicated tasks as disassembling and reassembling his M-1. Others, like Orme Beacotte, were not yet sufficiently physically fit to keep up without enormous physical exertion. Although Beacotte had lost fifteen pounds since his arrival, he was still at least twenty pounds overweight.

But it was Gabriel who worried Dutton the most, especially after he twice expressed fear that he'd end up in Simple City, the nickname given to the area where failures, psychotics, and misfits marked time awaiting medical or general discharges. Dutton did his best to bolster the timid recruit's confidence, but Gabriel was inconsolable. And fear of his failure was increasingly etched in his pallid face.

One Sunday afternoon, during a rare free hour for shining shoes, cleaning rifles, and polishing belt buckles, Gabriel uncharacteristically confided to Dutton that all his life he had been meek and withdrawn, that he instinctively shrank from any challenge that threatened to reveal his frailty, and this merely reinforced his sense of worthlessness. His father, who in his

youth had been a small but gritty athlete, was deeply disappointed in his son's lack of athletic ability and competitive spirit. He
went out of his way to hide that disappointment, but Gabriel felt
it, even saw it in his eyes. Yet the boy was helpless to do
anything about it.

By age seventeen he was a confirmed failure—in athletics,
with girls, even in the classroom, where his increasing sense of
futility caused him to quit studying except to earn the minimum
grades needed for graduation. He sensed that his only salvation,
the lone remaining opportunity he had to reverse this pattern of
futility, lay in confronting a challenge from which there was no
turning back, And so, several weeks before graduation, he
decided to join the Marine Corps.

His parents reacted as though he had taken leave of his
senses. He was surprised at his father's opposition, his fear that
this was not the path to salvation but to destruction. His few
friends were equally surprised, because it was clear to them he
didn't have what it took to make it. And the recruiting sergeant
was finally swayed by the shy, uncoordinated, bespectacled
youngster's plea only because he had a quota to fill and the
Korean War had taken a heavy toll in Marine manpower. "So
that's why I'm here," Gabriel concluded with a wry smile. "To
see if I'm worth anything at all."

Dutton was moved by Gabriel's inner conflict, but he didn't
want to encourage his pessimism. "Look, Jack, don't take it so
seriously. You aren't going to fail. Even if you did, it isn't the
end of the world. But you're going to make it, so no more talk
about failure."

Gabriel was about to reply when Sanders' voice boomed
out, "Fall in, on the double." Instead, he stood silent for a
second or two as his eyes filled with tears. Dutton hoped
they were tears of gratitude that someone cared whether or not he
made it, but he was afraid they were tears of hopelessness and
doubt.

Chapter
7

By the start of the fourth week, Platoon 486 had lost several recruits, including McGraw, who was reassigned to a newly formed recruit platoon when the injured tendons in the back of his knee failed to heal, making it impossible for him to keep up during the morning run that by now had been lengthened to one and three-quarter miles.

Two other recruits who were unable to execute even the most rudimentary commands were sent to Simple City for psychological examination and a probable discharge after more of their hair grew back. Almost every morning Gabriel began the day fearful he would not survive until the next day, yet equally fearful of remaining with a platoon being instructed by madmen.

Sanders was also opposed to many of the methods of his two colleagues, not so much of Krupe's brief, impartial flare-ups as of Bennett's prolonged harassment of certain recruits. Hoping to convey his distaste of these methods, one night when Bennett was in town with some drinking buddies from Third Battalion, Sanders asked Krupe if he didn't think it might be a good idea to order Bennett to stop picking on Gillian.

"I've thought about it," the tech sergeant replied tersely.

"And what did you decide?"

"I decided Gillian can take it. He's a pretty tough kid."

"Suppose he couldn't take it, though?" Sanders persisted. "Suppose he broke down, the way those other two gooney birds broke down and had to be sent to Simple City?"

The expression "gooney birds" was intended to allay any suggestion that he was blaming Krupe or Bennett for driving the two recruits to the special psychological section. But Krupe wasn't fooled. Looking up from the editorial page of the evening paper, he pushed back slowly in his chair, removed his glasses, and began polishing them with an oversized handkerchief he kept in his side desk drawer. "Are you trying to tell me something, Corporal?"

Sanders had just finished lighting a cigarette. He was tempted to avoid any unpleasantness or serious criticism beyond that already expressed. But after blowing out the match he said, "Now that you mention it, Krupe, I guess I am."

"Then be my guest," the tech sergeant said, settling back comfortably in his chair.

"I'm trying to tell you that I object to the way these recruits are mistreated. They're . . . they're treated like prisoners rather than boots—as though they were the enemy instead of kids we're supposed to be training to fight on our side."

This was the first time Sanders had ever called Krupe by his last name, devoid of the prefix "Sergeant," and it stang. "Does this mean you object to the way I run my platoon?"

In a voice surprisingly controlled, Sanders responded, "That's exactly what it means. I've had my fill of watching you, and especially that paranoiac Bennett, bully and beat these kids. You're not molding Marines, you're making savages out of them." He hadn't intended to be so blunt, but he decided that if Krupe was going to run him up before the C.O. for insubordination, it might as well be for unburdening himself of all his accumulated grievances.

But Krupe didn't betray any anger or emotion at his assistant's allegations. Instead, he leaned back farther in his chair, balancing it on its hind legs, and asked: "Is that the end of your sophomoric analysis?"

"No, it isn't all," Sanders said, dragging deeply on his cigarette. "Look, Krupe, I know all about there being a war on, and the need to turn out real Marines. But these kids won't be Marines, they'll be robots masquerading as Marines when they leave here—youngsters permanently scarred because of your ins . . . because of your unnatural preoccupation with obedience."

"You were about to say 'insane preoccupation.' Why didn't you—afraid you'd hurt my feelings?" When Sanders didn't reply, he said, "To you it's a preoccupation. To me it's an emphasis on obedience . . . on discipline. Discipline is what makes Marines, Sanders, the discipline hammered into them right here on this island. It's too late by the time they get to Korea. If they don't learn it here they'll never learn it, since few of them learn it at home, or school, or church.''

''But you're not teaching them discipline, you're teaching them fear. There's a big difference.''

''*Was mich nicht umbringt, macht mich starker.*''

When Sanders raised a quizzical eyebrow Krupe said, ''I'm surprised you don't recognize Nietzsche, Corporal: 'That which does not kill me, makes me stronger.' ''

''Nietzsche. I might have known. But that which doesn't kill can also cripple, mentally as well as physically. Besides, what guarantee do you have that Bennett won't kill one of those boots? He's damn lucky Gillian didn't land on that bayonet point while he was doing those pubh-ups.''

''Bennett won't do a stunt like that again. I've—''

''I know, I know, you warned him,'' Sanders said caustically, his voice rising slightly. ''So what if he doesn't do exactly that again? He's sure to do something just as stupid. He's lucky he didn't cripple Gillian when he had him on the ground and was kicking him. He's sadistic.''

''Sanders, what is it you want from me—an admission that Bennett isn't my idea of the perfect human being?'' His voice was irritable and tired. ''Okay, you have it. Bennett would torment his mother if he could. But I'm stuck with him, and that's all there is to it.''

''No, that isn't all there is to it,'' Sanders corrected. ''He takes his lead from you. He punches and kicks and bullies and terrorizes because you condone it. He's a bully, an extortionist, a—''

''An extortionist?'' Krupe furrowed his brow in genuine surprise.

''You mean you didn't know?''

''Didn't know what?''

''That he told the boots you were getting married after graduation and that they could show their good will by kicking in three dollars each?'' He calls it 'flight pay.' I thought he split it with you.''

Krupe reacted as though slapped across the face. ''Corporal, don't allow your uninformed judgment of my professional ability to warp your judgment of my personal ethics.'' The words themselves were not especially harsh, but the tone was unmistakable hostile.

"All right, I apologize. I'm sorry. But what are you going to do about making Bennett return the money?"

"Nothing."

"Why not?"

"If I could have prevented it, I would have," Krupe said, closing the newspaper and folding it. "But returning the money now would only lower the boots' opinion of their DIs."

"So you'll allow him to steal the money?"

"Those are pretty strong words. Especially since Bennett would probably reason that if they're that gullible they deserve to be taken advantage of. A fool and his money . . ."

"Sergeant," Sanders said irritably, "is there anything you wouldn't do to protect the reputation of an NCO?"

The question was intended as an insult, but Krupe regarded it as a backhanded compliment. "Offhand, Corporal, I can't think of anything."

"Then why do you allow brutality?" Sanders asked, changing his tone from accusatory to persuasive. "What could damage the entire Marine Corps quicker than that? Do you think these kids you've thumped are going to forget about it once they leave here? Most of them haven't read Nietzsche and never will. They don't understand about superman and the superiority of the masters. They'll have this crazy idea they were abused, not advancing the doctrines of philosophy."

Krupe sighed wearily, then recrossed his legs and shifted in his chair. Fixing his gaze directly on the corporal, his eyes magnified behind his thick eyeglass lenses, he said: "You're naive, Sanders. You act as though Bennett and I are the only two DIs on this island who raise our hands against recruits. Look around you, you have eyes. And you know why we're 'brutal'? Because we have only ten weeks to prepare these clowns for combat, and the quickest way—"

"Is not by brutalizing them," Sanders interrupted.

"Whoa, wait a minute, let me finish, then you can talk to your heart's content. First, your point about recruits complaining about the treatment they receive here. It shows you misjudge human nature—a serious failing in a potential officer. In the first place, those who wash out of boot camp, who crack up or get sent home, are too ashamed to do any talking. Even if they did complain, who would believe them? Obviously, they're malcontents who're disgruntled that they couldn't cut it."

He rose from his chair and began pacing slowly, talking—

the corporal felt—not so much to Sanders but to himself. "And boots who do graduate won't complain because they'll be full-fledged Marines when they leave—they'll be fraternity brothers, and what kind of person would denounce his own fraternity brothers?" Without waiting for an answer he continued, "But beyond that, those Marines who go to Korea will know soon enough why they were pushed so hard. And the ones who don't go will have too much respect for those who do, or will be too ashamed that they sat on their duffs here in the States, to say anything."

"So what you're saying is there's a conspiracy of silence, is that it?"

Krupe ignored him. "So ask yourself—who's going to believe it even if somebody, some crank, does complain about imaginary abuses?"

"Imaginary!" Sanders scoffed. "Was it imaginary when Bennett kicked Gillian unmercifully, or damn near crushed his neck? Is it imaginary when you elbow some seventeen-year-old in the gut or knock him to the deck?"

"Sanders, you really don't understand what discipline is all about, do you?" Krupe said wearily.

"Discipline, nothing. You're using that as an excuse to brutalize these kids."

"Your trouble is you keep mistaking discipline for brutality. The Corps is a fraternity of professional killers, and boot camp is merely the initiation, the rites of passage, that insure group solidarity through sharing a common experience."

Uncertain whether Krupe was stringing him along, Sanders said, "If brutality is necessary to inculcate 'fraternal spirit,' how do you account for Marine officers who don't go through P.I. or San Diego? They aren't abused, yet no one questions their devotion or *semper fi*. The ones I know are at least as gung-ho and capable as NCOs."

"Spoken like a loyal OCS candidate. And it may surprise you that I agree most officers are damn fine Marines. But don't compare them with these clowns, simpletons, mamas' boys, and goof-offs, who are sent to us by th trainload. Officers are carefully screened, most have been to college, and they're three or four years older. The jokers we're training are sworn in if their pulse is warm, then they're dumped here for us to weed out or make into Marines. And you can believe I intend to weed out every single bad one before he gets a chance to go to Korea and endanger real Marines.''

Sanders remained convinced Krupe's method was wrong, yet it troubled him that he found his arguments plausible, if not persuasive. As he lit another cigarette, Krupe drained his coffee cup and returned to his soliloquy. ''My idea of a disciplined Marine is one who respects life more than he disdains death, takes every precaution to stay alive but fights to the death if he has no other honorable alternative.''

''Yes, but—''

''Let me finish,'' Krupe demanded. ''Plenty of cultures have taught that man's most glorious achievement is to die in battle—to avenge ancestors, to attain everlasting life, or whatever. But despite their bravery many of them were defeated by rivals no more numerous or better equipped than they were. Why is that? I'll tell you why—because bravery is no match for bravery plus discipline.''

He was still pacing back and forth, talking faster than usual but very much in control of his words. ''Marines didn't earn their reputations as great fighters because they're braver than the enemy, or because we have God on our side, or because we're always right and the enemy is always wrong. We've outfought the enemy all through our history because of our loyalty to one another—because we know we can trust one another in combat, and because we believe it's better to die than to let down another Marine.''

''I don't understand what this has to do with my complaints,'' Sanders said uneasily.

''Don't you?'' Krupe was staring directly at him, as though sizing him up. ''Don't you understand yet that we're shaping individuals into Marines who think alike and respond alike, even it it means degrading and humiliating them? We even shave them bald in boot camp so they'll look alike.''

''So you're really doing them a favor by batting them around, is that it? You're testing them now instead of in Korea? You're being cruel only to be kind?''

''That's part of it.''

''So Bennett is not really a sadist or bully, but a wise counselor who deserves praise for testing Gillian's character under stress. Is that it?''

''How much do you know about Bennett?''

"Not much. But enough to know he's the type of person easily corrupted by power."

"Would you say he's brave?"

"I'd say he's basically a coward."

"It figures. Well, I hate to undermine your interesting analysis, Sanders but you might be interested to know that Bennett is the holder of the DSC— the Distinguished Service Cross, for bravery under fire. He also has two Purple Hearts."

Already confused by the unintended direction the conversation had taken, Sanders was astounded by this latest revelation. Bennett the Bully a hero? A medal winner for bravery in combat? "Who told you that?" he finally asked, although he knew he sounded foolish.

Krupe smiled omnisciently. "Ask to look at the chest wounds caused by two slugs from a burp gun. Or look through his Service Record Book. Or better yet, why not come down off your high pedagogical horse long enough to act civil so you can ask him about it. Ask how he crawled three times through heavy fire to rescue members of his squad when the Reds had them pinned down on the march out of Chosin?"

"Bennett was at Chosin?"

"The whole First Division was at Chosin. And they survived because they were tougher and better disciplined than the Chinese. Bennett was just one of dozens of heroes during those thirteen days. We lost four thousand killed and wounded, and almost twice that many were disabled from frostbite. But the casualty rate would have been at least double if it hadn't been for guys like Bennett."

Sanders was no longer worried about losing the argument; now he feared he was merely re-enforcing Krupe's opinion about the value of his harsh training methods. "Sergeant," he said, reverting to his traditional form of address, "okay, I was wrong about Bennett being a coward. But I'm not wrong about beating up these recruits. It's wrong, damn it."

"Sanders," Krupe said finally as he reached for his *cocomacaque* and cap, "who's a better judge of the best training methods for preparing Marines for combat? Bennett and I, or you?"

Phrased that way, Sanders couldn't think of an answer. "That's what I thought," said Krupe, fixing his cap at the proper angle before striding outside into the night.

*   *   *

Sanders' conversation had no visible restraining effect on Krupe's subsequent behavior He continued to punish the slightest infraction swiftly and indiscriminately, while Bennett continued to torment Gillian, Begay, and several other recruits.

A few nights after the confrontation in the DI hut, Sanders was awakened in the early hours by scuffling and a muted yell. He had taken to staying overnight with Susan a couple of times a week at the trailer, getting up at 3:45 A.M. in order to arrive at the DI hut before 5:00, but this night he had the duty and had gone to sleep shortly after 10:00 P.M. When he heard the noise he sprang from his rack, fumbled for a flashlight, and then—clad only in his skivvy shorts—ran outside, followed by a drowsy and muttering Bennett. "Fire watch!" Sanders hollered, hoping not to disturb the sleeping recruits.

"Fire watch!" Bennett repeated, hollering loudly in total disregard of the recruits.

"Down here," answered a voice from the direction of the head.

Sanders shined the light on an unrecognizable figure, then he and Bennett ran toward it. Krupe was hovering over a figure sprawled out on the grass, up on his elbows puking and interspersing shrill breathing sounds with deep gasps. "What's up?" Sanders asked, turning the beam toward the recruit, whom he finally recognized as Private Hosse.

"Go on, tell them. Sing out," Krupe commanded.

Hosse vomited again. After groaning once more he said, "Sir ... I ... don't know ... what happened. I was ... walking my—"

"You were walking around in a fog, weren't you, lad, not thinking about what you were doing, just trying to stay awake. Isn't that right?"

"I ... guess so, sir." He continued to gasp loudly.

"Don't tell me you guess. You were wool gathering, weren't you?"

"Yes ... sir."

"Then what happened?" Krupe persisted.

"Sir, I think somebody kicked me in the stomach. I ne—" He turned away, doubled up, and vomited once more.

"You weren't kicked, Hosse, you were struck with this," he said, brandishing his *cocomacaque*. "It was to remind you why you're walking guard duty. Suppose you were in Korea tonight instead of South Carolina, and suppose I were a North Korean or Chinese. What would have happened?''

"I'd . . . be . . . dead . . . sir.''

"You'd be dead! Who cares about you, Private? We'd *all* be dead, every officer and man of this platoon. You'd be responsible for more than seventy lives because you weren't paying attention.''

Initially angered at being roused from sleep, Bennett perked up when he considered how effectively Krupe had taught Hosse a lesson. He chimed in, "Do you think those Gooks announce themselves, lad? You think they give you fair warning?''

"No, sir,'' Hosse gasped, trying to rise by steadying himself on all fours.

"Fucking-A they don't, Private. They wear tennis shoes, even in the dead of winter, and they sneak up like big-assed birds and run you through with a bayonet or put a bullet through your brain. You ever seen anybody with a bullet through their brain?''

"No, sir,'' the youngster said, wobbling unsteadily on both feet.

"It's messy, lad, real messy. Ruins your looks to beat hell.''

Krupe cut in brusquely. "Get down to the head and clean up, then get back in the sack for tonight. You're to walk fire watch on this shift for the next three nights, is that understood?''

"Yes, sir.''

"Shine your flashlight over here so I can see what time it is,'' Krupe said to Sanders. "Zero-one-five. That means fifty-five extra minutes for the third fire watch to walk. Who is he?''

"Sergeant, I have an idea,'' a grinning Bennett said. "Let me wake up Private Gillian to finish out this shift. Three hours is pretty long to ask the next guy to walk, especially when we'll be drilling on the grinder most of tomorrow—or today, or whatever goddamn day this is.''

Sanders thought Krupe glanced at him for just a second, but it was too dark to be sure. "Okay,'' Krupe said finally, "wake Gillian. Me, I'm going home and hit the sack. See you in the mess hall in five hours.''

A number of recruits had heard the commotion, for Krupe and Bennett had made no attempt to lower their voices. But no one dared whisper as he lay there in the pitch darkness of the Quonsets. Yet by early morning, when Hosse was ordered to hose down the grass where he had thrown up, everyone knew about Krupe's latest assault.

Nevertheless, dramatic as the incident was, it did not prevent a similar attack by Bennett; indeed, he had been eager to imitate Krupe's success. Choosing an overcast night about a week later, he waited inside the DI hut until the fire watch on the midnight-to-two shift passed by on his appointed rounds. Then he quietly made his way down the far side of the huts and crouched behind a Dempster Dumpster, a large trash container.

He waited several minutes until Robert Begay drew alongside, then he lobbed a rock onto the roof of a nearby Quonset. Begay had actually been anticipating that Bennett would spring something on him—at least he decided to remain on guard against such a possibility during his tour. But when he whirled in the direction of the noise, Bennett sprang at him and felled him with two hard, sharp karate chops to the back of the neck.

"You call yourself an Injun?" he taunted in breath heavy with alcohol as the recruit writhed in pain—and humiliation, at having fallen for the oldest trick in the books, something out of every class-B Western movie. "You're a goddamn drugstore Injun, that's what you are," Bennett continued. "No wonder you lazy redskins got your asses whipped by the Doggies, can't even prevent being ambushed on fire watch."

Begay was sore for several days, but he was more chagrined than hurt. Bennett was so pleased by his success, regretful only that his victim had not been Gillian, that the next day he delivered a discourse to the entire platoon about the necessity of keeping alert at all times. His rambling talk detracted somewhat from the effectiveness of his message, pitched to the danger of relaxing one's guard in Korea, but the recruits were suitably impressed with the danger of relaxing while walking guard at Parris Island.

Bennett continued to inflict unique punishments. A special favorite, borrowed from a DI acquaintance over in Second Battalion, was to stomp on the instep of a recruit who got out of step and then say, "Pivot on the foot that hurts." When recruit Emerson Tillich failed to place his boondockers neatly under the bunk, Bennett made him carry a dress shoe suspended from his mouth by its laces for one full day. And Bennett delegated to Gillian the nightly task of spit-shinning the DI's shoes and holster (in which he carried only his cigarette pack), usually berating him afterward for what he claimed was an unsatisfactory job.

On top of everything else, Gillian's valet duties allowed him so little time for his own requirements—cleaning his rifle, shining his shoes, etc.—that he rarely found time to dash off other than a hasty note to his girl. One night Bennett came into the hut just before lights out and saw Gillian writing. "How long before you finish that letter, Janie?" he demanded.

"I just finished, sir," he replied.

"Who's it to?"

"My girl, sir." He saw the anger rising in Bennett. "I mean, it's to a girl I know."

"Read it," Bennett ordered, cocking his head and looking at him through malevolent half-closed eyes.

"Sir, you mean—"

"Goddamn it, Private, I mean read it. Now. Aloud."

Gillian thought that federal regulations governing the mails probably gave him the right to refuse, but he also knew such laws were unenforcible in Recruit Platoon 486 of the Sixth Battalion at Parris Island. He looked at Bennett once more, hoping he would change his mind, but the drill instructor's expression remained the same. "Gillian, you are one defiant son-of-a-bitch," Bennett said. "You read that letter aloud here and now or I'm going to rearrange your fairy features."

As Sanders entered the back door, Gillian looked toward him imploringly. But when the corporal didn't do or say anything Gillian reluctantly began reading: "Dearest Nancy, These lines—"

"Louder, damn it, Gillian, you're not loud enough. Dutton," he hollered, "can you hear him down there?"

Dutton was about to answer what was expected of him. But seized by a sudden impulse, some desire to offer Gillian encouragement and vicarious support, he replied, "Yes, sir." Bennett whirled angrily, but Dutton remained at rigid attention, facing forward. For a moment Bennett considered rushing down the squad bay to teach him a lesson, but he decided not to relax the pressure on Gillian.

"Louder, you fag. I want them to be able to hear it in the next hut."

The recruit began anew:

DEAREST NANCY,

These lines are written in haste, since I don't have too much time tonight. But I wanted you to know that everything is going well and that I'm getting along fine. It's tough and it's demanding, but that's what I expected when I joined and I wouldn't want it any other way.

I've been thinking of you a lot this past week, and please don't think my laxness in writing to you means any lessening of my love for you. I think about you all the time.

Remember what we learned in Mrs. Lynn's class: 'How do I love thee, let me count the ways'? I'm afraid I can't count that high, sweetheart, but just remember that I love you with all my heart and soul, and will always.

> Forever,
> Jim

Bennett didn't speak for several seconds, during which not a sound could be heard anywhere. Finally he said, "Give me that envelope," snatching it from Gillian's hand. "That's what I thought," he said. "This goddamned letter is addressed to a guy, to a Daniel Akimoto. All that crap was written to your boy friend."

"Sir," Gillian said firmly, "it's addressed to Miss Nancy Akimoto."

"I say it's addressed to a Mr. Daniel Akimoto," Bennett insisted, a sheepish grin creasing his face. "What is he, a Jap?"

"Yes, sir, *she's* a Japanese-American," Gillian persisted.

"You're getting me mad, you little ol' sweetheart, you. Is it true about Japs—I mean the reason they're called 'slants'? Is theirs really crosswise?"

"Sir, I don't know. I've only been—"

"That's right, you wouldn't know much about Jap women, would you? It's Greeks you're interested in. You got some Greek in you, don't you?" the drill instructor demanded, edging closer, his face less than an inch from the recruit, who was standing stiffly at attention with his thumbs locked along his trouser seams.

"No, sir, no Greek."

"But you have had some Greek in you, haven't you—just like you've had some Jap in you some nights."

"This letter's to a girl," Gillian shouted, snatching it from the drill instructor's hand and causing him to step backward in surprise. "It's to a girl, do yo hear, a girl?" he repeated, as tears of rage filled his eyes. "Corporal Sanders," he said, waving the letter toward the other drill instructor, "tell them this is to my girl."

"Why, you defiant, no good son-of-a-bitching bastard," exclaimed Bennett, who quickly recovered his aplomb and brought a knee swiftly up toward Gillian's groin. But the recruit managed to absorb most of the impact by twisting his body. That only fueled Bennett's anger, and after missing a right-hand punch to the face he kicked at Gillian again, this time catching the upper part of his left leg. Then he smashed an elbow under his chin that sent the recruit crashing into the locker and onto the deck.

Bennett, now consumed with rage, moved in on the prostrate recruit, who feared he might try to kill him if he struck back. Therefore he curled up in a fetal position to protect himself. But before Bennett landed more than two or three kicks, Sanders moved between them. "He's mine, Sergeant," Sanders said, turning his back to Bennett and reaching down and jerking Gillian up with both hands.

"What the Christ do you mean, he's yours?" Bennett exclaimed. "I'm going to work him over good this time, and nobody better try to stop me."

As though he hadn't heard, Sanders abruptly threw the recruit on the lower rack and turned menacingly toward Bennett. When the sergeant saw the anger blazing in Sanders' eyes, a good part of his own anger drained away. "No, Sergeant," Sanders said firmly, "you've had your fun with Gillian and now it's my turn. Just because you were having fun with him about this letter," he said, picking it up and examining the address with exaggerated interest, "is no excuse for the insubordination we've seen here. I intend to make sure it doesn't happen again."

Bennett was livid. But since he didn't know how far Sanders was prepared to go to keep him from getting at Gillian, he reluctantly decided he'd better not press too hard; if there was a showdown, there was no telling who the C.O. might stick up for. Besides, there was no sense making an issue of it in front of the troops, especially since Sanders at least tried to make it possible for him to back down without losing face. "All right, Corporal, he's all yours," he said grandly. "What are you going to do with him?"

"Gillian, get down to the DI hut and wait for me there," Sanders commanded. "And you better be at attention when I arrive."

"The rest of you, get those goddamned letters and things away," Bennett yelled. "It's time for lights out and I don't want none of you moving around after that light switch is thrown."

When they got outside, Bennett started to say something but Sanders cut him short. "Go over to the NCO Club. I'll be over shortly."

"Wait a goddamn minute, Corporal—don't you go giving me orders or I'll hang your ass higher than a kite," Bennett said bitterly.

"You won't do a damn thing, Bennett, or I'll give you the same treatment you gave Gillian. I don't give a damn where you go, but don't come back to the hut for at least another hour."

Bennett was pretty sure Sanders meant it and he wasn't particularly looking for trouble. Moreover, he told himself philosophically, he had no desire to antagonize a future officer. "Didn't you forget, Lieutenant," he said, his voice dripping with sarcasm, "that I can't go to the club while I'm on duty?"

"Now you can, Sergeant. You just designated me duty NCO for the rest of the night."

Bennett shrugged. "Remember that if Krupe drops around." Then he started toward the club.

When Sanders entered the hut Gillian was braced stiffly at attention. His neck was red and his eyes were still swollen from tears of anger and frustration, but otherwise he looked okay. "At ease, Private," Sanders said. But Gillian, suspicious, remained at attention. "Look, Gillian," Sanders said, "If you're not going to obey orders it's no wonder Bennett gets mad at you." He smiled, and when the recruit understood he was being friendly he slowly relaxed.

"How do you feel?"

"Good, sir. But, sir, I don't understand."

The corporal lit a cigarette and sat behind the desk. He took several deep drags. "Don't try to understand, Gillian. It can only get you in trouble. Do you smoke?" he asked, extending his pack of cigarettes.

"Sir, I don't . . . I mean, I better not—"

"Take it."

"Thank you, sir." Sanders offered a light.

"Tell me something, Gillian. Do you think you're going to make it through boot camp?"

The recruit lowered his eyes then muttered, "I guess so, sir. I don't really know, really. I mean . . . I know I could if—"

"Yea, and I could win the Korean War singlehanded if there was no enemy. I want to know if you think you'll make it."

"I want to, sir, I really want to. I know I can be a good Marine."

"I know it too, Jim," Sanders replied reassuringly. "So do it—make up your mind to make it."

Jim! And from a drill instructor, no less! Suddenly Gillian's bruises no longer hurt so much.

"And another thing. Are you still sleeping with that scrub brush?"

"Yes, sir."

"Well, from now on, don't. If Sergeant Bennett wants to know why, you tell him I ordered you not to."

"But, sir—"

"If he gives you a bad time, let me know. That's also an order. Do you understand?"

"Yes, sir," the boot said, relieved but also puzzled.

"What is this, a party?" Krupe demanded as he entered the Quonset. "Corporal, I assume Private Gillian is here smoking a cigarette with your permission." His voice was unusually cutting.

"Not only with my permission, Sergeant Krupe, but at my explicit order. I ordered him up here and made him smoke."

The tech sergeant looked quizzically at his assistant. "Do you mind telling me why?"

"Not at all. Private Gillian had a rough time of it a little while ago when Sergeant Bennett decided to remind him of the proper response expected from Marine Corps recruits. You can still see his neck is swollen and red."

"He disobeyed Sergeant Bennett and for that you reward him with a cigarette?"

"Not a reward, Sergeant. Merely something to help him recuperate. He had a somewhat nasty . . . fall."

"Well, he looks all right now," Krupe said, walking across the room toward his locker, "so get him back where he belongs."

"As you wish. Okay, Gillian, hit the sack and see if tomorrow you can avoid those loose locker boxes."

When Gillian had spun in the prescribed manner and hurried back to his darkened Quonset hut, Krupe wasted no time demanding an explanation. After Sanders described the incident he said, "That's the third time you've interceded to help Gillian, if I remember correctly."

"You remember correctly. And I'll intercede as often as my intercession is necessary to save him from getting his brains kicked out. Him or anyone else."

"Sanders," Krupe said as he reached in his desk drawer for a piece of chewing gum, "let me warn you—don't ever intercede if it's me who's working somebody over."

"Or what?"

"Just don't do it. I'm telling you for your own good, be cause I'm not Bennett and I wouldn't stand by while you made a fool of me."

"And I won't stand by and let even you maim or kill someone just to satisfy some fiendish impulse."

Krupe looked at the corporal appraisingly, then said, "You better not ever lift a finger."

"Don't bet on it, Sergeant. And don't bet I won't act before that time comes."

Krupe looked at him long and hard. "What is that supposed to mean?"

"Just this—that if you or Bennett mistreat anybody else the way you've done to some of these recruits, I'm going to report you to the C.O. And if that doesn't work, I'll go directly to Silverthorn, or Sheppard, or Secretary of the Navy Kimball, or Congress or President Truman. But I'll be damned if I'm going to be a party to any more cruelty."

"Bravo," Krupe said dryly. "Now, where's Bennett?"

When Sanders explained, the tech sergeant suggested that he also take the remainder of the night off.

Chapter
8

When Sanders entered the NCO Club, a plain white frame building partitioned off into an Enlisted Men's Club also, he was still smoldering and prepared to have it out then and there with Bennett, but Bennett was nowhere around, so he sat at the bar and ordered a beer. He thought about telephoning Susan and saying he'd be over to spend the night, but it was already after eleven and she was likely to be in bed or preparing to go. So he drained his glass and ordered another. As he raised it to his lips he heard a familiar voice behind him say loudly, "Don't tell me your lord and master let you and Bennett out on the same night?"

"How do you know Bennett's out?" Sanders asked, picking up the conversation as though they had been speaking for hours.

"I just saw him in Port Royal," said Pepper. "In the Harbor Inn—that's his hangout when he ain't at the Log Cabin in Beaufort. Hell, you and that tough-guy boss of yours are probably the only two DIs on this damn island who don't go there at least once in a while. Now Krupe, I know why he don't go there," Peppper said, walking toward the bar from his table, carrying his beer. "He thinks he's too good to associate with us common folk. But what's your excuse?"

"My excuse? My excuse is that like every other DI around here, I work about fifteen hours every day and then I have to study before I hit the sack." He decided not to mention Susan.

"Study? Oooh . . . that's right, you're going to OCS after your platoon graduates, ain't you? Bennett told me."

"I'm surprised you'd even talk with Bennett—I mean, a DI from a rival platoon."

Pepper laughed raucously. "Hell, Bennett ain't a bad guy. Did you know he was a hero in Korea?" Sanders nodded. "It's Krupe I have a hard-on for."

"No kidding," Sanders said with exaggerated wonder. After taking a long swallow he asked, "What I want to know is, why?"

"Two more beers here," Pepper hollered to the bartender, ignoring Sanders' polite refusal. "Why do I hate Krupe, you mean? Actually, Corporal—say, what's your name again?"

"Sanders."

"Actually, Sanders, I respect Krupe; I even admire him a little bit in some ways."

"You could have fooled me."

"Whoa, don't get me wrong—I hate the bastard personally, but I'm talking about professionally. He's a great Marine. I know two, three guys on this base right now who wouldn't be here today if it wasn't for Krupe."

"How's that?"

"In Korea. Man, they say he was a real tiger when the First Provisional Brigade relieved the Army's Twenty-seventh Regiment during the first Marine action of the war. And at the Frozen Chosin, too."

"He was at both those places?"

"That's affirmative. Right from Pendleton to the front lines. Old Krupe, he was in the thick of it right from the start. And he didn't miss much shooting between then and the time they reached Hamhung after breaking out of the Chinese trap at Chosin."

"And he was a good fighter?"

"One of the best. Hell, these guys I was telling you about, they claim Krupe was one of the most hated bastards in the world those two weeks at Chosin—making guys get up when they couldn't walk another step, not letting them take off their shoes or gloves so they wouldn't get frostbite, not letting them zip their sleeping bags at night so they could scramble out when the Gooks attacked. Yea, they hated him okay—until it was all over and they made it out in one piece, or with maybe just a finger or toe lost to frostbite. Then they appreciated his bullying."

"But you don't?"

"Hell, ain't his bullying bothers me—at least not his bullying of those cruds in that platoon of his now. You don't think I give my boots kid-glove treatment, do you?" He answered his own question with a loud, deep laugh.

"Then what's bugging you?"

"See these three stripes?" Pepper said angrily, tapping his chevrons for emphasis. "If it wasn't for that spit-and-polish bastard I'd have me four stripes now and be bucking for Tech."

"How so?"

"I was Krupe's assistant, same as you—except I was a Buck Sergeant. But I had passed my test for Staff and my name was on the list to be promoted. Only he wouldn't go to bat for me so I was dropped from the list—passed over and declared ineligible for Staff for eighteen months."

"Why wouldn't he defend you?"

"Some horse's ass of a Lieutenant Colonel put me on report for holding night drill back in Ribbon Creek—you know, the swamp grounds behind the butt area out at the rifle range. The C.O. was hopping mad; said somebody could drown or get lost at night, and that it was off limits."

"How'd the Lieutenant Colonel find out about it?"

"My rotten luck," Pepper said bitterly, taking a deep, satisfied swallow of beer. "While we was marching, some stupid son-of-a-bitch went and tripped over something in the dark and broke his leg. We got him back to the platoon area okay, but this officer just happened to be driving through and decided to investigate why the lights was burning after lights out."

"Oh God, then what?" Sanders asked, ordering another round.

"Then the shit hit the fan," Pepper remembered with amusement. "I tried to think of an excuse but there wasn't much I could say, since the boots was all muddy from slogging in Ribbon Creek."

"And you weren't court-martialed?"

"No—like I said, I got screwed out of my promotion and was restricted a few weeks. But I wouldn't of got that if Krupe woulda just said he never told me not to go back in the Ribbon Creek area."

"And he wouldn't do it?"

"You nuts or something? Floyd Krupe, *USMC*, defend a training violation?" His voice trailed off in anger.

"Had he told you not to march the platoon back near Ribbon Creek?"

Pepper furrowed his brow in amazement. "Yea, he told me. So what? What's that got to do with being a prick or a good guy? Hell, he could have covered for me."

"Did you ask him to?"

"Hell, yes, I asked him. But he said what I did showed poor judgment and lack of leadership. So he threw me to the wolves. Oh, he tried to be a nice guy after it was all over, saying he might have considered going to bat for me if it had been the first time. I'll bet he would of."

"You mean you'd done it before?"

"Once. One stinking other time I held night drill. Only nobody was hurt, and we didn't go near Ribbon Creek. What of it?" Pepper asked defensively. "It was good for those animals—they were salty, thought they knew all there was to know, but they couldn't march worth a damn. I was helping Krupe win his coveted Post Honor Platoon, only he didn't appreciate my help."

The two drank in silence for several minutes, then Pepper began chuckling. He nudged Sanders' arm confidentially with his elbow. "But Krupe hosed himself," he said. "He was supposed to make Master Sergeant last month, but they passed him over because of me. Since he was Senior DI, what happened was his responsibility. But that ain't enough for me," Pepper continued. "That don't help me any. And that ain't the end of it for Krupe. I'm gonna fix his ass, so help me God."

"How?"

"I got ways," he smiled. "But you can bet I ain't about to tell them to Krupe's assistant."

"Can't say I blame you," said Sanders, ordering still another round. "But you can say all you want to about that bastard Krupe—I've had it up to here with him," he said, drawing an imaginary line across his throat with his finger.

"Yea, ol' Bennett said you wasn't too much in love with Krupe; that's why I tole you as much as I have—that and 'cause this morning Platoon Four eighty-four passed its three-week inspection with flying colors. We're closing in on Post Honor Platoon, and you better believe I want it."

"Krupe wants it too."

"He would—he wants everything in sight. Got to prove to everybody around that he's the best Marine they ever was or ever will be."

"Sounds like you want to win yourself."

"Yea, but for a different reason. Krupe wants to win to show how good a Marine he is; I want to win to keep Krupe from winning."

"You really hate him, don't you?"

"Damn straight. The only good to come out of being deprived of my stripe was when they passed him over for Master Sergeant. It was damn near worth it."

"Sergeant Pepper," Sanders said, beginning to feel the effect of the beers, "I can appreciate how you feel, but think of it from Krupe's point of view. I mean, he's gung-ho all the way. He wouldn't disobey an order, and he thinks nobody else should. I'll bet it wasn't anything personal."

"That's just the point, Sanders," Pepper said impatiently. "It *wasn't* personal. It was as though I was a stranger rather than his assistant."

Uninterested in pursuing the argument, Sanders merely shook his head. "I don't know about Krupe—he's a strange one."

A few minutes later Pepper spotted some other DIs who were going to the Log Cabin to dance. Sanders thanked him for the offer to join them, but he said he was going to head back and hit the sack. Before he left, Pepper asked, "Hey, how'd Krupe react about that gooney bird from your platoon that my boys clobbered when he tried to break ranks?" When Sanders said Krupe blamed himself for the oversight, Pepper seemed disappointed. But he perked up when Sanders told what later became of Duvail.

*   *   *

Sanders sat brooding for half an hour longer, downing another couple of drinks as his resentment of Krupe and boot camp festered. Actually, he was more puzzled by Krupe than resentful, puzzled because he admired in him so many elements that went into the making of the perfect Marine—intelligence, fearlessness, pride, spirit, and his almighty discipline. But all those traits were negated or at least severely undermined, in Sanders' view, by Krupe's harsh treatment of recruits.

As he drank in silence, Sanders thought of Linda and wondered where in Europe she was at this moment. He thought of her small, dainty hands, the smart white hat and matching summer gloves she wore one evening two summers ago when they went to hear a concert in the park. And even as he pictured her sitting beside him, Susan's face intruded on his reverie and he was more confused than ever. Susan! Why did she ever wander into his life? he wondered. Was it possible to love one girl and be really fond of another? If so, which was which? The questions confused him but he could no longer deny that he thought about Linda less and less and about Susan more and more. It could simply have been a matter of opportunity, but he was beginning now to doubt it.

He asked the bartender for change, then staggered over to the telephone booth. He squinted in order to read the blurred instructions:

DO NOT DEPOSIT COIN
UNTIL PARTY ANSWERS
Automatic Electric Co.
Northlake, Ill., U.S.A.
United Telephone Co.
of the Carolinas, Inc.

Then he dialed the familiar number.

After the sixth or seventh ring someone siad, "Hello." The voice was barely audible.

"Susan?" he said. "This is Chris . . . Chris Sanders. Remember me?"

"Chris!" She tried to sound indignant but succeeded only in sounding sleepy. "Where are you? What time is it?"

"I'll bite—where am I and what time is it?"

"Chris," she scolded gently, "have you by any chance been drinking?"

"Not by any chance, my dear Susan. By design. With malice aforethought, or however that goes."

"Is anything wrong?"

"Wrong? No, nothing's wrong—at least nothing civilians would understand. Not even a civilian as checked-out as you."

"Civilian," he repeated, savoring the word. "What a nice sound that has to it."

"Well, don't let it sound good for another couple of years, at least not until you get your commission and put in your time."

"My commission." He laughed as though the word were a

joke. "I'm not fit to handle a recruit platoon, much less lead men into combat."

"Don't berate yourself," she said soothingly. "You'll be a great officer."

"I don't want to be an ossifer," he said, deliberately mispronouncing the word.

"Okay," she said. "So you don't want to be an ossifer. What do you want?"

"You don't really want me to say it, do you? I mean, the operator might be listening in and then I'll be arrested for . . . for whatever in hell sex maniacs are arrested for."

"Chris, you're naughty. Hey, aren't you on duty tonight?" She was fully awake now and the sleepiness was gone from her voice.

"I've been relieved for the duration of the night."

"Shall I come get you? I'll bundle up Amy and we'll be right out. We'll meet you at the main gate."

"I have to be back at zero-five-thirty. What time is it now?"

"About midnight, I think."

"No, I guess not. It'll take me that long to sober up."

"Then come tomorrow night after work. And the first Sunday you have off we'll go to Hilton Head again. How about it?"

There was a prolonged pause. Finally he said, "Okay, tomorrow night."

"Good. Good night Chris. Pleasant dreams."

"Good night." There was another pause. Finally he said, "Susan?"

"Yes, Chris?"

"Nothing."

"What is it, Chris?"

After a pause he said, "I forgot what I was going to say." Then he added, "Oh, yea, kiss Amy for me."

After hanging up he wove his way back to the bar and ordered a final beer. Shortly after the bartender announced last call, he left to return to the platoon area. It was a hot, muggy night, and even the stars seemed to radiate heat. As he walked unsteadily along he began softly singing the Marines' Hymn. But the farther he walked, the louder he sang, until a jeep pulled alongside and someone shone a flashlight in his face.

"Corporal," said the MP, "lights were out at ten o'clock. That means no noise. People are trying to sleep."

"You're absolutely right, my good man," Sanders replied avuncularly, stiffening while he snapped off an exaggerated salute. "I shall be quiet as a titmouse. Or is it church mouse? You'll forgive me if I seem to be confused tonight. You see, I'm praying for a deceased officer. Second Lieutenant Christopher Sanders. You know him?"

"No," the voice behind the flashlight replied. "Did he die in Korea?"

"That would be too easy, my friend. He died at Parris Island, tonight, in the Sixth Battalion."

The MP had not heard of any deaths aboard the base that day. He looked at his driver, a PFC who shook his head as if to indicate he didn't know what it was all about. "Can we give you a lift back to your area?" the MP asked finally.

"Thank you, but I think I'll walk. I'm in no condition to drive. Besides, I want to walk it off."

"Okay, but keep it down, will you?"

"Scout's honor. You have my word, as an officer and a gentleman."

Again the MPs looked at each other, shrugged, then drove away.

Five minutes later Sanders reached the platoon area. Still feeling the effects of the beer, he decided to use the recruits' head, rather than use the one in the DI hut and risk awakening Krupe. As he was washing his hands he looked in the mirror and saw the fire watch, who had come to investigate. Recognizing the recruit, Sanders pulled himself upright. "Well, well. Private Dutton," he said, "fancy meeting you here."

"Sir, I heard a noise and thought it might be one of our platoon members."

"You did the right thing," Sanders said gravely. "Sergeant Krupe would be proud of you. Hell, for that matter old Merv Silverthorn and Lem Sheppard would be proud of you. For all you knew I might have been Private Duvail trying to escape, isn't that right?"

When it dawned on him that Sanders had been drinking, Dutton said, "Sir, with your permission I'll continue walking my watch."

"Why do you need my permission when you already have

God's permission?'' When the recruit seemed puzzled, Sanders said, ''You have Sergeant Krupe's permission, and that's the same as God's. Don't *you* consider it the same as God's?''

''For the next seven weeks I do, sir.''

After he staggered over to sit on the front rim of a washtub Sanders said, ''Very good answer. Damn good answer, in fact. Tell me, Dutton, how do you feel about boot camp?''

The recruit, taken aback by this directness, wondered what kind of reply Sanders wanted. And he wondered whether an answer that might satisfy him tonight would satisfy him in the morning, after he sobered up. ''I don't mind it, sir,'' he said finally. ''It's all part of being a Marine.''

''Is it? Is that what made a Marine out of . . . what's his name, the guy who was presented the sword with the Mameluke hilt?''

''Lieutenant Presley N. O'Bannon, sir. At Tripoli.''

''Ah so, that's it . . . Presley N. O'Bannon. Very good, Private. You're studying your *Guidebook*, the way a good Marine should. Tell me, Dutton, you're an intelligent person, do you think this is the way to make Marines?''

''What way, sir?''

''You know what I mean—treating recruits the way we do. Don't let on you don't know what I'm talking about!''

''Sir, I don't have any opinion about it one way or the other. That's the system, and for the next seven weeks I'm part of it.'' The words sounded resigned, but there was a sharp edge to the recruit's voice.

''But you don't like it, do you?''

''Sir, I—''

''Be honest, Dutton.'' Sanders was becoming impatient. ''You don't like it, do you?''

Dutton thought about denying it, but something in Sanders' tone caused him to admit, ''No, sir, I don't like it—not for myself, but for Gillian and Gabriel and a few others.''

''Do they have a right to become Marines, Dutton?''

''I don't know about that, sir. But I do know they have a right to exist as human beings, and here they're in danger of losing even that.''

''You've thought a lot about it, haven't you?''

''Yes, sir—too much.''

''Why?''

''Why, sir? Because when I joined the Marine Corps I

believed in it, was proud of it. Now I've about reached the point where the only feeling I have is resentment.''

"How about fear?" Sanders asked as he winced, closed his eyes, and held his head. "Oooh," he groaned, "let this be a lesson, Dutton, keep away from Demon Rum."

The recruit smiled, then said, "Fear only lasted a week or two with me. But some of the others are still scared." He paused. "Sir, I hope I'm not talking out of line."

"Don't worry. It's nice to hear some candor for a change. I just about reached the conclusion that candor no longer existed within the sixty-six hundred acres of Parris Island. Did you know there were sixty-six hundred acres here, Dutton? Or that P.I. was founded in nineteen-eleven?"

"No, sir."

"Well keep it in mind, along with the information about Wesley O'Bannon, or whatever his name was. You never know when it may come in handy."

Dutton smiled. He liked Sanders. He admired his sense of fair play and justice.

The corporal righted himself without too much difficulty. "Good night, Dutton," he said, preparing to walk away.

"Good night, sir." Then he added, "Sir, I want to thank you for coming to Gillian's rescue tonight."

Sanders looked annoyed. "Did Gillian tell you that?"

"No, sir. He didn't have to."

Sanders brushed aside the thanks. "Is he going to make it?"

"He'll make it, unless Bennett—I mean Sergeant Bennett—cripples or kills him. But if he can still run and walk, he'll make it. He's plenty tough. He'll make a good Marine."

"Yea," Sanders said regretfully, "and the pity is, he'll graduate, leave here, then forgive and forget." With that he turned and walked unsteadily out of the head toward the darkened DI hut, leaving a bewildered Dutton to wonder about their conversation.

*   *   *

During the first month of boot camp, recruits attended a regular series of lectures by full-time instructors who briefed them on hygiene; the provisions of the Uniform Code of Military Justice; military customs, courtesy, and discipline; interior guard; military sanitation; and first aid. Lectures usually were held in large tents that were stiflingly hot. Boots already exhausted from a normal eighteen-hour day had to force themselves to remain awake, but they were stimulated in the effort by the sight of their DIs patroling during the lectures, on the lookout for eyes that could no longer be held open or heads that dropped involuntarily. When that happened, Krupe and Bennett could be depended upon to bowl the sleepy recruits onto the deck, toss clipboards at them, or make them stand in front of the class with their rifles fully extended overhead.

The few times classes were held outdoors the drill instructors stood flanking the instructor's rough wooden lectern, scrutinizing the recruits on the five-tiered benches. Even the two times the chaplain spoke to them, Krupe's and Bennett's eyes never stopped sweeping from one tier to the next and their visages never lost their look of brooding malevolence.

Once when the platoon marched over from the drill field and arrived at the classroom a few minutes early, Bennett snatched the M-1 from the hand of Herb Beeks, who had whispered something to a buddy, and without a word smashed the barrel over the recruit's head. The helmet liner absorbed most of the impact, but the force of the blow knocked Beeks's teeth together and chipped off the lower half of a top front tooth. When he saw what he had done, Bennett told Beeks to report to the dentist the next day to get it capped—and warned that if the infraction happened again he'd need a complete set of dentures.

In addition to the scheduled lectures, Krupe held his own informal lectures whenever he could squeeze in the time, using maps and graphs to trace the various Marine and Allied deployments in Korea. He discussed the Hermit Kingdom's geographical importance, bordering Manchuria and nestling between China and Japan. He traced the main battle lines, pointed out the principal cities of North and South Korea, and showed them Panmunjom, some thirty miles north of Seoul, where Major General William K. Harrison, Jr. was even then meeting with North Korea's Lieutenant General Nam Il in an effort to reach a settlement.

Sanders was surprised by this unexpected side of Krupe, surprised and favorably impressed. He hadn't expected Krupe the martinet to be also Krupe the military strategist. He could feel the pride in being Marines pass over the platoon, himself included, as Krupe described the landing at Inchon that he said changed the course of the war—a bold amphibious assault conceived by General MacArthur and executed by the Marines, which resulted in the liberation of Seoul and trapping thirteen North Korean infantry divisions about a hundred miles south of the Thirty-Eighth Parallel.

"The landing completely shattered the North Korean army," Krupe said. "Then UN forces advanced northward, captured the North Korean capital of Pyongyang, and shortly afterward reached the Yalu River, which flows between Korea and Manchuria. Just when the war seemed at an end, a couple of hundred thousand thousand Chinese soldiers swept across the Yalu in what marked the beginning of an entirely different phase of the war—in fact, a different war altogether. But the Inchon landing itself proved to be another brilliant demonstration of Marine Corps spirit, combat skill, and guts."

The only time Krupe lost his temper during the lectures was when Emerson Tillich asked his opinion about the wisdom of not bombing the hydroelectric plants on the Yalu. That was a question of national policy, Krupe scowled, and the only legitimate concern of professional military men was how best to execute that policy. He added that the fact that someone of MacArthur's stature was removed as Supreme Commander of the UN Forces in the Far East for expressing public disagreement with national policy should teach military men to keep their political opinions to themselves.

Krupe's one shortcoming as a lecturer was his undisguised contempt for the Army. At first Sanders thought the caustic references interspersed throughout his talks were really only semi-serious—that when Krupe compared the two branches he not unnaturally found the Army wanting. And at times, that was actually the case. Yet despite his uncharacteristic praise of MacArthur's Inchon strategy, his anti-Army attitude was readily apparent in matters meaningful and picayune.

Bennett enjoyed Krupe's vigorous indictment. Although he had known only a few of the facts—his hostility toward "Doggies" was almost totally osmotic—he liked the ring of historic truth attached to the names, dates, and locations.

The indictments were interspersed throughout the lectures in order to demonstrate the relative superiority of the Corps, but the cumulative effect was to present a singularly unflattering and at times demeaning picture of the Army. When Sanders and Krupe were alone, Sanders tried to point out that the Army had an entirely different mission—that it was not intended as a shock-troop military force, nor were most soldiers professionals in the sense that Marines were. In the early days of the Korean War many were civilian reservists who were exposed to military life only one weekend a month.

But Krupe insisted the Army was an inferior fighting organization because its troops lacked pride in themselves and their units . . . and they lacked pride because they lacked discipline . . . and they lacked discipline—here he shot a glance at Sanders—because they were pampered in basic training, and were not made to feel that everything they were being taught could become a matter of life or death.

He said that many enemy prisoners captured in Korea said they had been ordered to avoid the "Yellowlegs" wherever possible, to seek out the Army instead. That's when Marines began discarding their traditional khaki leggings. He also claimed that Army-trained ROK troops were less effective than Marine-trained ROKs, who were imbued with Marine *esprit* and pride.

When Sanders asked why he had given MacArthur such high marks for the Inchon landing, in view of his hatred of the Army, Krupe snapped: "I hate its frequent errors, not its occasional triumphs." Then he added that for years he harbored a grudge against MacArthur for not recommending the Fourth Marines for unit citations at Corregidor on grounds that the Marines had had their share of glory in World War I and he didn't want to give them any more. He said he didn't change his mind until MacArthur finally admitted in Korea that there wasn't a finer fighting organization in the world than the Marines.

Before long Sanders was sorry he ever got Krupe started, for if dislike of the Army surfaced in his lectures, it boiled over in private discussions. One night, for no reason at all, he was off on a tirade against the large number of "Doggies" he claimed bugged out in Korea, saying that in their race for the rear they deserted buddies and squad members, and discarded weapons and equipment all along the way. In violation of everything they had been taught about sanitation, they drank putrid water from infected ditches and then came down with dysentery. At Koto-ri, they left keys in the ignitions of vehicles they abandoned in their flight.

Another time, at noon chow, he claimed that in its flights the Army bequeathed the North Korean Army an arsenal of weapons second only to that supplied by the Russians. But what was unforgivable about the Army's performance in Korea was that during the Eighth Army's 275-mile retreat in January 1951, as Chinese troops crossed the Yalu and pushed into South Korea, officers and NCOs also took to their heels. "You can defend the enlisted reserves and draftees all you want," he said, "but what conceivable excuse is there for officers or NCOs not to stand fast unless they're ordered back in an orderly withdrawal?"

"No excuse, I guess," Sanders admitted.

"You *guess?* What is there to guess about?"

"From what I read," Sanders said by way of explanation, "even the officers and NCOs were inexperienced, young, and had no idea what the fighting was all about—why they were there, or even where they were."

"Exactly," Krupe said triumphantly. "But Marines have too much pride to run away. Any self-respecting Marine officer or NCO would sooner die than run."

The lectures were not all lengthy or historical. Krupe told them of the uncanny Chinese skill with mortar fire. The night before the recruits ran the bayonet course he informed them that more bayonet fighting had already occurred in Korea than in either World War, and said the main enemy of a successful bayonet charge was panic: Locked in a life-or-death struggle at close range, the temptation was strong to disregard everything one had been taught and to chop and thrust wildly.

He explained how the Chinese employed psychological warfare in order to unnerve their enemy during an attack. For instance, the way the sirens screamed on their tanks as their troops advanced behind them, to the accompaniment of bugles, cymbals, whistles, flutes, drums, and shepherds' pipes. Or the way they sometimes sounded a bugle charge in the dead of night, without launching an attack.

Krupe expressed respect for the ability, persistence, and adaptability of the Chinese troops, who often marched all night hauling packs half their own weight, yet whose entire day's provisions usually consisted of a small ball of dry rice. They were also resourceful, carrying a dirty white cloth with which to camouflage themselves in the snow and a straw mat to place over themselves in an open field to prevent detection from the air. And, he said, they were among the most formidable enemy troops Americans had ever faced.

"Gillian," Bennett broke in, squinting rapidly and directing his malevolent grin at the recruit, "tell that Gook boy friend of yours that his relatives might make good coolies and soldiers, but they still don't have shit for brains."

Chapter
9

Dutton didn't immediately recognize the return address on the upper lefthand corner of the envelope, and when he realized that the letter was from Hilda Conway he was reluctant to open it. The day he took his enlistment oath he had telephoned her to say good-by, and although he promised to write, he had not done so. He probably would have stopped writing completely had not Julie's daily letters shamed him into some sort of response, usually a hasty note asking forgiveness for the brevity of his letters but explaining he had been too busy to write at greater length.

The platoon *had* been kept busy, no doubt about it. In addition to endless hours spent on the drill field and at lectures, Krupe's own lectures, informative though they were, cut deeply into the available time. So did the time spent scrubbing clothes, and tedious hours cleaning rifles and polishing shoes and equipment in preparation for the fourth-week inspection, which they ultimately passed with high marks. Then there was the omnipresent *Guidebook*, first-aid procedures to memorize, and the map of Korea that Krupe demanded they familiarize themselves with. Even without the luxury of radio, TV, newspapers, and movies, time was a commodity in short supply.

But there was usually *some* time to write before lights out, now that boot camp was half over and therefore not quite so overwhelming, and some recruits managed to write to their girl friends almost every night. Dutton's inability to find time was partially of his own choosing, because he feared he might convey in his letters the bitterness he felt toward boot camp practices.

Despite this bitterness, though, he felt a curious ambivalence toward Krupe. On the one hand, he recoiled from the tech sergeant's volatile temper and sudden outbursts. Yet he respected Krupe's leadership qualities and rated his lectures on a par with the best he had heard in college. And he was mindful of the fact that Krupe's punishment was never personal.

Moreover, Dutton somehow felt that complaining about boot camp to an outsider, even to Julie, might be a betrayal of Corporal Sanders, who apparently was almost as repelled and embittered about boot camp as he was. After their discussion in the head that night, Sanders ignored Dutton for several days, as though implying it would be best to forget what he said under the influence of alcohol. Then one morning when Krupe and Bennett were away for an hour or two he summoned Dutton to clean the DI hut. At first he seemed to be absorbed with the newspaper while the recruit swept and swabbed. Finally he asked how Gillian was.

"The swellings have gone down, sir. He's okay."

"How's his mental outlook?"

"I think he's going to be all right. He hasn't said much, but then, he seldom does. I guess he's afraid Sergeant Bennett will consider him . . . you know . . . queer, if he fraternizes."

"Sure he's queer," Sanders scoffed, shifting in his seat and turning to look at Dutton. "He's different, isn't he? He has red hair, and in the tight little world of Sanford Bennett that's proof enough." He returned to his newspaper, but after a few moments he said, "Dutton, I was drafted into the Marine Corps. But you joined—why?"

The question was so direct, so lacking in subtlety, that the recruit couldn't think of an appropriate answer. Finally he replied, "I have sort of a personal mission, sir, and fulfilling it meant joining the Marine Corps—at least I thought so at the time."

"And now?"

"I don't know, sir. . . ."

At Krupe's return, the conversation ended. Ignoring the recruit, he rested his *cocomacaque* on the desk, poured a cup of coffee, and dropped into a nearby chair. He told Sanders Congress had recently voted forty-five dollars a month combat pay, retroactive to June 1950, for anyone who served in a combat unit for six days or more during any month. He also spoke of the new depot regulation assuring every DI of at least seven days' instruction and rest between recruit platoons. When it was apparent that Krupe planned to remain, Dutton, realizing his aborted conversation would have to await another time, finished cleaning and requested permission to depart.

Now as he stared at the letter from Hilda Conway he recalled that conversation with Sanders and wondered about his remaining missionary zeal. The real reason he hadn't written was the realization that his original motivation for joining the Marines, his compulsion to avenge Tim's death, was slowly being eroded by the bitterness he felt about the maltreatment he had witnessed.

Hilda Conway's letter was not unlike those of his mother, breezy and formal. She said she had received a letter from Julie the previous week, and she concluded by saying she shared his and Tim's pride in the Marine Corps.

Then he remembered that Tim *had* been proud of being a Marine, no doubt because it was one of the few things about which he could feel pride. And it was true that the Marines didn't care who or what your parents were, the sort of neighborhood you came from, what, if any, schools you attended. They cared only whether you measured up as a man, whether you could acquit yourself in combat.

In fact, that was all Krupe appeared concerned about. But Bennett was another matter. His undiminished bullying seemed rooted in some atavistic urge rather than in any attempt to transform ragged civilians into Marines.

*   *   *

The week before Platoon 486 was scheduled at the rifle range, Sixth Battalion sponsored a boxing smoker. All recruits were required to box two two-minute rounds in an elimination tournament, after which each platoon's division champs would compete against one another.

Wearing sneakers and blue bathing trunks under dungaree uniforms, late Friday afternoon Platoon 486 marched to the portable boxing ring in a large open field across from the Hostess House, the depot's guest house for overnight visitors. Platoon 484 was just finishing its elimination bouts when 486 arrived. "Krupe, I hope you got some fighters in that platoon of yours,"

Pepper taunted, "because I got some real bad-assed tigers in my group."

"Good for you, Pepper. You'll need them," Krupe said casually.

Pepper forced a hollow laugh, then said, "Those cruds of yours don't look like they could fight their way out of a wet rubber. Do they, Corporal Sayers?"

"Not hardly," his assistant replied, smiling enough to please Pepper but at the same time being careful not to anger Krupe.

"We'll see about that Wednesday night," Krupe said.

"Yea, we sure will, we sure as hell will. But if you expect to beat my boys you'll need that club you're carrying," Pepper said, looking at Krupe's *cocomacaque*.

"If it unnerves you," the tech sergeant said, "I'll leave it in the Quonset hut. That way you can't claim it intimidated your recruits."

"Don't worry about them, they aren't easily intimidated. Oh, by the way," he said with a satisfied smile, "how's Private . . . what's his name, Dubrell?"

"Duvail. Haven't you heard? He's no longer with us. I owe you one for that."

"So you do. A couple more of them and we'll be even, the way I figure it."

Krupe turned his back on Pepper and told Bennett and Sanders to pair off the recruits into approximately equal weights and have them strip to their bathing trunks. Bennett promptly matched Gabriel against Herb Beeks, a deliberate mismatch considering that Gabriel was no match for anyone in the platoon, much less for Beeks, who had acquitted himself well against the much larger Tew.

As a visibly scared Gabriel fumbled his way through the ropes into the ring, Dutton looked to Sanders, hoping to convey his fear of what might happen so the corporal would intercede. But the DI was busy acting as a second in Gabriel's corner—Bennett was in the other corner and Krupe was referee—and did not look up.

All that saved Gabriel from serious punishment was Beeks's compassion. Even though Bennett cursed and shouted, demanding he clobber the hapless recruit, Beeks remained at long range, hitting Gabriel with noisy but not really damaging body punches.

The few times Gabriel even swung, he was so awkward that Beeks could have finished him off at any time, yet he carried him both rounds, despite Bennett's incessant threats.

Toward the end of the evening Bennett tried to match Tew and Gillian, but Krupe mentioned there was at least a fifty-pound disparity. So Bennett backed away from that idea, suggesting instead a Tew-Dutton match. Although Tew still enjoyed a thirty-pound weight advantage, at least they were both heavyweights, so Krupe sanctioned the bout.

"Think you can take him?" Sanders asked as he helped Dutton on with his gloves.

"I don't know, sir. But I can give a better account of myself than Gabriel did."

"Good luck," Sanders said, tightening the laces. Then Krupe blew a whistle and Dutton walked to the center of the ring to touch gloves. At that instant a punch landed with terrific force on his nose and upper lip, sending him crashing to the canvas. It didn't actually hurt but he was stunned for several seconds, enough so that he couldn't comprehend what was happening. Then, from a distance, he heard a voice counting " . . .four . . . five . . . six . . . ," the counting interspersed with laughter.

Pulling himself up to his knees, he looked across the ring and saw Bennett grinning and shouting something up to a smiling Tew. Dimly he perceived that whatever had just happened—he still was not sure what—was the result of collusion between Tew and Bennett. Then he heard Sanders hollering for him to get up.

He was on his feet at eight, his brain still filled with cobwebs. "Don't let him hit you again, clinch with him," Sanders yelled. Tew moved in quickly, measuring Dutton for the kill. Dutton felt the blood trickling from his nose and it angered him. As Tew approached, Dutton whipped a straight left against the side of his head, followed with a right to the ribs, then started a left hook to the jaw. But before he could unload it, Tew caught him with a stinging right over the left ear that sent him sprawling again.

This time he remained conscious, but while he knew what was happening, he felt powerless to do anything about it. Tew's first sneak punch had been illegal, but the punch that dropped him the second time was legitimate. By then, though, his reflexes had been so badly dulled he hadn't even seen it.

This time he was up at nine. As Tew moved in, Dutton

threw two ineffective left jabs, blocked a right to the body with his elbow, and then forced a clinch. But the heavier Tew easily pushed him away, then moved in again, throwing powerful combinations that blunted Dutton's attempts to counterattack. He did manage to throw one good right, which caught the onrushing Tew in the neck and slowed him down. But he soon pressed forward again, pushing Dutton against the ropes and pounding him with a succession of hard lefts and rights.

Dutton never even saw the right cross that flattened him for good. When he came to he was still in the ring being attended by Sanders. Krupe ordered several recruits to drag him out on the grass, told Sanders to examine him and stanch the bleeding from his nose and mouth as best he could. Meanwhile the eliminations continued, with Tew, Beeks, and Robert Begay winning their divisions.

Dutton recovered sufficiently to sit up after a while and watch some of the bouts. He was ashamed that he hadn't given a better account of himself, but he was also infuriated by the sneak punch. Between bouts Tew came over to where he was stretched out on his elbows on the grass and asked, "How you feeling, Dutton?"

"I'll live, if that's what's worrying you." Both his words and tone of voice were sullen.

"Look," Tew said, feeling magnanimous, "it's nothing personal. It was either me or you. Hell, if you're worried about that first punch—"

"What's there to worry about?" Dutton interrupted, cutting him off in midsentence.

"That was . . . I mean, Sergeant Bennett said it—"

"It was Bennett's idea to throw a sneak punch?"

"Well . . . yea, he give me the idea, said Marines had to be prepared all the time."

"I should have known," Dutton said disgustedly. "You're not much of a sportsman, Tew, but you'll make a good DI once you get out of here."

Tew's humanitarian impulse was soon exhausted. Studying his defeated adversary for several seconds he finally said, "Fuck you," then turned and walked away.

After the last bout Krupe ordered the recruits to police the area, and he went on ahead. After they had picked up every scrap of litter, Bennett ordered them to attention. Wearing the sheepish grin that usually presaged trouble, he announced, "I've decided we should have one more bout—to determine the *worst* fighter in the platoon. Privates Gabriel and Lindsay, front and center on the double.''

When Sanders realized what was up, he began doing a slow burn. Bennett was deliberately matching the inept Gabriel against a kid who, in losing a reasonably close match to Beeks, showed he had ring savvy. Moreover, Lindsay was one of Hall's buddies from the first Quonset hut, so would be unlikely to go easy on Gabriel the way Beeks had. In fact, Gabriel was being deliberately set up for a beating, presumably to satisfy some inexplicable impulse of Bennett's.

"Sergeant Bennett, may I see you a second?"

"Can't it wait until after this bout?" Bennett replied with annoyance, overlooking the edge to Sanders' voice.

"I'd like to talk to you now," Sanders said, walking toward the wooden grandstands some twenty yards distant.

The exasperated sergeant ordered the platoon to run in place, then set off in pursuit of Sanders, protesting even as he overtook him. "Look, goddamn it, Corporal," he began, "if you think—''

"Just shut up and listen to me," Sanders said as he whirled on the startled Bennett. "You better forget your sadistic little plan or I promise you'll wish you had."

When he recovered from his surprise Bennett said, "Sanders, you seem to think you're running this mother-jumping platoon, only it's about time you learned differently."

"I *know* differently, you bullying bastard." Bennett was taken aback by the oath, the strongest he had ever heard out of Sanders. "But I'm warning you not to try it or you'll wish you never had."

"What are you going to do about it?" Bennett demanded.

"I'll *tell* you what. If you don't call it off, I'm going to get in that ring and publicly challenge you to a bout—in front of the entire platoon."

Bennett cocked his head to one side and studied the corporal, wondering whether he was hearing correctly. "Why, for Christ's sake, Sanders, you're crazy—you're a goddamn madman, anybody do a thing like that." His eyes were opening and closing furiously. "If you ever pulled such a crazy stunt your ass would be on report within the hour and you'd be in the brig by nightfall. This is the Marine Corps, not the god-damned—''

"I mean it, Bennett," Sanders persisted. "Unless you call it off I'm going to challenge you in fornt of the platoon."

"Corporal, you interfered with a senior NCO once before and I didn't say anything about it. You aren't crazy enough to do it again, are you?"

"Make up your mind," Sanders persisted.

"Kee-rist, Sanders," Bennett said, appearing to be reasonable, "how the hell is this going to look—"

"Which is it?"

"You'll never get to OCS if I report you."

"Which is it?"

Bennett stared at him, a mixture of loathing and disbelief etched into his face. "You bastard," he said finally. "Oooh, you bastard. Your ass has really had it now." With that he whirled and started back toward the platoon, trying to think of a face-saving excuse. Suddenly he changed direction and stalked off toward the platoon area, leaving Sanders alone with the recruits.

"I reminded Sergeant Bennett of a previous commitment," Sanders explained when he returned to the recruits, who were still double-timing, "so the final bout of the evening is postponed." He told Lindsay and Gabriel to return to ranks, then ordered a left flank and marched them back to the Sixth Battalion area.

*   *   *

When she saw his car turn into the carport, Susan ran to the door to greet him, smiling and waving as though he had been away for weeks rather than a couple of days. After they went inside and kissed and hugged, clinging tightly to each other, she said, "You'll never guess the good news."

He stepped back, surveying her at arm's length, and said, "You're not pregnant."

"Oh, Chris," she laughed, slapping him playfully as though he were an errant child. "Be serious."

"All right—you are pregnant. Is that what you wanted me to say?"

"Just for that I'm not going to tell you," she said coyly, making a halfhearted effort to pull herself away.

"Not tell the father of your expectant child? Or are you trying to tell me I'm not the father?"

"Chris!" she scolded. "You've got me so confused with all this talk about pregnancy and children that I can't remember what I started to tell you."

"Was it—"

"Oh, now I remember," she said happily, bouncing once or twice with excitement. "Chris, they're going to pay me the insurance money."

"What insurance money?"

"Dan's. His GI insurance. My . . . my widow's benefit." At the mention of the word she lowered her head.

"You mean it?" he asked, delighted with the news.

"Read this." She handed him an official-looking document saying the Department of Defense had been asked by Congressmen Wilde of Indiana and Propert of Pennsylvania to investigate the matter, untangle the mix-up, and expedite the claim as soon as possible. Accordingly, the U.S. Government was convinced she was the rightful beneficiary, and as soon as she advised them as to the method of payment she preferred the funds would be forthcoming. "'We very much regret the delay,'" he read aloud, "'and hope you will forgive any inconvenience.' Why, that's great, honey, that's terrific!" But no sooner had he said it than she began sobbing. "What's wrong, Susan? You should be happy, now that everything's worked out the way you wanted. You don't have to live hand-to-mouth anymore."

"Should I be happy, Chris?" She dabbed at her eyes with a handkerchief. "They're paying me for the life of my husband, so now we're all even, now we can close the book on our past, the future, this war—the whole thing. Well, I don't want it. I got along this far without it and I can get along from now on." She broke down and cried again. He didn't say anything for a while, he only tried to console her with kisses. Finally, as her tears subsided, he said, "Susan, I understand how you feel. But wouldn't Dan want you to have the money? For the two of you, you and Amy?"

"It's blood money," she said, sobbing again.

"It's not blood money. Dan didn't die because of the money, and refusing it won't bring him back to life. It'll just make it tougher for you and Amy."

"But how can you put a price on someone's life? How?"

"You can't. Not ten thousand or ten million. But if Dan could advise you, do you think he'd want you to accept or refuse the money?"

Her tear-stained face reflected her anguish. Finally she sank into his arms, overcome by the strain and the reawakened memories. "Oh Chris, Chris, Chris," she repeated mournfully.

"Hey, I almost forgot," he said a few minutes later, after he helped calm her down. He ran out to the car and returned holding several bunches of flowers purchased at a roadside stand. She sniffled her thanks and searched for some vases to put them in. She trimmed the stems and arranged the flowers in an attractive display, then kissed him again and thanked him for his thoughtfulness.

Afterward she managed to gain control of herself, and although she was subdued during dinner they talked and finished off the better part of two bottles of wine Chris had brought with him. As they lay together talking later that night, he denied any knowledge of what had prompted the governmental turnabout. He might have owned up if she had insisted, and she undoubtedly knew he or his family had something to do with applying the political pressure necessary to break the bureaucratic logjam. But she didn't press him about it and he saw no need to detail his family's influence in the state and federal corridors of power, influence he and Linda and others in their crowd took for granted.

He had trouble getting to sleep that night, thinking about his latest run-in with Bennett and everything else about boot camp that had bothered him. From time to time he looked over and watched as Susan slept, her face calm and innocent. After tossing and turning he got up a couple of times to check on Amy, then went into the bathroom and smoked a cigarette. Once Susan awoke while he was tossing and asked if everything was okay. He reassured her with a kiss, after which she drifted back to sleep. But when she awakened an hour later and he was sitting up with one arm behind his head, obviously deep in thought, she pulled herself upright and asked what was troubling him.

At first he pretended it was nothing, then said he was just restless, then said he was worrying that the platoon didn't seem to be progressing fast enough. But she deluged him with questions and before long he was expressing his disillusionment— with the methods being used in boot camp and with his inability to prevent what was happening.

"Why, that Sergeant Krupe sounds like a monster," Susan said, getting out of bed and putting on a pot of coffee.

"That's just it: He isn't a monster. Judged by his own standards of what Marines should be, he's exemplary. And I don't know a person I'd sooner go into combat with."

"Or a person you'd sooner avoid in civilian life."

"No, I'd sooner avoid Bennett, because I think he'd be a bully under any circumstances. But I don't feel that way about Krupe. Oddly enough, I think if he were a business executive he'd be efficient, capable, and probably even pleasant. Or if he were a teacher, I think he'd be ideal. But he's a Marine, and he has this obsession, this idea that it's up to him to save the Marine Corps's reputation from dishonor and from the weak and the cowardly."

Then he told her about Krupe—everything he had learned from Bennett, Pepper, and from the brief biographical sketch that appeared in the base newspaper, *Boot:*

Floyd Krupe enlisted in the Marines in January 1942 at age twenty, during the middle of his junior year in college. After boot camp he joined the newly formed First Raider Battalion under Colonel Merritt A. Edson. The Raiders were the first U.S. military organization designed specifically for raiding and guerrilla missions, and for that reason they stressed and restressed training and discipline. They learned to disarm and kill with their bare hands. They learned to live off the barren countryside for weeks at a time. They learned to make Molotov cocktails, to handle demolitions, and to assault enemy beaches in rubber rafts launched from submarines. They were trained to scout, patrol, and handle weapons and communications.

They braved withering enemy fire at Tulagi to crawl up to the mouth of caves and hurl satchel charges in on the Japanese defenders. At Guadalcanal they once again dislodged the tenacious Japanese defenders who had somehow survived the intense naval bombardment, this time after hand-to-hand combat. Because of heavy Raider casualties and his outstanding combat record, Krupe was promoted to sergeant.

Two months before war's end he was sent with twenty-five thousand Marine occupation forces to North China. On July 29, 1945, two weeks after local Communists had ambushed and captured seven Marine bridge guards, Krupe was among the forty enlisted men and one officer escorting six supply trucks from Tientsin to Peiping when they were ambushed. The officer was killed early in the four-hour fire fight, so Krupe took charge. Despite being taken by surprise, the outnumbered patrol fought bravely until an air-supported relief column arrived from Tientsin.

Krupe was discharged in July 1947 and completed his last two years of college. He re-enlisted shortly after the Korean War broke out, a day or two after President Truman in June 1950 ordered American ground forces to assist the air and sea units dispatched to Korea three days earlier.

Krupe joined the First Provisional Brigade when it was activated at Camp Pendleton on July 7, and on July 12 he was one of sixty-five hundred Marines on the way to relieve the Army's badly mauled Twenty-Seventh Regiment of the Twenty-Fifth Division at Chindongi-ni, fifty miles west of Pusan. The Brigade's official entry into battle came on August seventh—seven years to the day that the Marines landed on Guadalcanal. For a month it was used as a mobile reserve of "firemen," hopscotching across the 120-miles of mountains, plains, and rivers that comprised the perimeter, counterattacking to relieve the pressure from the threatened four Army and four ROK divisions, and sniping at the North Korean Army to keep it from coming any closer to Pusan than the thirty-five miles to which it had already advanced.

Krupe fought with the Brigade the entire time: When it routed the North Korean Sixth Division; at bloody No Name Ridge; and when it chased the North Korean Fourth Division to the Naktong River and decimated it. When the Brigade reverted to the Division in September, he fought with the Fifth Marines at Wolmi-do during the Ihchon landing, took part in the house-to-house battle in Seoul, and the following month joined the advance to Chosin.

After the withdrawal to Hungnam, Krupe was assigned to IX Corps and spent the next seven months fighting in east central Korea. He returned to the States in August, was given three weeks' vacation, reported to Parris Island for DI school, was assigned as assistant DI to a platoon that graduated in late January 1952, took over his own platoon the next month, picked up another one in mid-April, then, after a week's rest, picked up Platoon 486.

"The interesting thing," Sanders said reflectively, "is that he only talks about his military career if he's asked and then only minimally. You'd think anybody so gung-ho would be a glory boy, but he's not."

"Do you like him?" Susan asked.

Caught off-guard by so direct a question, Sanders replied, "I loathe him. At least I think I do."

"You *think* so?"

"That's the trouble, I'm not sure. That's why I don't just flat-out report him. I'm torn between despising his methods and admiring his intentions and results. I guess my confusion is because I've never been in combat. Maybe the way to prepare kids for war *is* to treat them so badly that they'll itch to be able to take it out on the enemy.''

''You don't really believe that, do you Chris?''

''I've reached the point where sometimes I really don't know,'' he said dejectedly. ''Three weeks ago, two weeks ago, last week . . . I would have said no. Then I was sure Krupe was one hundred percent wrong about everything. Now I'm all screwed up inside. I'm haunted by the fear that if I get Krupe removed and turn out to be wrong, the blood of any of those kids killed in Korea will be on my hands.''

''Oh, Chris, you can't feel that way.'' As she spoke she fluffed up his pillow and settled it more comfortably beneath his head.

''Maybe I shouldn't, but I do. I know one thing—the longer I'm with Krupe the more callous I become, and the tougher it is to arouse indignation, or horror, or pity, or disgust in me. Even most of the recruits seem to be becoming resigned to their treatment.''

''They probably have to, Chris, or they'd go out of their minds—or go AWOL. The important thing is not to let yourself be part of it, at least not willingly.''

He kept turning her advice over in his mind as he drove back toward the base, enjoying the early-morning coolness that would shortly give way to the stifling, oppressive heat and humidity. ''Don't let yourself be part of it, at least not willingly.'' It was wise, even admirable advice, but no matter how confused he was about judging Krupe, he knew there was no danger of his ever emulating his methods.

He passed through the checkpoint and pointed the car toward Sixth Battalion. A recruit platoon came marching smartly by in the dusk, getting an early start to somewhere and keeping perfect time to the DI's cadence. He waited patiently at the intersection, thinking again of Susan's advice, when suddenly a voice rang out, shattering the early-morning calm. ''Hey Corporal,'' Pepper bellowed. ''Don't you fraidy cats from Four eighty-six forget to show up for the boxing smoker on Wednesday.'' He laughed loudly and derisively, directing it as much toward his recruits as toward Sanders. The corporal leaned out the window, about to reply. Instead, he merely closed his eyes in disgust, shook his head, and muttered, ''Welcome to boot camp.''

Chapter
10

"Corporal Sanders reporting as ordered, sir," he said after being told to enter the office.

"At ease, Corporal." Major Knisely glanced up briefly, then returned to the papers spread across his desk. Unlike the usual trim, crew-cut Marine officer, Knisely's hair was closely trimmed on sides and back, but trained into a semi-pompadour in front. The faintest trace of a pot belly was visible below his belt. Sanders guessed him to be in his early to mid-forties.

"This makes interesting reading," he said, suddenly looking up and motioning toward his desk. "Recognize this?" he asked, picking up a brown booklet he had been poring over.

"No, sir."

"It's your Service Record Book. I was especially interested in the unqualified recommendations you've received for Officers Candidate School." He stared at Sanders as though expecting a reply, but none was forthcoming. "You may not realize it, Corporal," he continued, "but being a Marine officer is something special. Not the Officers Club, the salutes, the special privileges—they don't amount to a hill of beans. What counts is leadership. When those bars are pinned on your uniform, it means the Marine Corps has entrusted you with the most important responsibility of all—the responsibility to command and lead men." Again he looked at Sanders, but again Sanders made no reply. Finally Knisely asked, "What do you consider the main prerequisite of a Marine officer?"

"I'm not sure, sir. Probably the ability to command respect and loyalty."

"That's important all right," the C.O. agreed after some thought. "Mighty important, I would say. But there's something even more important in my book. Know what that is? It's the ability to command respect, loyalty, and *obedience*. And you know how that's done? By disciplining recruits, that's how. Through discipline earned on the drill field, at Lejeune, Pendleton—wherever else men are made into Marines. Do you follow what I'm saying?"

"I think so, sir."

"Good, 'cause you'll need to know it, Corporal, if you're going to be an officer." He looked at Sanders quizzically. "You do intend to become an officer, don't you?"

Sanders didn't reply.

"Well, do you or don't you?"

"I thought I did, sir."

The major looked surprised, unbelieving. "And now?" he asked.

"Now I'm no longer sure, sir. I do if I remain in the Marine Corps, but I'm not sure I'll remain in."

Knisely stared at him agape. "Not sure? What—"

"Personal reasons, sir," he said. "Reasons that didn't exist before I took my test for OCS."

"Corporal, I don't know what these reasons are, and it's not my business. But I can't believe you fully appreciate what you may be passing up. Your Record Book indicates you're officer material—that you have the potential to be an outstanding officer."

"Does it still show that, sir? I mean, after disobeying Sergeant Bennett?"

The major's eyebrows arched up in exaggerated surprise. "Then you admit you disobeyed Sergeant Bennett?"

"Yes, sir."

"Whatever in the world for, Sanders?" The question was almost a plea. "Don't you know that no offense is more serious in the Marine Corps than disobedience? What rhyme or reason would lead a future OCS candidate up that blind alley?"

"I have no excuse, sir."

"Corporal, you can't expect me to believe that of an intelligent person like you. Why, if a recruit gave such a lame answer you'd be all over him—at least I hope my Drill Instructors would be."

"Yes, sir," Sanders agreed, hoping that by acting evasive he could put an end to the questioning.

Knisely shifted uneasily, then lit a cigarette and drew two or three deep drags. "I don't understand you, Corporal," he persisted. "The average C.O. would bust you just like that for disobeying an order. But I'm trying to take the trouble to find out what makes you tick and you don't seem to care, much less appreciate it. How do you account for it?"

Sanders was only half listening. He was thinking at that moment of Susan and what she said about not letting himself be part of a brutal system. Then he heard the major's voice. "Well, do you want to explain?"

"I'm sorry, sir, I guess I didn't get that last part. Explain what?"

"Sanders, haven't you been listening to me?" Knisely asked exasperatedly.

"Major," Sanders said suddenly, "do you know what goes on in boot camp? I mean what *really* goes on?"

The C.O. recoiled as though slapped. "Your question is out of order, Sanders," he stammered. "I know what goes on in every platoon under my command every minute of the day."

"I didn't mean to be impertinent, sir, but neither do I think the question's out of order—unless you condone brutal treatment of recruits."

Knisely looked at him quizzically, nervously fingering his cigarette lighter. "What are you getting at, Sanders? Are you implying—"

"I'm not implying, sir, I'm saying. I'm saying that brutality is the rule and not the exception—at least in Platoon Four eighty-six."

There was a lengthy, uncomfortable silence. Then Knisely sighed deeply and said, "Sanders, you sound like those parents who've heard a lot of fairy tales about this place. Or some busy-body Congressman, usually an ex-soldier or sailor, out to make a name for himself at Marine Corps expense."

"But they go on rumors. My information is firsthand."

"I don't believe it," Knisely snapped.

"Then I'm sorry I mentioned it." Sanders paused, but only for a second. "Major, when was the last time you toured the recruit area unannounced?"

"What the hell are you trying to pull, Sanders? First you

disobey a superior NCO and now you're calling your Commanding Officer a liar.''

"I beg your pardon, Major, but I'm not calling you a liar. I only question whether you're really aware—''

"You only question whether I'm competent to run this command,'' Knisely said, banging his swagger stick down on the desk top and rising to his feet. "A punk Corporal who's never even been overseas, much less in combat.''

"Sir, I—''

"*I'm* doing the talking now, Corporal, and you're doing the listening.'' He began pacing the room. "I've given eighteen years of my life to the Marine Corps. I've served overseas almost half of that time. I've been shot at from every pay grade from Private to Buck Sergeant and from Second Lieutenant to Major. And you have the gall to come before me and question my competence. What in hell gives you the right even to presume to do that?''

When Sanders didn't speak, the major ordered, "Answer me, Corporal.''

"Sir, if I can explain my—''

"I'm listening.''

"I wasn't questioning your ability or your competence or your judgment—none of that. I merely wondered if you were aware that at least some recruits in the Sixth Battalion are being abused in violation of the UCMJ.''

Mention of the Uniform Code of Military Justice had an immediate sobering effect on Knisely; much of his anger drained quickly away. "Obviously you can't be every place at once,'' Sanders continued. "But if General Silverthorn ever got wind of—''

"How many of Four eighty-six's recruits have been 'brutalized,' as you call it?'' Knisely snapped.

"Most of them, sir.''

"*Most* of them?''

"All right—many.''

The major returned slowly to his desk and sat down heavily. In a few moments he said, "You're making a very serious charge against your senior Drill Instructors, I suppose you know.''

"I don't intend to make a formal charge, sir. I don't want anything to happen to either of them. But maybe if you could—''

"Why not a formal charge, Sanders? Afraid it might tarnish the reputation of the Corps?"

The question was sardonic, thus Knisely was unprepared when Sanders replied: "Yes, sir—that's exactly why I don't want to make a formal charge."

Knisely looked angry, bewildered, and hurt, all at once. Finally he said, "Report back to your platoon, Sanders. I won't take any formal action against you, even though it's against my better judgment. But don't ever come up before me again on a charge of disobeying orders. Is that understood?"

Sanders was about to say something more, but thought better of it. Finally he said, "Yes, sir."

"Dismissed," Knisely said. Then he spun around in his chair, deliberately turning his back on the corporal.

*   *   *

The telephone was ringing when Sanders walked into the empty DI hut. "Long distance calling for Private Thomas Dutton," said the operator.

"Private Dutton? I'm sorry, he isn't here. He's on the drill field."

After repeating the message to the party on the other end, the operator asked, "When do you expect him?"

"I don't expect him," Sanders said. "I mean, Private Dutton is a recruit. He can't come to the telephone."

"I'm sorry—" the operator began. Before she could relay the sentence an anxious voice at the other end said, "Oh, you mean it isn't possible to talk with him?" The question was almost a plea.

"No ma'am. Only if it's an emergency."

"Oh," the voice said dejectedly.

"Anything I can help you with, ma'am?"

"I don't know. I'm not sure . . ."

At that moment the operator interrupted their dialogue. "You sure it's not an emergency?" she asked the girl helpfully. "Or perhaps you'd like to speak to the party at the other end. Otherwise I'm afraid I'll have to disconnect."

"I'm Corporal Sanders, Private Dutton's Drill Instructor. I'd be glad to speak, ma'am, if you think I could be helpful."

"Oh, Corporal Sanders." She said it as though she recognized the name. "Yes, operator, I'll speak with him."

"Very good. Go ahead please."

"Hello, this is Corporal Sanders."

"Yes, Corporal Sanders, Tom has spoken of you. I'm Julie Cummings. His girl friend."

"How are you, Miss Cummings? Is anything wrong?"

"I'm fine, Corporal Sanders. I—"

"It's Chris, if you don't mind."

"Thank you, Chris. And I'm Julie. I'm fine, but I want to know if Tom is. That's why I'm phoning: I was so worried about him. Is he all right?"

"He's great. I saw him only this morning at chow—at breakfast. Right now he's out drilling. Why, did he say something was wrong?"

"Not exactly. Not in so many words."

"Well, then, may I ask why you're worried?"

She sighed, then said, "I'm not sure I can explain it. He went a couple of weeks without writing a single line and—"

"He's terribly busy, as you probably know. He must have told you how recruits are kept busy from four or five A.M. until ten P.M., didn't he?

"Yes, he did, and I know he's busy. That wasn't what bothered me so much. It's just that when he did write . . ." Her voice trailed away.

"Then what?"

"I'm not sure. He seemed to be telling me something, yet he didn't tell me. He sounded so . . . so, I guess you'd say disillusioned."

"That's not exactly unknown, Julie," Sanders said, laughing so as to allay her concern. "This is a big change from civilian life, and recruits typically hate it one day, love it the next, and hate it all over again. I can't imagine anything special is bothering him, at least nothing that a free half-hour wouldn't cure. He looks great and he seems happy whenever I talk with him."

"I know you two have talked. He told me about it. He has such high regard for you, that's why I told the operator I'd speak to you."

"That's very flattering, but I'm not sure it's deserved."

"But why would Tom be disillusioned?" Julie persisted. "When he left for Parris Island he was . . . obsessed with the idea of becoming a good Marine. Now his letters, when I receive them, read as though he's forgotten all of that. It just doesn't sound like him.''

"But Julie, you have to remember that seven days a week of nonstop training in sweltering temperature is enough to dampen anybody's enthusiasm.''

"Not Tom's. He's a born leader, and once he makes up his mind, nothing can change it. He's the most loyal person I know. That's why he's a Marine today, instead of a college student on summer vacation.''

"Julie, why did he join the Marines?''

"Didn't he tell you?'' She asked as though she were wary of betraying a confidence.

"He said something about a personal mission, but he didn't elaborate. I'd like to know, if you're at liberty to say.''

She hesitated at first, but then thought Tom wouldn't really mind if Corporal Sanders' knew. So she told him—told him about Tim's death and about Tom's youthful idealism. Her explanation reinforced Sanders' own impression of Dutton's character, but he was equally impressed by Julie's loyalty and devotion. "Now,'' she said, starting to cry, "the whole tone of his letters seems different. I thought if I could only talk to him . . . ''

"Julie,'' he said, trying to soothe someone who was little more than a faceless voice on the telephone, "I give you my word he's doing fine.''

"But couldn't I talk with him? Couldn't he phone me long enough to tell me in his own words he's all right?''

He was deeply touched by her appeal and wished he could promise he'd phone, but he couldn't. "Julie, it's against regulations—not only for Tom but for every recruit. I'm sorry.''

"Oh, it's my fault,'' she said, crying again. He could barely make out what she was saying between sobs. "I said I was going to fly down to see him and he wrote and pleaded with me not to. He told me then he couldn't even have contact with me by telephone. I shouldn't have phoned, but I was so worried I had to try.''

"It's okay,'' Sanders said soothingly. He didn't know how to comfort her by telephone, yet he did the best he could. "But you have my word he's fine and he'll be out of here in a few weeks. Then you'll see for yourself and you'll be proud of him.''

"I know. I know it.''

"Would you like me to tell him you called?"

She thought for a moment. "No. I guess not. No, please don't, Chris. It would probably upset him. But will you do me a favor?"

"Anything I can."

"Keep an eye on him, please Chris—not to give him preferential treatment or anything, but just talk to him if anything seems to be bothering him. He respects you and—"

"I promise. I'll talk to him tonight or tomorrow. And I won't say a word about your phone call."

"I'd appreciate it, I really would. And thank you, Chris. Now I know why Tom speaks so highly of you."

"Any time, Julie. If you're ever concerned again, don't hesitate to phone." He started to say good-by, then added, "But be sure to ask for me when you phone."

He didn't explain why and she didn't ask. Instead, she thanked him once more, wished him luck at OCS, and said she hoped they'd have a chance to meet one day soon. Then she hung up, and for a few moments he stared at the telephone receiver before returning it to its cradle.

Krupe barged into the Quonset hut, followed by Bennett, who was laughing and saying, "Did you see the way I scared the piss out of that lil' ole—" When he saw Sanders he stopped short. If Krupe was also surprised to see the corporal back at his post he didn't betray it by his expression. Instead he said, "Corporal, those clowns were mighty sloppy out there today. They're much too salty to suit me. I want you to drill them before and after chow tonight. Give them a lot of flanking movements and turns. If we're going to win Post Honor Platoon, we have a lot of catching up to do in a short time."

*   *   *

Early the next morning after chow, Krupe was bringing the recruits up to date on the latest events in Korea when suddenly he said, "Ten-shun," and snapped off a smart salute.

A grim Major Knisely returned the salute, then ordered the recruits to stand at ease. Positioning himself directly in front of the platoon, legs spread wide and both hands gripping an end of the swagger stick that rested across the small of his back, he said: "Less than two months ago the Marine Corps won one of the most important victories in its history—and it won it in the legislative halls of the U.S. Congress rather than on the battle-field.''

He paused for dramatic effect before continuing. ''Probably no military organization on earth has won so many shooting wars and lost so many legislative battles. But in mid-June Congress approved raising our troop strength to four hundred thousand, almost double our present strength. Senator Paul Douglas, an ex-Marine, said he hoped this will prevent the Marine Corps from becoming extinct as a combat organization, and will insure that the Commandant is consulted on Marine matters.

''Gentlemen,'' he said, forgetting for the moment that he was addressing recruits, ''I shouldn't have to tell you how important that is. Because as you know—or should know—the Marine Corps has powerful enemies who like nothing better than to blacken our reputation, disparage our accomplishments, ridicule our training methods.'' He glanced toward Sanders, who was standing off to one side, certain he knew what was coming.

''Our most powerful enemies are the other services, which forever try to tarnish our military record and do their best to drag the Marine Corps down to their level. Their powerful lobbies work overtime in Washington trying to convince anybody who will listen that Marines are obsolete, that our usefulness ended with World War Two. Korea proved them wrong, but don't you think for one minute they've given up. The entire history of the Corps has been a history of fighting for survival against political pressures. Andrew Jackson, in his first message to Congress in eighteen twenty-nine, proposed that the Marine Corps be merged with the infantry or artillery. And before the Second World War began, there were fewer Marines on active duty than there were cops on the New York City police force. Think about that for a while.

''And two weeks after the Korean War began, when MacArthur asked the Joint Chiefs of Staff for a Marine regimental combat team and supporting air group in Korea, we had fewer than seventy-five thousand men. To top it all off, a well-known political leader—an ex-*Army* artillery officer, I might add—gratuitously described the Marines as just the Navy's police force, and said we have a propaganda machine almost equal to Stalin's. So you can see what we're up against—and have been since Commandant Archibald Henderson, way back in eighteen twenty, wrote to the Secretary of the Navy complaining about Army and Navy pressures to kill off the Corps.''

He shifted the swagger stick to his left armpit, as though in emulation of Krupe, who occasionally shifted his *cocomacaque* as he listened attentively. Then Knisely began pacing slowly, raising his voice as he proceeded. "But we don't intend to let the Corps be killed off, and that could happen if a lot of wild charges began making the rounds . . . a lot of unfounded accusations that can only help the other services' lobbies and our enemies. As your Commanding Officer, I feel I have a duty to squelch those rumors and accusations right now, before they get out of hand— before even *you* begin believing them and start writing home, scaring the wits out of your folks and having them run to their Congressmen.

"As I've been talking, I've carefully looked at each one of you, expecting to see a bunch of cripples or sick-bay candidates, but you all look pretty healthy to me. Looks to me like the chow and your daily exercise agree with you." He smiled, and Bennett snickered sycophantically. "The wildest rumor I've heard is that some of you have been mistreated—'abused,' is the word I think was used. I know, I know, it's easy to laugh," he said, although only Bennett so much as smiled, "but this is the sort of rumor that has to be nipped right in the bud. So now I'm going to ask you, before we drop this unpleasant subject once and for all, how many of you feel you've been abused? Those who do, step forward."

No one stirred.

"Let me put it another way," he said. "If any of you knows of any mistreatment to yourselves or others by any of your Drill Instructors, since the day you arrived at Parris Island, step forward."

Again no one moved.

"Am I right, then, in assuming this rumor is just that—a rumor? With no basis in fact?"

When no one responded, Krupe said, "Major Knisely asked you a question—have you been mistreated by any of your Drill Instructors?"

"No, sir," came the prompt reply.

"Are you sure?" asked Knisely.

"Yes, sir!" came an even louder reply.

Turning to Krupe, the major said, "Sergeant, I apologize for questioning your recruits like this, but unless I questioned them in full view and hearing of everybody concerned, these rumors might never get squelched."

"I understand perfectly, sir."

"Good. And are you satisfied that the inquiry was fair to everyone concerned?"

"No question about it, sir."

Turning to Bennett, he asked, "And you, Sergeant—are you satisfied?"

"You know it, sir," Bennett agreed enthusiastically.

"Very good," he said, abruptly turning away. But at that moment Sanders blurted out, "Major."

"What is it, Corporal?" Knisely asked, turning around slowly, his eyes betraying annoyance and malice.

Sanders hesitated for an instant, trying to think of a way of thwarting the charade without appearing defiant or insubordinate. As Knisely waited impatiently, Krupe interrupted. "May I make a suggestion, sir?"

"Of course, Sergeant."

"I was thinking, just so there won't be any misunderstanding, any doubt in anyone's mind, why don't you question several recruits individually? Then they can't claim later that the reason they didn't step forward was because they were shy, or some other reason. Corporal Sanders could designate three or four recruits, any ones he wants, and you can question them directly."

"Excellent idea," replied the major, impressed with Krupe's sagacity. "Who would you like me to ask first, Corporal?"

Sanders wondered why Krupe dared press his luck when he was already home free. Didn't he understand this suggestion was not only bold but potentially reckless as well? Finally he said, "Ask Private Gabriel."

"Private Gabriel, front and center," Krupe ordered.

When the confused recruit came to attention as best he could in front of the platoon, Knisely said, "State your name, rank, and serial number."

"Private Jonathan Gabriel, sir. Serial number 1338578."

"Private Gabriel," said the major, "since you've been a member of this platoon have you witnessed or do you know of brutality or mistreatment to yourself or anyone else?"

The recruit blinked several times, as though mustering his courage. He swallowed twice, then a third time. Finally he replied in a tremulous voice, "No, sir."

"Thank you, Private. That's all."

"Aye, aye, sir," Gabriel replied. He started to turn away,

then at the last second remembered to salute. The major returned it wearily.

"Who do you want to call now, Corporal?"

Sanders hadn't really expected Gabriel to admit to maltreatment, knowing his fear of what might happen was probably greater than his fear of what had already cocurred. But he had reason to believe his next choice might testify. "I'd like to call Private Gillian, sir."

Gillian likewise reported in and likewise was asked if he was aware of any brutality. Bennett, who had sidled toward Knisely when Sanders suggested Gillian's name, edged closer until he was peering over the major's shoulder.

Gillian remained silent. "Well?" said Knisely.

For one brief moment Gillian thought about blowing the whistle on them, particularly on Bennett. But he didn't want to give them the satisfaction of thinking they had beaten him down, that he couldn't take it. Punishment would hurt Bennett's career, but Gillian's graduating from boot camp in spite of the incessant badgering would hurt Bennett even more because it would damage his pride. Finally Gillian replied, "No, sir."

"That's all, Private. Return to ranks." He looked impatiently at his watch. "One more should do it, Corporal. Who's your final candidate?"

Sanders had hoped not to involve Dutton, and he knew the testimony of Gabriel and Gillian, the two most frequently abused recruits, had made it virtually impossible for anyone else to contradict them. He should have nominated Dutton first, but since he hadn't, he was hesitant to put him on the spot now. But Knisely and Krupe were waiting, watching him, expecting him to reply. Finally he said, "Private Dutton."

"Dutton," Major Knisely said after the recruit announced himself in the prescribed manner, "you've heard what I asked your buddies. Have you been maltreated during boot camp?"

Dutton had had a hunch Sanders would single him out. In fact, when Krupe made his surprising proposal to Knisely, he expected to be the first one picked and he resolved to protest the treatment of Gillian and Gabriel. But now that was no longer feasible. And as he stood before the major he thought, what a perversion of justice, being hauled before a kangaroo court in which the prosecutors also served as the jury.

"I'm waiting for your answer," Knisely said. "Have you been brutalized?"

"No, sir, not I. Not personally."

Sanders held his breath. Say it, Dutton, he urged silently. Say what they won't dare ask me publicly. Say it and I'll back you up all the way to the commandant.

"Not personally? Does that mean you've seen others maltreated?"

For God's sake, say it, Sanders implored him silently. Say that one word, Yes.

Suppose he said yes, Dutton asked himself, then what? The answer, most likely, was that it would only make things worse for everybody. Even if Krupe and Bennett were made to end the physical abuse—even if they were removed from duty—Dutton felt sure Gillian and Gabriel would be subjected to unremitting physical and mental stress. He didn't exactly welcome reprisals directed against himself, but he especially didn't want to make it any worse for them. And what could he say? That they had lied to their commanding officer?

"Private, my patience is growing thin. I don't have all day."

"Sir, I . . ."

"You what?"

"I . . ." All at once he thought of Tim, how proud he had been to be a Marine, and how saddened he'd be if anyone harmed the Corps's reputation. He thought of Gillian and Gabriel, telling himself that if they decided not to admit to the brutality, at least they shouldn't have made it impossible for him to go to bat for them. And how did he know Knisely really wanted to know the truth? What if the whole episode had already been rehearsed between the major and Krupe?

"Speak up," Knisely snapped, an unmistakable tone of finality in his voice.

Dutton paused. Finally he said softly, "I don't know of any violations, sir."

"You're sure?"

"Yes, sir."

"Good. That's what I thought—a pack of lies, a lot of wild charges designed to destroy the Marine Corps's effectiveness." Turning to Krupe he said, "Sergeant, carry on. Maybe you can make something of this platoon yet."

"Thank you, Major," Krupe replied, returning the salute. "They still have a long way to go, but I'm hoping they'll shape up by the time we return from the rifle range."

"I hope so. You and Four eighty-four are running neck and neck for Post Honor Platoon at the halfway point, and it looks like you're gonna be in a dead heat down to the wire. The scores on the range and the final inspection will probably determine the winner. Good luck."

"Thank you, sir." Then Krupe called the platoon to attention as the commanding officer hurried away. After he was gone Krupe said, with just the slightest hint of satisfaction, "Now that this unpleasantness is out of the way, let's continue learning how to be Marines. "Ten-shun. For-ward . . . harch."

Even before Knisely departed, even as he watched Dutton wrestle with his dilemma, Sanders understood that Krupe had known all along that none of the recruits would testify to the maltreatment, least of all those who had been most abused. Somehow Krupe knew that the pride, determination, or whatever it was that impelled recruits to join the Marine Corps would exert itself at that moment. He knew Gabriel had too much shame and Gillian too much pride to cause trouble. That left only someone like Dutton, someone not directly affected but personally appalled. Yet Krupe had been confident enough of his mastery of the situation to run the risk.

* * *

"I could have told you it wouldn't work," Krupe said later that night, casual and unruffled, putting aside his news magazine. "Going to the C.O. I mean."

Sanders didn't bother replying; he merely lay on his rack gazing at the ceiling, reliving the incident. "The funny thing is, Sanders, you have contempt for Bennett and me," Krupe persisted, "yet either of us could have told you it wouldn't work. The textbook psychology you think you know, old semi-educated Bennett knows better than you. It's the difference between theoretical and applied psychology."

Sanders started to reply but Krupe continued: "It's the psychology of man under stress—*innere Schweinehund*, the coward lurking in the soul of every man."

"You believe in that two-dimensional world, don't you?" Sanders said with hostility. "Man and superman, weak and strong, powerful and puny?"

"Of course. And so would you believe it if you'd open your eyes. How many heroes did you find when it came time for a showdown? Exactly none," he said, discussing the incident clinically, as though it were a chapter in a textbook. "Where was Dutton, the athlete? Where was Gillian, the recruit you've rescued several times at the risk of your stripes and your career? So you see, with all your preaching to me these past weeks about motivation and leadership, it turns out that you, a future officer, know less about those subjects than someone like Bennett, who I'm sure you consider beneath you."

Sanders hated Krupe at that moment, but he knew he was right, or at least mostly right, and this made him dislike him all the more. Somehow Krupe instinctively understood what Yeats had observed long ago—that "The best lack all conviction, while the worst are full of passionate intensity." And somehow he, Sanders, had become enmeshed in a web of contradiction and confusion, and his attempt at reforms, rather than forcing an end to the abuses, seemed to succeed only in strengthening Krupe's and Bennett's hands.

*　　*　　*

The next morning Krupe summoned Loyal Reese to the DI hut. "Private Reese," he said, "are you happy here?"

"Happy, sir? Yes, sir, I'm happy." His face betrayed his apprehension.

Krupe produced an envelope and waved it in front of him. "Recognize this?"

"I . . . I think so, sir." It was evident that he did.

"Do you make it a practice of corresponding with your Congressman, Reese?"

"Answer up, pinhead," growled Bennett, who was sitting half-dressed on his locker box scratching himself.

The recruit turned a deep red. "Not . . . often, sir."

"I thought not," Krupe said. "Yet two days ago you decided to write to him. Why?"

Fearful that Krupe was about to pounce on him, Reese replied, "Sir, it's . . . it's a personal matter."

"Does that mean you don't intend to answer?" The words did not sound challenging, but there was no mistaking the intent.

Reese cast his eyes downward but said nothing. Krupe continued, "Private, would you like to open the letter and read us what you have written?"

"No, sir," Reese said. Krupe detected a look of panic in his eyes.

"Yet you still want to send this letter?"

"I . . . I did, sir."

"Did? Or do?"

"Sir," he implored, "that letter was written two days ago, before Major Knisely's talk to us yesterday."

"Oh, I see. Are you implying that if you had it to do over, you wouldn't write to your Congressman?"

"Yes, sir," he replied, sensing that perhaps he was being offered a way out of his contretemps.

"Would you like to have this letter back, then, Private?" He dangled it like a metronome before the wary recruit.

"Yes, sir. I would, sir," Reese said eagerly. "I'd like to destroy it," he volunteered.

"Of your own volition—entirely of your own choice?" Krupe continued to tantalize him by dangling the letter back and forth.

"Yes, sir. I really would, sir."

"Here," said Krupe, returning the unopened letter.

"Thank you, sir," the recruit replied.

After a few seconds Krupe said, "Well?"

"Well what, sir?"

"The letter, Private, the letter. Or do you want it for your scrap book?"

"Oh, no, sir," Reese said. "I don't want it at all."

"In that case," the drill instructor said, sliding a GI can across the floor over to the recruit, "perhaps you'll want to dispose of it now, rather than later. But remember, it has to be entirely your choice. Because if you really want to send it, Corporal Sanders will mail it for you this morning."

"No, sir," Reese said, relieved to be on the verge of extricating himself from a potentially dangerous situation. "I really don't want to send it." He tore it to pieces as he spoke.

"I admire your judgment, Reese. You're excused. Oh—one thing more. The next time you feel an urge to write your Congressman, why don't you give the letter to one of us to mail, so we can do it personally? You know how important it is to be prompt in writing to anyone as important as a Congressman."

"Yes, sir," the recruit agreed.

"I thought you'd understand. Dimisssed."

"Thank you, sir," said Reese, pivoting as directed.

"Oh, Reese," Krupe called as he headed for the doorway and temporary freedom.

"Sir?" he said, turning again.

"Since you seem to have time on your hands, you won't mind walking the midnight fire watch shift the next three nights, will you?"

"No, sir, not at all."

"Good. That's all." A moment later Krupe rose and hitched on his cartridge belt, asking Sanders to fall-in the platoon for some close-order drill.

*   *   *

The boxing smoker between Platoons 484 and 486 was postponed three successive nights because of a driving rainstorm that lashed the South Carolina coast. Finally, despite considerable muttering by Pepper, he and Krupe agreed to hold it during the final week of boot camp, after both platoons had returned from the rifle range and from a week of mess duty. Not even Pepper suggested holding the bouts while the recruits were at the range, for fear of eye injuries to the boxers.

The day Platoon 486 marched to the Elliot's Beach Training Area at the far end of the island it was still raining heavily. Nevertheless, Krupe led the platoon, in full sixty-pound marching packs and waterproof ponchos, as it jogged and doubled-timed the entire six miles through frequent cloudbursts.

They spent the day scouting, examining emplacements, learning how to erect trip wires, crawling through mud and water, rehearsing fire team formations, bridging barbed wire, patrolling, studying the compass, and deploying into combat formations signaled by fire-team leaders.

That night they ate rations mixed with rain, were given instructions in moving in the dark, and embarked on scouting maneuvers. At 10:00 P.M., after everyone was accounted for, they sacked out in tents they had pitched in the water and mud.

The thunder rumbled ominously most of the night, but the rain stopped by morning, although it was uncommonly chilly and the ground was a thick layer of mud. After breakfast rations, the recruits policed the area, picking up every scrap of paper and cigarette butt. Then they filed in relays into the stone gas chamber, wearing their gas masks.

Standing in the midst of the chamber, Krupe ordered them to begin singing the Marines' Hymn. After a few minutes he told them to remove the masks long enough to whiff the tear gas. Then they were ordered outside.

Gabriel was the only casualty. He had not placed his gas mask on properly, allowing the gas to seep in, momentarily blinding him and making his eyes water. By the time the order was given to remove the masks, he was gasping violently. Krupe dragged him outside, berating him for his stupidity, which, the DI said, would have rendered him a casualty in a real gas attack.

Several hours later the platoon jogged back to mainside, sloshing through the mud at a pace just under double-time. The slippery underfooting, added to the weight of the packs and rifles, made the jog all the more difficult. And before long, despite Krupe's and. Bennett's threats, several recruits lagged behind. When Orme Beacotte tumbled face downward in the mud, four other recruits, acting on Krupe's explicit orders, stepped squarely on his back before he managed to roll off to the side, out of the way. When the main group of recruits reached the platoon area, they were ordered to line up in two columns along the street and then turn their backs on stragglers.

Gabriel, his glasses splattered with mud, was the last to appear, Bennett cursing and threatening alongside him. The recruit could be heard gasping almost a hundred yards from the platoon area. As he approached, his rifle trailed down by his belt buckle, rather than at high port. About fifteen yards from the finish he suddenly buckled and half-slipped to the ground. He righted himself momentarily, ran another step or two, then pitched forward on his face in the mud. Moaning, he tried to get up but couldn't. He crawled toward his rifle, as all the while Bennett cursed and threatened to have him court-martialed for misusing government property. He stretched out his fingers, grasping for his rifle. Finally he brushed the barrel and managed to nudge it toward him. But just as he wrapped his fingers around it, he emitted a final loud moan, the left side of his face dropped into the mud, and he lay motionless.

Bennett prodded him in the ribs with his foot, but Gabriel didn't stir. "You lily-livered son-of-a-bitch," Bennett screamed. "You no-good chicken-shit bastard. You're worthless, you hear, you're worthless!" Turning toward the two rows of recruits standing with their backs to the drama, he shouted, "Well, what are you waiting for? Get moving—run over him, step on him and grind him into the mud."

They turned and did as ordered, each recruit stepping on Gabriel's prostrate form. Dutton and several others were careful to step on his buttocks or the upper part of his back, lest they injure him. But those who feared antagonizing the irate Bennett stepped hard on the small of Gabriel's back.

Standing off to the side, Sanders watched the first one or two recruits run over the outstretched Gabriel. Then he turned his back on the incident.

*   *   *

The pace of training made it difficult for recruits to form deep friendships, yet bonds of friendship managed to develop nonetheless—friendships snatched from a free minute here, a rest period there, from whispered conversations during those few moments before lights out. Dutton remained close to Herb Beeks, his acquaintance from the train ride to South Carolina, and he was friends with Jim Gillian, whom he respected for refusing to break under Bennett's goading and abuse. But over the days and weeks he forged his closest ties with Robert Begay, who had proven himself to be the outstanding recruit in the platoon. His intelligence, determination, and athletic ability marked him as a natural leader—so much so that Sanders took him aside one evening and asked whether he had given any thought to becoming an officer.

Begay replied that he was not planning to make a career of the military; his ultimate ambition was to return to college and then to the reservation as a teacher or tribal administrator. Right now, though, his concern was to do well in boot camp, he said. But he was so pleased by Sanders' interest that a day later he mentioned it to Dutton.

This was unusual for Begay, who rarely spoke unless spoken to; his stoicism and silence were the only ways in which he fitted the stereotype of the Indian. Yet he reciprocated Dutton's friendship, the two of them sharing phatic communication during those infrequent moments at rest when they sought each other out. Once when Dutton asked Begay why he had joined the Marines, he merely shrugged and lapsed again into silence, indicating that he didn't intend to discuss it.

Bennett, though, kept after him—not with the same degree of hostility he directed toward Gillian, but in any number of petty ways. His being an Indian appeared to have a great deal to do with it, since Bennett almost always called him "Injun"—not in the offhanded manner in which some recruits called him "chief," but maliciously, in a tone of voice apparently intended to convey inferiority or loathsomeness. Dutton once made a stumbling effort to apologize, telling Begay not to let it bother him but rather to consider the source. Begay nodded appreciatively. A moment later he said, "Bennett doesn't bother me. I don't worry about crude, ignorant people, only the ones who know better."

But Bennett did his best to bother him, and most likely would have done even more if he hadn't had Gillian to keep him occupied. Still, one night when Begay and Dutton began walking back from the head, the familiar sound rang out from the darkness: "Get over here, Injun." Begay recognized the voice but he hesitated because the sergeant was in civvies, a pair of chartreuse slacks and a checkered sport shirt open at the neck. It was the first time he had ever seen him out of uniform. "You better snap shit when I talk to you, Injun," Bennett demanded, catching himself just as he started to stumble.

Finally the recruit walked over to him and drew himself up to attention. "Yes, sir?"

"What kind of Injun did you say you were?" Bennett's eyes were half-closed, as usual, and his head was tilted to one side.

"I'm Navajo, sir."

"Not your fucking ancestry, or tribe, or whatever in hell it is. Your goddamn religion, boy." His breath reeked of alcohol and he was weaving unsteadily.

"I'm Mormon, sir."

"That's it, Mormon. They're them freaks that don't believe in smoking, drinking, or fucking, ain't that right?"

"No, sir, Mormons don't smoke or drink."

Bennett's red-faced smile turned into a leer. "What about fucking, Injun, they believe in that?"

Dutton was mortified, but his friend appeared unruffled. "Sir, sex is sinful only outside of marriage."

"Who's talking about sex—I said fuckin'." At that he broke into uncontrolled laughter, until he noticed Dutton standing off to the side. "What the hell you looking at, Private?"

"Nothing, sir. I was walking back to the hut with Private Begay and—"

"Then keep on walking," Bennett said, adding a lengthy string of obscenities.

"Yes, sir," Dutton replied, looking anxiously toward Begay before departing.

When he had gone, Bennett said, "Let's you and me have a

party tonight, Injun, what do you say?" The recruit looked at him warily but made no move to reply. "You know what a party is, don't you, Injun?" he persisted.

When the boot said that he did, Bennett said, "Good, then follow me." He turned and walked to the back of the Quonset huts, then headed toward the DI hut. Begay had a sudden impulse not to follow, not knowing whether recruits were required to obey drill instructors who were out of uniform as well as under the influence of alcohol. But he felt certain that, regardless of rules or regulations, a DI's word was always law. So he followed, reluctantly, hoping Sergeant Krupe or Corporal Sanders would be at the DI hut.

However, the hut was lighted but empty. Bennett banged against the screen door, then stumbled through the doorway and sprawled against the side of the desk. When Begay knocked and asked permission to enter, Bennett made him repeat the procedure twice more. Finally he said, "Get your ass on in here, Injun."

The recruit approached the desk, stopped, and stood stiffly at attention, still dressed in only his shorts with a towel draped around his neck. Bennett took a bottle from his back pocket and extended it to him. "Have some firewater, Injun."

Begay began to be concerned. "Sir, I don't drink," he said.

"Oh, that's right. It's against your religion, isn't it? Tell me, Injun, is it against your religion if I have a drink?"

"No, sir."

"Well thank you all to hell." He put the bottle to his mouth, tilted back his head, and took a long swallow. "Mmmmm," he said, smacking his lips with loud satisfaction. "This stuff'll put hair on your pecker." He flopped wearily into the chair behind the desk. "Tell me something, Injun," he asked almost solicitously. "Is it true that Injun girls love to fuck?"

"Sir?"

Had Bennett's senses not been dulled by drink he would have realized Begay was not only embarrassed by but angry at the question. As it was, he said, "You really do have a hearing problem, don't you, Injun? Like that time on fire watch when I smacked you upside the head." He took another swig and again offered the bottle to Begay. "Sure you won't have one?" When Begay declined, he said, "I asked you if it's true that Injun girls love to fuck. Reason I asked, an old buddy of mine, a Sergeant in Ko-rea, he was from Wyoming or Arizona or somewhere out there in cowboy country, lots of times he told me about how they were always putting the boots to Injuns. I 'member, his favorite expression about any girl was, 'She probably fucks like an Injun.' "

He raised the bottle to his lips to take another drink, but he broke out laughing so hard he had to set it down. "J. D. Setliff—that was this old cowboy's name, J.D. Setliff. Never will forget, one night we was in Hong Kong on some R and R, and we got ourselves some of that Chinese poontang. Next morning when we woke up I asked him, I said, 'Was she any good?' And the first thing he answered, he says, 'Man, that lil ole gal fucks like a skinny Injun.' "

He laughed again, louder than ever, pounding the desk for emphasis. "Right then and there I thought I'd bust a gut laughing—ten thousand miles away in a chink whorehouse and he says she fucks like a skinny Injun." He laughed so hard he began coughing and choking. Finally he sat back in the chair smiling, his eyes almost closed. He might have fallen off to sleep in that position if Begay hadn't said, "Did you ever think he might not have known what he was talking about, sir?"

For a moment Bennett remained in his near-comatose state, his face frozen into a mean grin. Still without opening his eyes he finally said, "Who? Who you talking about?"

"Your friend, sir. J.D. Setliff."

At the mention of the name, Bennett opened his eyes and blinked rapidly, as though emerging from a nap. "J.D. Setliff? What're you talking about, Injun?"

"I'm talking about what he said about Indian girls." He drew himself up even more erect. "How do you know he wasn't repeating hearsay, the kind of lies Indians have had to live down all their lives from people who claim to know them?" He spoke softly, not much above a whisper, but loud enough to be heard.

Yet Bennett reacted as though all he had heard was someone questioning his friend's veracity. "Jesus Christ, Injun," he said, laying his bottle down and trying to push himself out of the chair. "Do you know who you're talking about? Sergeant Setliff was killed in Ko-rea, shot by a bullet that might have been meant for me. He probably saved my life." His voice rose as he tried once more to lift himself out of the chair. "And you . . . you, a goddamn Injun, stand there and tell me he was a liar. Nobody tells me a damn thing about Sergeant Setliff."

"Sir, I didn't say he was a liar."

Bennett struggled to his feet. "There ain't an Injun alive who's fit to kiss his ass," he screamed, blinking and squinting. For emphasis he swept his arm across the desk, sending papers and books sailing across the room. "Pick 'em up, you bastard," he ordered, "pick ever' last one of them up." Bennett hovered over the recruit as Begay did as ordered. Shortly after he finished and resumed his previous stance the sergeant said, "Here!" and thrust the bottle at him." "Drink!"

"Sir, I—"

"I don't give a rat's ass about your religion," he said, his words slurred and indistinct. "I'm ordering you to drink."

Prepared for the worst, Begay said: 'I can't, sir."

"You think I'm a fool, Injun?" he said. "You think I don't know that Injuns love alcohol? Don't drink!" he spat. "My ass you don't drink. You take this bottle right goddamn now."

Begay reluctantly accepted the bottle. "You take a drink this fucking minute, Injun, or you've had it." Bennett's anger appeared to be having a sobering effect on him; his words were still slurred but his coordination was not much worse than usual.

"Sir," Begay replied with a note of finality, "I'm sorry but I won't drink it. I can't."

Bennett snatched the bottle from his hand in a rage and said, "You—"

At that instant Krupe opened the screen door, followed by Major Knisely. "At ease," the C.O. said, even though Bennett had been too surprised to do other than stare at them before setting the bottle down flat alongside a stack of books. Finally he said, "Evening Major, Sergeant."

Krupe nodded, then looked from Bennett to Begay to the desk, quickly sizing up the situation. "Sit down, sir," he said, walking toward the desk and interposing himself between Knisely's line of vision and the desk top.

"Thanks, I think I will. I'm pooped."

"Private, go over there and get us each a cup of coffee," Krupe said, pointing to the urn across the room.

Begay wasted no time doing as ordered, and when he looked up a moment later the bottle was nowhere in sight.

"What brings you here at night, Major?" Bennett asked, his familiar grin back in place and sounding perfectly sober.

"Troubles, Sergeant, troubles, what else?"

"Troubles, sir?"

"Some foul-ball private in Platoon Four eighty-seven went

berserk and started threatening everybody with a bayonet. Slashed two other recruits and sliced Sergeant Miller's arm in a couple of places. But they're okay."

"What about that boot, what'cha do with him?"

"Had the MPs haul him away, what else? Either the brig or Simple City for him. Another lad who couldn't cut it in the Marines." He shook his head in disgust, although he perked up when Begay gave him coffee.

"Simple City," Bennett repeated, kicking off his shoes and settling atop his rack with his clothes still on. "That's where half these recruits today belong, if you want to know the truth— Simple City or the brig."

Krupe ordered Begay to return to his Quonset and soon afterward Knisely finished his coffee and announced, "Time for me to get along. Don't get up," he said as he stood and put on his hat. "Thanks again, Krupe, for your help."

"Any time, sir," he replied. "Good night."

After Knisely left, the tech sergeant walked over to the desk, opened the top drawer, and pulled out the whiskey bottle. "What was this doing here?" he demanded.

"Now, don't sweat it, Sergeant," Bennett said amiably. "I was going over to my buddy's hut in another battalion. I just stopped off here to get some cigarettes out of my locker. I caught Begay grass-assing on the way back from the shower, and brought him up here for you to chew out. We was waiting for you to come back."

Krupe eyed him suspiciously. Without another word he opened the bottle, walked to the sink, and emptied its contents down the drain. "Hey, what's that for?" Bennett moaned, starting to sit up but then having to lie back down while his head throbbed.

"Bennett, I told you the first day I don't want a drop of alcohol anywhere on these premises, not even a beer."

"Jeez Christ, Sergeant Krupe, I—"

"If you had been on duty tonight and had liquor around, even on your breath, I would have turned you over for court-martial without a second thought. And if you ever bring liquor around here again, on duty or not, I'll personally put you on report. You understand?"

"All right, all right, my mistake," Bennett said, holding his head with both hands.

"Just see that you don't do it again."

Two days later Krupe summoned Begay to the DI hut. "I've been looking over your personnel file," he said. "You have a good record." Sanders was surprised by his subdued tone.

"Thank you, sir," he said, wondering how long before he would be punished for having disobeyed Bennett.

"Why'd you join the Marines when you were doing so well at Dartmouth?"

"Sir, I plan to return to school after my enlistment's up."

"But why did you join up now? And why the Marines?"

When Dutton had asked a somewhat similar question, he had evaded it. But Krupe was staring at him—demanding, not asking, his reasons. Finally Begay said, "Because there's a war on now. And because my father was a Marine."

"The Old Corps?"

"Yes, sir. World War Two."

"Did he see combat?"

"Yes, sir."

"Where?"

"All over the Pacific, sir."

Krupe pushed back in his chair and rested both hands behind his head, interlocking his fingers. It was the first time the recruit ever remembered seeing him relax. "So you decided to follow in his footsteps?"

"Yes, sir. Well, not exactly, sir. The Marines don't have any code talkers anymore."

Krupe raised his hands slowly in a gesture that said "of course." "A code talker, I might have known."

"What's that?" asked Sanders.

"Tell him, Begay."

"Sir," said the recruit, turning toward the corporal, "code talkers were a few hundred Navajo Marines in the Pacific who used an unbreakable code to call in air strikes and direct artillery bombardment."

"And it was unbreakable? What was it, the Navajo language itself?"

"No, sir. They spoke in Navajo but used a special coded alphabet."

"At ease," Krupe finally told him. "What was the key to the alphabet?"

The recruit noticed that for once the drill instructor's tone and demeanor were inquisitive rather than inquisitorial. "I'm not really sure," he said. "My father never told me exactly how they did it. But he said that instead of the alphabet, they used clan names for military units, bird names for airplanes, and fish for ships. It had something like forty primary symbols, plus a few auxiliary terms."

"And it worked?" Sanders asked.

"Perfectly," Krupe replied. "They were the best two-man teams ever devised."

"Why don't we have them now?" the corporal wondered aloud.

"We fight a different kind of warfare now. Or maybe warfare is too 'scientific' or too 'modern.' Who knows?" Turning again toward Begay he said, "How'd your father wind up as a code talker?"

"Sir, he heard about it at a trading post, and he decided then and there to join even though he was one of the oldest Navajos in the Marines. He was in his mid-thirties when he went to boot camp at San Diego, then to Field Signal Battalion at Camp Pendleton."

"Was he proud of being a Marine?" Sanders wasn't exactly sure why he asked, except that he intended it for Krupe more than for the Navajo youngster.

"Yes, sir, terribly proud. I can remember . . . "

"Go on," Krupe urged.

"I was in boarding school at Phoenix Indian School," he said slowly, "and he came down to see me just before he shipped out. He and my mother, they hitchhiked down from Many Farms on the Reservation, about three hundred miles. I couldn't get off from school to visit them so they came to see me. My father had on dress blues and my mother was in her traditional velveteen shirt and calico skirt. And she had on her best turquoise jewelry and squash-blossom necklace. My mother was so proud of my father and I was proud of him, especially that my classmates had a chance to see him."

"What's he now?" Bennett asked. "One of them medicine men sitting around a tepee?"

"Sir, Navajos don't live in tepees. And my father's dead."

Even Bennett looked repentant. "Was he killed in the war?" asked Krupe.

"No, sir. He and my mother were killed in a crash on the reservation a couple of months after he was discharged." Glancing toward Bennett he added, "They were hit by a drunken driver as they started to drive to Phoenix and bring me home from school for the summer."

For a moment no one knew exactly what to say. Sanders and Krupe both muttered something about being sorry. Finally Krupe told him he was dismissed. As he turned to go out the door the tech sergeant added: "I want you to hold that platoon banner a little higher from now on. Like you're also proud to be a Marine."

"Yes, sir," Begay said. "I'll do my best, sir."

Chapter 11

On Sunday, August tenth, members of Platoon 486 made up their packs, filled their seabags, and loaded them aboard a van. Then they marched to the rifle range where they officially became part of the Second Recruit Training Battalion. Boot camp was more than halfway over. Now the drill instructors had the platoon only part of each day; the remainder of the time it was under the tutelage of rifle coaches.

Their second day at the range the recruits were issued padded shooting jackets, cartridge belts, and scorebooks. From then on they were on the school range each morning at 6:45, where they were instructed in the use of the .22, the .45, the BAR, rifle grenades, and machine guns. They observed demonstrations of bazookas and portable flame throwers. And they threw hand grenades on the practice range, falling flat behind the chest-high brick compounds after getting rid of the grenade.

Most platoon members seemed to have a natural aptitude for tossing grenades, especially after Krupe told them during one of his lectures that anyone at all athletically inclined could throw a grenade properly. "Forget that nonsense of lobbing grenades over your head like they do in the movies," he said. "That's only necessary if you're trying to lob over a bunker or an incline. Otherwise just throw it naturally, with a little arc, and be sure to keep covered."

In the afternoons the recruits began the agony of "snapping in"—contorting the body during painful practice sessions that eventually enabled them to get into the proper positions from which to fire—kneeling, prone, standing, and sitting. Each day the snapping-in process became a little easier, and the alternate pleading and threatening of rifle instructors and DIs diminished accordingly. The taut rifle slings felt as though they would shut off the flow of blood at the biceps, but the coaches stressed so often the importance of using the sling to steady the rifle and absorb the recoil that most recruits winced but bore it.

Most drill instructors kept away from the range itself, except to march the recruits over the back. Krupe, however, was a notable exception. He regularly paced back and forth among the sprawled-out recruits, offering encouragement, helping some place elbows under their body properly, showing others how to steady the rifle. No platoon could win Post Honor Platoon without a good score at the range, and he felt that if his recruits were not good marksmen it wouldn't be because he didn't take an active interest in helping them.

Even Pepper realized the importance of the three weeks spent at the range, for when he ran into Krupe he usually passed by in silence. He didn't consider this the place to say or do anything that might upset the recruits unnecessarily, and he and his assistants generally adopted a hands-off policy.

Evenings were as busy as they had been at mainside. Soon after the recruits arrived at the range they were marched to the indoor swimming pool and made to swim the entire fifty-six-yard length. Non-swimmers were given extra instruction at night until they could manage the distance, while those who qualified either attended lectures or marched, marched, marched.

The lectures were Krupe's idea. He used the opportunity to remind them how important it was for squad leaders to check everyone's ammunition, canteens, packs, equipment, and bayonets before going into battle. He reiterated the danger of firing from unprotected areas, and showed them how to roll away after firing, before return shots could be directed at the position. And he explained the psychology of infantry fighting—the loneliness of the soldier who is being shot at by an enemy he can't see ... the strange feeling of being part of a rifle team when often you can't see even your nearby buddies ... of not knowing how the battle is going, even when you are being overrun or are overwhelming the enemy. He credited Army General S.L.A. Marshall with the observation that there is no such thing as "battle-seasoned" troops in the sense that experienced soldiers ever manage to overcome their fears. The difference, he said, is that seasoned troops learn to do things well instead of badly, and as they become more knowledgeable they usually become less susceptible to wild imaginings.

Finally, he raised even Sanders' eyebrows by saying that Medical Corps psychiatrists have found that fear of killing and fear of failure caused greater stress than did fear of being killed.

"It's an established fact," he said, "that in any combat situation a large percentage of troops simply won't fire their weapons. The percentage was estimated as high as seventy-five percent in the army during World War Two, which means that in some fire fights only one-quarter of the troops were really engaging the enemy. This percentage was a lot better for the Marines, and it's probably higher for both services now, but it's still not good enough. So long as even one infantryman isn't firing, he's betraying his buddies, making it easier for the enemy. The battlefield is the worst possible place to begin agonizing over moral or ethical questions about killing. It's either kill or be killed. And the tragedy is that your own buddies may die unless you keep firing."

He held the rifle aloft in his right arm, in the classic pose of infantrymen, and shook it as though it were an extension of his arm. "Each time you squeeze off a round on this rifle range," he said, "I want you to consider that bull's eye an enemy—an enemy who's waiting to kill you, who's waiting to squeeze off a bullet into your brain, who wants you to die in Korea. You've got to tell yourself you don't want to die, you're not going to die. You have to tell yourself that the reputation of the Marine Corps and the life of your buddies rest with you, and so you can't fail. Is that understood?"

After the recruits shouted agreement he added, "Don't forget, your enemy is your country's enemy, but he's also your personal enemy. Even though you never met him, and probably won't get close enough to see what he looks like, you have to kill or he'll kill you. Let him get out of your sights and he'll kill someone else, maybe your best friend. This is war, it's for keeps, and a lot of you are going to be involved in it by this time next year."

*   *   *

Even though they were at the rifle range where harassment was usually kept to a minimum, Bennett continued to dog Gillian. Oftentimes after lights out he would appear at the foot of

Gillian's rack and shine a flashlight on his own face, the beam pointing upward from his chin, making him appear grotesque. The first time it happened Gillian bolted upright in surprise and fear. Other times Bennett appeared the instant the lights were thrown on in the morning, and then proceed to tumble the recruit onto the floor. And he dogged the recruit in numerous other ways, whenever he got a chance—or whenever he could force an opportunity.

After the platoon had been at the range almost a week, Bennett collected close to three hundred dollars from the recruits by claiming he was going on emergency leave to attend his father's funeral. Sanders learned about the shakedown when one of the recruits innocently inquired about Bennett's ailing father, and he immediately reported it to Krupe. When Bennett returned from his weekend at Myrtle Beach, Krupe ordered him to concoct some story for the recruits and then return every cent the following payday. Bennett unblushingly explained that he had only intended it to be a loan, and he insisted he thought the recruits understood as much at the time.

Usually Sanders took advantage of any time off to spend it with Susan, about whom he now cared a great deal. Many nights when either or both got off work it was too late for a movie or drive, so they sat at home talking. She had pretty well decided by now that before long she'd return to Indiana, but neither of them talked very much about the future. For the first time in a long while Susan found pleasure in the present, in the here and now, and she wanted to savor as much of it as possible.

As a result, Sanders was spending little free time at the base, but one night when he had the duty he was surprised when Krupe walked into the DI hut shortly before lights out and inquired if everything was okay. Sanders, who had been decidedly cool to Krupe since soon after the incident with Knisely, replied: "Okay, considering that a mere mortal is in charge." Then he resumed reading, stretched out on his bunk.

"Still have a chip on your shoulder, huh?" Krupe asked indifferently, going over to his desk, opening the drawer, and leafing through some papers. "It's okay, just so you know who to be disgusted with—your three shy recruits or yourself."

"Oh?" Sanders replied acidly. "So now you've become the psychoanalyst."

Krupe laughed. "I guess I have at that. It's a common

failing of humans—doing what they warn others not to do." He said it affably enough, but he was eyeing Sanders, expecting a reaction.

It wasn't long in coming. Sanders lowered his book and said, "Of *some* humans, but not all."

"I guess not." Krupe appeared prepared to concede the point rather than spoil the evening with argument. But Sanders was not to be put off.

"In any case," said the corporal, "I can't imagine I'd ever be as corrupted by power and authority as you are."

Krupe's lips tightened, his eyes narrowed, and for a moment his body seemed to stiffen. "I wouldn't begin to compare the two of us in most things," he said crisply. "I should think you'd be more careful yourself."

Sanders raised up on his elbow and said, "Krupe, you'd be the last person I'd ever want to compare myself with." He hadn't meant to be so abrasive, and his words were harsher than intended, but he had no intention of modifying them.

For a moment Krupe said nothing. Then he asked, "Why is that, Sanders? Because you think I'm cruel . . . or because in looking for faults in me you've found imperfections in yourself? A lack of conviction, maybe?"

"Look, Krupe, if—"

"I'm talking about the courage of your convictions, actually. The courage to fight for something you believe in. You don't seem to have that courage, you—"

"You're wrong, Krupe," Sanders interrupted. "I believe in decency, and fair play, and decent treatment for these recruits."

"And what did you do when you were put to the test?" You submitted, just as docilely as any of your three recruits—not because you aren't a good barroom brawler, but because at the last minute you weren't sure whether you were doing the right thing."

"If Knisely had asked me I would have told him," he declared, now sitting up with his legs dangling over the side of the rack. "I *wanted* him to ask me."

"I'm sure you did. But even Knisely isn't that stupid. The point is, if you had really had the kind of courage the situation called for, you would have found some way not to put those recruits on the spot. Why do you think your three shining examples deserted you? I'll tell you why," he said, warming to his subject. "Gabriel is so ashamed of himself he needs—he craves—Bennett's punishment to remind him of his pitiful state. Gillian is almost convinced there just might be something wrong with him, so he wouldn't dare talk. And Dutton, he's a lot like you—quick to make neat, simplistic moral judgments that break down the minute they're challenged.''

"You must feel like a king, Krupe, ruling over your own small kingdom.''

"On the contrary, I feel like a warden guarding a prison full of moral delinquents and defectives.'' He looked at Sanders, but his gaze appeared to be turned inward. Finally he said, "I don't expect you to believe this, but if I had a kingdom, I'd give it up to find a recruit willing to stand up to me—not with his fists, necessarily, but with his entire being. Someone proudly defiant.''

"Nonsense, Krupe,'' Sanders said. "That's bull and you know it. What chance would a recruit have to stand up to you? If you didn't smash him senseless, Bennett would cripple him—with your indulgence, if not your approval. Stand up to you! They'd be lucky to stand at all.''

Krupe ignored him as he began filling out forms, the mission that apparently inspired his visit. Sanders returned to reading, and afterward made a tour of the barracks area. When he returned Krupe was still at it. Sanders resumed reading, but after a while, in an effort to defrost the chill between them, he asked whether Krupe had ever tried to become an officer, and if not, why not?

Krupe looked at him archly, almost as though the question didn't deserve an answer. Then he said, "Does that mean you consider me fit to associate with proper gentlemen like you'll soon be?''

"I'm serious,'' Sanders said, opening a new pack of cigarettes and offering one to Krupe. "Why would you be content to be a Tech Sergeant, or even a Master Sergeant, if you could be an officer? Why would you want to be bossed around, or at least in a position to be bossed around, instead of doing the bossing?''

"My answer wouldn't satisfy you, Corporal,'' Krupe said brusquely, returning to his paperwork.

"Maybe not, but I'd still like to hear it.''

"To you,'' Krupe said, setting aside his pen, "being an officer probably means being looked up to—being saluted, eating in the officers' mess, sitting in the middle seats at the base theater, being called 'sir' by enlisted men with twice your time in the military. It satisfies your ego. I can understand that. But to me it means being an administrator rather than someone who gets things done, a watchdog rather than an attack dog, a—"

"A gentleman rather than a peon."

"Exactly. A gentleman." He emphasized the word carefully, almost disdainfully. "But I prefer being a peon. I prefer to train Marines in the art of survival, rather than delegate that responsibility to others."

"But doesn't it annoy you to have to salute some inexperienced kid a lot younger than yourself?"

"That's the system," he replied, sidestepping an answer. "I didn't invent it, I'm powerless to do anything about it, so I accept it."

"Krupe, how can you accept a—"

"I'm not trying to talk you out of going to OCS, if that's what you want," Krupe said, rising and looking at the prone Sanders. "Go, earn your gold bar and the piece of paper that shows you're my superior. You won't be the first officer to feel that way, or the last."

"You know I didn't mean that."

"Maybe not, but that seems to be what you're implying. Just why are you anxious to become an officer?"

Sanders thought about it, almost as though for the first time. "Krupe, I don't know if this answer will satisfy you," he said, trying hard to phrase his reply precisely, "but I was raised to try to excel. Not that I always did excel, but I was raised to try. That means I was raised to believe it's better to be a Corporal than a Private, better to be a Sergeant than a Corporal. Better to be a Lieutenant than a Sergeant. Not that the Lieutenant is the better *person*, or the Sergeant or the Corporal. Just that the *rank* is better; it carries greater responsibility and therefore is worth striving for. Is that attitude wrong?"

Now it was Krupe's turn to pause, as well as his turn to evade a direct question. "Maybe if my career had begun like yours I'd do the same thing," he said. "But by the time I knew the difference between officers and enlisted men, I was in the middle of a war, where we were almost all the same, being shot at by an enemy that was no respecter of rank. And after the war I decided to become a civilian again, so rank didn't make any difference."

"Why did you come back in?"

Krupe appeared to be mulling it over, trying to decide whether to answer. Then he said, "This will give you a good laugh, since I don't expect you to understand. But I'm a Marine. Just as some people are teachers, or musicians, or scientists, or insurance agents—I'm a Marine.''

"But all that schooling—Bennett told me you were taking home-study courses in Chinese language and Asian geography and politics. Why?"

"Do you consider education wasted effort?" Krupe asked, turning the question back on Sanders. "Do you think ignorance is prerequisite for being a career Marine?"

"But what possible use can your knowledge of Far Eastern affairs be when you're on patrol in Korea?"

"That's like asking what good your ability to print or write is after you learn to type. I don't know exactly what good it will do, but it may come in handy in the future. I have a feeling that China is going to be very important someday—not just big, but powerful."

"So you burn the midnight oil studying its language and culture."

" 'Know thine enemy,' Sanders. I shouldn't have to tell you that. But it's more than that. I've spent almost seven of the past ten years in the Far East. It interests me—its culture, its values, its art, its folklore. Some people—even Marine NCOs, it may surprise you to learn—are Civil War buffs, others know everything there is to know about the First World War. I'm interested in Asia. I happen to think that's where much of our history is going to be written during the last half of this century." As though getting carried away by his subject he added, "Even if it isn't, I'd still be interested."

"I still think your education isn't being utilized fully as an enlisted man."

Suddenly Krupe lapsed into a strange tongue: *"Shinuru yamai kusuri nomaji to omoeru wo urusaku hito no kusuri nome to yu."*

Sanders arched his eyebrows. "What's all that?"

"A Japanese *waka*—light verse."

"What's it mean?"

"Roughly:

> 'Sick unto death,
> I have no desire
>   For medicine,
> But people keep
> Urging me to take it!' ''

"Is that a hint?" Sanders asked, the trace of a smile beginning to play at the corners of his mouth.

"Nebba hotchie, Joe," Krupe replied in the pidgin English common to veterans of Korea and Japan. "You know we Orientals never say things outright; we have other people adopt our suggestions as their own. It's our way of saving face."

It was the first time Sanders had viewed Krupe's light side. He considered bantering with him but then decided against it. Instead, without knowing exactly what impelled him, he said: "Yea, I've noticed how often Sergeants Krupe and Bennett have tried to save face for their recruits."

Krupe immediately became silent and the smile vanished completely. Without another word he gathered up his papers and departed for the night, slamming the screen door behind him.

Chapter
12

The recruits first fired the M-1 during their second week at the range. Platoons were divided into four relays. Two remained on the firing line while the others worked the butts—concrete dugouts ten feet below ground from where the butt crews marked a shooter's progress by plugging the bullet holes in the six-foot square targets with "spotters," small cardboard discs on wooden spindles.

Crew members lowered the targets on a sliding chain after each shot or series of shots, placed the spotter in the hole, then signaled the value of the shot by raising the corresponding colored metal discs attached to long, slender poles. Then they lowered the target once more, pasted a white or black patch over the bullet hole, and raised it again. A shot that missed the target completely received the ultimate ignominy: "Maggie's Drawers," signaled by waving a red flag from the butts.

The range was divided into sections A through D, each containing fifty targets. Rifle coaches, wearing shooting jackets and old-style campaign hats, helped each recruit sight-in his rifle properly and encouraged them to relax while firing. The coaches were also alert to any carelessIness on the part of recruits, which they punished immediately and with force. Positioned midway between the lines of shooters, atop a wooden platform raised six feet off the ground, a rifle coach—wearing his campaign hat but stripped to his T-shirt sans his dungaree jacket—remained in constant communication with the rifle pits via a field phone. He also instructed shooters over a loudspeaker system situated off to the side:

"All ready on the right. . . . All ready on the left. . . . All ready on the firing line. Load and lock. Shooters face your targets. . . . Fire."

From prone, standing or kneeling position, recruits sighted-in on the targets and commenced rapid or slow fire. Although the targets looked at first to be thousands of yards distant, they were never more than a hundred yards away. Even with cotton stuffed into their ears, the recruits still heard the loud pop of explosions all around them as they fired.

Afterward, their ears still ringing, recruits were ordered by the fire master to pick up their empty cartridge shells and deposit them in nearby buckets. When given the word, they retreated to the empty ammunition boxes some ten yards behind the firing line while another relay prepared to fire. A large sign attached to the fire master's platform warned recruits to keep bolts open at all times, except when ordered to load and lock.

After two relays finished firing the course, they were marched to the rifle pits to change places with the two relays working the butts. Afterward all recruits spent an hour or so cleaning their rifles, removing every trace of carbon, dirt, and dust accumulated during the firing.

Even Bennett was unusually restrained when the recruits were on the firing line, although he decked Paul Mathern after the recruit carelessly wandered off the firing line carrying his rifle as though preparing to fire it from the hip. But away from the firing line he was the same old Bennett, roughing up Gillian and Begay from time to time.

At night the DIs drilled the recruits endlessly on the function and operation of the M-1. "Name the parts of the barrel and receiver group," Krupe would demand of a recruit. "Explain the functioning of the M-1," he ordered another. "What do you do if the bolt doesn't lock?" he challenged a third. "What if the rifle fails to feed—what do you do then?" "What if it fails to extract?"

Krupe demanded immediate answers, and those who failed to provide them were ordered to strip down the rifle, then reassemble it in minutes. Then they were asked a different question, and if they were unable to answer that, they were made to repeat the process.

Krupe also insisted that each recruit close his eyes and learn to set the sights on his rifle by listening to the clicks. This, he explained, would help them sight-in in the dark, an ability that might mean the difference between life and death in Korea.

During the final week at the range, each recruit fired the full course every morning leading up to Friday's scheduled qualification round. When more than a third of the platoon failed to qualify the first day, Krupe didn't seem especially concerned.

When a dozen failed the second day, he still didn't seem upset.

But when Beacotte, Gabriel, Hosse, and five others failed on Wednesday, two days before final qualification, he dropped his insouciant attitude and castigated them in front of everyone. "This in not the Army, this is the United States Marine Corps," he announced when they returned to the platoon area and the recruits finished reporting their scores to him. "A Marine who can't fire a rifle isn't a Marine at all. If those cooks, and bakers, and clerks, and mechanics at Chosin hadn't learned to fire their M-1s, the Division would never have broken out of the Chinese trap. Now, you people listen up. Tomorrow afternoon I want every one of you to qualify, and God help those who don't."

The next day only Gabriel and Sam Bayard failed to fire the minimum score of 190. Because Bayard missed by only two points, Krupe merely glowered and warned that he better qualify the next day. When Gabriel reported his score, Krupe exploded. "One . . . hundred . . . and . . . thirty . . . six?" he asked incredulously. "Is that some kind of joke, Private?"

"No . . . sir."

"No sir," Krupe growled. "Is that all you can say? What excuse, what possible excuse, have you for such a miserable score?"

The trembling recruit swallowed hard. "No excuse, sir."

Krupe rose slowly, deliberately, gripping his *cocomacaque* and struggling to control his anger. "Gabriel, do you know the best thing you could do for me? Do you?"

"No, sir."

"You could leave—run away, right now, tonight. Like Duvail tried to do. Duck out, so you wouldn't be here tomorrow to ruin Four eighty-six's chances of making Post Honor Platoon. You're not a Marine, Gabriel. It's an insult to the Marine Corps, to the guys who are dying in Korea, to call you a Marine. You're not even man enough to make a good Doggie. Go on, get out of my sight. You sicken me."

In tears, Gabriel turned away and fell in at attention with the rest of the platoon. He knew Krupe was right, and he didn't mind the public humiliation as much as he hated himself for his abject weakness. But he was too frightened of the consequences to take Krupe's advice.

The next day, however, he wished he had run away, for he was the only member of Platoon 486 who failed to qualify; he shot 171, the next lowest being a three-way tie at 192. Altogether six recruits, led by Begay and including Herb Beeks, fired expert. Dutton, Tew, Gillian, and Beacotte were among the twenty-six who fired sharpshooter. And except for Gabriel, all the remainder were marksmen.

Bennett threatened Gabriel with a beating. But Krupe's anger was tempered when he learned that two recruits from Pepper's platoon had failed to qualify. Moreover, only four members of 484 shot expert and twenty-three fired sharpshooter. So he said not another word to Gabriel, did not even acknowledge his existence. He had hoped for one hundred percent, but even failing that, it had been a rewarding three weeks at the rifle range.

*   *   *

The next day, August 29, a hurricane slammed into the South Carolina coast, packing winds which that evening reached eighty miles per hour. All that day work parties of recruits nailed mattresses against windows inside huts, moved bedding and locker boxes to the second floor of the brick barracks at the far end of the rifle range, and lashed down everything that might not withstand the wind.

Dozens of three-ton trucks lined the sidewalks opposite the barracks, awaiting evacuation instructions. Gas and electricity were shut off in every barracks. That evening each recruit sat with an emergency bucket of water alongside his rack as he reviewed General Orders, committed to memory every possible malfunction of the M-1, or silently reviewed his experiences in boot camp, which for 486's members was finally drawing to an end. Fire watches and drill instructors in ponchos patrolled with flashlights, ducking in and out of doorways in futile attempts to avoid being soaked.

The main thrust of the winds, resulting from a tropical disturbance off the Florida coast, hit shortly before midnight. It tore up shrubs, uprooted trees, knocked down power lines, shattered glass, and damaged several buildings. And although it threatened to topple several barracks and Quonsets, the storm finally blew itself out in the early-morning hours and soon the skies were clear once more.

After morning chow the recruits were put to work again, removing mattresses from the windows and restoring things to normal. It was a tiresome task, but Bennett claimed it would be a picnic compared with the week of mess duty before a final week of review, then graduation.

The night of the storm, while awaiting its full impact, Sanders asked Krupe if he meant what he had said to Gabriel on Thursday. "Of course I meant it," Krupe replied adamantly. "Why?"

Asleep on the rack that had been set near the center of the hut, Bennett punctuated Krupe's reply with muted snores.

"Because Gabriel may not be a good Marine, but he is a human being. And that sort of public chewing-out can only destroy his confidence in himself."

"Sanders, when are you going to learn?" Krupe asked impatiently, raising his voice above the storm. "Any confidence that misfit has in himself is misplaced. And I wasn't evaluating his worth as a human being, only as a Marine. He's worthless and you know it. His platoon members know it and I know it. So why shouldn't he know it?" He still can't even keep up on the morning run."

"But he's almost home free. Another two-and-a-half weeks he'll be gone—he'll be out of your hair, sitting behind a desk somewhere."

"That's what you think."

"What do you mean?" Sanders asked, moving toward his desk.

"I mean that I'm recommending Gabriel be dropped back to another platoon in the beginning of training, so he can go all through boot camp again. Either that or that he be given a General Discharge."

Sanders leaned across the desk imploringly. "You can't do that. It isn't fair to him. He's come all this way—"

"He's come all this way as a totally incompetent recruit whose one asset is that he didn't foul up badly enough at any one time for me to send him back."

"But he deserves some credit for joining the Marine Corps, some credit for not waiting to be drafted into the Army or joining the Navy."

Krupe was tapping a pencil impatiently, getting more irritated by the minute. "There's no such thing as deserving credit where it comes to being a Marine," he said finally. "Not where other people's lives are involved. I can't have it on my conscience that I allowed an incompetent like Gabriel to graduate from my platoon. I'd never forgive myself, thinking I could be sending him to Korea where he'd be a menace to every other Marine."

Searching for arguments that might dissuade Krupe, Sanders finally said, "What gives you the right to sit in judgment on everybody? Where do you get your moral superiority?"

"Not moral superiority, Sanders—just good judgment as to who will and won't make a good Marine. And Gabriel won't. He'll crack at the very first strain, and other Marines will suffer." He resumed tapping his pencil, looking at Sanders. Finally he asked, "Would you lead Gabriel into combat with you? Tell the truth—after you get commissioned, would you like him in your rifle squad?"

"Once he got out of boot camp he could be a typist or a clerk. There are lots of them—"

"Whoa, hold on a minute," Krupe interrupted. "This isn't the Civil Service. We don't train recruits to be typists and clerks. We train them to become Marines. Some of them eventually become deskbound, but we train them to be Marines."

Sanders slumped down on the bed and lit a cigarette. He drew on it deeply several times, then said: "Krupe, this will infuriate you, but I still don't know who or what makes a good Marine. I mean it—how do you know how anybody will react under fire? I'm not sure I'd be a good Marine under fire. Okay, you've proven yourself under combat conditions, but how do you know next time you won't break and run? Courage isn't something you have forever or lack as long as you live. It's something all of us have at some time and lack at other times, depending on a whole lot of variables."

"That's where you're wrong, Corporal. I wouldn't break and run, because I know myself. I'd die before I'd break and run."

"Maybe so, Krupe," Sanders said. "But if so, you're one

of the few wholly predictable people in this world. Most of us are predictable only in our unpredictability. People we say are brave are brave at a particular time, or for longer periods than most others. Cowards aren't always without courage."

"That's rationalization, Corporal." He withdrew a handkerchief and began polishing his eyeglasses, breathing on the lenses and wiping them clean. Sanders noticed that he looked less ferocious without them. "Courage isn't something that comes and goes like a virus infection. It's a way of life, a code of honor."

"All fanatics have courage," Sanders replied. "But it can't take the place of judgment."

"I told you before that discipline was more important than raw courage," Krupe said, putting his glasses back on. "But Gabriel doesn't have discipline or courage."

"Maybe he does. Maybe it only has to be given a chance to develop."

"Then it can develop at home, on his own time, where he can't harm anybody." With that Krupe reached for a book and opened it, signaling that the subject was closed. Sanders began pacing the Quonset hut, annoyed by the conversation and anxious to telephone Susan to make sure she was safe, but not while Krupe or Bennett were about. Besides, he didn't even know if the telephones were still working during the storm. Krupe, meanwhile, had set down his book and was staring off into space. Sanders thought he was listening to the wind and rain, but in a few moments he said, "Suppose you were an Air Force pilot, shot down over North Korea. You're captured and accused of spreading germ warfare. You're told to sign a confession. Do you do it?"

"What is this, Twenty Questions?"

"Would you sign?" Krupe persisted.

"No. Not voluntarily, anyhow. What's—"

"Voluntarily? What does that mean when you're a prisoner of war, an enemy who has been shot down after dropping bombs on your captors?"

"Since you put it that way, there doesn't seem to be much of a distinction," Sanders said.

"'Exactly. So obviously you won't voluntarily sign a confession. But my question is, do you ever sign?" He leaned back as far as the chair would go as Sanders considered the question.

Instead of answering, Sanders had a question of his own: "You know, of course, what the North Koreans do to captured Air Force pilots?"

"That's not what I asked. What would you do if *you*, a Marine, were captured?"

"I'd resist as long as I possibly could."

Krupe dropped forward in the chair and flipped his book closed. "Sanders, what kind of answer is that from a potential Marine Officer?" he asked disgustedly. "As long as you possibly could. Suppose you could only hold out a half-hour?"

"How do I know how long I could hold out? How does anybody know? I'm a human being, in uniform or out. Human beings are capable of withstanding just so much torture, but they all have a breaking point."

"Correction—we have a breaking point if we're not willing to die for what we believe in. Or if we don't believe strongly in anything."

"For what—"

It began as a question, but Krupe interrupted. "Yea, for what we believe in. I believe in the United Sates Marine Corps, as irrational as that sounds to you. I'm willing to die rather than disgrace it. Nothing could make me betray it."

The words were forceful but not dramatic. Indeed, Krupe looked wistful and sounded almost matter-of-fact.

"I believe you mean it," Sanders said. "But my contention is that you'll never know unless you're put to the test."

"With your attitude," Krupe snapped, "you shouldn't be heading for OCS, you should be in the Army."

"Krupe," Sanders said, lowering his voice until it could barely be heard over the storm, "I don't pretend to be a hero. I'm a human being, with all the virtues and faults of the species. I'm not scornful, just realistic. Maybe I'm a better soldier because I'm a Marine and not in the Army, but basically I'm the same guy. Believe me, nothing would please me more than to be a superman, but I'm not. I recognize my limitations."

Krupe shook his head and contorted his face into a look of pained displeasure. "People like you . . ." he said. "You've got brains, ability—everything but convictions. You remind me of my brother."

"Your brother?"

"Vernon Krupe. Ever heard of him?" He studied Sanders as the corporal turned the name over in his mind.

"Vernon Krupe . . . Vernon Krupe," Sanders repeated almost to himself. "I don't think I—"

"You've heard of him. At least you've read about him. Everybody has. Major Vernon Krupe, U.S. Air Force."

Sanders' mouth flew open and he stood transfixed. Finally he said, "Not Major Krupe, the—"

"The turncoat, that's right."

"Turncoat? I thought—"

"That he's merely a traitor?"

"No—that he made propaganda broadcasts for the Reds. But I didn't think he joined them."

"Maybe you can find satisfaction in the distinction," Krupe said as he removed his eyeglasses once again and rested them upside down on his desk as he rubbed his eyes. "But I can't find any satisfaction or any consolation." As he said it he looked fatigued and greatly troubled.

Major Vernon Krupe! And it had never occurred to him. The papers had carried endless accounts, but even with the similarity of the names, who would have thought . . .

"Krupe, I'm sorry, I really am," Sanders said sympathetically. "I had no idea . . . but you've got to look at it from his viewpoint. He—"

"Article Seventeen of the Geneva Convention of nineteen forty-nine says that every prisoner of war is bound to give only his surname, first name and rank, date of birth, and serial number."

"But you can't live by a literal interpretation of that Article," Sanders protested, walking over as though to lay a comforting hand on Krupe but finally just standing alongside him. "It's a rule governing a prison of war's conduct. It doesn't say anything about confessing to torture."

Krupe unlocked the bottom drawer of his desk and withdrew a thick stack of newspaper clippings. He thumbed through them until he found the article he was looking for. "Read this," he said, pushing it toward Sanders, who picked it up and began reading to himself as the wind whistled and howled past the Quonset hut:

Tokyo, July 19 (AP)—U.S. Air Force Major Vernon Krupe, believed killed when his F-86 Sabre jet fighter crashed in North Korea after being downed by enemy ground fire, was reported alive today by an Australian journalist who claims that Krupe confessed to waging germ warfare against North Korea.

According to reports monitored here, Krupe, 26, who previously was credited with downing four MIG-15s in dogfights over Korean skies, said that he "regretted" his part in the bombing and strafing raids against "the People's Republic of North Korea" and against "humanity everywhere."

Asked by touring journalist Willard Skiffington whether he voluntarily signed his name to an anti-U.S. article that appeared in *Towards Truth and Peace*, the newspaper published by progressive prisoners in the Communist Chinese POW camp at Pyoktong, Krupe replied, "I stand by every word in it."

The newspaper article said, in part:

"My name is Vernon Krupe. I've been in the Air Force five years and I finally learned how my government has tricked me and my friends and family.

"Until I came to Pyoktong, I didn't understand how capitalist warmongers like Truman and MacArthur forced me to fight against the People's Government. But my generous allies of the Democratic People's Republic of Korea have forgiven me for my germ-warfare raids on them, and have provided me with good food, warm clothing, and health services.

"My fellow servicemen, I appeal to you to end this barbaristic, aggressive action to promote the capitalistic interests of the American monopolists. Let us fight for right against wrong, bravely opposing mobilization for this unjust war."

When Skiffington asked Krupe if he planned to return home, the father of a son and daughter replied, "Only if the capitalists and warmongers no longer run the government of the U.S."

Sanders had skimmed the news story when it had appeared originally, but this time he read every word. He stared at the clipping long after he finished reading, unable to raise his eyes to Krupe's.

"Do you condone that?" Krupe demanded. "Does any sort of treatment by his captors justify such . . . such treason?"

Sanders finally returned Krupe's gaze. "I know how you

must feel, but think of him," he said. "Think of what they must have done to him to make him say things like that."

Krupe seemed not to hear. He arose and walked slowly toward the map of Korea. Sanders thought he detected him swallowing hard, but he couldn't be sure, since the tech sergeant's back was to him. Without turning around, Krupe said, "He was a lot like you. Or you're a lot like him."

Apprehensively, Sanders asked, "In what way?"

"He was never sure of himself either. He was always finding excuses for the other guy, always refusing to embrace anything wholeheartedly. He wanted to know why, he was never content to accept anything on faith. And like you, he was sure he could change the world."

"Is there something wrong with that?"

Krupe turned slowly from the map and fixed Sanders with a look that bordered on resignation. "There was plenty wrong— that's why he disgraced himself, his country, and his family. He thought he could change the world and he couldn't even manage himself."

"Floyd," Sanders said, using Krupe's Christian name for the first time, "none of us can sit in judgment of your brother until we know what he's gone through. How do we know how much he resisted? I've read stories about what they do to those pilots to get them to confess—they throw them outside, naked, in cages in sub-zero temperatures in the snow, and they make them stay there for weeks. They put them in cages constructed so they can't sit, stand, or lie down. They make them wallow in their own filth, and they isolate them for days. They starve them, they beat them, they question them for days and nights on end. Then they threaten to kill them. Sometimes they actually march them out to open pits, put a pistol behind their heads, and offer them a final chance to 'confess' or have their brains blown out."

"Then he should have let them blow his brains out," Krupe said. "That's right, my own brother—he should have let them kill him rather than make a whimpering traitor out of him. He would have been better off dead than living with that stain forever on his Conscience."

"Who are we to say he should die?" Sanders asked, using the plural pronoun in hopes of overcoming the barrier Krupe had erected between them. "When you're kneeling over an open pit thousands of miles from anywhere, your hands bound behind your back, and you know no one will ever know what happened to you, whether you lived or died—then codes of proper behavior don't seem too important. I'm willing to bet he resisted for weeks before he 'confessed.'"

Krupe shook his head vigorously. "They even have him in their 'Progressives' Camp,' the worst camp of all. He's a coward, and that's all there is to it."

"That isn't all there is to it. You can torture a man into confessing anything—anything. He'll betray his God, his wife, his children, his parents, his country—anything and everything. Did you ever read *Nineteen Eighty-Four?*"

Krupe nodded. "So? What's that got to do with my brother?"

"It has everything to do with him. Don't you remember . . . what was his name? Smith . . . Yea, Winston Smith. His only fear was rats. He endured everything else, except when confronted with a cage full of rats that could only escape by eating through his face. Remember his torturer explaining that many humans will resist pain even to the point of death, but that everybody has something he can't endure—his own rats? And that fear isn't cowardice."

"It's easy to be philosophical when you're not to blame," Krupe said, twisting his *cocomacaque* nervously in one hand.

"Neither are you. Neither is your brother, probably."

"Sanders, you can find an excuse for anything, can't you?" It was less a question than an accusation. "I'm his older brother, don't you understand? Whatever he is, I helped shape him—or at least had a chance to make him into something else."

"You're wrong, Krupe, absolutely wrong." He was about to say more but the wind was raging and it would have been difficult to hear him. As it died down again Krupe said:

"You think it's wrong because you don't believe in absolutes. He was like that too—everything was relative, everything was tinged with gray. There were no black or white values."

"If there are, your sense of responsibility isn't one of them. No human being is entirely shaped by brotherly influences. We're a jumble of genes and of what we learned at home, in school, and on our own. Of how we've been treated by others. And yes, whether we were loved as children."

"He was loved by his parents and by his wife and two kids," Krupe insisted angrily. "But he didn't love any of them enough to spare them shame and humiliation."

"I'm not as convinced of his disgrace or failure as you

are,'' Sanders said, watching as Krupe sat still twisting his *cocomacaque*. Sanders lit another cigarette and poured each of them a cup of coffee. Bennett began snoring loudly, as though to drown out the storm. Presently Sanders asked, ''Do you recognize in Gabriel the same weaknesses you saw in your brother?''

''Gabriel? Gabriel isn't *half* the man my brother is. Or was. That's why he's being sent back as soon as I can arrange it.'' He stirred his coffee absently, then he said: ''The pity is that Vern had most of the qualities it takes to be courageous rather than cowardly. I think if he had been a Marine, he wouldn't have given in to his captors.''

Sanders had his coffee cup halfway to his lips when he stopped and stared at Krupe in amazement. ''You can't be serious,'' he said.

''I am serious. How many Marine POWs have signed germ-warfare confessions or betrayed their country?''

''That isn't fair. It's—''

''How many?''

''It's the pilots they're trying to force confessions from, not foot soldiers. It fits in with their propaganda about germ-warfare bombings. They make a special effort to get Air Force pilots to confess.''

''I'll tell you how many,'' Krupe persisted, as though he hadn't heard. ''None. Not any. Zero. No Marine pilot, officer, or enlisted man would ever betray everything he was taught to believe in, the way my brother did.''

''You're wrong, dead wrong. Maybe some wouldn't, just as some Air Force pilots haven't signed those phony confessions. And maybe Marines, because of their special pride, could hold out a little longer. But its delusion to believe Marines don't have limitations like everybody else.''

''It's obvious you have yours,'' Krupe said curtly.

''I know you mean that as an insult, Krupe, but it doesn't faze me. You're right, I admit to my limitations. One is not to harbor illusions of omnipotence. You prefer Nietzsche and I prefer Aristotle—his understanding that a person doesn't expose himself to danger needlessly, but will give his life for the right cause, knowing that under certain conditions it isn't worthwhile living.''

''It must be nice to be guided by such a convenient philosophy,'' Krupe said drolly.

''That's where you're all wrong. Comfort comes from

knowing absolutely what's right and what's wrong, from having something as unfailing as the UCMJ or Marine Corps regulations to guide you and light the way."

"In other words, your argument is that the weakling, the traitor who denounces his country, is a better man than the one who resists out of faith in himself or his unit. Is that it?"

"I'm not saying that," Sanders replied heatedly. "What I'm saying is that the ability to withstand torture and punishment isn't the essence of a human being—or even the ultimate mark of a soldier. You should know that, Krupe."

The sergeant started to reply but thought better of it. Instead, he drained his coffee cup as the wind continued blowing and Bennett shifted fitfully in bed. Finally he said, "The day his letter arrived telling me he had joined the Air Force and was on his way to flight school, I telephoned him from Pendleton, where I was awaiting discharge. I tried to talk him out of it. I tried to talk him into the Marine flight training program, but he said he wasn't gung-ho enough to be a Marine. He said he didn't think he 'had the temperament for the Marine Corps. Now I know that he meant 'guts,' not temperament."

Krupe returned the clippings to his desk drawer and locked it. Neither of them spoke. Then Bennett stirred, rolled over, and opened his eyes, trying to get his bearings. "Son-of-a-bitch," he said as he listened to the rain beating down on the tin hut, "it's raining harder than a double-donged cow pissing off a flat rock."

Chapter
13

After helping to return the rifle range to its original condition the next day, after the storm passed and the sun and humidity returned, Platoon 486 ran all the way back to mainside and to the barracks it was to occupy for the remainder of boot camp. After the recruits settled into the new quarters, Krupe had them out on the grinder, putting them through their paces.

If he had been pleased with their performance at the range, he didn't betray it. Instead, he seemed determined to regain that fine precision edge they had lost during the past three weeks. But after only one day, he had to relinquish them for a week of mess duty.

Reveille for messmen was at 3:30 A.M. and they worked straight through until almost 9:30 at night. They hit the rack at 10:00 P.M. and began all over again five-and-a-half hours later. It was an exhausting week—although since 486 spent an extra day at the range during the hurricane, it drew only six days of mess duty—and it was made all the more trying by cooks and bakers who rode the messmen unendingly, as though to remind them they were still lowly recruits. In return, some messmen on the serving line took out their frustrations on the newer recruits who passed through the chow line, although usually berating them only whenever no one else was around to hear.

Dutton was assigned to the garbage shed behind the rear entrance of the mess hall. Aesthetically, it was unpleasant having to scour dozens of GI cans after emptying their contents into garbage trucks from nearby farms. He also had to help scrub down the back of the mess hall three times a day, police the area,

213

unload meat as well as cases of milk and other provisions, and do whatever else the cooks ordered. But there were compensations, especially the opportunity of being by himself much of the time, rather than under the scrutiny of irascible cooks.

Gabriel, Gillian, and Hosse were nowhere as lucky; Bennett had them assigned to the worst task of all, cleaning pots and pans the entire time. He told the cooks they were foul-balls and troublemakers, and so the cooks were only too glad to berate and occasionally lash out at their new helpers. Theirs was a dirty, grueling, wearisome task.

Dutton looked forward twice each day to talking with the garbage truck driver, a pleasant old rustic from a farm not far outside the nearby town of Pritchardville. Their conversations were never memorable or intellectually stimulating, but the farmer represented the world outside the gate and this made him something special at Parris Island.

One time, after a particularly abusive cook, a corporal, chewed out Dutton for some imaginary infraction, the old man stared at him with obvious disapproval. When the corporal saw the old man looking at him, he tried to make light of his outburst, saying with an apologetic laugh, "Some of these goddamn messmen, they can't do nothin' right unless you holler at 'em."

Without the trace of a smile in return, the old man said sourly, "So it would appear."

When the cook retreated, with a halfhearted command that Dutton shape up, the driver said, "Don't let him get you down none. In a little while this'll all be over."

It couldn't be over soon enough to suit Dutton. His disillusionment—with the system and with everyone in authority except Sanders—had grown with the passage of boot camp, rather than abated. Now he was counting the days, the hours, until he was off the island. He thought of Julie constantly, even as he emptied and cleaned the garbage cans. She wrote at least five times a week, often every day. Her most recent letter said how proud she was that he was nearing the end of boot camp, and how proud his parents were also. She added that Hilda Conway had written, wondering if everything was well. Dutton smiled at Julie's gentle reminder that he hadn't written to Tim's mother, as promised. He was ashamed but had decided he really couldn't bring himself to write to the Conways unless he changed his attitude about boot camp. And any transformation was unlikely until long after he departed Parris Island.

As he worked, he often found himself humming the words to the song that reminded him of Julie:

> "Ev'ry time we say goodbye,
> I die a little.
> Ev'ry time we say goodbye,
> I wonder why a little.
> Why the gods above me,
> Who must be in the know,
> Think so little of me
> They'd allow you to go. . . ."

Innocent Julie, who in her wildest flights of fancy couldn't imagine a place like Parris Island in the summer of 1952: Thank God he had dissuaded her from her visiting.

When he wasn't thinking about her or about graduating from boot camp, Dutton thought often about Tew—how he had tricked him during their boxing bout. Ordinarily he might have been willing to chalk it up to experience, to let it serve as a reminder so that never again would somebody pull a sneak attack on him. But the entire boot camp experience had made him unwilling to turn the other cheek, lest someone smash that one too. Besides, Tew epitomized the bullying and callousness Dutton so detested about boot camp; it was easy for him to picture Tew as the typical brutal DI. So he looked forward to another confrontation with Tew as a chance to atone for not telling the truth when Major Knisely had inquired about maltreatment. He wasn't ashamed of the lie, under the circumstances, since he realized the whole episode had been a charade. But he was certain Sanders hadn't been in on the charade and therefore he felt he had let him down. In any event, Sanders hadn't spoken to him or acknowledged his presence since the incident.

On the next-to-last day of mess duty, Tew, still exploiting every advantage from his quasi-supervisory role as platoon leader, came out the back door of the mess hall after noon chow intent on sneaking a smoke. He strutted into the garbage shack, forgetting Dutton was working there. When he spotted him scouring the Gi cans with a steam hose, Tew started to back out—not out of fear, but because he was in no mood just then to argue. Sensing someone had entered, Dutton looked up. "What do you want?" he demanded.

Angered by Dutton's tone, Tew replied, "What's it to you?"

"You're not Platoon Leader in here, Tew. This is my domain and you're not welcome, so shove off."

Tew was rankled, yet he decided to be conciliatory. "What's ailing you, man? I just came in here for a smoke. I'm not asking for a hard time."

"Tough. That's what you're getting, so get moving."

Tew clenched, then unclenched, his fists. His nostrils flared, virtually flattening out his nose in anger. But he was determined not to be goaded. "You still sore about our boxing match?" He asked it offhandedly, as though it had been only a joke more or less.

"That's right, Tew, that's what I'm mad about. You fouled me, remember?"

"You think you'd have won if I hadn't hit you first? Because if you do, you're kidding yourself, let me clue you."

Walking over to turn off the steam hose, Dutton kept his eyes on Tew. "You're entitled to your opinion," he said grandly, his tone much less hostile. "Maybe so, maybe not. But now we'll never know, will we?"

"I guess not," Tew said, forcing a let-bygones-be-bygones laugh. He was so relieved to have avoided trouble that he hadn't noticed Dutton edging closer while rolling a dripping GI can in his direction. Suddenly a fist came hurtling toward him and he heard a voice say, "Let's find out."

Tew instinctively threw his head to the side in order to minimize the force of the punch. The abrupt reaction knocked him off balance and sent him reeling backward, unable to stop until he slammed against the wall. He heard Dutton laughing, and when he tried to find out where he had been hit and whether he was badly hurt, he realized Dutton hadn't hit him at all; he had pulled his punch just before impact, causing Tew to make a fool of himself.

"Why, you no-good bastard," Tew said between clenched teeth, straightening up and coming toward Dutton, no longer concerned about avoiding a fight. "I'm gonna break your lousy neck."

"Sure you are, Tew," Dutton replied calmly, his fists in a semi-relaxed position near his belt. "I'm waiting."

Then Tew began circling, his eyes blazing with anger. Dutton followed, studying his larger opponent cautiously. For several seconds they stared at each other. Then Tew rushed blindly, bent on knocking Dutton against the wall and pinning him there, where he could thrash him into unconsciousness. But as he moved forward on the slippery wet floor, both hands suddenly flew up and out, his head snapped backward, and he struggled to retain his footing. At that instant Dutton stepped in and smashed his fist into Tew's exposed neck, forcing a horrible gasping sound from the bigger recruit. He was unconscious before he hit the floor, his head smashing against the side of a GI can, then onto the steam hose, which helped cushion the blow.

"What in the fuck do you call this?" demanded an almost hysterical voice. Dutton didn't answer. He just studied Bennett, who was standing in the doorway, an expression of amazement and fury on his face. "Answer me!" Bennet commanded at the top of his voice. "What did you do to him?" His eyes blinked rapidly, fluttering like hummingbirds.

"We had a fight, sir." Dutton's voice was anything but repentant.

"A fight? A fight? Jesus Christ, you've killed this man," Bennett said, advancing toward the inert body of Tew and bending over him.

Dutton kneeled beside the drill instructor, who felt Tew's pulse. Some thirty seconds later, when he was satisfied Tew was alive, Bennett suddenly lashed out sideways with the flat edge of his hand and caught Dutton flush on the nose. He fell backward as blood spurted from his nostrils. Almost instantly two cooks, including the corporal who had given Dutton a bad time earlier, barged into the shack. "What's wrong, Sergeant?" the corporal asked.

Bennett explained as best he could, although he was barely coherent because he was so choked with anger. He strode over to Dutton, who now was standing holding a handkerchief against his nose, and threw a punch at the recruit's face. Dutton ducked and the punch glanced high off the back of his head.

"Did you see that?" Bennett demanded of the cooks. "Did you see him defy me?"

"I wouldn't take that off that salty son-of-a-bitch," said the corporal. "I'll teach him to obey a Noncom." With that he rushed Dutton, smashing him flush in the face and splitting his lower lip.

"Goddamn you," Dutton spat, vaguely aware of what he was letting himself in for but too mad and resentful to care.

"Get that son-of-a-bitch, kill him," Bennett shrieked. He raced toward Dutton as each cook grabbed an arm. Dutton tried to shake them off so he could defend himself from the onrushing Bennett, who was screaming incoherently. He began flailing away with punches at the pinioned recruit, then finally stepped back and aimed a kick at Dutton's groin. It would have landed on target had Dutton not twisted sideways, catching the blow higher than Bennett intended. But the force was still sufficient to double him up, and while he was bent over Bennett brought the heel of his hand down hard on Dutton's neck, sending him crashing to the floor.

When Dutton came to, he was in his rack. His neck pained him agonizingly, and when he swallowed he thought his head was going to explode. He sat up slowly, then gingerly put one leg at a time over the edge of the rack while he tried to reconstruct what had happened.

Before Dutton regained his senses Bennett's voice boomed throughout the empty squad bay from the DI quarters at the far end: "Get up here, Private, before I come down there after you." He rose painfully, but started to topple backward; he had to steady himself against the top rack. Everything began spinning, so he shut his eyes for a moment hoping to steady himself. When he reopened them the vertigo had gone, but he was still in great pain. He walked unsteadily to the DI room, knocked and announced himself, then entered at Bennett's command.

"Sergeant Bennett tells me you picked a fight with Tew, is that right?" Krupe asked. He was seated at his desk, examining Dutton with icy eyes.

"I guess so, sir."

"What do you mean, you guess so? Did you or didn't you?"

"I got even with him for fouling me during the boxing tournament."

"Got even? You're lucky you didn't kill him. What did you hit him with, a baseball bat?"

Dutton's head began throbbing, causing him to wince. "No, sir, with my fist. He was off balance when I hit him so—"

"You believe in fighting dirty, is that it?"

"No, sir."

"You believe in getting even?"

"Yes, sir."

Krupe eyed him with obvious distaste, although Sanders sensed this was because he had interrupted the drill instructor's routine, not because Dutton had avenged himself on Tew. "How do you feel?" Krupe asked finally.

"Sir, I feel lousy. My neck is killing me and I'm sore all over."

"Well, sore or dying, you're going back on duty and you're going to stay with this platoon until it graduates, you understand? Private Tew is in the dispensary, thanks to you, and may be there another couple of days, in which case he'll be dropped from this platoon—set back another week. I'm not about to lose two recruits with only about a week to go . . . am I, private?"

"No, sir." Dutton was even more eager to remain with 486 than Krupe was for him to stay.

"Good. Now get out of my sight. And God help you if you raise your hand to anyone else the rest of the time you're in my platoon, you understand?"

"Yes, sir."

"You better. Now, get."

The recruit turned to leave, ignoring Bennett altogether and wondering why he wasn't being court-martialed or at least beaten up for cursing a superior. When he reached the door Krupe said, "Private, how do you propose getting even with Sergeant Bennett or me?"

"Sir?" Dutton asked, stalling so he could think of a noncommittal reply.

"You said you believe in getting even. So how do you propose to get even with us? You do feel maltreated, don't you?"

Dutton considered the question. Finally he said, "I had my chance, sir. When Major Knisely questioned us."

"And?"

"And . . ." He paused. "I decided to give the answer I thought was expected of me."

"I see," Krupe said, shifting in the chair and squaring his huge shoulders. "And now?"

"Now I plan to take out my grievances on the enemy."

"Good idea, Private. Maybe you have more sense than I've been giving you credit for. Or else you're already good at saying what you think people want to hear. Now, get out of here and don't let me see you again."

*   *   *

Sanders volunteered to stay around DI quarters during the week Platoon 486's recruits were on mess duty. But Krupe said he intended to be there much of the time catching up on paperwork, so he told Sanders to rest up for the last ten days of boot camp after mess duty ended.

Sanders welcomed the chance to spend more time with Susan—to the delight of Amy, who had taken a great liking to "Kwis," as she called him. He had taken a great liking to her also, and spent much of their time together picking her up and swinging her, giving her a ride on one leg crossed over the other, and lavishing affection on her. It didn't surprise him that he was smitten by Amy, for he had always loved children. Much more surprising were his feelings toward Susan, feelings no longer compounded of loneliness, pity, and helpfulness. Whenever he began thinking their relationship went well beyond mere affection, he forced himself to concentrate on other matters. It would have been unfair for her to fall for another Marine officer and run the same risks all over again. And his own future was still a large question mark.

For a long while, or what seemed like a long while, he had worried about Linda, worried that he was somehow being unfaithful. Perhaps he was, by conventional standards. But their relationship had never been conventional, which was the case with many of their friends. It wasn't that they were incapable of love, merely that romantic love wasn't considered as important as family ties, breeding, and good schools. It wasn't so much aloofness as lack of passion.

Therefore, as Susan became a more important part of his life, he began to understand that what he and Linda felt for each other was not passion but a polished mutual respect. She was a "nice girl," refined, well-met and cultivated, not an unsophisticated bone in her body. Their courtship—if their accretion of a lifelong friendship could really be called that—had been eminently respectable, agreeable, even fun. He was proud of the way she dressed and handled herself in social situations. He enjoyed the envious glances of classmates who were infatuated by her delicate good looks. He was comforted by the knowledge that by marrying her, both families would consider themselves fortunate.

The only problem was, he didn't love her. Respect, fondness, pride—all these feelings added up to affection, but none added up to love. He was sure it was the same with her, but the problem was that she might never discover that—at least not while she considered herself bound to Chris. She was loyal by training and breeding, and so she would never allow herself to experience any romance other than that offered by Chris. To her, enduring love meant fidelity and propriety more than it meant passion.

And who could deny her definition of love? Chris mused. After all, romantic love, love built around sexual attraction and passion, hadn't enjoyed that good a batting average—at least to judge from the divorce rate and the available statistics. The ideal arrangement, it seemed to him, was one in which passion existed side by side with fidelity, honor, and all those other virtues Linda and her family held so dear. It was obvious that Susan exemplified fidelity and honor, just as there was no doubting the passion she brought to their relationship. It was a pent-up passion at first, yet even after the initial fury subsided it seemed to derive from some inner amatory reserve. And it was a passion kindled by innocence, for he had been only the second man she had ever known.

Both of them had come close to admitting their feelings for the other, yet neither could do so. Even if it had not been improper for women to confess their love, she would have been restrained by her own upbringing and moral dilemma. A decent girl, a girl who had truly loved her husband, didn't fall in love with the first guy who came along after her husband's death. It was bad enough even to think of another man while her husband's memory was still warm, but it verged on sinfulness to allow thoughts of another man to eclipse the memory of someone as beloved as Dan had been. Susan was increasingly beset by conflict and guilt.

Yet she hadn't sought someone to help her out of her loneliness and melancholy—she would have been offended if anyone other than Sal had even suggested it would be a good idea to do so—and she had turned down without second thought or regret every invitation from customers for a date. She still wasn't sure why she had agreed to go out with Chris, except that he seemed so completely different from everyone else who asked her. Nevertheless, she would have refused even him except that she felt she owed him an explanation for her rudeness. Still, once he drove away after promising to pick her up after work, she immediately regretted saying yes. She would have begged off even then if she had known where to telephone him. Then she toyed for a while with the thought of not showing up at all, but that would only complicate things. Besides, she had agreed to go out with him to atone for being rude, and now to compound her rudeness by standing him up seemed the height of inconsideration. And so she forced herself to meet him as planned, and ever since her life had become infinitely happier but also infinitely more complicated.

She loved him, she was sure of it. In the beginning she was willing to hide the truth from her innermost self, ready to believe she was merely grateful to him for easing her loneliness. Later it became much harder to carry on the pretense, while at the same time it became harder to put off those questions she had tried to submerge entirely: Would Dan approve? Would he understand? Or forgive?

For a while she rationalized her feelings and motives, assuring herself Dan would not have wanted her to go on being lonely forever, nursing a broken heart the rest of her life, or ending up a grieving widow raising a fatherless daughter. Still, she was not the only young woman who had ever lost a husband or boy friend. And her anguish and grief would end one day, would harden into a permanent numbness, whereas his sacrifice was forever. The very thought unlocked another torrent of tears.

Yet her new-found happiness with Chris *had* been accompanied by a lessening of the persistent grief, and even of some of her memories of Dan. She fought against it, even pretended to be busy once when Chris telephoned two nights in succession to ask her out. But her resistance crumbled the third night he phoned. Then she was plagued by guilt from another direction: She told herself she was beginning to like Chris precisely in order to rid herself of the pain associated with memories of Dan.

One night when she couldn't stand the confusion and guilt any longer, she went and talked it over with Mary Rose, Sal's wife. Mary Rose wasn't a worldly or sophisticated woman, any more than Sal himself was worldly or sophisticated, but she had two sterling qualities admired by everyone who knew her: She was absolutely candid whenever anyone asked her advice, and she was absolutely devoted to Sal. In fact, her devotion went beyond love for the man she married and embraced the very institution of marriage and sanctity of the family. So Susan went, knowing her advice might not be what she wanted to hear— knowing Mary Rose was likely to be much more concerned about what was fundamentally right, according to her beliefs and intuition at any rate, than about what was easiest for Susan or for assuaging her guilt.

To her great relief, Mary Rose consoled and assured her. Later she and Sal had a chance to talk with Chris and both of them took to him at once. He seemed so much more mature and serious than most of the young servicemen they saw in their restaurant and in the surrounding communities. Those qualities and his sincerity had been what prompted Sal to give him Susan's address the morning he came knocking on the restaurant door, are what inspired in Sal a confidence based on a lifetime of dealing with the public and having to try to size up everyone from royalty to reprobates.

Mary Rose, as petite as Sal was heavy, was a delicate black-eyed beauty with a radiant smile. She explained to Susan that it was natural to feel guilty under the circumstances, and that some guilt was probably good to act as a brake on any runaway emotions—and to stop her from forgetting the past too quickly. We have to absorb and assimilate the experiences of the past, she said, not merely use them up and cast them aside. And so Susan had to remember the joy and happiness her marriage had brought her and the pain of death. She had no right to deny either one, Mary Rose went on, but neither had she the right to deny herself the opportunity for happiness if it presented itself.

Without a hint of embarrassment or reticence she asked what Chris's intentions and future plans were, and she made no bones about saying she would have liked it better if he had talked marriage. "After all," she said, "you're not only a young widow, you're also a mother." But Susan convinced her that even if marriage had crossed his mind he wouldn't mention it, in order to spare her additional grief, since he was almost certainly bound for Korea after OCS. Besides, she wasn't even sure how deep his feelings for her ran.

"Do you love him?" Mary Rose demanded. After a pause, during which Susan searched for a graceful way to parry the question, she said she probably did. "What's this probably business?" Mary Rose insisted. "You love somebody or you don't, at least you did when I was your age. There's no probably about it." But she didn't press for a stronger declaration after Susan explained that she couldn't allow herself to think in terms implying commitment, not until the war ended or Chris was discharged.

"Will he wait for you?" Mary Rose asked. "And just as important, will you wait for him?"

They had been sitting in Mary Rose and Sal's kitchen, drinking coffee, and suddenly Susan turned and stared out the window. Mary Rose admired her beautiful profile, her small upturned nose that bespoke determination. "I think he'd wait," she replied. "And I know I would. I've grown good at it," she added with just a trace of pity in her voice. She turned back to her friend. "I've learned how to count the weeks and months, wishing away this year and the next. Yes, Mary Rose, I'd wait. But I doubt if he wants it that way. Everything's been so fast, maybe too fast. And he's scared of what it would do to me if he went to Korea and the same thing . . ." Her voice trailed away and she lowered her head; some of the old sadness and anguish crept back.

"But what's the difference," Mary Rose demanded, "if something happened to him and you were married, and something happened and you weren't married but in love—not that anything's going to happen."

"There is a difference, there really is, and that's what he's thinking of. If we were married, it would be like raising up our hopes, mine and Amy's, and then destroying them again. I don't know if I could ever recover from that a second time."

"And if you were just girl friend and boy friend?"

"Then the pain would be as sharp but maybe not as longlasting. I wouldn't seem so much like a marked woman, maybe. And I could always console myself that he was just another guy who passed in and out of my life. Mine and Amy's."

Some of this was beyond Mary Rose, who had been brought up to believe love and marriage were inseparable, not acts to be analyzed and compartmentalized. Nevertheless, she realized that times and attitudes were changing and were likely to keep on changing, and not for the better. Moreover, Susan's explanation maybe made sense—not for her and women of her upbringing and generation, but for younger girls who weren't so bound by tradition. Finally she said, "I have just two questions. First, do he and Amy get along?"

"They love each other. Like father and daughter."

"Okay," she said, as though now she was coming down to basics. "We've discussed all the possibilities and how he feels and what he wants. What do you want? Would you be willing to marry another Marine officer who you knew might be sent to combat?"

At that Susan bit her lip and some of the color drained from her face. Finally she answered, "I had hoped you wouldn't ask. Would I risk it? If I had to go through . . . it . . . another . . . the same thing once more, I don't think I'd have the strength to overcome the pain and heartache again. But would I risk it?" She looked away. Eventually she said, "I guess I'd risk it, yes. I'd risk it because love *means* taking risks. Or because a love that isn't worth taking risks for must be a very weak love." She was talking slowly now, as much to herself as to Mary Rose. "And I'd risk it because I'm not ready yet to be beaten down by fate or circumstance. Oh, sure, I can go home to Indiana—in fact, that's probably what I'm going to do—and hang around hoping he comes back to me when it's all over. But that seems to be a bigger risk even than remarrying."

Mary Rose gave Susan one bit of advice before she left. Let Chris know her feelings. Don't pressure him into anything or play on his sympathies. Just make sure he got the message that she loved him and was willing to marry him, no matter what. Susan promised she would, and after thanking Mary Rose, she left. And she really did try to let Chris know, not by anything direct but in those thousand-and-one unspoken ways lovers communicate their feelings. He seemed to understand, and often in return he expressed his feelings for her by the same tacit methods. He also said he wished circumstances could be different. Eventually he told her that he realized no matter what became of the two of them, it was all over between him and Linda. All that was left was to find an honorable way to break the news to her.

He had wanted time and again to confess the depth of his feeling for Susan, but he too was beset by conflict. He didn't know at first how much of what he felt was really love and how much was sympathy for the young widow with the child. As the days and weeks passed, he realized that sympathy had very little to do with his feelings, or at least those feelings that mattered most. What did matter was Susan herself—not only her charm and good looks, but also her courage and pride and honor. Some of his friends and their parents—Linda's parents, for example— would be apt to turn up their noses at her. Oh, they would have admired her working to support her fatherless child, since they professed to admire the work ethic, but they infinitely preferred some kinds of work to others. Working as a waitress was certainly more admirable than allowing her parents or in-laws to support her, but the job required no special intelligence or ability. Besides, while she was pretty and personable, it would not be overlooked that she had never attended, much less graduated from, college. Therefore, for all her personal charm and independence, she would be out of place among most of his friends.

Yet none of this bothered Chris very much. His friends ultimately were likely to accept anyone he liked, and his parents were fundamentally decent people whom Susan could easily win over. What annoyed him was that he had been guilty of similarly pigeonholing her on the basis of her occupation when they first met. He was not that way ordinarily, in fact not ever before, that he could remember, and certainly would never be again. Each time they were together he appreciated her all the more. He wanted to take her in his arms and propose to her. But there was still Korea—a risk he did not intend to subject her to a second time.

And there was one other thing, stemming from his problems with Krupe and Knisely. They had had an unsettling effect on him, making him less sure of himself in many things. Less than two months before he had believed with Orwell that there was truth and there was untruth, and if you clung to the truth against even the whole world you were not mad. Now he was less certain about that elusive concept, truth. If it existed at all, maybe it did reside on the side of Krupe and those who had the courage of their convictions. Maybe the meek and the uncertain were destined to end up—not inheriting the earth, but begging for mercy in some prisoner-of-war camp in North Korea. Maybe it was better after all to reign in Hell than serve in Heaven.

Nevertheless, the romance grew in intensity and feeling. His happiest moments were those times he was with her, each time he saw her anew after driving over from Parris Island, and she came out of her trailer and greeted him with a hug and kiss. The moments they spent together were the fondest he could ever remember, and the six days Platoon 486 was on mess duty were among the most memorable—days of swimming at Hilton Head, horseback riding and hiking, nights of love and unrestrained passion.

Their joy must have shone in their faces. One night when they were to retrieve a sleeping Amy from Mrs. Bletz's trailer, she gave them a detailed report of the child's activities and then, after they talked a while longer, said finally, "I hope you both will forgive me for saying so, but I can't ever remember seeing a couple so much in love."

They both laughed, although not without blushing, and assured her they didn't mind her saying it. And just before they went to sleep that night Chris asked, "Do you think Mrs. Bletz is right—are our feelings really so obvious?" Snuggled against him beneath the sheet, Susan said she hadn't thought it showed. Long after she fell asleep in his arms, Chris lay awake trying to sort out his thoughts and feelings.

Chapter 14

When Sergeant Pepper ran into Bennett the week both platoons were on mess duty, he reminded him the boxing smoker was to be held the final week of boot camp. When Bennett relayed the news, Krupe seemed annoyed. This meant disruption of his tight schedule, yet there was really no graceful way out. Finally he told Bennett to have Pepper schedule the bouts for any night that suited him, give them twenty-four hours' notice, and 486 would be there.

After making sure Major Knisely and some lesser brass would be in attendance, Pepper selected the following Monday evening, at seven-thirty. He personally invited DIs from several other Battalion platoons to bring their recruits to watch, and several agreed to do so. Krupe thought about ordering Dutton to represent 486 in the heavyweight division, in place of Tew, who just that very day had been released from the infirmary and reassigned to another platoon. But he finally abandoned the idea when Sanders convinced him Dutton's neck injury was real and they shouldn't risk losing yet another recruit. Instead, Krupe settled on Leslie Potter, a stocky but awkward recruit who had lost easily to Tew in the interplatoon preliminaries and didn't figure to be much of a match for a good boxer.

Krupe and Pepper agreed on six bouts, a maximum of three three-minute rounds each, the winner to be decided by a referee and timekeeper appointed by Major Knisely. By the time Platoon 486 arrived at ringside, after a thorough drill en route, several recruit platoons were already ensconced in the makeshift chairs and bleachers. A handful of officers and their wives occupied seats in the center section, close to ringside.

"I was beginning to think you weren't going to show," Pepper hollered the moment he spotted Krupe. Ignoring him, the DI ordered his boxers to fall out and the other recruits to file noiselessly into the bleachers. Platoon 484's entrants, stripped to their blue bathing trunks and T-shirts, were already shadow-boxing to warm up. Platoon 486's contestants quickly stripped to their trunks and likewise began shadowboxing, skipping imaginary rope, and hopping up and down nervously.

The referee, a DI from the Second Battalion, explained that the boxers were to fight fair, were to obey his instructions immediately, were not to hit on the break, and that there was to be no "fancy Danning or showboating—get in there and mix it up from the opening bell." With that Krupe and Pepper returned to their respective corners to deliver final instructions to the boxers. In Krupe's case, this amounted to telling them to carry the fight to their opponents, rather than sitting back waiting for the opponents to come to them.

In the first bout, the recruit from Platoon 484 overwhelmed his outclassed opponent, knocking him down twice in the second round before the referee stopped it.

In the second fight, Robert Begay knocked down his taller opponent three times before the referee halted it.

Herb Beeks gave 486 a one-fight advantage when he thrashed his opponent, chasing him around the ring for three rounds, battering him almost at will whenever he caught up with him.

The best fight of the evening involved Gillian and an opponent who, in aggressiveness and toughness, resembled Beeks. He was easily the most experienced fighter in either platoon, always pursuing, willing to trade two punches for the opportunity of landing one solid one. Gillian fought gamely, bouncing back up after being floored by a solid overhand right to the chin and later by a left hook to the jaw. Although outgunned, he slugged it out toe-to-toe rather than backpedal in hopes of keeping out of range. Yet even while he was being bloodied because of his refusal to give ground, suffering a split lip and a deep cut over the left eye, Bennett threatened and derided him, keeping up a steady stream of ridicule and invective.

Midway in the second round, when Gillian was knocked down the second time, some recruits in Pepper's platoon—taking their lead from Bennett—began yelling, "Get up, Janie," or "Come on, girl, friend, it was only a love tap." Walking to his corner at the end of the round, Gillian heard the scattered catcalls and taunts and recognized Bennett's voice prominent among the chorus of hecklers. But the jeers couldn't cover up the fact that Gillian had courage to spare. From the second the bell signaled the start of the final round, Gillian traded one punch after another with his more skillful opponent, flailing away and refusing to budge. Twice they hammered each other repeatedly, and both times it was Gillian's opponent who finally gave ground when he was too weary to throw another punch. He had landed the stronger punches, but took a number of solid shots, and he knew he had been in an unforgettable brawl.

When the bell finally ended the fight, Knisely led the other officers and some exuberant recruits in standing to cheer and applaud. Sanders was so overwhelmed by Gillian's gritty performance that he hurried to his corner and, in full view of Bennett and everyone else, threw his arm around the recruit's shoulder in tribute. Even Krupe looked well-pleased. Gillian smiled appreciatively, pressing a towel against his face to stop the bleeding. When the decision was announced, Gillian's victorious opponent walked across the ring to congratulate him, saying it had been far and away his toughest fight ever.

Bothered by the sudden adulation for Gillian, Bennett started clambering through the ropes, cursing and threatening as he came. Gillian's opponent spotted the advancing DI and wisely lit out across the ring, where Pepper berated him for fraternizing with the enemy. When Bennett saw Sanders sidle up alongside Gillian, he simmered down immediately. Feeling foolishly conspicuous standing in the ring, he said impatiently, "Let's get started—let's get these bouts over with."

The final two bouts were dull, especially by comparison with the previous slugging match. But Leslie Potter lost on a technical knockout when the referee wisely halted the fight to prevent him from being cut up worse by his opponent, an unspectacular fighter whom Sanders was certain would have presented little difficulty for Tew or Dutton. And Paul Thorn won a sluggish split decision.

The instant the bell ended the final round, Pepper, without waiting to congratulate his or 486's fighters, bounded over to where the Kniselys were sitting, and huddled with the major. Sanders saw them look toward Krupe several times, but he couldn't make out what was being said. Finally Knisely said, "Sergeant Krupe, will you come here a minute?"

Krupe knew from the look on Pepper's face that something was up. The major said, "Sergeant Pepper has an idea to resolve this three-three tie, and I'm inclined to go along with it. He suggested a final bout between him and you."

Krupe looked puzzled. "Here? Now?"

"Yea, Krupe," Pepper said with a smirk. "Here and now."

"Look, Major," Krupe said, calm and composed. "I'll gladly accommodate Pepper right now if that's what you want. But I think I should remind you that fights between Drill Instructors could have harmful consequences on the recruits in the platoon of the losing DI."

"That's your problem," Pepper cut in. "Besides, you're not worried about the effect on the recruits. You're worried about your ass. Oh, excuse me, Mrs. Knisely," he said, turning toward the timid middle-aged woman who had not said a word all evening. Turning back to Krupe he said, "You're worried about yourself."

Without changing his expression or calm outward demeanor, the tech sergeant said to Knisely, "Major, all I need is your permission and you've got yourself a fight."

Ordinarily Knisely would never have consented, for Krupe was right—It was bad policy to allow impressionable recruits to see their superiors compromised or embarrassed. But the evening was still early. And, more to the point, he was piqued with Krupe. Okay, so he was the best drill instructor in his command— probably the best on the entire island, if not in the entire Corps—but Krupe had caused him trouble. First Duvail ran away. Then there was the regrettable incident with Sanders. Then Private Tew had to be set back so near to the end of boot camp. Maybe, he thought, it would be good for Krupe to lose a fight. What's more, it might be good for the future of the Corps to drum a little humility into him. And if he won, why, Pepper could use a lesson in humility also. "Proceed," he said finally. "And may the best man win."

When the referee announced that Sergeant Pepper and Tech Sergeant Krupe had agreed to fight five three-minute rounds in order to break the deadlock, those officers and NCOs who had started to leave quickly returned to their places. As a murmur swept across the audience, Sanders wondered how Krupe had ever allowed himself to take part in an event, a virtual stunt, that could undermine his leadership. But he didn't have long to think about it, for soon both drill instructors stripped to the waist and removed their shoes and socks. When they met in center ring to receive the referee's instructions, Sanders was surprised to see that Pepper was noticeably taller and broader than Krupe. Moreover, without his eyeglasses, Krupe seemed somehow less awesome.

Pepper wore a contemptuous smile, almost a sneer, during the referee's brief instructions. Krupe was impassive, seemingly absorbed in thought. Shortly after they returned to their respective corners, the bell rang. They approached center ring and touched gloves. Pepper connected first, a stinging right high on Krupe's left ear. He missed with a left hook, took a straight left to the ribs, and connected with an overhand left.

Several times Pepper started to charge behind a barrage of lefts and rights, but each time Krupe slowed his attack by slipping the punches and countering with straight left jabs to Pepper's head and face. One straight left caused blood to trickle from his right nostril, but it was more annoying than serious.

Halfway through the round, just after the jab on the nose, Pepper decided to take greater advantage of his size. He started forward again, missed a straight right to Krupe's kidney, then, after shooting out a left to the body, he aimed a hard left hook to the face. But the instant he fired the punch his head was snapped back from another straight left, causing his own punch to fall far short. Annoyed, Pepper wondered whether Krupe had set him up for the punch or whether he had just guessed right or taken advantage of a lucky opening.

When, seconds later, Krupe beat him to the punch with another straight left some of Pepper's confidence began to desert him. He had known of Krupe's reputation as a brawler, but he hadn't imagined Krupe was anything special in the boxing ring, as he himself had been. That's why he had set him up, scheduling six bouts and making sure his recruit lost the final bout so the two platoons would end up in a standoff. Now, though, it— At that moment a hard right-cross stung him on the mouth, another right slammed into his ribs and knocked some of the wind out of him. Having slowed Pepper's charge, Krupe determined to nullify Pepper's height and weight advantage by beating him to the punch.

At the beginning of round two Pepper hurried across the ring and threw a left-right combination, Krupe blocked both

punches and jabbed Pepper twice in the face and once in the ribs.
When Pepper felt the blood trickling down his nostril again he
cursed Krupe and moved toward him angrily. Just as he fired a
wild right that Krupe caught high on his glove, a powerful right
uppercut smashed Pepper flush on the chin and almost lifted him
off the canvas. Had it been two inches shorter it would have
knocked him flat, instead of propelling him backward into the
ropes.

Thoroughly shaken by now, the cockiness completely gone,
Pepper began yielding ground grudgingly. Until then Krupe had
remained well out of range, content to counterpunch and wear
down his opponent. But once he noticed that Pepper was no
longer pressing the attack, Krupe began to stalk his quarry.

After he had methodically worked Pepper into a corner and
hit him hard with several combinations, Krupe unloaded a
wicked right that drove Pepper's own glove back into his face
when he raised it to block the punch. Then Krupe backed off.

When Krupe cornered him and backed off several times
more, a puzzled Pepper realized he had badly underestimated
Krupe's boxing skills. Nevertheless, he still felt he could win if
he used his height-and-weight advantage. His best hope, he
concluded, lay in standing in midring and slugging it out, if need
be, rather than keep backtracking into a corner.

In the third round Krupe again tried to move Pepper out of
center ring by jabbing and hooking, yet Pepper stood his ground,
circling but refusing to back up. Suddenly he exploded a right
hand over Krupe's heart and moved in with a barrage of
punches, any of which could have ended the fight. But Krupe
managed to slip some and block others, then he tied up Pepper in
a clinch.

At the break, Pepper unloaded a hard left hook that caught
Krupe flush on the jaw and knocked him to one knee. Before the
ref could warn Pepper against committing another foul, the
sergeant moved in and threw a short, powerful uppercut just as
Krupe was rising. It would have torn the tech sergeant's head off
had it landed squarely, but Krupe managed to absorb much of its
impact with his upraised glove. Nevertheless, the force knocked
him flat on the canvas. Boos rained down on Pepper, but he did
not hear them, so intently was he watching Krupe struggling to
get up. He scented victory, and he was eager to get it.

Krupe knelt on one knee at the count of four and finally
stood at the count of eight. Even before the ref finished wiping

his gloves, Pepper closed for the kill. But a that moment a broad smile—the first hint of emotion he had displayed all night—creased Krupe's face. Confused, Pepper hesitated. Then he charged again, landed a left to Krupe's ribs, and missed with a wild right before Krupe tied him up again. This time, at the break, Krupe shoved Pepper out of range, as the bell signaled the end of the round.

Krupe spurned Sanders' offer of water, but he accepted a towel to press against his cut and swollen nose. By the time the ten-second warning was announced, the flow had almost stopped.

Determined to pick up where he had left off, Pepper fired a left. Krupe ducked under, blocked another left, just missed with a right-cross to Pepper's face, then doubled him over with a hard left jab to the stomach. A left to the face straightened him up, then Krupe floored him with a right-cross.

Pepper was up at four but Krupe moved straight in on him, pounding away with left-right combinations, jabs and hooks, solo punches and combinations. Pepper went down again. This time he took a nine count, trying to clear his head. He was still dazed and floundering when action resumed, yet Krupe stayed at long range, jabbing him repeatedly, snapping his head back twice and keeping him disoriented.

At the start of the final round, Krupe picked up where he had left off, jabbing at the bleeding Pepper almost at will. But with about a minute to go Pepper stuck out two straight lefts, ducked under a return jab, then rushed Krupe and clinched with him, banging Krupe's ribs and punching the back of his muscular neck with his free hand. Before the referee could step between them, Pepper crashed a knee up into Krupe's groin; the tech sergeant crashed in a loud heap and writhed on the floor.

Even some recruits from Platoon 484, temporarily forgetting the risks of retribution, joined in the chorus of boos that issued from the shocked spectators. Then quieted down only after one of Pepper's assistants grabbed a recruit by the throat and began choking him. Meanwhile, Sanders vaulted into the ring and berated the confused referee, forcing him to stop counting.

Krupe struggled to one knee but did not seem to know what was happening. For several minutes everything was bedlam, during which several officers stood and yelled through cupped hands, "Foul! Foul!" keeping it up until Knisely finally climbed into the ring and signaled for silence. Pepper, meanwhile, nervously paced the far ring, eager to resume the attack.

When things eventually quieted down, Knisely announced: "It appears that was an unintentional foul—" At that Sanders and Bennett, joined by several officers and their wives, jeered and protested, while recruits from most of the platoons booed and hooted surreptitiously. Knisely waited patiently for the noise to subside. "It appears as though there was an unintentional foul," he repeated, again to an accompaniment of jeers and laughter. Casting a malevolent look at Pepper, he continued. "In which case, the only fair solution is to declare a draw and give each platoon three victories and a tie." The announcement sparked another loud, derisive outburst.

Sanders had been standing against the ropes inside the ring, and now he walked over to Knisely. "I beg your pardon, sir," he said above the noise, "but you're rewarding Pepper for fouling an opponent. You—"

Knisely was livid; his face became so contorted with rage that he sputtered when he tried to reply. Yet Sanders never flinched, and he was prepared to argue his point further. But someone interrupted: "The fight's not over yet, Major. We still have more than a minute left."

Knisely turned to face Krupe, who had struggled unsteadily to his feet. "But there's no more time left after tonight," Knisely protested. "Our job is to train recruits, not put on another Roman Circus."

"I'm talking about tonight. Now."

"You're out of your mind. You can't fight any more tonight. Hell's bells, man, you've just been kneed in the—in the jewels. I won't hear of it."

As Knisely started to turn away, Krupe laid his glove firmly on the officer's arm. "Major, I have another minute on that clock and I damn well want it. Every second."

Sanders was surprised at the sharp tone Krupe adopted toward a superior officer.

"I'm trying to tell you, you're in no—"

"And I'm trying to tell *you* I only need a ten-minute rest."

Knisely wished he had never listened to Pepper, or to Krupe now. He'd be goddamn glad when this was all over. Finally he sighed, "Very well, Krupe, it's your funeral."

When he announced that round five would be fought from

the beginning, after a fifteen-minute intermission, the crowd buzzed with surprise, then cheered. When Pepper started across the ring to say something, Knisely spun on his heel and climbed through the ropes.

"How you feeling?" Sanders asked as Krupe crouched in the corner, wincing with each deep breath. "Are you going to make it?"

Krupe looked at him through glazed eyes. Finally he said, "I'll be okay—as long as Pepper doesn't turn any rats loose to eat through my face."

As Sanders wondered what to make of the reply, a gleam came into Krupe's eyes and the trace of a smile played at the corners of his mouth. Sanders knew then that Krupe would be okay.

At the bell Pepper began circling warily, as though trying to determine what condition Krupe was in. He flicked out two harmless left jabs, faked a left, then landed a solid right hand to Krupe's ribs. When Krupe just kept circling, Pepper threw two quick left jabs, followed by a quick overhand right. But the moment he dipped his left elbow ever so slightly, about to launch a left hook to Krupe's jaw, from out of nowhere something smashed against the side of his face and knocked him to one knee. Pepper bounced right up, though, even before Krupe could go to a neutral corner, and he started after the tech sergeant without waiting for the referee to wipe his gloves.

Pepper fired a wild left over Krupe's head, and an aimless right grazed Krupe's arm. But before Pepper could step back out of range, Krupe turned and bombarded him with a left to the face, a hard right into his ribs, and a left uppercut to the stomach. As Pepper's head drooped, Krupe smashed it with a powerful right, sending him sprawling.

Pepper was up at nine, cut and bleeding profusely. He tried to back-pedal but Krupe caught him and battered him repeatedly. Yet each time it looked as though the next punch would end it, Krupe backed away. Then, a few seconds later, he resumed the onslaught.

When Knisely realized that Krupe was systematically chopping up Pepper, he hollered to the referee to stop the bout. But the battered Pepper heard the command and warned the referee through swollen lips that he damn well better not stop it. By the time Krupe hit him several more times, Pepper had cuts over both eyes, his nose was bleeding, and his defense nonexistent. When the ref still didn't stop the fight, Krupe backed off and turned to walk toward his corner.

As he did, Pepper, humiliated and hurt, charged after him and caught Krupe in the back of the neck with the best righthand punch he could muster. Krupe angrily whirled and angrily shoved him away. But when Pepper came at him again, Krupe split his bottom lip with a left jab. Then he flattened him with a short right on the chin.

This time Pepper lay stretched out on the canvas, unable to move. The audience, by then swollen by passers-by and visitors to the nearby Hostess House, erupted in cheers and applause.

*   *   *

That night Bennett again made Gillian walk fire watch. After berating the boot for losing his fight he decided he'd go "tie one on" to celebrate Krupe's—and by extension, 486's—great victory. Sanders had mixed feelings about Krupe's triumph. He wanted him to whip Pepper, all right, because he saw in Pepper the very cruel traits he disliked in Krupe, but he knew Pepper was nowhere near the leader Krupe was. On the other hand, he had been hoping Krupe would receive some kind of comeuppance, although preferably at the hands of someone who shared his own disgust over maltreatment.

When Krupe greeted Sanders and a hung-over Bennett the next morning, he made no reference to the night before, and the only telltale sign was an ugly red welt over his left eye. Finally Sanders said, "Nice going last night."

"Thanks," Krupe said. Then he added, "I would have thought you'd be disappointed by the outcome."

"Not against Pepper. Against a lot of others, maybe, but not Pepper."

"Pepper," Krupe scoffed. "Now maybe he'll tone down that big mouth of his, at least while I'm around. I suppose everybody who ever hears his version of the fight will think I fouled him, or had the ref slug him when he wasn't looking."

Bennett poured three cups of coffee, then groaned as he slumped into a chair.

"You made it look easy. Was it?"

"Well, Pepper's strong. If he had connected on some of those shots he could have done a lot of damage. So I wasn't taking him for granted."

"Where'd you learn to box?"

"In college," he said, sitting and unfolding the Charleston newspaper. "I wasn't anything special—unless you consider being heavyweight champion of my college a big deal, which it wasn't. There were a lot of college heavyweights that year who could whip me . . . in the ring, anyhow."

"And out of the ring?"

"I don't know," he said, turning the question over in his mind. "I learned a long time ago never to concede victory before the fight starts—on the street or in battle."

"Why in hell didn't you knock Pepper on his ass when you had him staggered?" Bennett mumbled. "Looked like you could have cold-cocked him whenever you wanted."

Krupe leaned back and gripped his *cocomacaque*. "I'll tell you why: Because of those recruits in his platoon—kids who should feel that their Drill Instructor is the toughest, meanest Marine in the entire Corps. I wasn't about to let Pepper win, but I couldn't let him be humiliated either."

"Why? He was always bad-mouthing you," Sanders said. "He didn't care if he humiliated you."

"That's because Pepper doesn't have better sense. For instance, he berates his recruits to make himself feel important."

"And you?"

Krupe seemed annoyed at the question. "I berated them because that's the way to teach them to survive in combat," he said wearily. "If I humiliated Pepper I would have been humiliating the Marine Corps in the eyes of his recruits. This way, okay he lost—there had to be a loser. But at least he went down fighting."

"He kept his honor clean?" Sanders asked sarcastically, parodying the Marines' Hymn.

"Exactly."

"Even when he fouled you?"

"That *was* overdoing it some, wasn't it? The trouble with Pepper is that he doesn't know how to pick his spots. That's why he's being transferred after graduation," he said triumphantly.

Almost in the same breath Bennett and Sanders demanded to know how Krupe knew, but he just smiled. "Take my word for it," he said. "His days as a DI are over."

"You seem plenty pleased," Sanders said.

"I am. That man shouldn't be instructing recruits," he said, twisting the club in his massive hands. "He's a liability to the Corps."

"Damn," Bennett said, adding still more sugar to his coffee, "you sound almost glad he fouled you."

"I wasn't sure he'd take the bait," Krupe said slyly, "but I should have known he didn't have better sense."

"What do you mean, take the bait?" Sanders asked suspiciously.

"The idea about kneeing me, of course."

"You mean—"

"Exactly," Krupe said with a satisfied air. "Twice in the clinches I warned him not to knee me."

"—knowing he'd do exactly that," said a gleeful Bennett.

"I was pretty sure he would, once he was convinced he was going to lose. The hard part was making sure the match between the platoons ended up in a tie."

"Because you knew what solution Pepper would propose to break the tie?" Sanders asked.

Krupe grinned. "It was close. I figured Potter would lose but I wasn't sure how to figure Gillian or Thorn. If they had both lost I'd have been out of luck."

"Or if they had both won," Bennett said.

"Not a chance. Even if I had to order Thorn not to throw a single punch."

"You'd have done that?"

"Let's just say the bouts went according to my script— mine and Pepper's, because I'm pretty sure he would have done everything he needed to do to assure that three-three tie. The only thing that didn't go according to his script was the final bout," he said with a look of satisfaction. "Now, how about the two of you marching the platoon to chow?"

* * *

Gabriel was stunned when Krupe said he was being set back, that he would be transferred on Sunday to a platoon in Second Battalion about to begin its second week of training. Dutton was sympathetic, but deep down he knew Gabriel had failed to measure up. Maybe if boot camp had been different . . . perhaps it the threats and intimidation had been removed . . . maybe in another eight weeks . . . But he also understood why Gabriel felt crushed by the news; why, instead of considering the move correctional, he regarded it as further evidence of his failure.

Dutton was even more upset than he might otherwise have

been, because during their last week on the rifle range he had received a letter from Gabriel's mother. It was ostensibly a thank-you note for helping Jonathan as much as Jonathan had indicated in his letters to her. But as he read further he realized the letter was also a plea for him to continue watching over her son. She hinted at some of the things Gabriel had himself admitted—including the fact that, as the mother put it, "he seemed to have trouble excelling in athletics." The letter was a touching blend of pride that her son would soon graduate as a Marine and fear that he still might fail during the remaining days of boot camp. In any event, Lorraine Gabriel concluded, she was grateful to Dutton for everything, she knew he would not mention the letter to Jonathan.

Gabriel told Dutton on Saturday night about Krupe's decision. Through tear-swollen eyes he said he wouldn't have bothered mentioning it at all—he would simply have departed without telling anyone—if it wasn't that he had to have everything packed by noon the next day in preparation for his transfer. Dutton tried to cheer him, but none of the usual words or phrases seemed appropriate. That night, while Dutton was shining his shoes before lights out, Gabriel finally broke down altogether. Tearfully he repeated the history of his failure, asking over and over, "What can I do? What can I do?"

"Do the best you can, Jack," Dutton comforted him, not knowing what else to say. "Give it all you've got. You can make it. Those extra eight weeks count toward your enlistment, the same as if you were at Lejeune, or Pendleton, or in Korea. So take them as they come and you'll be all right."

"They'll kill me," Gabriel said. "I'll never get off this island alive." Before, he had been crestfallen, but now he looked scared.

"That's silly," Dutton said reassuringly. "It won't be anywhere near as tough as the time you've already put in with Krupe."

"That's easy for you to say, especially when you'll be gone from here this week." His voice was suddenly angry and accusatory.

"I'm sorry," Dutton replied. "I really am. I tried my best to help."

"Sure, sure," Gabriel sobbed. "You tried, Krupe tried, Bennett tried."

"Wait a minute," Dutton said, taking offense. "Why are you comparing me with them? I *did* try, you know that."

"Then why am I being sent back?" he demanded.

Ordinarily, Dutton would have tried to explain, tried to reassure his frightened and confused friend. But he too had been feeling the mounting pressures of the final days of boot camp, as well as guilt for not keeping his promise to Hilda Conway. So without stopping to think he snapped: "Goddamn it, Gabriel, how do I know why you're being set back? I guess because you're a screw-up, so why cry about it to me? I have enough damn troubles of my own. You shouldn't have joined the Marines if you're going to act like a baby."

Even before all the words were out, Dutton realized he had made a mistake, even though there was truth in what he said. Mistake or not, however, at that moment he could not bring himself to do much more than apologize halfheartedly.

But it's unlikely Gabriel even heard Dutton's apology. He merely listened to the words of censure, then slumped against his rack, still seated atop the locker box. Surprisingly, he stopped sobbing almost immediately. Then, without a word, he rose and began packing his clothes and toilet articles in preparation for the next day's transfer. It was as though Dutton's words had restored him to his senses.

After lights were out, Dutton leaned down from his rack to apologize once again. But Gabriel didn't reply; instead, he continued staring into space. Dutton decided to try again in the morning. But Gabriel was already at the head cleaning up when Dutton dragged himself from the sack—Sunday being the one morning he didn't hop out of his bed the second the lights flashed on, since it was the one day a momentary laggardness didn't invite being overturned onto the deck by Bennett or Krupe. So there was no opportunity early that morning for Dutton to apologize. And later, before the Catholic recruits returned from mass, Gabriel had already moved his seabag, rifle, and foot locker toward the front of the Quonset hut, in preparation for his transfer.

By then everyone knew about Gabriel's misfortune, and although several recruits expressed regrets, most were indifferent, others thought it was the right decision, and all were glad it wasn't they who had to go through boot-camp hell again. By the time the recruits returned from mass, Gabriel had gone. Dutton felt remorseful, and resolved to write him a letter that night apologizing for his thoughtlessness and promising to keep in touch.

Even after he heard the blast, Dutton didn't pay any attention. Then he heard hollering outside and saw people running past the Quonset hut in the direction of the head. "Gabriel." He didn't know what made him say it, nor did he know what the blast signified, but his intuition told him it had something to do with Gabriel. He dashed quickly toward the front door and started outside. Someone—he thought it was Krupe—said something about getting a doctor, and a moment later Bennett ran past, headed toward the DI hut and, Dutton guessed, on his way to telephone for help. "Get in those huts, you sons-of-bitches," he hollered at recruits who crowded the doorways. "Get inside, get in," he raged.

Sanders and Krupe had been reading the morning newspapers when they heard the shot. Bennett was still in the sack, trying to sleep off the effects of being out late the night before. Krupe didn't ordinarily come in on Sundays until midmorning, but this last Sunday of boot camp he wanted to put the platoon through additional drill in preparation for the final inspection. When he heard the shot, Krupe sprang up and bolted directly toward the head, with Sanders in close pursuit. When the corporal arrived, Krupe was bent over Gabriel, who was sprawled out grotesquely on the shower floor, his rifle stretched beside him. Sanders almost threw up when he saw the blood pulsating from a gaping hole near the recruit's heart. It wasn't until Krupe roared for Bennett to get help that Sanders noticed Gabriel was still alive.

Moving silently and swiftly, without a wasted motion, Krupe unloosened Gabriel's belt and trousers and applied pressure to his body in an effort to slow the bleeding. But it continued to flow, most of it coming from beneath him. Sanders took this to mean the recruit's back had been blown away.

Gabriel's eyes opened and he smiled wanly as though in recognition. For a few seconds he lay there staring, moving his lips. Then, with great effort, he said: "I . . . guess I . . . won't have to . . . to . . . sleep with my . . . rifle . . . tonight for dropping it. . . ." He smiled again, then his eyes closed.

Krupe felt his pulse. "How is he?" Sanders asked.

"Dying," Krupe said solemnly, his voice almost a whisper.

Then he said, "Order two recruits to stand guard outside the doors and keep everybody out. I'll stay here until Bennett gets back, then I'll hunt up the duty officer and make a report."

Sanders stepped outside and hollered, "Two recruits, get down on the double." Dutton had been pressed against the door trying to see what was happening and took off running, sprinting past two slower recruits from the closer Quonset hut. "Private Dutton reporting as ordered, sir."

"Get back to your hut and get your duty belt," Sanders said, "then go stand outside the back door and don't let any recruits inside." After posting another recruit outside the front door, Sanders went back inside the head to await Bennett's arrival. Krupe, meanwhile, had covered the recruit with his shirt, and was still applying pressure to Gabriel's chest. The only sound was that of labored breathing coming at infrequent intervals. The recruit's right shoe and sock were off, indicating that he had probably bent over the rifle muzzle and gripped the trigger with the big toe.

When he couldn't look any longer at the dying recruit, Sanders stormed outside. When he saw Dutton again his pent-up emotions suddenly exploded. "You bastard," he hollered, walking over to him. "You're no better than any of the others." Before Dutton could reply, Sanders smacked him hard against the side of the face with his open hand. "You're worse than they are because you know better." Then he swung again, only this time Dutton backed away, causing the blow to whiz by harmlessly.

"What's all this for . . . sir?" he demanded.

Sanders grabbed him by the neck with both hands and shook him vigorously. "That's your friend Private Gabriel in on the floor there, with life oozing out of him. He's dying, Dutton, dying, you hear? And you helped kill him." Dutton looked at him and swallowed several times, remembering his hostile treatment of Gabriel the night before, but he did not reply. "Why didn't you speak up when Knisely questioned you? Huh? Why didn't you? You had your chance then, and you didn't do it. Now Gabriel's dying." As he released Dutton he punched him in the stomach, doubling the recruit over. Dutton gasped for breath, but still he didn't say a word. When he finally stood upright, his eyes blazed with anger at this unexpected betrayal. Yet at the same time he almost hoped Sanders would stomp him—not for not participating in the stacked deck involving Knisely, but for losing his own temper with Gabriel when he needed encouragement.

Suddenly, however, the anger drained from Sanders' face and was immediately replaced by remorse. "My God, what the hell am I doing? What the hell am I doing. . . ." He dropped his hands to his side. "I'm sorry, Dutton, I really am," he said. "Hell, it wasn't you. It's me, and I'm just taking it out on you."

"Forget it," Dutton said, dabbing at the trickle of blood that had formed in the corner of his mouth. "We're all to blame—me, Krupe, Bennett."

"And me. Gabriel's a victim of us all . . . a victim to a way of life." He shook his head in sorrow. "I really am sorry, Dutton."

"No problem, sir," Dutton said, pressing a handkerchief to his lip. Then he added, "You really want to know why I didn't tell the Major about what goes on here?"

"It's not necessary to explain."

"I'd like you to know, sir."

Sanders studied the recruit. "Okay."

"Because I didn't believe it would do any good. Because I didn't believe he was interested in the truth, or justice. He was looking to see who the troublemakers were. Am I right?"

Sanders shrugged. "I'm not sure. I think Knisely really hoped there wasn't any brutality, or if there was, he didn't want to be told about it. If learning about it was unavoidable, my guess is he would have done something to prevent a recurrence. But you couldn't have known that, so of course you were wary."

"You mean if I had told the truth, Gabriel might not be stretched out in there right now?"

Sanders shook his head vigorously. "What happened in there has nothing to do with you and Major Knisely. I hope it doesn't have anything to do with me. Hell, I don't know—maybe it doesn't have anything to do with Krupe and Bennett." When the recruit wrinkled his brow, Sanders added: "Maybe I'm rationalizing, and God knows I feel sick about Gabriel bleeding to death on the deck in there. But did he really have what it takes to be a Marine? Maybe Krupe was right about him after all. I mean, would a stable guy shoot himself just because he was being set back?" When Dutton didn't reply, Sanders said, "Answer me honestly—did Gabriel deserve to graduate?"

For a moment Dutton looked away, as though in the thought. Finally he said, "I'm not sure. But he didn't deserve to die."

"Of course he didn't. But from the standpoint of an infantryman who might have had to fight alongside Gabriel, did he have what it takes?"

A lump formed in Dutton's throat. He had liked Gabriel, notwithstanding his impatience with him the day before. He badly wanted him to graduate with 486, for Gabriel's own sake and for his mother's. But did he have what it takes? Dutton just stared at Sanders, unable to reply.

"I guess that's as good as an answer," the drill instructor said softly. With that he opened the door and walked back inside the head, and in a moment the ambulance drove up.

Krupe directed the removal of the unconscious Gabriel as several MPs and officers crowded around asking questions. Soon Major Knisely arrived, and, after being told what happened, expressed the common opinion that Gabriel must have smuggled the bullet from the rifle range. He paced nervously back and forth, muttering what a tragic thing Gabriel had done, his expressions wavering between sympathy and worry about the likelihood of unfavorable publicity.

Even before the corpsmen closed the ambulance doors, preparing to take Gabriel to the Naval Hospital at Beaufort, Sanders walked out of the head, passed Dutton without a word, and returned to the DI hut. He flopped wearily on his rack and closed his eyes, as though to shut out the horror of what he had just seen.

Soon after Gabriel was placed in the ambulance and the door slammed shut, Bennett returned and sent Gillian to the head with orders to clean the shower, swab up every trace of blood, and disinfect the entire area. As Gillian worked, Bennett stood over him baiting him, saying he wished it had been he rather than Gabriel, swearing he would break Gillian in the remaining three days. Claiming that the recruit splashed him with water from the mop, he kicked Gillian and sent him reeling headfirst across the shower floor.

Gillian never responded except to answer direct questions. Less than seventy-two hours left; now he knew he could take whatever Bennett could throw at him. Moreover, despite this final attempt at intimidation, he realized Platoon 486 could ill afford another unsavory incident. So did Bennett realize it, which is why he finally drew back each time he appeared on the verge of working the recruit over.

By the time the ambulance arrived at the hospital, Gabriel was dead.

Late that afternoon and again the next day Krupe, both assistants, and random members of Platoon 486 were questioned about Gabriel—his state of mind, reasons why he might kill himself, whether he had been a good Marine up until the time he killed himself, etc. The questions were more or less routine; Krupe's official report, corroborated by Knisely, had already made clear what kind of recruit Gabriel had been, where he was being transferred, and why.

Sanders, busy attending to last-minute details connected with graduation, was not asked anything out of the ordinary. Even if he had been, he doubted he would have said anything to contradict the overall picture of Gabriel as a misfit.

*   *   *

He mourned for Gabriel, but he also mourned for himself. What a total wreck he had made of things—he, the idealist and wishful thinker who supposed he could reform Krupe and Bennett. Not only was he unable to reform them, he had even failed to save Gabriel. His good intentions had been for naught. He had simply been overwhelmed by a system he was powerless to alter. If only he could have resisted Krupe more forcefully. If only he had presented his case more convincingly to Knisely. If only he had been more emphatic . . .

He heard someone calling him. Turning on his side he saw Krupe standing in the doorway. "Take the platoon out and drill them until I return," he said, outwardly unmoved by what had happened. "I have to make out some reports, but I'll be back soon." Sanders stared without responding. "You feeling okay?" Krupe asked.

"Why wouldn't I be? Didn't we just rid the Marine Corps of one more subspecies of human being—something not even fit for the Army?"

"Sanders, I'm in no mood to humor you right now, so back off."

"Or what, Sergeant? You'll add my notch to your club, right alongside the one for Gabriel?"

Krupe bounded suddenly across the room and in one quick motion toppled Sanders on the deck. Before the corporal knew it, Krupe was astride him, pressing the *cocomacaque* across his windpipe, "I'll kill you if you ever say anything like that again," he hissed.

"Go ahead, choke me," Sanders gasped between clenched

teeth. "If I were you I wouldn't want anyone telling the truth about me either."

Krupe suddenly relaxed the pressure, then rose. "The truth!" he scoffed. "What do you know about the truth?"

"I know that Gabriel would still be in one piece if you hadn't set him back," replied Sanders, rising and massaging his throat.

"Yea, he'd still be here. But how many others would be dead next month or next year because of him? What kind of combat Marine would a person make who can't even face another eight weeks of boot camp? But why ask you? You're going to be an officer, and won't have to worry yourself about training recruits."

"Correction—I'm going to be a *civilian*, and won't have to worry about training recruits . . . or about burying them."

Krupe looked at him warily. "What do you mean, civilian?"

"Exactly that. I'm not going to Quantico, I'm going home. I'm getting out. *Sayonara*."

"When did you decide that?" There was an edge of suspicion to Krupe's voice, but it was clear that he wasn't certain whether Sanders was telling the truth.

"Ten minutes ago. Ten days. Ten weeks—what's the difference? The point is, I'm getting out, leaving."

Krupe removed his eyeglasses and wiped them clean. "How very brave—to 'protest' in a way that doesn't cost anything. Going home to a life where you can settle down to a nine-to-five job, complain about taxes, and forget there's a war on. No more responsibility or obligation."

"While you do my fighting for me. Is that it?"

"While I train the Marines to do your fighting for you—Marines who stand between you and whatever you consider we're fighting for in Korea."

In a final attempt to get through to him, Sanders said, "Don't you see, Krupe, that what those Marines are fighting for in Korea you're undermining here?" His question was almost a plea. "What difference does it make to Gabriel or his family whether we win in Korea or not? His war was here, his front not a hundred yards from here. Soon he'll be as much a casualty of war as any Marine who died at Inchon or at the Chosin."

"That's sentimental rubbish, and you know it. He's dead because he was a weakling. Nobody drove him to suicide. He shot himself because he came face to face with his own inadequacy. Look at how Gillian has been treated, yet he'll graduate this week as a man. He could have chosen the easy way out, but instead he chose to brave it through."

"Krupe, you make me sick," Sanders said finally, after it was clear he hadn't gotten through to him. "All this talk about manhood and weaklings. I admire Gillian—but I despise Bennett for putting him through the 'test' you so much admire. St. Augustine said no one is fit to inflict punishment until he's overcome hate in his own heart. Do you qualify under that definition?" Without awaiting an answer Sanders continued, "Gabriel was no worse than a lot of others who graduated from here. Or from other places. Were his weaknesses any worse than your brother's?"

He wanted to hurt Krupe, even if it meant hitting him with a low blow. Yet instead of recoiling at the remark, the tech sergeant replied: "I guess not. Maybe they weren't even as bad. But that doesn't say much for Gabriel."

He whirled and walked away, slamming the door behind him. Sanders began changing into a freshly pressed uniform, in preparation for falling the platoon in for drill.

Chapter
15

The final examination the next afternoon went off with the snap
and precision Krupe had worked for two-and-a-half months to
attain. Following the banner held aloft by Robert Begay, the
banner that reflected Krupe's pride and boundless confidence in
the Marine Corps, Platoon 486 strutted by the reviewing platform in perfect unison. Farther and farther it went, the sixty-five
surviving recruits responding to Krupe's cadence, floating effortlessly
across the quiet drill field like a proud, billowing windjammer,
deftly executing each command.

   Even the personal and rifle inspections went off without a
hitch, although a still-smoldering Major Knisely hoped to be able
to find fault. It wasn't that he wanted 484 to win Post Honor
Platoon; he had no use for Pepper and was only too glad to
recommend that he be removed from drill-instructor duty. But he
hoped to be able to take Krupe down a peg or two, to show him
he wasn't quite as high and mighty as he thought. The problem
was, he *was* high and mighty—at least when it came to taking
the raw human material that washed up on the shores of Parris
Island and transforming it into Marines. The mamas' boys, the
sissies, the braggarts and malcontents and bullies, kids who had
been coddled their entire lives and were never made to finish
anything they ever started—by God, somebody had to take them
and mold them into fighting men. He didn't always agree with
Krupe's methods, or at least what he had been hearing lately
about Krupe's methods, but this wasn't the Boy Scouts. Everybody in the world knew the Marines were tough, damn tough,
and nobody was forced to join. Each recruit damn well made his

own bed, he concluded as he watched the platoon float in front of the reviewing platform once again, and it served them right if they had to sleep in it with Sergeant Krupe.

The only discordant note at the outset was the black armband worn by Corporal Sanders. He had talked to Susan about making some sort of symbolic protest, or some symbolic tribute to Gabriel. At first he thought about ordering the recruits who had lined up in front of and behind Gabriel to leave the normal interval just before they drew near the reviewing platform. But he decided it would be cowardly to implicate or involve others in his protest. That's when he thought of the armband. "Someone has to do it," he explained, "even if it's only that pitiful gesture." He told her that what probably saddened him most about Gabriel's suicide was its insignificant effect on the recruits. Except for Dutton and possibly two or three others, their attitudes ranged from indifference to unconcern. He wondered whether the North Koreans and Chinese placed as little value on human life.

When Bennett saw the armband he complained, "Jesus, Sanders, ain't you ever gonna let up?"

Krupe never even acknowledged it, although before the inspection started he briefed both assistants on their assignments and the formations he proposed to employ. Knisely's eyes flamed like red-hot coals when he saw the armband, and it was all he could do to stifle the impulse to charge Sanders with insubordination. But Sanders would soon be out of his hair, out of the Marine Corps's hair, for that matter, so it was best to endure it as stoically as possible. Besides, he thought he remembered hearing that Sanders' family was influential, so no sense stirring up trouble when it would soon be all over.

Knisely delivered a brief talk, congratulating them and wishing them luck, and promising to buy them a drink the next time they met. Tossing off a crisp salute he said to Krupe, "Carry on, Sergeant." But Sanders stepped forward and said:

"Major, I'd like to request a moment of silence in memory of Private Jonathan Gabriel, a former member of this platoon." He said it rapidly, as though to avoid being interrupted, but he said it distinctly.

Knisely's jaw dropped open and he looked apoplectic. But Sergeant Krupe, imperturbable as ever, said, "That would be a fine idea," and proceeded to bow his head. Even Bennett appeared properly reverent, although twice he looked up in anticipation before Krupe finally said, "Amen."

On the march back to the platoon area Krupe dropped back alongside Sanders. "I'm glad you thought of that tribute," he said. Sanders expected to encounter mockery or a hint of irony in Krupe's expression, but there was none.

That afternoon Krupe gathered the platoon together and read the official orders assigning the recruits to new duty stations:

Paul Mathern was assigned to Marine Barracks, Great Lakes Naval Base, Illinois.

Paul Thorn was assigned to the Marine Corps Air Station at Cherry Point, North Carolina.

Loyal Reese was assigned to a service school at Camp Lejeune, North Carolina.

Dave Hall, three of his buddies, and eight or nine others were assigned to the Naval Air Station at Jacksonville, Florida, for the twelve-week airmen's school, before assignment to the Marine Air Wing.

Dutton, Gillian, Robert Begay, Herb Beeks, Otis McGraw, Jackson Hosse, and twenty-three others received orders to report, after ten days' leave, to Camp Pendleton, California, to undergo Advanced Infantry Training for subsequent reassignment to the First Marine Division in Korea.

When he heard the announcement Sanders glanced at Dutton, and saw a look of wry satisfaction.

*   *   *

Tuesday's graduation amounted to little more than a parade involving Platoons 486, 484, and two others from the Battalion. A small but spirited band played martial music as the platoons passed the reviewing stand to pay respects to the reviewing officers. From the staff carried smartly by Robert Begay, atop even the platoon banner, flew the proud ensign designating 486 as Post Honor Platoon. Krupe accepted the award graciously, ignoring the presence of Sergeant Pepper, who still wore patches over the bridge of his nose and over one eye.

Finally it was all over. After chow that evening each graduate of 486's honor platoon was permitted to sew a PFC stripe on his khaki shirt. The next morning, most of them would be put aboard buses and transported home on leave.

For Dutton this meant riding all day and all night to Philadelphia, but he was looking forward to it with unconcealed eagerness. He wanted to telephone Julie and tell her when he would arrive, but Krupe forbade calls, saying they could telephone whenever the bus stopped en route.

Krupe was taking ten days off, during which time he and his wife planned to tour the Carolinas, two states they had lived in but hadn't had time to explore. When Krupe mentioned his plans, it occurred to Sanders that it was one of the few times he had ever mentioned his wife. After his leave was up, Krupe was scheduled to pick up another recruit platoon and begin the ten-week cycle anew.

Bennett was also given ten days off, with orders to report back for assignment as senior drill instructor. "Senior DI." He repeated the words several times, savoring their meaning. Now he was going to be top dog of his own platoon, something he had looked forward to for a long time.

Sanders was to report to Casual Company to await final processing and discharge. In a little more than a week he would be a civilian, readjusting to a world far removed from Parris Island, instant obedience, and total authority. But it shouldn't be difficult, he thought, since Susan and Amy would be making the adjustment with him.

He had thought about it endlessly, agonized over it, and each time realized anew that he didn't want to leave without her. Whether she was in South Carolina or Indiana, he would always miss her, always worry about her, always regret that he left without her. It was one thing to walk away from a system of brutality he seemed powerless to influence, but quite a different matter to walk away from something as good and as honorable as that wonderful girl.

When he proposed to her she was not only elated but tearful, overcome by emotion, and all the more so when she became convinced his resignation from the Corps had nothing to do with his unwillingness to put her through another ordeal. Somehow she almost wanted him to stay in and work for reforms from inside, but she knew junior officers carried little more weight than corporals. But she didn't want to think of the Marine Corps now, or Sergeant Krupe, or Parris Island. She wanted to think only about *them*, and how Amy would wonder why "Kwis" was now suddenly "Daddy."

Maybe in her heart of hearts she would always wonder whether she had done the right thing, shown the proper respect for her dear Dan. Yet somehow she felt she could deal with that question, and that Dan would have understood and approved. Again and again she had asked herself if she had fallen in love with Chris merely in order to have someone, anyone, to ease her loneliness. Again and again her answer was no. But if she wasn't entirely free of conflict, she began to understand that, for whatever reason, she was being granted a second chance. A lucky few find someone they adore once in their lives, but how many ever find two people they truly love? She didn't know, but she thanked God she was one of them.

So she accepted Chris's proposal without hesitation, without concern, and even without regret—even, she kidded him, without making him ask Sal's permission to marry a soon-to-be-rich widow. Chris explained that there were likely to be some awkward questions from friends—everything from her previous marriage to his decision to get out to what happened between him and Linda. He had already written to Linda in Europe a week or two previously, trying tactfully to explain he was not suited for her. He didn't mention Susan, for he had not then decided to leave the Marine Corps and therefore had not proposed. But she would know, later he would write again and tell her, and perhaps in time she would forgive him.

There were any number of unresolved questions about their future—where they would live, how he would make a living. Fortunately, he laughed, these were mere details, not vital concerns; what was important was that they would always be together. Sal and Mary Rose said they'd take care of selling the trailer for Susan, and the two of them cried with happiness. They made them promise to bring Amy with them to the restaurant the night before they departed in order to have a farewell dinner, "a real Italian sendoff." After that their plans were indefinite, except to be wed at the first town that didn't require a waiting period or any rigmarole. Perhaps they would wed in Elkton, Maryland, then go on to suburban Philadelphia to begin their new life.

"What about your parents?" Susan asked apprehensively.

"Don't worry," Chris assured her, "you'll like them—and they'll like you. They're not like Dan's parents, even though a lot of their friends are. You'll get along just fine. And as soon as we get settled, it's off to Indiana."

* * *

On the last night of boot camp Bennett ordered Gillian to walk fire watch from midnight until two. Shortly after midnight he summoned Gillian from his rounds and ordered him to remain at the post until 4:00 A.M., ostensibly because he didn't respond quickly enough when called. Begay had expected Bennett to tap him also, and was pleasantly surprised as well as mystified when he did not.

Early the next morning Krupe led the platoon on its final run, setting a fast pace and maintaining it the entire three miles, right up to the mess hall door. By now even Bennett and Orme Beacotte were able to keep up, although neither one without some difficulty.

As they lined up outside the mess hall, Dutton watched as frightened new recruits marched and straggled by, verbally lashed by drill instructors who periodically charged into their midst to thrash unsuspecting boots. He wondered how many of them would not be around at graduation, like Gabriel—or even like Duvail or Tew? He wondered what had become of Tew, and whether he was still bragging about all the girls he was going to lay and the beer he was going to drink and the asses he was going to whip. He had difficulty believing this was his last meal at Parris Island, and that by this time tomorrow he would be in Ocean Point with Julie. Ten whole days in which to hold her, to walk with her along beaches by now almost deserted, and to tell her how much he missed her and loved her. This time he wouldn't neglect to say what he should have said those last nights before he left for Parris Island. He thought of her singing to him, and it filled him with nostalgia and longing:

"Ev'ry time we say goodbye,
I die a little.
Ev'ry time we say goodbye,
I wonder why a little. . . ."

She would go with him, of course, when he visited the Conways and tried to explain his failure to write; whatever his excuse, he was sure he would spare them the real reason.

He was so engrossed in thinking about Julie that he couldn't comprehend what was happening when he heard Bennett yelling, "Get him, get that man." But he turned in time to see a recruit from another platoon trying to cross between 486's first and second sections, the way Duvail had attempted to split 484's ranks. As several of his platoon mates began battering the unsuspecting boot, Dutton also bolted ranks and ran toward the melee. By the time he reached it, the bloodied stranger was slumped on the ground.

"That's enough, that's enough," Krupe commanded, annoyed at the intrusion, although totally unconcerned about the recruit. "Let him up, we can't waste time."

The injured youth—his shaved head revealed he had been on the island less than a week—scrambled up, bleeding profusely from the nose and mouth. His dungaree jacket was torn at the buttonholes and the pocket was ripped off. He didn't utter a sound. Instead, he eyed his attackers warily, and when he saw he wasn't about to be attacked again, he took off, running toward the relative safety of his platoon some distance up the street.

Before the youngster bolted, Dutton caught a glimpse of fright in his eyes, and it reminded him of Gabriel. A chill enveloped him as he thought about the dying Gabriel being carried out on the stretcher, and he shuddered. Then he realized that only a minute before he had run toward the fray—not to assist the helpless recruit who was being beaten but to join in the beating.

He thought about it during the meal—about how, under the tutelage of Bennett and Krupe, he had learned his lesson well . . . about how disappointed Julie and Tim would have been by his action . . . about the look of disappointment on Sanders' face when he passed him on the way back into ranks. Even Begay greeted him with a puzzled look. Was it possible, they seemed to be asking, that even Dutton had finally joined the mob?

After chow Krupe summoned everyone to one end of the squad bay and said: "Some of you wonder whether what you went through here was worth it. I can tell you that it was—but you're not likely to believe it until you've been in combat. You might try asking somebody like Begay's father," he continued, turning and looking at the astonished youth. "You didn't know it, but his father won the Congressional Medal of Honor as a Marine in World War Two. It would be interesting to hear a hero's opinion on the subject of hard work and discipline."

A feeling of pride welled up in Dutton as many recruits turned and looked at his friend, who was trying not to show his pride but who also couldn't understand how Krupe had learned about his father's decoration. After that he had difficulty concentrating on what Krupe was saying, until the very end of the talk. "You've been a good platoon and I'm proud of each of you," he said. "There isn't one of you I'd be afraid to take into battle with me, and that's the ultimate tribute one Marine can pay another. I don't much care how you feel about me, now or when you leave here. But I do care that you never forget you're Marines, members of the finest fighting organization on the face of the earth. You earned the right to call yourselves Marines because of the ten weeks you sweated and strained here. Now you must never disgrace the uniform whose traditions you all volunteered to uphold, the uniform that was worn by Marines like Peter Begay. Good luck to every one of you."

Most of the recruits flocked to shake hands with Krupe, and some with Bennett, who had stationed himself nearby. Sanders stood off to one side in the rear of the squad bay, where almost all the recruits sought him out to say good-by. Many of them also crowded around Begay, who had become the reluctant but proud center of attention.

Dutton didn't bother shaking hands with either Krupe or Bennett; instead, he walked directly over to Sanders with his hand outstretched and said, "Good-by, sir, and thanks for everything."

Sanders waved, as though to say don't mention it. "Pendleton?" he asked without elaboration.

"Pendleton. Then Korea."

"Are you glad?"

Dutton nodded. "I figure I'll need that time overseas to adjust to being a human being again. I can channel my aggressions against the enemy."

"Is that the only reason you're happy to be going to Korea?"

"I'm not sure I understand, sir."

"You once told me you joined the Marines for personal reasons, and I assumed the purpose was to go to Korea. Was I right?"

A look of remembrance crossed Dutton's face. "You know, I almost forgot about that. Isn't that incredible?" Sanders remembered his conversation with Julie, but didn't think it right to probe any deeper.

Then a chartered bus pulled up outside, its motor roaring impatiently. Krupe announced that those going north should begin loading.

"I understand you're getting out," Dutton said.

Sanders nodded. "Next week at the latest."

"Then what?"

"I haven't thought it through yet. I'm going to get married as soon as I leave here. Then, who knows? First I have to let my battle scars heal."

"Battle scars?"

"Sure, the Battle of P.I., July to September, nineteen fifty-two. I was wounded in action and for a while presumed lost."

Dutton studied him with a quizzical look. "Sir—"

"It's Chris now—Private First Class," Sanders smiled.

Dutton grinned. "Okay, Chris. I'd like to get together after I come back, when we're both around the Philly area."

"That's a long way off."

"Not really. And I mean it. I wouldn't say it to anyone else—not Krupe or Bennett," he said emphatically. "I never want to see either of them again. But I'm serious about getting together with you and your wife. I'd like to."

"You mean you forgive me for shaking you up the other day?" Sanders said it lightly, but he was obviously still mortified by the incident.

"I've already forgotten it. besides, I didn't exactly exercise self-restraint outside the mess hall this morning. Are you in the telephone book?"

"Not yet. But my father is—same name as mine. He's a lawyer. He or my mother can tell you my whereabouts."

"Okay, it's a promise. If I return . . ." He corrected himself quickly. "*When* I return home, I'll give you a call. I'll introduce you to my girl Julie. Only by then she'll be my wife. You and your wife will like her a lot."

"I'm sure we will, Tom."

The bus horn sounded impatiently. "Let's hurry it up, let's get moving," the driver hollered.

"Chris, if you ever get to Ocean Point, look up my parents. They'd love to invite you both in for a drink, or to spend the weekend. Do it."

"Thanks," Chris said, shaking hands again. "Maybe I will. And good luck, Tom. Be careful in Korea—for Julie's sake."

Gillian interrupted. "I just wanted to say good-by sir. It's been a pleasure serving under you." He extended his hand.

"A pleasure?" Sanders asked, returning the handshake. "Have you forgotten what you've gone through here?"

"No, sir, I haven't forgotten. But you weren't responsible. In fact, without your help I might not have made it at all."

Begay also came by to say good-by to Sanders. "Think about what I said about going to OCS," the drill instructor told him. "Your father would be proud."

"I will, sir," he replied. "I was sorry to hear you're not going to officers' school."

"Personal reasons," Sanders replied. "But you'd be foolish not to. You have the leadership and ability. It would be a waste of talent for you not to go."

Sanders started to wish all of them good luck when Bennett approached, wearing a sheepish smile and exuding forced bonhomie. When they ignored him he said with a chuckle, "Well, Private Gillian, I guess you'll soon be in the arms of your Jap girlfriend, huh?"

"Japanese," Gillian corrected coolly, deliberately omitting the word "sir."

"Hey," Bennett said confidentially, adopting a sudden tone of familiarity, as though they were old friends, "you never did tell me—you know, whether a Gook girl's is slanted." He nudged him knowingly. "Do you really get a new slant on life screwing them?"

Ignoring him, Gillian turned again toward Sanders and thanked him once more. "Good luck, Jim," Sanders replied.

"Didn't you hear me talking to you, Gillian?" Bennett demanded, suddenly dropping the buddy-buddy routine and all pretense of cheerfulness.

"I heard you, all right. So what?"

For a second the air was charged with tension as Bennett began blinking rapidly and his face darkened with anger. "Then you goddamn well answer me, Private."

"Here's your answer, Bennett," Gillian replied calmly, staring him in the eye with hatred. "Fuck you."

Bennett lunged at the defiant recruit but ran immediately into Sanders' outstretched arms. "Where are your manners, Sergeant?" he asked. "Didn't you see me talking with PFC Gillian?"

Gillian and Dutton smiled as Bennett cursed and threatened but made no move to push Sanders' arm aside.

"Don't you want to shake hands good-by with Sergeant Bennett?" Sanders asked.

Gillian smiled contemptuously. "Bennett has touched me for the last time," he spat. "The second that bus leaves this island his authority over me ends. If he's wise, he'll stay away from me for good."

"Jesus Christ Almighty, Gillian, are you threatening me?" Bennett raged, again lunging at the recruit but again allowing himself to be restrained by Sanders.

"On the contrary, Sergeant," he said, "I'm warning you as a brother—a brother Marine."

"I'd say it was pretty good advice," added Sanders. "Now, if you'll let us alone . . ."

"You son-of-a-bitch," Bennett hissed at Sanders. "You no good son-of-a-bitch."

"Better make that 'civilian son-of-a-bitch,' " he said. "Come to think of it, you better run along now or I'll turn Jim here loose on you."

Bennett turned, cursing under his breath. "Here Sanford, here's a present for you." When Bennett turned, Gillian threw a scrub brush at his feet. "My bed companion, remember? It's a going-away present so you'll think of me at night."

When Sanders joined Gillian, Dutton, and Begay in laughing at him, Bennett looked toward Krupe for support, but the tech sergeant had momentarily disappeared into the DI hut. Eventually Bennett stomped away, muttering and cursing.

Dave Hall drifted over and congratulated Begay. Then he turned to Gillian and congratulated him too, apologizing for having questioned his courage. Gillian said forget it, and the two of them shook hands warmly.

"Oh, oh," said Dutton. "Better batten down the hatches around Edgemont Street, because Marine Private First Class Beeks is on his way."

"You better believe it!" said the Philadelphian proudly, walking up rubbing his hand over his head to call attention to the fact that much of his hair had finally grown in. "Now Norma's gonna know what they mean about Marines being great lovers. She's even gonna love this capped job," he said, pointing to the tooth lost when Bennett had hit him over the head with a rifle barrel. "My first battle wound," he said, throwing out his chest amid their laughter. "Haven't been gone three months yet and already I'm returning home a hero."

Even before their laughter died down, Krupe intercepted one of the recruits who was approaching the steps leading inside the bus. "Private, what's your name, rank, and serial number?"

The recruit didn't know whether Krupe was kidding or not, but he decided against trying to find out. "PFC Jackson T. Hosse, sir, USMC 1335844," he replied.

"Your sixth General Order," Krupe demanded of Otis McGraw.

"Sir, my sixth General Order is 'To receive, obey, and pass on to the sentry who relieves me all orders from the commanding officer, field officer of the day, officer of the day, and officers and noncomissioned officers of the guard only.'"

"All right, get aboard, all of you," Krupe ordered, his voice as harsh and his look as threatening as the day they had arrived. The driver gunned the motor, sending clouds of gray smoke billowing from the exhaust. Then the bus started to creep forward. Dutton, Gillian, and Begay waved a final good-by to Sanders and ran to board it.

Krupe edged over toward Sanders as the bus rounded the bend and began its journey down Blvd. de France, a journey that would take them past Iron Mike and the Iwo Jima Monument that had been dedicated twelve days previously. "Well, there they go," Sanders said, staring after the bus. "Tell me something, Krupe—do you have any doubts or regrets or second thoughts about the past ten weeks?" He turned and stared at the tech sergeant.

Without hesitating Krupe replied, "None—and I won't have until wars are a thing of the past. Now, you tell me," he said, shifting his *cocomacaque* under his other arm, "what do you plan to do after you return to the safety of your Main Line womb, where war is an abstraction and while other people's kids are being killed in Korea?"

Sanders turned back to look at the bus, all the while considering Krupe's question. Then the slightest grin began playing at the corners of his mouth. "I'm thinking of maybe getting into politics," he said.

"Oh, you're going to be President, is that it?" He wasn't sure whether Sanders was serious or stringing him along.

"I'd settle for chairmanship of the Senate or House Armed Services Committees," Sanders replied, again without revealing whether he meant it or not. "Or even Secretary of the Navy—

head of the Marine Corps. Yea, the more I think of it, the better I like that idea.''

"Sorry to disappoint you, Sanders, but I'll be long gone from the Corps by them.''

"Don't worry, there'll be a lot more Krupes. The Marine Corps will never run out of Krupes, not until someone revamps the system.''

"And you're going to be that person?''

At last Sanders smiled, but it was a smile of anticipation. "I just might be,'' he said. "I very well just might be.''

Far down the road a voice rang out from an open window in the bus. "Hey Krupe, see you in Korea.''

"Be sure not to turn your back,'' yelled someone else.

Krupe's mouth hardened and he tightened the grip on his *cocomacaque*. Eventually his fingers began to relax. Then, still following the path of the bus, he said, "That's what I mean about recruits not having discipline.'' He turned toward Sanders and smiled, as though nothing had happened since their last conversation about that subject.

Sanders didn't bother to reply. When the bus finally disappeared from view, he turned and walked back toward his room. He still had to begin packing in preparation for his move to Casual Company. Then, in a few more days, he would pick up Susan and Amy and he, too, would be on his way home.

ABOUT THE AUTHOR

EDWIN MCDOWELL, an ex-Marine sergeant trained at Parris Island, is a writer for *The New York Times*. He has, as well, written for the *Wall Street Journal*, *Reader's Digest*, the *Saturday Review*, and many other newspapers and magazines. He is also the author of the novel *Three Cheers and a Tiger*.

**A towering novel of friendship,
betrayal and love**

THE LORDS
OF DISCIPLINE

by Pat Conroy
author of The Great Santini

This powerful and passionate novel is the story
of four cadets who become bloodbrothers. Together they will encounter the hell of hazing
and the rabid, raunchy and dangerously secre-
tive atmosphere of an arrogant and proud
military institute. Together, they will brace
themselves for the brutal transition to manhood . . . and one will not survive.

Pat Conroy sweeps you dramatically into
the turbulent world of these four friends—and
draws you deep into the heart of his rebellious
hero, Will McLean, an outsider forging his
personal code of honor, who falls in love with
Annie Kate, a mysterious and whimsical beauty who first appears to him one midnight in
sunglasses and raincoat.

(#14716-1 • $3.75)